this novel journal
belongs to:

_____

and you're sharing it
with J. M. barrie

Write between the lines of some of the best literature the world has to offer with your Novel Journal. Whether you're an aspiring writer crafting the next great novel or a journaler recording life's memorable events, you'll be able to write over, under, and within the words of the world's greatest writers. Each Novel Journal contains the complete text of the classic work; in some cases, that text repeats to allow for standard journal lengths. Important quotes and lines from each novel are highlighted in a different color throughout so that the inspiring words of your favorite authors are never far away.

All children, except one, grow up. They soon know that they will grow up, and the way Wendy knew was this.

One day when she was two years old she was playing in a garden, and she plucked another flower and ran with it to her mother. I suppose she must have looked rather delightful, for Mrs. Darling put her hand to her heart and cried, "Oh, why can't you remain like this for ever!" This was all that passed between them on the subject, but henceforth Wendy knew that she must grow up. You always know after you are two. Two is the beginning of the end. Of course they lived at 14, and until Wendy came her mother was the chief one. She was a lovely lady, with a romantic mind and such a sweet mocking mouth. Her romantic mind was like the tiny boxes, one within the other, that come from the puzzling East, however many you discover there is always one more; and her sweet mocking mouth had one kiss on it that Wendy could never get, though there it was, perfectly conspicuous in the right-hand corner. The way Mr. Darling won her was this: the many gentlemen who had been boys when she was a girl discovered simultaneously that they loved her, and they all ran to her house to propose to her except Mr. Darling, who took a cab and nipped in first, and so he got her. He got all of her, except the innermost box and the kiss. He never knew about the box, and in time he gave up trying for the kiss. Wendy thought Napoleon could have got it, but I can picture him trying, and then going off in a passion, slamming the door. Mr. Darling used to boast to Wendy that her mother not only loved him but respected him. He was one of those deep ones who know about stocks and shares. Of course no one really knows, but he quite seemed to know, and he often said stocks were up and shares were down in a way that would have made any woman respect him. Mrs. Darling was married in white, and at first she kept the books perfectly, almost gleefully, as if it were a game, not so much as a Brussels sprout was missing; but by and by whole cauliflowers dropped out, and instead of them there were pictures of babies without faces. She drew them when she should have been totting up. They were Mrs. Darling's guesses. Wendy came first, then John, then Michael. For a week or two after Wendy came it was doubtful whether they would be able to keep her, as she was another mouth to feed. Mr. Darling was frightfully proud of her, but he was very honourable, and he sat on the edge of Mrs. Darling's bed, holding her hand and calculating expenses, while she looked at him imploringly. She wanted to risk it, come what might, but that was not his way; his way was with a pencil and a piece of paper, and if she confused him with suggestions he had to begin at the beginning again. "Now don't interrupt," he would beg of her. "I have one pound seventeen here, and two and six at the office; I can cut off my coffee at the office, say ten shillings, making two nine and six, with your eighteen and three makes three nine seven, with five naught naught in my cheque-book makes eight nine seven—who is that moving?—eight nine seven, dot and carry seven—don't speak, my own—and the pound you lent to that man who came to the door—quiet, child—dot and carry child—there, you've done it!—did I say nine nine seven? yes, I said nine nine seven; the question is, can we try it for a year on nine nine seven?" "Of course we can, George," she cried. But she was prejudiced in Wendy's favour, and he was really the grander character of the two. "Remember mumps," he warned her almost threateningly, and off he went again. "Mumps one pound, that is what I have put down, but daresay it will be more like thirty shillings—don't speak—measles one five, German measles half a guinea, makes two fifteen six—don't waggle your finger—whooping cough, say fifteen shillings"—and so on it went, and it added up differently each time; but at last Wendy just got through, with mumps reduced to twelve six, and the two

kinds of measles treated as one. There was the same excitement over John, and Michael had even a narrower squeak; but both were kept, and soon you might have seen the

three of them going in a row to Miss Fulsom's Kindergarten school, accompanied by their nurse. Mrs. Darling loved to have everything just so, and Mr. Darling had a passion

for being exactly like his neighbours; so, of course, they had a nurse. As they were poor, owing to the amount of milk the children drank, this nurse was a prim Newfoundland

dog, called Nana, who had belonged to no one in particular until the Darlings engaged her. She had always thought children important, however, and the Darlings had

become acquainted with her in Kensington Gardens, where she spent most of her spare time peeping into perambulators, and was much hated by careless nursemaids, whom

she followed to their homes and complained of to their mistresses. She proved to be quite a treasure of a nurse. How thorough she was at bath-time; and up at any moment

of the night if one of her charges made the slightest cry. Of course her kennel was in the nursery. She had a genius for knowing when a cough is a thing to have no patience

with and when it needs stocking round your throat. She believed to her last day in old-fashioned remedies like rhubarb leaf, and made sounds of contempt over all this new-

fangled talk about germs, and so on. It was a lesson in propriety to see her escorting the children to school, walking sedately by their side when they were well behaved, and

butting them back into line if they strayed. On John's footer days she never once forgot his sweater, and she usually carried an umbrella in her mouth in case of rain. There

is a room in the basement of Miss Fulsom's school where the nurses wait. They sat on forms, while Nana lay on the floor, but that was the only difference. They affected to

ignore her as of an inferior social status to themselves, and she despised their light talk. She resented visits to the nursery from Mrs. Darling's friends, but if they did come

she first whipped off Michael's pinafore and put him into the one with blue braiding, and smoothed out Wendy and made a dash at John's hair. No nursery could possibly

have been conducted more correctly, and Mr. Darling knew it, yet he sometimes wondered uneasily whether the neighbours talked. He had his position in the city to consider.

Nana also troubled him in another way. He had sometimes a feeling that she did not admire him. "I know she admires you tremendously, George," Mrs. Darling would assure

him, and then she would sign to the children to be specially nice to father. Lovely dances followed, in which the only other servant, Liza, was sometimes allowed to join. Such

a midget she looked in her long skirt and maid's cap, though she had sworn, when engaged, that she would never see ten again. The gaiety of those romps! And gayest of all

was Mrs. Darling, who would pirouette so wildly that all you could see of her was the kiss, and then if you had dashed at her you might have got it. There never was a simpler

happier family until the coming of Peter Pan. Mrs. Darling first heard of Peter when she was tidying up her children's minds. It is the nightly custom of every good mother

after her children are asleep to rummage in their minds and put things straight for next morning, repacking into their proper places the many articles that have wandered

during the day. If you could keep awake (but of course you can't) you would see your own mother doing this, and you would find it very interesting to watch her. It is quite

like tidying up drawers. You would see her on her knees, I expect, lingering humorously over some of your contents, wondering where on earth you had picked this thing up, making discoveries sweet and not so sweet, pressing this to her cheek as if it were as nice as a kitten, and hurriedly stowing that out of sight. When you wake in the

morning, the naughtinesses and evil passions with which you went to bed have been folded up small and placed at the bottom of your mind, and on the top, beautifully aired,

are spread out your prettier thoughts, ready for you to put on. I don't know whether you have ever seen a map of a person's mind. Doctors sometimes draw maps of other

parts of you, and your own map can become intensely interesting, but catch them trying to draw a map of a child's mind, which is not only confused, but keeps going round

all the time. There are zigzag lines on it, just like your temperature on a card, and these are probably roads in the island; for the Neverland is always more or less an island,

with astonishing splashes of colour here and there, and coral reefs and rakish-looking craft in the offing, and savages and lonely lairs, and gnomes who are mostly tailors, and

caves through which a river runs, and princes with six elder brothers, and a hut fast going to decay, and one very small old lady with a hooked nose. It would be an easy map

if that were all; but there is also first day at school, religion, fathers, the round pond, needlework, murders, hangings, verbs that take the dative, chocolate pudding day,

getting into braces, say ninety-nine, three-pence for pulling out your tooth yourself, and so on, and either these are part of the island or they are another map showing

through, and it is all rather confusing, especially as nothing will stand still. Of course the Neverlands vary a good deal. John's, for instance, had a lagoon with flamingoes

flying over it at which John was shooting, while Michael, who was very small, had a flamingo with lagoons flying over it. John lived in a boat turned upside down on the

sands, Michael in a wigwam, Wendy in a house of leaves deftly sewn together. John had no friends, Michael had friends at night, Wendy had a pet wolf forsaken by its parents,

but on the whole the Neverlands have a family resemblance, and if they stood still in a row you could say of them that they have each other's nose, and so forth. On these

magic shores children at play are for ever beaching their coracles. We too have been there; we can still hear the sound of the surf, though we shall land no more. Of all

delectable islands the Neverland is the snuggest and most compact, not large and sprawly, you know, with tedious distances between one adventure and another, but nicely

crammed. When you play at it by day with the chairs and table-cloth, it is not in the least alarming, but in the two minutes before you go to sleep it becomes very nearly real.

That is why there are night-lights. Occasionally in her travels through her children's minds Mrs. Darling found things she could not understand, and of these quite the most

perplexing was the word *Peter*. She knew of no Peter, and yet he was here and there in John and Michael's minds, while Wendy's began to be scrawled all over with him. The

name stood out in bolder letters than any of the other words, and as Mrs. Darling gazed she felt that it had an oddly cocky appearance. "Yes, he is rather cocky," Wendy

admitted with regret. Her mother had been questioning her. "But who is he, my pet?" "He is Peter Pan, you know, mother." At first Mrs. Darling did not know, but after

thinking back into her childhood she just remembered a Peter Pan who was said to live with the fairies. There were odd stories about him, as that when children died he went

part of the way with them, so that they should not be frightened. She had believed in him at the time, but now that she was married and full of sense she quite doubted whether

there was any such person. "Besides," she said to Wendy, "he would be grown up by this time." "Oh no, he isn't grown up," Wendy assured her confidently, "and he is just my size." She meant that he was her size in both mind and body; she didn't know how she knew it, she just knew it. Mrs. Darling consulted Mr. Darling, but he smiled pooh-pooh. "Mark my words," he said, "it is some nonsense Nana has been putting into their heads; just the sort of idea a dog would have. Leave it alone, and it will blow over." But it would not blow over; and soon the troublesome boy gave Mrs. Darling quite a shock. **Children have the strangest adventures without being troubled by them.** For instance, they may remember to mention, a week after the event happened, that when they were in the wood they met their dead father and had a game with him. It was in this casual way that Wendy one morning made a disquieting revelation. Some leaves of a tree had been found on the nursery floor, which certainly were not there when the children went to bed, and Mrs. Darling was puzzling over them when Wendy said with a tolerant smile: "I do believe it is that Peter again!" "Whatever do you mean, Wendy?" "It is so naughty of him not to wipe," Wendy said, sighing. She was a tidy child. She explained in quite a matter-of-fact way that she thought Peter sometimes came to the nursery in the night and sat on the foot of her bed and played on his pipes to her. Unfortunately she never woke, so she didn't know how she knew, she just knew. "What nonsense you talk, precious. No one can get into the house without knocking." "I think he comes in by the window," she said. "My love, it is three floors up." "Were not the leaves at the foot of the window, mother?" It was quite true; the leaves had been found very near the window. Mrs. Darling did not know what to think, for it all seemed so natural to Wendy that you could not dismiss it by saying she had been dreaming. "My child," the mother cried, "why did you not tell me of this before?" "I forgot," said Wendy lightly. She was in a hurry to get her breakfast. Oh, surely she must have been dreaming. But, on the other hand, there were the leaves. Mrs. Darling examined them carefully; they were skeleton leaves, but she was sure they did not come from any tree that grew in England. She crawled about the floor, peering at it with a candle for marks of a strange foot. She rattled the poker up the chimney and tapped the walls. She let down a tape from the window to the pavement, and it was a sheer drop of thirty feet, without so much as a spout to climb up by. Certainly Wendy had been dreaming. But Wendy had not been dreaming, as the very next night showed, the night on which the extraordinary adventures of these children may be said to have begun. On the night we speak of all the children were once more in bed. It happened to be Nana's evening off, and Mrs. Darling had bathed them and sung to them till one by one they had let go her hand and slid away into the land of sleep. All were looking so safe and cosy that she smiled at her fears now and sat down tranquilly by the fire to sew. It was something for Michael, who on his birthday was getting into shirts. The fire was warm, however, and the nursery dimly lit by three night-lights, and presently the sewing lay on Mrs. Darling's lap. Then her head nodded, oh, so gracefully. She was asleep. Look at the four of them, Wendy and Michael over there, John here, and Mrs. Darling by the fire. There should have been a fourth night-light. While she slept she had a dream. She dreamt that the Neverland had come too near and that a strange boy had broken through from it. He did not alarm her, for she thought she had seen him before in the faces of many women who have no children. Perhaps he is to be found in the faces of some mothers also. But in her dream he had rent the film that obscures the Neverland, and she saw Wendy and John and Michael peeping through the gap. The dream by itself would have been a trifle, but while she was dreaming the window of the nursery blew open, and a boy did drop on the floor. He was accompanied by a strange light, no bigger than your fist, which darted about the room like a living thing; and I think it must have been this light that wakened Mrs. Darling. She started up with a cry, and saw the boy, and somehow she knew at once that he was Peter Pan. If you or I or Wendy had been there we should have seen that he was very like Mrs. Darling's kiss. He was a lovely boy, clad in skeleton leaves and the juices that ooze out of trees; but the most entrancing thing about him was that he had all his first teeth. When he saw she was a grown-up, he gnashed the little pearls at her. CHAPTER II *The Shadow* Mrs. Darling screamed, and, as if in answer to a bell, the door opened, and Nana entered, returned from her evening out. She growled and sprang at the boy, who leapt lightly through the window. Again Mrs. Darling screamed, this time in distress for him, for she thought he was killed, and she ran down into the street to look for his little body, but it was not there; and she looked up, and in the black night she could see nothing but what she thought was a shooting star. She returned to the nursery, and found Nana with something in her mouth, which proved to be the boy's shadow. As he leapt at the window Nana had closed it quickly, too late to catch him, but his shadow had not had time to get out; slam went the window and snapped it off. You may be sure Mrs. Darling examined the shadow carefully, but it was quite the ordinary kind. Nana had no doubt of what was the best thing to do with this shadow. She hung it out at the window, meaning "He is sure to come back for it; let us put it where he can get it easily without disturbing the children." But unfortunately Mrs. Darling could not leave it hanging out at the window; it looked so like the washing and lowered the whole tone of the house. She thought of showing it to Mr. Darling, but he was totting up winter greatcoats for John and Michael, with a wet towel round his head to keep his brain clear, and it seemed a shame to trouble him; besides, she knew exactly what he would say: "It all comes of having a dog for a nurse." She decided to roll the shadow up and put it away carefully in a drawer, until a fitting opportunity came for telling her husband. Ah me! The opportunity came a week later, on that never-to-be-forgotten Friday. Of course it was a Friday. "I ought to have been specially careful on a Friday," she used to say afterwards to her husband, while perhaps Nana was on the other side of her, holding her hand. "No, no," Mr. Darling always said, "I am responsible for it all. I, George Darling, did it. *Mea culpa, mea culpa.*" He had had a classical education. They sat thus night after night recalling that fatal Friday, till every detail of it was stamped on their brains and came through on the other side like the faces on a bad coinage. "If only I had not accepted that invitation to dine at 27," Mrs. Darling said. "If only I had not poured my medicine into Nana's bowl," said Mr. Darling. "If only I had pretended to like the medicine," was what Nana's wet eyes said. "My liking for parties, George." "My fatal gift of humour, dearest." "My touchiness about trifles, dear master and mistress." Then one or more of them would break down altogether; Nana at the thought, "It's true, it's true, they ought not to have had a dog for a nurse." Many a time it was Mr. Darling who put the handkerchief to Nana's eyes. "That fiend!" Mr. Darling would cry, and Nana's bark was the echo of it, but Mrs. Darling never upbraided Peter; there was something in the right-hand corner of her mouth that wanted her not to call Peter names. They would sit there in the empty nursery, recalling fondly every smallest detail of that dreadful evening. It had begun so uneventfully, so precisely like a hundred other evenings, with Nana putting on the water for Michael's bath and carrying him to it on her back. "I won't go to bed," he had shouted, like one who still believed that he had the last word on the subject, "I won't, I won't. Nana, it isn't six o'clock yet. Oh dear,

oh dear, I shan't love you any more, Nana. I tell you I won't be bathed, I won't, I won't!" Then Mrs. Darling had come in, wearing her white evening-gown. She had dressed

early because Wendy so loved to see her in her evening-gown, with the necklace George had given her. She was wearing Wendy's bracelet on her arm; she had asked for the

loan of it. Wendy so loved to lend her bracelet to her mother. She had found her two older children playing at being herself and father on the occasion of Wendy's birth, and

John was saying: "I am happy to inform you, Mrs. Darling, that you are now a mother," in just such a tone as Mr. Darling himself may have used on the real occasion. Wendy

had danced with joy, just as the real Mrs. Darling must have done. Then John was born, with the extra pomp that he conceived due to the birth of a male, and Michael came

from his bath to ask to be born also, but John said brutally that they did not want any more. Michael had nearly cried. "Nobody wants me," he said, and of course the lady

in evening-dress could not stand that. "I do," she said, "I so want a third child." "Boy or girl?" asked Michael, not too hopefully. "Boy." Then he had leapt into her arms.

Such a little thing for Mr. and Mrs. Darling and Nana to recall now, but not so little if that was to be Michael's last night in the nursery. They go on with their recollections.

"It was then that I rushed in like a tornado, wasn't it?" Mr. Darling would say, scorning himself; and indeed he had been like a tornado. Perhaps there was some excuse for

him. He, too, had been dressing for the party, and all had gone well with him until he came to his tie. It is an astounding thing to have to tell, but this man, though he knew

about stocks and shares, had no real mastery of his tie. Sometimes the thing yielded to him without a contest, but there were occasions when it would have been better for

the house if he had swallowed his pride and used a made-up tie. This was such an occasion. He came rushing into the nursery with the crumpled little brute of a tie in his

hand. "Why, what is the matter, father dear?" "Matter!" he yelled; he really yelled. "This tie, it will not tie." He became dangerously sarcastic. "Not round my neck! Round

the bed-post! Oh yes, twenty times have I made it up round the bed-post, but round my neck, no! Oh dear no! begs to be excused!" He thought Mrs. Darling was not

sufficiently impressed, and he went on sternly, "I warn you of this, mother, that unless this tie is round my neck we don't go out to dinner to-night, and if I don't go out to

dinner to-night, I never go to the office again, and if I don't go to the office again, you and I starve, and our children will be flung into the streets." Even then Mrs. Darling

was placid. "Let me try, dear," she said, and indeed that was what he had come to ask her to do, and with her nice cool hands she tied his tie for him, while the children stood

around to see their fate decided. Some men would have resented her being able to do it so easily, but Mr. Darling was far too fine a nature for that; he thanked her carelessly,

at once forgot his rage, and in another moment was dancing round the room with Michael on his back. "How wildly we romped!" says Mrs. Darling now, recalling it. "Our

last romp!" Mr. Darling groaned. "O George, do you remember Michael suddenly said to me, "How did you get to know me, mother?" "I remember!" "They were rather

sweet, don't you think, George?" "And they were ours, ours! and now they are gone." The romp had ended with the appearance of Nana, and most unluckily Mr. Darling

collided against her, covering his trousers with hairs. They were not only new trousers, but they were the first he had ever had with braid on them, and he had to bite his lip to prevent the tears coming. Of course Mrs. Darling brushed him, but he began to talk again about its being a mistake to have a dog for a nurse. "George, Nana is a treasure."

"No doubt, but I have an uneasy feeling at times that she looks upon the children as puppies." "Oh no, dear one, I feel sure she knows they have souls." "I wonder," Mr.

Darling said thoughtfully, "I wonder." It was an opportunity, his wife felt, for telling him about the boy. At first he pooh-poohed the story, but he became thoughtful when

she showed him the shadow. "It is nobody I know," he said, examining it carefully, "but he does look a scoundrel." "We were still discussing it, you remember," says Mr.

Darling, "when Nana came in with Michael's medicine. You will never carry the bottle in your mouth again, Nana, and it is all my fault. Strong man though he was, there is

no doubt that he had behaved rather foolishly over the medicine. If he had a weakness, it was for thinking that all his life he had taken medicine boldly; and so now, when

Michael dodged the spoon in Nana's mouth, he had said reprovingly, "Be a man, Michael." "Won't; won't," Michael cried naughtily. Mrs. Darling left the room to get a

chocolate for him, and Mr. Darling thought this showed want of firmness. "Mother, don't pamper him," he called after her. "Michael, when I was your age I took medicine

without a murmur. I said "Thank you, kind parents, for giving me bottles to make me well." He really thought this was true, and Wendy, who was now in her night-gown,

believed it also, and she said, to encourage Michael, "That medicine you sometimes take, father, is much nastier, isn't it?" "Ever so much nastier," Mr. Darling said bravely,

"and I would take it now as an example to you, Michael, if I hadn't lost the bottle. **He had not exactly lost it; he had climbed in the dead of night to the top of the wardrobe**

and hidden it there. What he did not know was that the faithful Liza had found it, and put it back on his wash-stand. "I know where it is, father," Wendy cried, always glad

to be of service. "I'll bring it," and she was off before he could stop her. Immediately his spirits sank in the strangest way. "John," he said, shuddering, "it's most beastly

stuff. It's that nasty, sticky, sweet kind." "It will soon be over, father," John said cheerily, and then in rushed Wendy with the medicine in a glass. "I have been as quick as I

could," she panted. "You have been wonderfully quick," her father retorted, with a vindictive politeness that was quite thrown away upon her. "Michael first," he said

doggedly. "Father first," said Michael, who was of a suspicious nature. "I shall be sick, you know," Mr. Darling said threateningly. "Come on, father," said John. "Hold your

tongue, John," his father rapped out. Wendy was quite puzzled. "I thought you took it quite easily, father." "That is not the point," he retorted. "The point is, that there is

more in my glass than in Michael's spoon." His proud heart was nearly bursting. "And it isn't fair; I would say it though it were with my last breath; it isn't fair." "Father, I

am waiting," said Michael coldly. "It's all very well to say you are waiting; so am I waiting." "Father's a cowardy custard." "So are you a cowardy custard." "I'm not

frightened." "Neither am I frightened." "Well, then, take it." "Well, then, you take it." Wendy had a splendid idea. "Why not both take it at the same time?" "Certainly,"

said Mr. Darling. "Are you ready, Michael?" Wendy gave the words, one, two, three, and Michael took his medicine, but Mr. Darling slipped his behind his back. There was

a yell of rage from Michael, and "O father!" Wendy exclaimed. "What do you mean by 'O father?'" Mr. Darling demanded. "Stop that row, Michael. I meant to take mine,

but I—I missed it." It was dreadful the way all the three were looking at him, just as if they did not admire him. "Look here, all of you," he said entreatingly, as soon as Nana had gone into the bathroom, "I have just thought of a splendid joke. I shall pour my medicine into Nana's bowl, and she will drink it, thinking it is milk!" It was the colour

of milk; but the children did not have their father's sense of humour, and they looked at him reproachfully as he poured the medicine into Nana's bowl. "What fun," he said

doubtfully, and they did not dare expose him when Mrs. Darling and Nana returned. "Nana, good dog," he said, patting her, "I have put a little milk into your bowl, Nana."

Nana wagged her tail, ran to the medicine, and began lapping it. Then she gave Mr. Darling such a look, not an angry look: she showed him the great red tear that makes us

so sorry for noble dogs, and crept into her kennel. Mr. Darling was frightfully ashamed of himself, but he would not give in. In a horrid silence Mrs. Darling smelt the bowl.

"O George," she said, "it's your medicine!" "It was only a joke," he roared, while she comforted her boys, and Wendy hugged Nana. "Much good," he said bitterly, "my

wearing myself to the bone trying to be funny in this house." And still Wendy hugged Nana. "That's right," he shouted. "Coddle her! Nobody coddles me. Oh dear no! I

am only the breadwinner, why should I be coddled, why, why, why!" "George," Mrs. Darling entreated him, "not so loud; the servants will hear you." Somehow they had

got into the way of calling Liza the servants. "Let them," he answered recklessly. "Bring in the whole world. But I refuse to allow that dog to lord it in my nursery for an

hour longer." The children wept, and Nana ran to him beseechingly, but he waved her back. He felt he was a strong man again. "In vain, in vain," he cried; "the proper place

for you is the yard, and there you go to be tied up this instant." "George, George," Mrs. Darling whispered, "remember what I told you about that boy." Alas, he would not

listen. He was determined to show who was master in that house, and when commands would not draw Nana from the kennel, he lured her out of it with honeyed words,

and seizing her roughly, dragged her from the nursery. He was ashamed of himself, and yet he did it. It was all owing to his too affectionate nature, which craved for

admiration. When he had tied her up in the back-yard, the wretched father went and sat in the passage, with his knuckles to his eyes. In the meantime Mrs. Darling had put

the children to bed in unwonted silence and lit their night-lights. They could hear Nana barking, and John whimpered, "It is because he is chaining her up in the yard," but

Wendy was wiser. "That is not Nana's unhappy bark," she said, little guessing what was about to happen; "that is her bark when she smells danger." Danger! "Are you sure,

Wendy?" "Oh yes." Mrs. Darling quivered and went to the window. It was securely fastened. She looked out, and the night was peppered with stars. They were crowding

round the house, as if curious to see what was to take place there, but she did not notice this, nor that one or two of the smaller ones winked at her. Yet a nameless fear clutched

at her heart and made her cry, "Oh, how I wish that I wasn't going to a party to-night!" Even Michael, already half asleep, knew that she was perturbed, and he asked, "Can

anything harm us, mother, after the night-lights are lit?" "Nothing, precious," she said; "they are the eyes a mother leaves behind her to guard her children." She went from

bed to bed singing enchantments over them, and little Michael flung his arms round her. "Mother," he cried, "I'm glad of you." They were the last words she was to hear

from him for a long time. No. 27 was only a few yards distant, but there had been a slight fall of snow, and Father and Mother Darling picked their way over it deftly not to

soil their shoes. They were already the only persons in the street, and all the stars were watching them. Stars are beautiful, but they may not take an active part in anything, they must just look on for ever. It is a punishment put on them for something they did so long ago that no star now knows what it was. So the older ones have become glassy-eyed and seldom speak (winking is the star language), but the little ones still wonder. They are not really friendly to Peter, who has a mischievous way of stealing up behind them and trying to blow them out; but they are so fond of fun that they were on his side to-night, and anxious to get the grown-ups out of the way. So as soon as the door of 27 closed on Mr. and Mrs. Darling there was a commotion in the firmament, and the smallest of all the stars in the Milky Way screamed out: "Now, Peter!" CHAPTER III

Come Away, Come Away! For a moment after Mr. and Mrs. Darling left the house the night-lights by the beds of the three children continued to burn clearly. They were awfully nice little night-lights, and one cannot help wishing that they could have kept awake to see Peter; but Wendy's light blinked and gave such a yawn that the other two yawned also, and before they could close their mouths all the three went out. There was another light in the room now, a thousand times brighter than the night-lights, and in the time we have taken to say this, it has been in all the drawers in the nursery, looking for Peter's shadow, rummaged the wardrobe and turned every pocket inside out. It was not really a light; it made this light by flashing about so quickly, but when it came to rest for a second you saw it was a fairy, no longer than your hand, but still growing. It was a girl called Tinker Bell exquisitely gowned in a skeleton leaf, cut low and square, through which her figure could be seen to the best advantage. She was slightly inclined to *embonpoint*. A moment after the fairy's entrance the window was blown open by the breathing of the little stars, and Peter dropped in. He had carried Tinker Bell part of the way, and his hand was still messy with the fairy dust. "Tinker Bell," he called softly, after making sure that the children were asleep, "Tink, where are you?" She was in a jug for the moment, and liking it extremely; she had never been in a jug before. "Oh, do come out of that jug, and tell me, do you know where they put my shadow?" The loveliest tinkle as of golden bells answered him. It is the fairy language. You ordinary children can never hear it, but if you were to hear it you would know that you had heard it once before. Tink said that the shadow was in the big box. She meant the chest of drawers, and Peter jumped at the drawers, scattering their contents to the floor with both hands, as kings toss ha'pence to the crowd. In a moment he had recovered his shadow, and in his delight he forgot that he had shut Tinker Bell up in the drawer. If he thought at all, but I don't believe he ever thought, it was that he and his shadow, when brought near each other, would join like drops of water; and when they did not he was appalled. He tried to stick it on with soap from the bathroom, but that also failed. A shudder passed through Peter, and he sat on the floor and cried. His sobs woke Wendy, and she sat up in bed. She was not alarmed to see a stranger crying on the nursery floor; she was only pleasantly interested. "Boy," she said courteously, "why are you crying?" Peter could be exceedingly polite also, having learned the grand manner at fairy ceremonies, and he rose and bowed to her beautifully. She was much pleased, and bowed beautifully to him from the bed. "What's your name?" he asked. "Wendy Moira Angela Darling," she replied with some satisfaction. "What is your name?" "Peter Pan." She was already sure that he must be Peter, but it did seem a comparatively short name. "Is that all?" "Yes," he said rather sharply. He felt for the first time that it was a shortish name. "I'm so sorry," said Wendy Moira Angela. "It doesn't matter," Peter gulped. She asked where he lived. "Second to the right," said Peter, "and then straight on till morning." "What a funny address!" Peter had a sinking. For the first time he felt that perhaps it was a funny address. "No, it isn't," he said. "I mean," Wendy said

nicely, remembering that she was hostess, "is that what they put on the letters?" He wished she had not mentioned letters. "Don't get any letters," he said contemptuously.

"But your mother gets letters?" "Don't have a mother," he said. Not only had he no mother, but he had not the slightest desire to have one. He thought them very overrated

persons. Wendy, however, felt at once that she was in the presence of a tragedy. "O Peter, no wonder you were crying," she said, and got out of bed and ran to him. "I wasn't

crying about mothers," he said rather indignantly. "I was crying because I can't get my shadow to stick on. Besides, I wasn't crying." "It has come off?" "Yes." Then Wendy

saw the shadow on the floor, looking so draggled, and she was frightfully sorry for Peter. "How awful!" she said, but she could not help smiling when she saw that he had

been trying to stick it on with soap. How exactly like a boy! Fortunately she knew at once what to do. "It must be sewn on," she said, just a little patronisingly. "What's sewn?"

he asked. "You're dreadfully ignorant." "No, I'm not." But she was exulting in his ignorance. "I shall sew it on for you, my little man," she said, though he was as tall as

herself; and she got out her housewife, and sewed the shadow on to Peter's foot. "I daresay it will hurt a little," she warned him. "Oh, I shan't cry," said Peter, who was

already of opinion that he had never cried in his life. And he clenched his teeth and did not cry; and soon his shadow was behaving properly, though still a little creased.

"Perhaps I should have ironed it," Wendy said thoughtfully; but Peter, boylike, was indifferent to appearances, and he was now jumping about in the wildest glee. Alas, he

had already forgotten that he owed his bliss to Wendy. He thought he had attached the shadow himself. "How clever I am," he crowed rapturously, "oh, the cleverness of

me!" It is humiliating to have to confess that this conceit of Peter was one of his most fascinating qualities. To put it with brutal frankness, there never was a cockier boy. But

for the moment Wendy was shocked. "You conceit," she exclaimed, with frightful sarcasm; "of course I did nothing!" "You did a little," Peter said carelessly, and continued

to dance. "A little!" she replied with hauteur. "If I am no use I can at least withdraw;" and she sprang in the most dignified way into bed and covered her face with the blankets.

To induce her to look up he pretended to be going away, and when this failed he sat on the end of the bed and tapped her gently with his foot. "Wendy," he said, "don't

withdraw. I can't help crowing, Wendy, when I'm pleased with myself." Still she would not look up, though she was listening eagerly. "Wendy," he continued, in a voice that

no woman has ever yet been able to resist, "Wendy, one girl is more use than twenty boys." Now Wendy was every inch a woman, though there were not very many inches,

and she peeped out of the bed-clothes. "Do you really think so, Peter?" "Yes, I do." "I think it's perfectly sweet of you," she declared, "and I'll get up again," and she sat

with him on the side of the bed. She also said she would give him a kiss if he liked, but Peter did not know what she meant, and he held out his hand expectantly. "Surely you

know what a kiss is?" she asked, aghast. "I shall know when you give it to me," he replied stiffly; and not to hurt his feelings she gave him a thimble. "Now," said he, "shall

I give you a kiss?" and she replied with a slight primness, "If you please." She made herself rather cheap by inclining her face toward him, but he merely dropped an acorn

button into her hand, so she slowly returned her face to where it had been before, and said nicely that she would wear his kiss on the chain round her neck. It was lucky that she did put it on that chain, for it was afterwards to save her life. When people in our set are introduced, it is customary for them to ask each other's age, and so Wendy, who always liked to do the correct thing, asked Peter how old he was. It was not really a happy question to ask him; it was like an examination paper that asks grammar, when what you want to be asked is Kings of England. "I don't know," he replied uneasily, "but I am quite young." He really knew nothing about it; he had merely suspicions, but he said at a venture, "Wendy, I ran away the day I was born." Wendy was quite surprised, but interested; and she indicated in the charming drawing-room manner, by a touch on her night-gown, that he could sit nearer her. "It was because I heard father and mother," he explained in a low voice, "talking about what I was to be when I became a man." He was extraordinarily agitated now. "I don't want ever to be a man," he said with passion. "I want always to be a little boy and to have fun. So I ran away to Kensington Gardens and lived a long, long time among the fairies." She gave him a look of the most intense admiration, and he thought it was because he had run away, but it was really because he knew fairies. Wendy had lived such a home life that to know fairies struck her as quite delightful. She poured out questions about them, to his surprise, for they were rather a nuisance to him, getting in his way and so on, and indeed he sometimes had to give them a hiding. Still, he liked them on the whole, and he told her about the beginning of fairies. "You see, Wendy, when the first baby laughed for the first time, its laugh broke into a thousand pieces, and they all went skipping about, and that was the beginning of fairies." Tedious talk this, but being a stay-at-home she liked it. "And so," he went on good-naturedly, "there ought to be one fairy for every boy and girl." "Ought to be? Isn't there?" "No. You see children know such a lot now, they soon don't believe in fairies, and every time a child says, 'I don't believe in fairies,' there is a fairy somewhere that falls down dead." Really, he thought they had now talked enough about fairies, and it struck him that Tinker Bell was keeping very quiet. "I can't think where she has gone to," he said, rising, and he called Tink by name. Wendy's heart went flutter with a sudden thrill. "Peter," she cried, clutching him, "you don't mean to tell me that there is a fairy in this room!" "She was here just now," he said a little impatiently. "You don't hear her, do you?" and they both listened. "The only sound I hear," said Wendy, "is like a tinkle of bells." "Well, that's Tink, that's the fairy language. I think I hear her too." The sound came from the chest of drawers, and Peter made a merry face. No one could ever look quite so merry as Peter, and the loveliest of gurgles was his laugh. He had his first laugh still. "Wendy," he whispered gleefully, "I do believe I shut her up in the drawer!" He let poor Tink out of the drawer, and she flew about the nursery screaming with fury. "You shouldn't say such things," Peter retorted. "Of course I'm very sorry, but how could I know you were in the drawer?" Wendy was not listening to him. "O Peter," she cried, "if she would only stand still and let me see her!" "They hardly ever stand still," he said, but for one moment Wendy saw the romantic figure come to rest on the cuckoo clock. "O the lovely!" she cried, though Tink's face was still distorted with passion. "Tink," said Peter amiably, "this lady says she wishes you were her fairy." Tinker Bell answered insolently. "What does she say, Peter?" He had to translate. "She is not very polite. She says you are a great ugly girl, and that she is my fairy." He tried to argue with Tink. "You know you can't be my fairy, Tink, because I am a gentleman and you are a lady." To this Tink replied in these words, "You silly ass," and disappeared into the bathroom. "She is quite a common fairy," Peter explained apologetically, "she is called Tinker Bell because she mends the pots and kettles." They were together in the armchair by this time, and Wendy plied

him with more questions. "If you don't live in Kensington Gardens now—" "Sometimes I do still." "But where do you live mostly now?" "With the lost boys." "Who are

they?" "They are the children who fall out of their perambulators when the nurse is looking the other way. If they are not claimed in seven days they are sent far away to

the Neverland to defray expenses. I'm captain." "What fun it must be!" "Yes," said cunning Peter, "but we are rather lonely. You see we have no female companionship."

"Are none of the others girls?" "Oh no; girls, you know, are much too clever to fall out of their prams." This flattered Wendy immensely. "I think," she said, "it is perfectly

lovely the way you talk about girls; John there just despises us." For reply Peter rose and kicked John out of bed, blankets and all; one kick. This seemed to Wendy rather

forward for a first meeting, and she told him with spirit that he was not captain in her house. However, John continued to sleep so placidly on the floor that she allowed him

to remain there. "And I know you meant to be kind," she said, relenting, "so you may give me a kiss." For the moment she had forgotten his ignorance about kisses. "I thought

you would want it back," he said a little bitterly, and offered to return her the thimble. "Oh dear," said the nice Wendy, "I don't mean a kiss, I mean a thimble." "What's

that?" "It's like this." She kissed him. "Funny!" said Peter gravely. "Now shall I give you a thimble?" "If you wish to," said Wendy, keeping her head erect this time. Peter

thimbled her, and almost immediately she screeched. "What is it, Wendy?" "It was exactly as if some one were pulling my hair." "That must have been Tink. I never knew

her so naughty before." And indeed Tink was darting about again, using offensive language. "She says she will do that to you, Wendy, every time I give you a thimble." "But

why?" "Why, Tink?" Again Tink replied, "You silly ass." Peter could not understand why, but Wendy understood; and she was just slightly disappointed when he admitted

that he came to the nursery window not to see her but to listen to stories. "You see I don't know any stories. None of the lost boys know any stories." "How perfectly awful,"

Wendy said. "Do you know," Peter asked, "why swallows build in the eaves of houses? It is to listen to the stories. O Wendy, your mother was telling you such a lovely

story." "Which story was it?" "About the prince who couldn't find the lady who wore the glass slipper." "Peter," said Wendy excitedly, "that was Cinderella, and he found

her, and they lived happy ever after." Peter was so glad that he rose from the floor, where they had been sitting, and hurried to the window. "Where are you going?" she cried

with misgiving. "To tell the other boys." "Don't go, Peter," she entreated, "I know such lots of stories." Those were her precise words, so there can be no denying that it

was she who first tempted him. He came back, and there was a greedy look in his eyes now which ought to have alarmed her, but did not. "Oh, the stories I could tell to the

boys!" she cried, and then Peter gripped her and began to draw her toward the window. "Let me go!" she ordered him. "Wendy, do come with me and tell the other boys."

Of course she was very pleased to be asked, but she said, "Oh dear, I can't. Think of mummy! Besides, I can't fly." "I'll teach you." "Oh, how lovely to fly." "I'll teach you

how to jump on the wind's back, and then away we go." "Oo!" she exclaimed rapturously. "Wendy, Wendy, when you are sleeping in your silly bed you might be flying about

with me saying funny things to the stars." "Oo!" "And, Wendy, there are mermaids." "Mermaids! With tails?" "Such long tails." "Oh," cried Wendy, "to see a mermaid!"

He had become frightfully cunning. "Wendy," he said, "how we should all respect you." She was wriggling her body in distress. It was quite as if she were trying to remain

on the nursery floor. But he had no pity for her. "Wendy," he said, the sly one, "you could tuck us in at night." "Oo!" "None of us has ever been tucked in at night." "Oo,"

and her arms went out to him. "And you could darn our clothes, and make pockets for us. None of us has any pockets." How could she resist. "Of course it's awfully

fascinating!" she cried. "Peter, would you teach John and Michael to fly too?" "If you like," he said indifferently, and she ran to John and Michael and shook them. "Wake

up," she cried, "Peter Pan has come and he is to teach us to fly." John rubbed his eyes. "Then I shall get up," he said. Of course he was on the floor already. "Hallo," he said,

"I am up!" Michael was up by this time also, looking as sharp as a knife with six blades and a saw, but Peter suddenly signed silence. Their faces assumed the awful craftiness

of children listening for sounds from the grown-up world. All was as still as salt. Then everything was right. No, stop! Everything was wrong. Nana, who had been barking

distressfully all the evening, was quiet now. It was her silence they had heard! "Out with the light! Hide! Quick!" cried John, taking command for the only time throughout

the whole adventure. And thus when Liza entered, holding Nana, the nursery seemed quite its old self, very dark; and you could have sworn you heard its three wicked

inmates breathing angelically as they slept. They were really doing it artfully from behind the window curtains. Liza was in a bad temper, for she was mixing the Christmas

puddings in the kitchen, and had been drawn away from them, with a raisin still on her cheek, by Nana's absurd suspicions. She thought the best way of getting a little quiet

was to take Nana to the nursery for a moment, but in custody of course. "There, you suspicious brute," she said, not sorry that Nana was in disgrace. "They are perfectly

safe, aren't they? Every one of the little angels sound asleep in bed. Listen to their gentle breathing." Here Michael, encouraged by his success, breathed so loudly that they

were nearly detected. Nana knew that kind of breathing, and she tried to drag herself out of Liza's clutches. But Liza was dense. "No more of it, Nana," she said sternly,

pulling her out of the room. "I warn you if you bark again I shall go straight for master and missus and bring them home from the party, and then, oh, won't master whip

you, just." She tied the unhappy dog up again, but do you think Nana ceased to bark? Bring master and missus home from the party! Why, that was just what she wanted.

Do you think she cared whether she was whipped so long as her charges were safe? Unfortunately Liza returned to her puddings, and Nana, seeing that no help would come

from her, strained and strained at the chain until at last she broke it. In another moment she had burst into the dining-room of 27 and flung up her paws to heaven, her most

expressive way of making a communication. Mr. and Mrs. Darling knew at once that something terrible was happening in their nursery, and without a good-bye to their

hostess they rushed into the street. But it was now ten minutes since three scoundrels had been breathing behind the curtains; and Peter Pan can do a great deal in ten minutes.

We now return to the nursery. "It's all right," John announced, emerging from his hiding-place. "I say, Peter, can you really fly?" Instead of troubling to answer him Peter

flew round the room, taking the mantelpiece on the way. "How topping!" said John and Michael. "How sweet!" cried Wendy. "Yes, I'm sweet, oh, I am sweet!" said Peter,

forgetting his manners again. It looked delightfully easy, and they tried it first from the floor and then from the beds, but they always went down instead of up. "I say, how do you do it?" asked John, rubbing his knee. He was quite a practical boy. "You just think lovely wonderful thoughts," Peter explained, "and they lift you up in the air." He showed them again. "You're so nippy at it," John said; "couldn't you do it very slowly once?" Peter did it both slowly and quickly. "I've got it now, Wendy!" cried John, but soon he found he had not. Not one of them could fly an inch, though even Michael was in words of two syllables, and Peter did not know A from Z. Of course Peter had been trifling with them, for no one can fly unless the fairy dust has been blown on him. Fortunately, as we have mentioned, one of his hands was messy with it, and he blew some on each of them, with the most superb results. "Now just wriggle your shoulders this way," he said, "and let go." They were all on their beds, and gallant Michael let go first. He did not quite mean to let go, but he did it, and immediately he was borne across the room. "I flewed!" he screamed while still in mid-air. John let go and met Wendy near the bathroom. "Oh, lovely!" "Oh, ripping!" "Look at me!" "Look at me!" "Look at me!" They were not nearly so elegant as Peter, they could not help kicking a little, but their heads were bobbing against the ceiling, and there is almost nothing so delicious as that. Peter gave Wendy a hand at first, but had to desist, Tink was so indignant. Up and down they went, and round and round. Heavenly was Wendy's word. "I say," cried John, "why shouldn't we all go out!" Of course it was to this that Peter had been luring them. Michael was ready: he wanted to see how long it took him to do a billion miles. But Wendy hesitated. "Mermaids!" said Peter again. "Oo!" "And there are pirates." "Pirates," cried John, seizing his Sunday hat, "let us go at once." It was just at this moment that Mr. and Mrs. Darling hurried with Nana out of 27. They ran into the middle of the street to look up at the nursery window; and, yes, it was still shut, but the room was ablaze with light, and most heart-gripping sight of all, they could see in shadow on the curtain three little figures in night attire circling round and round, not on the floor but in the air. Not three figures, four! In a tremble they opened the street door. Mr. Darling would have rushed upstairs, but Mrs. Darling signed to him to go softly. She even tried to make her heart go softly. Will they reach the nursery in time? If so, how delightful for them, and we shall all breathe a sigh of relief, but there will be no story. On the other hand, if they are not in time, I solemnly promise that it will all come right in the end. They would have reached the nursery in time had it not been that the little stars were watching them. Once again the stars blew the window open, and that smallest star of all called out: "Cave, Peter!" Then Peter knew that there was not a moment to lose. "Come," he cried imperiously, and soared out at once into the night, followed by John and Michael and Wendy. Mr. and Mrs. Darling and Nana rushed into the nursery too late. The birds were flown. CHAPTER IV *The Flight*

Second to the right, and straight on till morning." That, Peter had told Wendy, was the way to the Neverland; but even birds, carrying maps and consulting them at windy corners, could not have sighted it with these instructions. Peter, you see, just said anything that came into his head. At first his companions trusted him implicitly, and so great were the delights of flying that they wasted time circling round church spires or any other tall objects on the way that took their fancy. John and Michael raced, Michael getting a start. They recalled with contempt that not so long ago they had thought themselves fine fellows for being able to fly round a room. Not so long ago. But how long ago? They were flying over the sea before this thought began to disturb Wendy seriously. John thought it was their second sea and their third night. Sometimes it was dark and sometimes light, and now they were very cold and again too warm. Did they really feel hungry at times, or were they merely pretending, because Peter had such a jolly new way of feeding them? His way was to pursue birds who had food in their mouths suitable for humans and snatch it from them; then the birds would follow and snatch it back; and they would all go chasing each other gaily for miles, parting at last with mutual expressions of good-will. But Wendy noticed with gentle concern that Peter did not seem to know that this was rather an odd way of getting your bread and butter, nor even that there are other ways. Certainly they did not pretend to be sleepy, they were sleepy; and that was a danger, for the moment they popped off, down they fell. The awful thing was that Peter thought this funny. "There he goes again!" he would cry gleefully, as Michael suddenly dropped like a stone. "Save him, save him!" cried Wendy, looking with horror at the cruel sea far below. Eventually Peter would dive through the air, and catch Michael just before he could strike the sea, and it was lovely the way he did it; but he always waited till the last moment, and you felt it was his cleverness that interested him and not the saving of human life. Also he was fond of variety, and the sport that engrossed him one moment would suddenly cease to engage him, so there was always the possibility that the next time you fell he would let you go. He could sleep in the air without falling, by merely lying on his back and floating, but this was, partly at least, because he was so light that if you got behind him and blew he went faster. "Do be more polite to him," Wendy whispered to John, when they were playing "Follow my Leader." "Then tell him to stop showing off," said John. When playing Follow my Leader, Peter would fly close to the water and touch each shark's tail in passing, just as in the street you may run your finger along an iron railing. They could not follow him in this with much success, so perhaps it was rather like showing off, especially as he kept looking behind to see how many tails they missed. "You must be nice to him," Wendy impressed on her brothers. "What could we do if he were to leave us?" "We could go back," Michael said. "How could we ever find our way back without him?" "Well, then, we could go on," said John. "That is the awful thing, John. We should have to go on, for we don't know how to stop." This was true; Peter had forgotten to show them how to stop. John said that if the worst came to the worst, all they had to do was to go straight on, for the world was round, and so in time they must come back to their own window. "And who is to get food for us, John?" "I nipped a bit out of that eagle's mouth pretty neatly, Wendy." "After the twentieth try," Wendy reminded him. "And even though we became good at picking up food, see how we bump against clouds and things if he is not near to give us a hand." Indeed they were constantly bumping. They could now fly strongly, though they still kicked far too much; but if they saw a cloud in front of them, the more they tried to avoid it, the more certainly did they bump into it. If Nana had been with them, she would have had a bandage round Michael's forehead by this time. Peter was not with them for the moment, and they felt rather lonely up there by themselves. He could go so much faster than they that he would suddenly shoot out of sight, to have some adventure in which they had no share. He would come down laughing over something fearfully funny he had been saying to a star, but he had already forgotten what it was, or he would come up with mermaid scales still sticking to him, and yet not be able to say for certain what had been happening. It was really rather irritating to children who had never seen a mermaid. "And if he forgets them, so quickly," Wendy argued, "how can we expect that he will go on remembering us?" Indeed, sometimes when he returned he did not remember them, at least not well. Wendy was sure of it. She saw recognition come into his eyes as he was about to pass them the time of day and go on; once even she had to tell him her name. "I'm Wendy," she said agitatedly. He was very sorry. "I say, Wendy," he whispered to her, "always if you see me forgetting you, just keep on saying 'I'm Wendy,' and then I'll remember." Of course this was rather unsatisfactory. However, to make amends he showed them how to lie out flat on a strong wind that was going their way, and this was such a pleasant change that they tried it several times and found they could sleep thus with security. Indeed they would have slept longer, but Peter tired quickly of sleeping, and soon he would cry in his captain voice, "We get off here." So with occasional tiffs, but on the whole rollicking, they drew near the Neverland; for after many moons they did reach it, and, what is more, they had been going pretty straight all the time, not perhaps so much owing to the guidance of Peter or Tink as because the island was out looking for them. It is only thus that any one may sight those magic shores. "There it is," said Peter calmly. "Where, where?" "Where all the arrows are pointing." Indeed a million golden arrows were pointing out the island to the children, all directed by their friend the sun, who wanted them to be sure of their way before leaving them for the night. Wendy and John and Michael stood on tiptoe in the air to get their first sight of the island. Strange to say, they all recognised it at once, and until fear fell upon them they hailed it, not as something long dreamt of and seen at last, but as a familiar friend to whom they were returning home for the holidays. "John, there's the lagoon!" "Wendy, look at the turtles burying their eggs in the sand." "I say, John, I see your flamingo with the broken leg!" "Look, Michael, there's your cave!" "John, what's that in the brushwood?" "It's a wolf with her whelps. Wendy, I do believe that's your little whelp!" "There's my boat, John, with her sides stove in!" "No, it isn't! Why, we burned your boat." "That's her, at any rate. I say, John, I see the smoke of the redskin camp!" "Where? Show me, and I'll tell you by the way the smoke curls whether they are on the war-path." "There, just across the Mysterious River." "I see now. Yes, they are on the war-path right enough." Peter was a little annoyed with them for knowing so much, but if he wanted to lord it over them his triumph was at hand, for have I not told you that anon fear fell upon them? It came as the arrows went, leaving the island in gloom. In the old days at home the Neverland had always begun to look a little dark and threatening by bedtime. Then unexplored patches arose in it and spread, black shadows moved about in them, the roar of the beasts of prey was quite different now, and above all, you lost the certainty that you would win. You were quite glad that the night-lights were in. You even liked Nana to say that this was just the mantelpiece over here, and that the Neverland was all make-believe. Of course the Neverland had been make-believe in those days, but it was real now, and there were no night-lights, and it was getting darker every moment, and where was Nana? They had been flying apart, but they huddled close to Peter now. His careless manner had gone at last, his eyes were sparkling, and a tingle went through them every time they touched his body. They were now over the fearsome island, flying so low that sometimes a tree grazed their feet. Nothing horrid was visible in the air, yet their progress had become slow and laboured, exactly as if they were pushing their way through hostile forces. Sometimes they hung in the air until Peter had beaten on it with his fists. "They don't want us to land," he explained. "Who are they?" Wendy whispered, shuddering. But he could not or would not say. Tinker Bell had been asleep on his shoulder, but now he wakened her and sent her on in front. Sometimes he poised himself in the air, listening intently, with his hand to his ear, and again he would stare down with eyes so bright that they seemed to bore two holes to earth. Having done these things, he went on again. His courage was almost appalling. "Would you like an adventure now," he said casually to John, "or would you like to have your tea first?" Wendy said "tea first" quickly, and Michael pressed her hand in gratitude, but the braver John hesitated. "What kind of adventure?" he asked cautiously. "There's a pirate asleep in the pampas just beneath us," Peter told him. "If you like, we'll go down and kill him." "I don't see him," John said after a long pause. "I do." "Suppose," John said a little huskily, "he were to wake up." Peter spoke indignantly. "You don't think I would kill him while he was sleeping! I would wake him first, and then kill him. That's the way I always do." "I say! Do you kill many?"

"Tons." John said "how ripping," but decided to have tea first. He asked if there were many pirates on the island just now, and Peter said he had never known so many. "Who is captain now?" "Hook," answered Peter; and his face became very stern as he said that hated word. "Jas. Hook?" "Ay." Then indeed Michael began to cry, and even John could speak in gulps only, for they knew Hook's reputation. "He was Blackbeard's bo'sun," John whispered huskily. "He is the worst of them all. He is the only man of whom Barbecue was afraid." "That's him," said Peter. "What is he like? Is he big?" "He is not so big as he was." "How do you mean?" "I cut off a bit of him." "You!" "Yes, me," said Peter sharply. "I wasn't meaning to be disrespectful." "Oh, all right." "But, I say, what bit?" "His right hand." "Then he can't fight now?" "Oh, can't he just!" "Left-hander?" "He has an iron hook instead of a right hand, and he claws with it." "Claws!" "I say, John," said Peter. "Yes." "Say, 'Ay, ay, sir.'" "Ay, ay, sir." "There is one thing," Peter continued, "that every boy who serves under me has to promise, and so must you." John paled. "It is this, if we meet Hook in open fight, you must leave him to me."

"I promise," John said loyally. For the moment they were feeling less eerie because Tink was flying with them, and in her light they could distinguish each other. Unfortunately she could not fly so slowly as they, and so she had to go round and round them in a circle in which they moved as in a halo. Wendy quite liked it, until Peter pointed out the drawback. "She tells me," he said, "that the pirates sighted us before the darkness came, and got Long Tom out." "The big gun?" "Yes. And of course they must see her light, and if they guess we are near it they are sure to let fly." "Wendy!" "John!" "Michael!" "Tell her to go away at once, Peter," the three cried simultaneously, but he refused. "She thinks we have lost the way," he replied stiffly, "and she is rather frightened. You don't think I would send her away all by herself when she is frightened!"

For a moment the circle of light was broken, and something gave Peter a loving little pinch. "Then tell her," Wendy begged, "to put out her light." "She can't put it out. That is about the only thing fairies can't do. It just goes out of itself when she falls asleep, same as the stars." "Then tell her to sleep at once," John almost ordered. "She can't sleep except when she's sleepy. It is the only other thing fairies can't do." "Seems to me," growled John, "these are the only two things worth doing." Here he got a pinch, but not a loving one. "If only one of us had a pocket," Peter said, "we could carry her in it." However, they had set off in such a hurry that there was not a pocket between the four of them. He had a happy idea. John's hat! Tink agreed to travel by hat if it was carried in the hand. John carried it, though she had hoped to be carried by Peter. Presently

Wendy took the hat, because John said it struck against his knee as he flew; and this, as we shall see, led to mischief, for Tinker Bell hated to be under an obligation to Wendy.

In the black topper the light was completely hidden, and they flew on in silence. It was the stillest silence they had ever known, broken once by a distant lapping, which Peter explained was the wild beasts drinking at the ford, and again by a rasping sound that might have been the branches of trees rubbing together, but he said it was the redskins sharpening their knives. Even these noises ceased. To Michael the loneliness was dreadful. "If only something would make a sound!" he cried. As if in answer to his request, the air was rent by the most tremendous crash he had ever heard. The pirates had fired Long Tom at them. The roar of it echoed through the mountains, and the echoes seemed to cry savagely, "Where are they, where are they, where are they?" Thus sharply did the terrified three learn the difference between an island of make-believe and the same island come true. When at last the heavens were steady again, John and Michael found themselves alone in the darkness. John was treading the air mechanically, and Michael without knowing how to float was floating. "Are you shot?" John whispered tremulously. "I haven't tried yet," Michael whispered back. We know now that no one had been hit. Peter, however, had been carried by the wind of the shot far out to sea, while Wendy was blown upwards with no companion but Tinker Bell. It would have been well for Wendy if at that moment she had dropped the hat. I don't know whether the idea came suddenly to Tink, or whether she had planned it on the way, but she at once popped out of the hat and began to lure Wendy to her destruction. Tink was not all bad: or, rather, she was all bad just now, but, on the other hand, sometimes she was all good. Fairies have to be one thing or the other, because being so small they unfortunately have room for one feeling only at a time. They are, however, allowed to change, only it must be a complete change. At present she was full of jealousy of Wendy. What she said in her lovely tinkle Wendy could not of course understand, and I believe some of it was bad words, but it sounded kind, and she flew back and forward, plainly meaning "Follow me, and all will be well." What else could poor Wendy do? She called to Peter and John and Michael, and got only mocking echoes in reply. She did not yet know that Tink hated her with the fierce hatred of a very woman. And so, bewildered, and now staggering in her flight, she followed Tink to her doom. CHAPTER V *The Island Come True* Feeling that Peter was on his way back, the Neverland had again woke into life. We ought to use the pluperfect and say wakened, but woke is better and was always used by Peter. In his absence things are usually quiet on the island. The fairies take an hour longer in the morning, the beasts attend to their young, the redskins feed heavily for six days and nights, and when pirates and lost boys meet they merely bite their thumbs at each other. But with the coming of Peter, who hates lethargy, they are all under way again: if you put your ear to the ground now, you would hear the whole island seething with life. On this evening the chief forces of the island were disposed as follows. The lost boys were out looking for Peter, the pirates were out looking for the lost boys, the redskins were out looking for the pirates, and the beasts were out looking for the redskins. They were going round and round the island, but they did not meet because all were going at the same rate. All wanted blood except the boys, who liked it as a rule, but to-night were out to greet their captain. The boys on the island vary, of course, in numbers, according as they get killed and so on; and when they seem to be growing up, which is against the rules, Peter thins them out; but at this time there were six of them, counting the twins as two. Let us pretend to lie here among the sugar-cane and watch them as they steal by in single file, each with his hand on his dagger.

They are forbidden by Peter to look in the least like him, and they wear the skins of bears slain by themselves, in which they are so round and furry that when they fall they

roll. They have therefore become very sure-footed. The first to pass is Tootles, not the least brave but the most unfortunate of all that gallant band. He had been in fewer

adventures than any of them because the big things constantly happened just when he had stepped round the corner; all would be quiet, he would take the opportunity of

going off to gather a few sticks for firewood, and then when he returned the others would be sweeping up the blood. This ill-luck had given a gentle melancholy to his

countenance, but instead of souring his nature had sweetened it, so that he was quite the humblest of the boys. Poor kind Tootles, there is danger in the air for you to-night.

Take care lest an adventure is now offered you, which, if accepted, will plunge you in deepest woe. Tootles, the fairy Tink who is bent on mischief this night is looking for

a tool, and she thinks you the most easily tricked of the boys. 'Ware Tinker Bell. Would that he could hear us, but we are not really on the island, and he passes by, biting his

knuckles. Next comes Nibs, the gay and debonair, followed by Slightly, who cuts whistles out of the trees and dances ecstatically to his own tunes. Slightly is the most

conceited of the boys. He thinks he remembers the days before he was lost, with their manners and customs, and this has given his nose an offensive tilt. Curly is fourth; he

is a pickle, and so often has he had to deliver up his person when Peter said sternly, "Stand forth the one who did this thing," that now at the command he stands forth

automatically whether he has done it or not. Last come the Twins, who cannot be described because we should be sure to be describing the wrong one. Peter never quite knew

what twins were, and his band were not allowed to know anything he did not know, so these two were always vague about themselves, and did their best to give satisfaction

by keeping close together in an apologetic sort of way. The boys vanish in the gloom, and after a pause, but not a long pause, for things go briskly on the island, come the

pirates on their track. We hear them before they are seen, and it is always the same dreadful song: "Avast belay, yo ho, heave to, A-pirating we go, And if we're parted by a

shot We're sure to meet below!" A more villainous-looking lot never hung in a row on Execution dock. Here, a little in advance, ever and again with his head to the ground

listening, his great arms bare, pieces of eight in his ears as ornaments, is the handsome Italian Cecco, who cut his name in letters of blood on the back of the governor of the

prison at Gao. That gigantic black behind him has had many names since he dropped the one with which dusky mothers still terrify their children on the banks of the Guadjo-

mo. Here is Bill Jukes, every inch of him tattooed, the same Bill Jukes who got six dozen on the *Walrus* from Flint before he would drop the bag of moidores; and Cookson,

said to be Black Murphy's brother (but this was never proved); and Gentleman Starkey, once an usher in a public school and still dainty in his ways of killing; and Skylights

(Morgan's Skylights); and the Irish bo'sun Smee, an oddly genial man who stabbed, so to speak, without offence, and was the only Nonconformist in Hook's crew; and

Noodler, whose hands were fixed on backwards; and Robt. Mullins and Alf Mason and many another ruffian long known and feared on the Spanish Main. In the midst of

them, the blackest and largest jewel in that dark setting, reclined James Hook, or as he wrote himself, Jas. Hook, of whom it is said he was the only man that the Sea-Cook feared. He lay at his ease in a rough chariot drawn and propelled by his men, and instead of a right hand he had the iron hook with which ever and anon he encouraged them to increase their pace. As dogs this terrible man treated and addressed them, and as dogs they obeyed him. In person he was cadaverous and blackavized, and his hair was dressed in long curls, which at a little distance looked like black candles, and gave a singularly threatening expression to his handsome countenance. His eyes were of the blue of the forget-me-not, and of a profound melancholy, save when he was plunging his hook into you, at which time two red spots appeared in them and lit them up horribly. In manner, something of the grand seigneur still clung to him, so that he even ripped you up with an air, and I have been told that he was a *raconteur* of repute. He was never more sinister than when he was most polite, which is probably the truest test of breeding; and the elegance of his diction, even when he was swearing, no less than the distinction of his demeanour, showed him one of a different caste from his crew. A man of indomitable courage, it was said of him that the only thing he shied at was the sight of his own blood, which was thick and of an unusual colour. In dress he somewhat aped the attire associated with the name of Charles II, having heard it said in some earlier period of his career that he bore a strange resemblance to the ill-fated Stuarts; and in his mouth he had a holder of his own contrivance which enabled him to smoke two cigars at once. But undoubtedly the grimmest part of him was his iron claw. Let us now kill a pirate, to show Hook's method. Skylights will do. As they pass, Skylights lurches clumsily against him, ruffling his lace collar; the hook shoots forth, there is a tearing sound and one screech, then the body is kicked aside, and the pirates pass on. He has not even taken the cigars from his mouth. Such is the terrible man against whom Peter Pan is pitted. Which will win? On the trail of the pirates, stealing noiselessly down the war-path, which is not visible to inexperienced eyes, come the redskins, every one of them with his eyes peeled. They carry tomahawks and knives, and their naked bodies gleam with paint and oil. Strung around them are scalps, of boys as well as of pirates, for these are the Piccaninny tribe, and not to be confused with the softer-hearted Delawares or the Hurons. In the van, on all fours, is Great Big Little Panther, a brave of so many scalps that in his present position they somewhat impede his progress. Bringing up the rear, the place of greatest danger, comes Tiger Lily, proudly erect, a princess in her own right. She is the most beautiful of dusky Dianas and the belle of the Piccaninnies, coquettish, cold and amorous by turns; there is not a brave who would not have the wayward thing to wife, but she staves off the altar with a hatchet. Observe how they pass over fallen twigs without making the slightest noise. The only sound to be heard is their somewhat heavy breathing. The fact is that they are all a little fat just now after the heavy gorging, but in time they will work this off. For the moment, however, it constitutes their chief danger. The redskins disappear as they have come like shadows, and soon their place is taken by the beasts, a great and motley procession: lions, tigers, bears, and the innumerable smaller savage things that flee from them, for every kind of beast, and, more particularly, all the man-eaters, live cheek by jowl on the favoured island. Their tongues are hanging out, they are hungry to-night. When they have passed, comes the last figure of all, a gigantic crocodile. We shall see for whom she is looking presently. The crocodile passes, but soon the boys appear again, for the procession must continue indefinitely until one of the parties stops or changes its pace. Then quickly they will be on top of each other. All are keeping a sharp look-out in front, but none suspects that the danger may be creeping up from behind. This shows how real the island was. The first to fall out of the moving circle was the boys. They flung themselves down on the sward, close to their underground home. "I do wish Peter would come back," every one of them said nervously, though in height and still more in breadth they were all larger than their captain. "I am the only one who is not afraid of the pirates," Slightly said, in the tone that prevented his being a general favourite; but perhaps some distant sound disturbed him, for he added hastily, "but I wish he would come back, and tell us whether he has heard anything more about Cinderella." They talked of Cinderella, and Tootles was confident that his mother must have been very like her. It was only in Peter's absence that they could speak of mothers, the subject being forbidden by him as silly. "All I remember about my mother," Nibs told them, "is that she often said to father, 'Oh, how I wish I had a cheque-book of my own.'" I don't know what a cheque-book is, but I should just love to give my mother one." While they talked they heard a distant sound. You or I, not being wild things of the woods, would have heard nothing, but they heard it, and it was the grim song: "Yo ho, yo ho, the pirate life, The flag o' skull and bones, A merry hour, a hempen rope, And hey for Davy Jones." At once the lost boys—but where are they? They are no longer there. Rabbits could not have disappeared more quickly. I will tell you where they are. With the exception of Nibs, who has darted away to reconnoitre, they are already in their home under the ground, a very delightful residence of which we shall see a good deal presently. But how have they reached it? for there is no entrance to be seen, not so much as a large stone, which if rolled away would disclose the mouth of a cave. Look closely, however, and you may note that there are here seven large trees, each with a hole in its hollow trunk as large as a boy. **These are the seven entrances to the home under the ground, for which Hook has been searching in vain these many moons.** Will he find it to-night? As the pirates advanced, the quick eye of Starkey sighted Nibs disappearing through the wood, and at once his pistol flashed out. But an iron claw gripped his shoulder. "Captain, let go," he cried, writhing. Now for the first time we hear the voice of Hook. It was a black voice. "Put back that pistol first," it said threateningly. "It was one of those boys you hate. I could have shot him dead." "Ay, and the sound would have brought Tiger Lily's redskins upon us. Do you want to lose your scalp?" "Shall I after him, captain," asked pathetic Smee, "and tickle him with Johnny Corkscrew?" Smee had pleasant names for everything, and his cutlass was Johnny Corkscrew, because he wriggled it in the wound. One could mention many lovable traits in Smee. For instance, after killing, it was his spectacles he wiped instead of his weapon. "Johnny's a silent fellow," he reminded Hook. "Not now, Smee," Hook said darkly. "He is only one, and I want to mischief all the seven. Scatter and look for them." The pirates disappeared among the trees, and in a moment their captain and Smee were alone. Hook heaved a heavy sigh; and I know not why it was, perhaps it was because of the soft beauty of the evening, but there came over him a desire to confide to his faithful bo'sun the story of his life. He spoke long and earnestly, but what it was all about Smee, who was rather stupid, did not know in the least. Anon he caught the word Peter. "Most of all," Hook was saying passionately, "I want their captain, Peter Pan. 'Twas he cut off my arm." He brandished the hook threateningly. "I've waited long to shake his hand with this. Oh, I'll tear him!" "And yet," said Smee, "I have often heard you say that hook was worth a score of hands, for combing the hair and other homely uses." "Ay," the captain answered, "if I was a mother I would pray to have my children born with this instead of that," and he cast a look of pride upon his iron hand and one of scorn upon the other. Then again he frowned. "Peter flung my arm," he said, wincing, "to a crocodile that happened to be passing by." "I have often," said Smee, "noticed your strange dread of crocodiles." "Not of crocodiles," Hook corrected him, "but of that one crocodile." He lowered his voice. "It liked my arm so much, Smee, that it has followed me ever since, from sea to sea and from land to land, licking its lips for the rest of me." "In a way," said Smee, "it's a sort of compliment." "I want no such compliments," Hook barked petulantly. "I want Peter Pan, who first gave the brute its taste for me." He sat down on a large mushroom, and now there was a quiver in his voice. "Smee," he said huskily, "that crocodile would have had me before this, but by a lucky chance it swallowed a clock which goes tick tick inside it, and so before it can reach me I hear the tick and bolt." He laughed, but in a hollow way. "Some day," said Smee, "the clock will run down, and then he'll get you." Hook wetted his dry lips. "Ay," he said, "that's the fear that haunts me." Since sitting down he had felt curiously warm. "Smee," he said, "this seat is hot." He jumped up. "Odds bobs, hammer and tongs I'm burning." They examined the mushroom, which was of a size and solidity unknown on the mainland; they tried to pull it up, and it came away at once in their hands, for it had no root. Stranger still, smoke began at once to ascend. The pirates looked at each other. "A chimney!" they both exclaimed. They had indeed discovered the chimney of the home under the ground. It was the custom of the boys to stop it with a mushroom when enemies were in the neighbourhood. Not only smoke came out of it. There came also children's voices, for so safe did the boys feel in their hiding-place that they were gaily chattering. The pirates listened grimly, and then replaced the mushroom. They looked around them and noted the holes in the seven trees. "Did you hear them say Peter Pan's from home?" Smee whispered, fidgeting with Johnny Corkscrew. Hook nodded. He stood for a long time lost in thought, and at last a curdling smile lit up his swarthy face. Smee had been waiting for it. "Unrip your plan, captain," he cried eagerly. "To return to the ship," Hook replied slowly through his teeth, "and cook a large rich cake of a jolly thickness with green sugar on it. There can be but one room below, for there is but one chimney. The silly moles had not the sense to see that they did not need a door apiece. That shows they have no mother. We will leave the cake on the shore of the mermaids' lagoon. These boys are always swimming about there, playing with the mermaids. They will find the cake and they will gobble it up, because, having no mother, they don't know how dangerous 'tis to eat rich damp cake." He burst into laughter, not hollow laughter now, but honest laughter. "Aha, they will die. Smee had listened with growing admiration. "It's the wickedest, prettiest policy ever I heard of," he cried, and in their exultation they danced and sang: "Avast, belay, when I appear, By fear they're overtook; Nought's left upon your bones when you Have shaken claws with Cook." They began the verse, but they never finished it, for another sound broke in and stilled them. It was at first such a tiny sound that a leaf might have fallen on it and smothered it, but as it came nearer it was more distinct. *Tick tick tick tick!* Hook stood shuddering, one foot in the air. "The crocodile," he gasped, and bounded away, followed by his bo'sun. It was indeed the crocodile. It had passed the redskins, who were now on the trail of the other pirates. It oozed on after Hook. Once more the boys emerged into the open; but the dangers of the night were not yet over, for presently Nibs rushed breathless into their midst, pursued by a pack of wolves. The tongues of the pursuers were hanging out; the baying of them was horrible.

"Save me, save me!" cried Nibs, falling on the ground. "But what can we do, what can we do?" It was a high compliment to Peter that at that dire moment their thoughts

turned to him. "What would Peter do?" they cried simultaneously. Almost in the same breath they added, "Peter would look at them through his legs." And then, "Let us

do what Peter would do." It is quite the most successful way of defying wolves, and as one boy they bent and looked through their legs. The next moment is the long one;

but victory came quickly, for as the boys advanced upon them in this terrible attitude, the wolves dropped their tails and fled. Now Nibs rose from the ground, and the others

thought that his staring eyes still saw the wolves. But it was not wolves he saw. "I have seen a wonderfuller thing," he cried, as they gathered round him eagerly. "A great

white bird. It is flying this way." "What kind of a bird, do you think?" "I don't know," Nibs said, awestruck, "but it looks so weary, and as it flies it moans, 'Poor Wendy.'"

"Poor Wendy?" "I remember," said Slightly instantly, "there are birds called Wendies." "See, it comes," cried Curly, pointing to Wendy in the heavens. Wendy was now

almost overhead, and they could hear her plaintive cry. But more distinct came the shrill voice of Tinker Bell. The jealous fairy had now cast off all disguise of friendship,

and was darting at her victim from every direction, pinching savagely each time she touched. "Hullo, Tink," cried the wondering boys. Tink's reply rang out: "Peter wants

you to shoot the Wendy." It was not in their nature to question when Peter ordered. "Let us do what Peter wishes," cried the simple boys. "Quick, bows and arrows." All but

Tootles popped down their trees. He had a bow and arrow with him, and Tink noted it, and rubbed her little hands. "Quick, Tootles, quick," she screamed. "Peter will be so

pleased." Tootles excitedly fitted the arrow to his bow. "Out of the way, Tink," he shouted; and then he fired, and Wendy fluttered to the ground with an arrow in her breast.

CHAPTER VI *The Little House* Foolish Tootles was standing like a conqueror over Wendy's body when the other boys sprang, armed, from their trees. "You are too late,"

he cried proudly, "I have shot the Wendy. Peter will be so pleased with me." Overhead Tinker Bell shouted "Silly ass!" and darted into hiding. The others did not hear her.

They had crowded round Wendy, and as they looked a terrible silence fell upon the wood. If Wendy's heart had been beating they would all have heard it. Slightly was the

first to speak. "This is no bird," he said in a scared voice. "I think it must be a lady." "A lady?" said Tootles, and fell a-trembling. "And we have killed her," Nibs said hoarsely.

They all whipped off their caps. "Now I see," Curly said; "Peter was bringing her to us." He threw himself sorrowfully on the ground. "A lady to take care of us at last,"

said one of the twins, "and you have killed her." They were sorry for him, but sorrier for themselves, and when he took a step nearer them they turned from him. Tootles'

face was very white, but there was a dignity about him now that had never been there before. "I did it," he said, reflecting. "When ladies used to come to me in dreams, I said,

'Pretty mother, pretty mother.' But when at last she really came, I shot her." He moved slowly away. "Don't go," they called in pity. "I must," he answered, shaking; "I am

so afraid of Peter." It was at this tragic moment that they heard a sound which made the heart of every one of them rise to his mouth. They heard Peter crow. "Peter!" they

cried, for it was always thus that he signalled his return. "Hide her," they whispered, and gathered hastily around Wendy. But Tootles stood aloof. Again came that ringing crow, and Peter dropped in front of them. "Greeting, boys," he cried, and mechanically they saluted, and then again was silence. He frowned. "I am back," he said hotly,

"why do you not cheer?" They opened their mouths, but the cheers would not come. He overlooked it in his haste to tell the glorious tidings. "Great news, boys," he cried,

"I have brought at last a mother for you all." Still no sound, except a little thud from Tootles as he dropped on his knees. "Have you not seen her?" asked Peter, becoming

troubled. "She flew this way." "Ah me," one voice said, and another said, "Oh, mournful day." Tootles rose. "Peter," he said quietly, "I will show her to you," and when the

others would still have hidden her he said, "Back, twins, let Peter see." So they all stood back, and let him see, and after he had looked for a little time he did not know what

to do next. "She is dead," he said uncomfortably. "Perhaps she is frightened at being dead." He thought of hopping off in a comic sort of way till he was out of sight of her,

and then never going near the spot any more. They would all have been glad to follow if he had done this. But there was the arrow. He took it from her heart and faced his

band. "Whose arrow?" he demanded sternly. "Mine, Peter," said Tootles on his knees. "Oh, dastard hand," Peter said, and he raised the arrow to use it as a dagger. Tootles

did not flinch. He bared his breast. "Strike, Peter," he said firmly, "strike true." Twice did Peter raise the arrow, and twice did his hand fall. "I cannot strike," he said with

awe, "there is something stays my hand." All looked at him in wonder, save Nibs, who fortunately looked at Wendy. "It is she," he cried, "the Wendy lady; see, her arm."

Wonderful to relate, Wendy had raised her arm. Nibs bent over her and listened reverently. "I think she said 'Poor Tootles,'" he whispered. "She lives," Peter said briefly.

Slightly cried instantly, "The Wendy lady lives." Then Peter knelt beside her and found his button. You remember she had put it on a chain that she wore round her neck.

"See," he said, "the arrow struck against this. It is the kiss I gave her. It has saved her life." "I remember kisses," Slightly interposed quickly, "let me see it. Ay, that's a kiss."

Peter did not hear him. He was begging Wendy to get better quickly, so that he could show her the mermaids. Of course she could not answer yet, being still in a frightful

faint; but from overhead came a wailing note. "Listen to Tink," said Curly, "she is crying because the Wendy lives." Then they had to tell Peter of Tink's crime, and almost

never had they seen him look so stern. "Listen, Tinker Bell," he cried, "I am your friend no more. Begone from me for ever." She flew on to his shoulder and pleaded, but

he brushed her off. Not until Wendy again raised her arm did he relent sufficiently to say, "Well, not for ever, but for a whole week." Do you think Tinker Bell was grateful

to Wendy for raising her arm? Oh dear no, never wanted to pinch her so much. Fairies indeed are strange, and Peter, who understood them best, often cuffed them. But what

to do with Wendy in her present delicate state of health? "Let us carry her down into the house," Curly suggested. "Ay," said Slightly, "that is what one does with ladies."

"No, no," Peter said, "you must not touch her. It would not be sufficiently respectful." "That," said Slightly, "is what I was thinking." "But if she lies there," Tootles said,

"she will die." "Ay, she will die," Slightly admitted, "but there is no way out." "Yes, there is," cried Peter. "Let us build a little house round her." They were all delighted.

"Quick," he ordered them, "bring me each of you the best of what we have. Gut our house. Be sharp." In a moment they were as busy as tailors the night before a wedding.

They scurried this way and that, down for bedding, up for firewood, and while they were at it, who should appear but John and Michael. As they dragged along the ground they fell asleep standing, stopped, woke up, moved another step and slept again. "John, John," Michael would cry, "wake up. Where is Nana, John, and mother?" And then

John would rub his eyes and mutter, "It is true, we did fly." You may be sure they were very relieved to find Peter. "Hullo, Peter," they said. "Hullo," replied Peter amicably,

though he had quite forgotten them. He was very busy at the moment measuring Wendy with his feet to see how large a house she would need. Of course he meant to leave

room for chairs and a table. John and Michael watched him. "Is Wendy asleep?" they asked. "Yes." "John," Michael proposed, "let us wake her and get her to make supper

for us," but as he said it some of the other boys rushed on carrying branches for the building of the house. "Look at them!" he cried. "Curly," said Peter in his most captainy

voice, "see that these boys help in the building of the house." "Ay, ay, sir." "Build a house?" exclaimed John. "For the Wendy," said Curly. "For Wendy?" John said, aghast.

"Why, she is only a girl." "That," explained Curly, "is why we are her servants." "You? Wendy's servants!" "Yes," said Peter, "and you also. Away with them." The

astounded brothers were dragged away to hack and hew and carry. "Chairs and a fender first," Peter ordered. "Then we shall build the house round them." "Ay," said

Slightly, "that is how a house is built; it all comes back to me." Peter thought of everything. "Slightly," he ordered, "fetch a doctor." "Ay, ay," said Slightly at once, and

disappeared, scratching his head. But he knew Peter must be obeyed, and he returned in a moment, wearing John's hat and looking solemn. "Please, sir," said Peter, going

to him, "are you a doctor?" The difference between him and the other boys at such a time was that they knew it was make-believe, while to him make-believe and true were

exactly the same thing. This sometimes troubled them, as when they had to make-believe that they had had their dinners. If they broke down in their make-believe he rapped

them on the knuckles. "Yes, my little man," anxiously replied Slightly, who had chapped knuckles. "Please, sir," Peter explained, "a lady lies very ill." She was lying at their

feet, but Slightly had the sense not to see her. "Tut, tut, tut," he said, "where does she lie?" "In yonder glade." "I will put a glass thing in her mouth," said Slightly; and he

made-believe to do it, while Peter waited. It was an anxious moment when the glass thing was withdrawn. "How is she?" inquired Peter. "Tut, tut, tut," said Slightly, "this

has cured her." "I am glad," Peter cried. "I will call again in the evening," Slightly said; "give her beef tea out of a cup with a spout to it;" but after he had returned the hat

to John he blew big breaths, which was his habit on escaping from a difficulty. In the meantime the wood had been alive with the sound of axes; almost everything needed

for a cosy dwelling already lay at Wendy's feet. "If only we knew," said one, "the kind of house she likes best." "Peter," shouted another, "she is moving in her sleep." "Her

mouth opens," cried a third, looking respectfully into it. "Oh, lovely!" "Perhaps she is going to sing in her sleep," said Peter. "Wendy, sing the kind of house you would like

to have." Immediately, without opening her eyes, Wendy began to sing: "I wish I had a pretty house, The littlest ever seen, With funny little red walls And roof of mossy

green." They gurgled with joy at this, for by the greatest good luck the branches they had brought were sticky with red sap, and all the ground was carpeted with moss. As

they rattled up the little house they broke into song themselves: "We've built the little walls and roof And made a lovely door, So tell us, mother Wendy, What are you

wanting more?" To this she answered rather greedily: "Oh, really next I think I'll have Gay windows all about, With roses peeping in, you know, And babies peeping out."

With a blow of their fists they made windows, and large yellow leaves were the blinds. But roses—? "Roses," cried Peter sternly. Quickly they made-believe to grow the loveliest roses up the walls. Babies? To prevent Peter ordering babies they hurried into song again: "We've made the roses peeping out, The babes are at the door, We cannot make ourselves, you know, 'Cos we've been made before." Peter, seeing this to be a good idea, at once pretended that it was his own. The house was quite beautiful, and no doubt Wendy was very cosy within, though, of course, they could no longer see her. Peter strode up and down, ordering finishing touches. Nothing escaped his eagle eye. Just when it seemed absolutely finished, "There's no knocker on the door," he said. They were very ashamed, but Tootles gave the sole of his shoe, and it made an excellent knocker. Absolutely finished now, they thought. Not a bit of it. "There's no chimney," Peter said; "we must have a chimney." "It certainly does need a chimney," said John importantly. This gave Peter an idea. He snatched the hat off John's head, knocked out the bottom, and put the hat on the roof. **The little house was so pleased to have such a capital chimney that, as if to say thank you, smoke immediately began to come out of the hat.** Now really and truly it was finished. Nothing remained to do but to knock. "All look your best," Peter warned them; "first impressions are awfully important." He was glad no one asked him what first impressions are; they were all too busy looking their best. He knocked politely; and now the wood was as still as the children, not a sound to be heard except from Tinker Bell, who was watching from a branch and openly sneering. What the boys were wondering was, would any one answer the knock? If a lady, what would she be like? The door opened and a lady came out. It was Wendy. They all whipped off their hats. She looked properly surprised, and this was just how they had hoped she would look. "Where am I?" she said. Of course Slightly was the first to get his word in. "Wendy lady," he said rapidly, "for you we built this house." "Oh, say you're pleased," cried Nibs. "Lovely, darling house," Wendy said, and they were the very words they had hoped she would say. "And we are your children," cried the twins. Then all went on their knees, and holding out their arms cried, "O Wendy lady, be our mother." "Ought I?" Wendy said, all shining. "Of course it's frightfully fascinating, but you see I am only a little girl. I have no real experience." "That doesn't matter," said Peter, as if he were the only person present who knew all about it, though he was really the one who knew least. "What we need is just a nice motherly person." "Oh dear!" Wendy said, "you see I feel that is exactly what I am." "It is, it is," they all cried; "we saw it at once." "Very well," she said, "I will do my best. Come inside at once, you naughty children; I am sure your feet are damp. And before I put you to bed I have just time to finish the story of Cinderella." In they went; I don't know how there was room for them, but you can squeeze very tight in the Neverland. And that was the first of the many joyous evenings they had with Wendy. By and by she tucked them up in the great bed in the home under the trees, but she herself slept that night in the little house, and Peter kept watch outside with drawn sword, for the pirates could be heard carousing far away and the wolves were on the prowl. The little house looked so cosy and safe in the darkness, with a bright light showing through its blinds, and the chimney smoking beautifully, and Peter standing on guard. After a time he fell asleep, and some unsteady fairies had to climb over him on their way home from an orgy. Any of the other boys obstructing the fairy path at night they would have mischiefed, but they just tweaked Peter's nose and passed on. CHAPTER VII *The Home Under*

The Ground One of the first things Peter did next day was to measure Wendy and John and Michael for hollow trees. Hook, you remember, had sneered at the boys for thinking they needed a tree apiece, but this was ignorance, for unless your tree fitted you it was difficult to go up and down, and no two of the boys were quite the same size. Once you fitted, you drew in your breath at the top, and down you went at exactly the right speed, while to ascend you drew in and let out alternately, and so wriggled up. Of course, when you have mastered the action you are able to do these things without thinking of them, and then nothing can be more graceful. But you simply must fit, and Peter measures you for your tree as carefully as for a suit of clothes: the only difference being that the clothes are made to fit you, while you have to be made to fit the tree. Usually it is done quite easily, as by your wearing too many garments or too few; but if you are bumpy in awkward places or the only available tree is an odd shape, Peter does some things to you, and after that you fit. Once you fit, great care must be taken to go on fitting, and this, as Wendy was to discover to her delight, keeps a whole family in perfect condition. Wendy and Michael fitted their trees at the first try, but John had to be altered a little. After a few days' practice they could go up and down as gaily as buckets in a well. And how ardently they grew to love their home under the ground; especially Wendy. It consisted of one large room, as all houses should do, with a floor in which you could dig if you wanted to go fishing, and in this floor grew stout mushrooms of a charming colour, which were used as stools. A Never tree tried hard to grow in the centre of the room, but every morning they sawed the trunk through, level with the floor. By tea-time it was always about two feet high, and then they put a door on top of it, the whole thus becoming a table; as soon as they cleared away, they sawed off the trunk again, and thus there was more room to play. There was an enormous fireplace which was in almost any part of the room where you cared to light it, and across this Wendy stretched strings, made of fibre, from which she suspended her washing. The bed was tilted against the wall by day, and let down at 6.30, when it filled nearly half the room; and all the boys except Michael slept in it, lying like sardines in a tin. There was a strict rule against turning round until one gave the signal, when all turned at once. Michael should have used it also; but Wendy would have a baby, and he was the littlest, and you know what women are, and the short and the long of it is that he was hung up in a basket. It was rough and simple, and not unlike what baby bears would have made of an underground house in the same circumstances. But there was one recess in the wall, no larger than a bird-cage, which was the private apartment of Tinker Bell. It could be shut off from the rest of the home by a tiny curtain, which Tink, who was most fastidious, always kept drawn when dressing or undressing. No woman, however large, could have had a more exquisite boudoir and bed-chamber combined. The couch, as she always called it, was a genuine Queen Mab, with club legs; and she varied the bedspreads according to what fruit-blossom was in season. Her mirror was a Puss-in-boots, of which there are now only three, unchipped, known to the fairy dealers; the wash-stand was Pie-crust and reversible, the chest of drawers an authentic Charming the Sixth, and the carpet and rugs of the best (the early) period of Margery and Robin. There was a chandelier from Tiddly-winks for the look of the thing, but of course she lit the residence herself. Tink was very contemptuous of the rest of the house, as indeed was perhaps inevitable, and her chamber, though beautiful, looked rather conceited, having the appearance of a nose permanently turned up. I suppose was all especially entrancing to Wendy, because those rampageous boys of hers gave her so much to do. Really there were whole weeks when, except perhaps with a stocking in the evening, she was never above ground. The cooking, I can tell you, kept her nose to the pot, and even if there was nothing in it, even though there was no pot, she had to keep watching that it came aboil just the same. You never exactly knew whether there would be a real meal or just a make-believe, it all depended upon Peter's whim: he could eat, really eat, if it was part of a game, but he could not stodge just to feel stodgy, which is what most children like better than anything else; the next best thing being to talk about it. Make-believe was so real to him that during a meal of it you could see him getting rounder. Of course it was trying, but you simply had to follow his lead, and if you could prove to him that you were getting loose for your tree he let you stodge. Wendy's favourite time for sewing and darning was after they had all gone to bed. Then, as she expressed it, she had a breathing time for herself; and she occupied it in making new things for them, and putting double pieces on the knees, for they were all most frightfully hard on their knees. When she sat down to a basketful of their stockings, every heel with a hole in it, she would fling up her arms and exclaim, "Oh dear, I am sure I sometimes think spinsters are to be envied." Her face beamed when she exclaimed this. You remember about her pet wolf. Well, it very soon discovered that she had come to the island and it found her out, and they just ran into each other's arms. After that it followed her about everywhere. As time wore on did she think much about the beloved parents she had left behind her? This is a difficult question, because it is quite impossible to say how time does wear on in the Neverland, where it is calculated by moons and suns, and there are ever so many more of them than on the mainland. But I am afraid that Wendy did not really worry about her father and mother; she was absolutely confident that they would always keep the window open for her to fly back by, and this gave her complete ease of mind. What did disturb her at times was that John remembered his parents vaguely only, as people he had once known, while Michael was quite willing to believe that she was really his mother. These things scared her a little, and nobly anxious to do her duty, she tried to fix the old life in their minds by setting them examination papers on it, as like as possible to the ones she used to do at school. The other boys thought this awfully interesting, and insisted on joining, and they made slates for themselves, and sat round the table, writing and thinking hard about the questions she had written on another slate and passed round. They were the most ordinary questions—"What was the colour of Mother's eyes? Which was taller, Father or Mother? Was Mother blonde or brunette? Answer all three questions if possible." "(A) Write an essay of not less than 40 words on How I spent my last Holidays, or The Carakters of Father and Mother compared. Only one of these to be attempted." Or "(1) Describe Mother's laugh; (2) Describe Father's laugh; (3) Describe Mother's Party Dress; (4) Describe the Kennel and its Inmate." They were just everyday questions like these, and when you could not answer them you were told to make a cross; and it was really dreadful what a number of crosses even John made. Of course the only boy who replied to every question was Slightly, and no one could have been more hopeful of coming out first, but his answers were perfectly ridiculous, and he really came out last: a melancholy thing. Peter did not compete. For one thing he despised all mothers except Wendy, and for another he was the only boy on the island who could neither write nor spell; not the smallest word. He was above all that sort of thing. By the way, the questions were all written in the past tense. What was the colour of Mother's eyes, and so on. Wendy, you see, had been forgetting too. Adventures, of course, as we shall

see, were of daily occurrence; but about this time Peter invented, with Wendy's help, a new game that fascinated him enormously, until he suddenly had no more interest in

it, which, as you have been told, was what always happened with his games. It consisted in pretending not to have adventures, in doing the sort of thing John and Michael

had been doing all their lives: sitting on stools flinging balls in the air, pushing each other, going out for walks and coming back without having killed so much as a grizzly

To see Peter doing nothing on a stool was a great sight; he could not help looking solemn at such times, to sit still seemed to him such a comic thing to do. He boasted that he

had gone a walk for the good of his health. For several suns these were the most novel of all adventures to him; and John and Michael had to pretend to be delighted also;

otherwise he would have treated them severely. He often went out alone, and when he came back you were never absolutely certain whether he had had an adventure or not.

He might have forgotten it so completely that he said nothing about it; and then when you went out you found the body; and, on the other hand, he might say a great deal

about it, and yet you could not find the body. Sometimes he came home with his head bandaged, and then Wendy cooed over him and bathed it in lukewarm water, while he

told a dazzling tale. But she was never quite sure, you know. There were, however, many adventures which she knew to be true because she was in them herself, and there

were still more that were at least partly true, for the other boys were in them and said they were wholly true. To describe them all would require a book as large as an English

Latin, Latin-English Dictionary, and the most we can do is to give one as a specimen of an average hour on the island. The difficulty is which one to choose. Should we take

the brush with the redskins at Slightly Gulch? It was a sanguinary affair, and especially interesting as showing one of Peter's peculiarities, which was that in the middle of

fight he would suddenly change sides. At the Gulch, when victory was still in the balance, sometimes leaning this way and sometimes that, he called out, "I'm redskin to-day

what are you, Tootles?" And Tootles answered, "Redskin; what are you, Nibs?" and Nibs said, "Redskin; what are you, Twin?" and so on; and they were all redskin; and of

course this would have ended the fight had not the real redskins, fascinated by Peter's methods, agreed to be lost boys for that once, and so at it they all went again, more

fiercely than ever. The extraordinary upshot of this adventure was—but we have not decided yet that this is the adventure we are to narrate. Perhaps a better one would be

the night attack by the redskins on the house under the ground, when several of them stuck in the hollow trees and had to be pulled out like corks. Or we might tell how Peter

saved Tiger Lily's life in the Mermaids' Lagoon, and so made her his ally. Or we could tell of that cake the pirates cooked so that the boys might eat it and perish; and how

they placed it in one cunning spot after another; but always Wendy snatched it from the hands of her children, so that in time it lost its succulence, and became as hard as

stone, and was used as a missile, and Hook fell over it in the dark. Or suppose we tell of the birds that were Peter's friends, particularly of the Never bird that built in a tree

overhanging the lagoon, and how the nest fell into the water, and still the bird sat on her eggs, and Peter gave orders that she was not to be disturbed. That is a pretty story

and the end shows how grateful a bird can be; but if we tell it we must also tell the whole adventure of the lagoon, which would of course be telling two adventures rather than just one. A shorter adventure, and quite as exciting, was Tinker Bell's attempt, with the help of some street fairies, to have the sleeping Wendy conveyed on a great floating leaf to the mainland. Fortunately the leaf gave way and Wendy woke, thinking it was bath-time, and swam back. Or again, we might choose Peter's defiance of the lions, when he drew a circle round him on the ground with an arrow and defied them to cross it; and though he waited for hours, with the other boys and Wendy looking on breathlessly from trees, not one of them dared to accept his challenge. **Which of these adventures shall we choose? The best way will be to toss for it.** I have tossed, and the lagoon has won. This almost makes one wish that the gulch or the cake or Tink's leaf had won. Of course I could do it again, and make it best out of three; however, perhaps fairest to stick to the lagoon. CHAPTER VIII *The Mermaids' Lagoon* If you shut your eyes and are a lucky one, you may see at times a shapeless pool of lovely pale colours suspended in the darkness; then if you squeeze your eyes tighter, the pool begins to take shape, and the colours become so vivid that with another squeeze they must go on fire. But just before they go on fire you see the lagoon. This is the nearest you ever get to it on the mainland, just one heavenly moment; if there could be two moments you might see the surf and hear the mermaids singing. The children often spent long summer days on this lagoon, swimming or floating most of the time, playing the mermaid games in the water, and so forth. You must not think from this that the mermaids were on friendly terms with them; on the contrary, it was among Wendy's lasting regrets that all the time she was on the island she never had a civil word from one of them. When she stole softly to the edge of the lagoon she might see them by the score, especially on Marooners' Rock, where they loved to bask, combing out their hair in a lazy way that quite irritated her; or she might even swim, on tiptoe as it were, to within a yard of them, but then they saw her and dived, probably splashing her with their tails, not by accident, but intentionally. They treated all the boys in the same way, except of course Peter, who chatted with them on Marooners' Rock by the hour, and sat on their tails when they got cheeky. He gave Wendy one of their combs. The most haunting time at which to see them is at the turn of the moon, when they utter strange wailing cries; but the lagoon is dangerous for mortals then, and until the evening of which we have now to tell, Wendy had never seen the lagoon by moonlight, less from fear, for of course Peter would have accompanied her, than because she had strict rules about every one being in bed by seven. She was often at the lagoon, however, on sunny days after rain, when the mermaids come up in extraordinary numbers to play with their bubbles. The bubbles of many colours made in rainbow water they treat as balls, hitting them gaily from one to another with their tails, and trying to keep them in the rainbow till they burst. The goals are at each end of the rainbow, and the keepers only are allowed to use their hands. Sometimes a dozen of these games will be going on in the lagoon at a time, and it is quite a pretty sight. But the moment the children tried to join in they had to play by themselves, for the mermaids immediately disappeared. Nevertheless we have proof that they secretly watched the interlopers, and were not above taking an idea from them; for John introduced a new way of hitting the bubble, with the head instead of the hand, and the mermaids adopted it. This is the one mark that John has left on the Neverland. It must also have been rather pretty to see the children resting on a rock for half an hour after their midday meal. Wendy insisted on their doing this, and it had to be a real rest even though the meal was make-believe. So they lay there in the sun, and their bodies glistened in it, while she sat beside them and looked important. It was one such day, and they were all on Marooners' Rock. The rock was not much

larger than their great bed, but of course they all knew how not to take up much room, and they were dozing or at least lying with their eyes shut, and pinching occasionally

when they thought Wendy was not looking. She was very busy, stitching. While she stitched a change came to the lagoon. Little shivers ran over it, and the sun went away

and shadows stole across the water, turning it cold. Wendy could no longer see to thread her needle, and when she looked up, the lagoon that had always hitherto been such

a laughing place seemed formidable and unfriendly. It was not, she knew, that night had come, but something as dark as night had come. No, worse than that. It had not come,

but it had sent that shiver through the sea to say that it was coming. What was it? There crowded upon her all the stories she had been told of Marooners' Rock, so called

because evil captains put sailors on it and leave them there to drown. They drown when the tide rises, for then it is submerged. Of course she should have roused the children

at once; not merely because of the unknown that was stalking toward them, but because it was no longer good for them to sleep on a rock grown chilly. But she was a young

mother and she did not know this; she thought you simply must stick to your rule about half an hour after the midday meal. So, though fear was upon her, and she longed to

hear male voices, she would not waken them. Even when she heard the sound of muffled oars, though her heart was in her mouth, she did not waken them. She stood over

them to let them have their sleep out. Was it not brave of Wendy? It was well for those boys then that there was one among them who could sniff danger even in his sleep.

Peter sprang erect, as wide awake at once as a dog, and with one warning cry he roused the others. He stood motionless, one hand to his ear. "Pirates!" he cried. The others

came closer to him. A strange smile was playing about his face, and Wendy saw it and shuddered. While that smile was on his face no one dared address him; all they could

do was to stand ready to obey. The order came sharp and incisive. "Dive!" There was a gleam of legs, and instantly the lagoon seemed deserted. Marooners' Rock stood

alone in the forbidding waters, as if it were itself marooned. The boat drew nearer. It was the pirate dinghy, with three figures in her, Smee and Starkey, and the third a

captive, no other than Tiger Lily. Her hands and ankles were tied, and she knew what was to be her fate. She was to be left on the rock to perish, an end to one of her race

more terrible than death by fire or torture, for is it not written in the book of the tribe that there is no path through water to the happy hunting-ground? Yet her face was

impassive; she was the daughter of a chief, she must die as a chief's daughter, it is enough. They had caught her boarding the pirate ship with a knife in her mouth. No watch

was kept on the ship, it being Hook's boast that the wind of his name guarded the ship for a mile around. Now her fate would help to guard it also. One more wail would go

the round in that wind by night. In the gloom that they brought with them the two pirates did not see the rock till they crashed into it. "Luff, you lubber," cried an Irish voice

that was Smee's; "here's the rock. Now, then, what we have to do is to hoist the redskin on to it and leave her there to drown." It was the work of one brutal moment to land

the beautiful girl on the rock; she was too proud to offer a vain resistance. Quite near the rock, but out of sight, two heads were bobbing up and down, Peter's and Wendy's.

Wendy was crying, for it was the first tragedy she had seen. Peter had seen many tragedies, but he had forgotten them all. He was less sorry than Wendy for Tiger Lily;

was two against one that angered him, and he meant to save her. An easy way would have been to wait until the pirates had gone, but he was never one to choose the easy way. There was almost nothing he could not do, and he now imitated the voice of Hook. "Ahoy there, you lubbers," he called. It was a marvellous imitation. "The captain," said the pirates, staring at each other in surprise. "He must be swimming out to us," Starkey said, when they had looked for him in vain. "We are putting the redskin on the rock," Smee called out. "Set her free," came the astonishing answer. "Free!" "Yes, cut her bonds and let her go." "But, captain—" "At once, d'ye hear," cried Peter, "or I'll plunge my hook in you." "This is queer," Smee gasped. "Better do what the captain orders," said Starkey nervously. "Ay, ay," Smee said, and he cut Tiger Lily's cords. At once like an eel she slid between Starkey's legs into the water. Of course Wendy was very elated over Peter's cleverness; but she knew that he would be elated also and very likely crow and thus betray himself, so at once her hand went out to cover his mouth. But it was stayed even in the act, for "Boat ahoy!" rang over the lagoon in Hook's voice, and this time it was not Peter who had spoken. Peter may have been about to crow, but his face puckered in a whistle of surprise instead. "Boat ahoy!" again came the cry. Now Wendy understood. The real Hook was also in the water. He was swimming to the boat, and as his men showed a light to guide him he had soon reached them. In the light of the lantern Wendy saw his hook grip the boat's side; she saw his evil swarthy face as he rose dripping from the water, and, quaking, she would have liked to swim away, but Peter would not budge. He was tingling with life and also top-heavy with conceit. "Am I not a wonder, oh, I am a wonder!" he whispered to her, and though she thought so also, she was really glad for the sake of his reputation that no one heard him except herself. He signed to her to listen. The two pirates were very curious to know what had brought their captain to them, but he sat with his head on his hook in a position of profound melancholy. "Captain, is all well?" they asked timidly, but he answered with a hollow moan. "He sighs," said Smee. "He sighs again," said Starkey. "And yet a third time he sighs," said Smee. "What's up, captain?" Then at last he spoke passionately. "The game's up," he cried, "those boys have found a mother." Affrighted though she was, Wendy swelled with pride. "O evil day," cried Starkey. "What's a mother?" asked the ignorant Smee. Wendy was so shocked that she exclaimed, "He doesn't know!" and always after this she felt that if you could have a pet pirate Smee would be her one. Peter pulled her beneath the water, for Hook had started up, crying, "What was that?" "I heard nothing," said Starkey, raising the lantern over the waters, and as the pirates looked they saw a strange sight. It was the nest I have told you of, floating on the lagoon, and the Never bird was sitting on it. "See," said Hook in answer to Smee's question, "that is a mother. What a lesson. The nest must have fallen into the water, but would the mother desert her eggs? No." There was a break in his voice, as if for a moment he recalled innocent days when—but he brushed away this weakness with his hook. Smee, much impressed, gazed at the bird as the nest was borne past, but the more suspicious Starkey said, "If she is a mother, perhaps she is hanging about here to help Peter." Hook winced. "Ay," he said, "that is the fear that haunts me." He was roused from this dejection by Smee's eager voice. "Captain," said Smee, "could we not kidnap these boys' mother and make her our mother?" "It is a princely scheme," cried Hook, and at once it took practical shape in his great brain. "We will seize the children and carry them to the boat: the boys we will make walk the plank, and Wendy shall be our mother." Again Wendy forgot herself. "Never!" she cried, and bobbed. "What was that?" But they could see nothing. They thought it must have been but a leaf

in the wind. "Do you agree, my bullies?" asked Hook. "There is my hand on it," they both said. "And there is my hook. Swear." They all swore. By this time they were on

the rock, and suddenly Hook remembered Tiger Lily. "Where is the redskin?" he demanded abruptly. He had a playful humour at moments, and they thought this was one

of the moments. "That is all right, captain," Smee answered complacently; "we let her go." "Let her go!" cried Hook. "'Twas your own orders," the bo'sun faltered. "You

called over the water to us to let her go," said Starkey. "Brimstone and gall," thundered Hook, "what cozening is here?" His face had gone black with rage, but he saw that

they believed their words, and he was startled. "Lads," he said, shaking a little, "I gave no such order." "It is passing queer," Smee said, and they all fidgeted uncomfortably.

Hook raised his voice, but there was a quiver in it. "Spirit that haunts this dark lagoon to-night," he cried, "dost hear me?" Of course Peter should have kept quiet, but of

course he did not. He immediately answered in Hook's voice: "Odds, bobs, hammer and tongs, I hear you." In that supreme moment Hook did not blanch, even at the gills,

but Smee and Starkey clung to each other in terror. "Who are you, stranger, speak?" Hook demanded. "I am James Hook," replied the voice, "captain of the *Jolly Roger*."

"You are not; you are not," Hook cried hoarsely. "Brimstone and gall," the voice retorted, "say that again, and I'll cast anchor in you." Hook tried a more ingratiating

manner. "If you are Hook," he said almost humbly, "come tell me, who am I?" "A codfish," replied the voice, "only a codfish." "A codfish!" Hook echoed blankly; and it

was then, but not till then, that his proud spirit broke. He saw his men draw back from him. "Have we been captained all this time by a codfish!" they muttered. "It is lowering

to our pride." They were his dogs snapping at him, but, tragic figure though he had become, he scarcely heeded them. Against such fearful evidence it was not their belief

in him that he needed, it was his own. He felt his ego slipping from him. "Don't desert me, bully," he whispered hoarsely to it. In his dark nature there was a touch of the

feminine, as in all the great pirates, and it sometimes gave him intuitions. Suddenly he tried the guessing game. "Hook," he called, "have you another voice?" Now Peter

could never resist a game, and he answered blithely in his own voice, "I have." "And another name?" "Ay, ay." "Vegetable?" asked Hook. "No." "Mineral?" "No."

"Animal?" "Yes." "Man?" "No!" This answer rang out scornfully. "Boy?" "Yes." "Ordinary boy?" "No!" "Wonderful boy?" To Wendy's pain the answer that rang out

this time was "Yes." "Are you in England?" "No." "Are you here?" "Yes." Hook was completely puzzled. "You ask him some questions," he said to the others, wiping his

damp brow. Smee reflected. "I can't think of a thing," he said regretfully. "Can't guess, can't guess," crowed Peter. "Do you give it up?" Of course in his pride he was

carrying the game too far, and the miscreants saw their chance. "Yes, yes," they answered eagerly. "Well, then," he cried, "I am Peter Pan." Pan! In a moment Hook was

himself again, and Smee and Starkey were his faithful henchmen. "Now we have him," Hook shouted. "Into the water, Smee. Starkey, mind the boat. Take him dead or

alive." He leaped as he spoke, and simultaneously came the gay voice of Peter. "Are you ready, boys?" "Ay, ay," from various parts of the lagoon. "Then lam into the

pirates." The fight was short and sharp. First to draw blood was John, who gallantly climbed into the boat and held Starkey. There was a fierce struggle, in which the cut-was torn from the pirate's grasp. He wriggled overboard and John leapt after him. The dinghy drifted away. Here and there a head bobbed up in the water, and there was a

flash of steel followed by a cry or a whoop. In the confusion some struck at their own side. The corkscrew of Smee got Tootles in the fourth rib, but he was himself pinked

in turn by Curly. Farther from the rock Starkey was pressing Slightly and the twins hard. Where all this time was Peter? He was seeking bigger game. The others were all

brave boys, and they must not be blamed for backing from the pirate captain. His iron claw made a circle of dead water round him, from which they fled like affrighted fishes.

But there was one who did not fear him: there was one prepared to enter that circle. Strangely, it was not in the water that they met. Hook rose to the rock to breathe, and at

the same moment Peter scaled it on the opposite side. The rock was slippery as a ball, and they had to crawl rather than climb. Neither knew that the other was coming. Each

feeling for a grip met the other's arm: in surprise they raised their heads; their faces were almost touching; so they met. Some of the greatest heroes have confessed that just

before they fell to they had a sinking. Had it been so with Peter at that moment I would admit it. After all, this was the only man that the Sea-Cook had feared. But Peter had

no sinking, he had one feeling only, gladness; and he gnashed his pretty teeth with joy. Quick as thought he snatched a knife from Hook's belt and was about to drive it home,

when he saw that he was higher up the rock than his foe. It would not have been fighting fair. He gave the pirate a hand to help him up. It was then that Hook bit him. Not

the pain of this but its unfairness was what dazed Peter. It made him quite helpless. He could only stare, horrified. Every child is affected thus the first time he is treated

unfairly. All he thinks he has a right to when he comes to you to be yours is fairness. After you have been unfair to him he will love you again, but he will never afterwards

be quite the same boy. No one ever gets over the first unfairness; no one except Peter. He often met it, but he always forgot it. I suppose that was the real difference between

him and all the rest. So when he met it now it was like the first time; and he could just stare, helpless. Twice the iron hand clawed him. A few minutes afterwards the other

boys saw Hook in the water striking wildly for the ship; no elation on his pestilent face now, only white fear, for the crocodile was in dogged pursuit of him. On ordinary

occasions the boys would have swum alongside cheering; but now they were uneasy, for they had lost both Peter and Wendy, and were scouring the lagoon for them, calling

them by name. They found the dinghy and went home in it, shouting "Peter, Wendy" as they went, but no answer came save mocking laughter from the mermaids. "They

must be swimming back or flying," the boys concluded. They were not very anxious, they had such faith in Peter. They chuckled, boylike, because they would be late for

bed; and it was all mother Wendy's fault! When their voices died away there came cold silence over the lagoon, and then a feeble cry. "Help, help!" Two small figures were

beating against the rock; the girl had fainted and lay on the boy's arm. With a last effort Peter pulled her up the rock and then lay down beside her. Even as he also fainted he

saw that the water was rising. He knew that they would soon be drowned, but he could do no more. As they lay side by side a mermaid caught Wendy by the feet, and began

pulling her softly into the water. Peter, feeling her slip from him, woke with a start, and was just in time to draw her back. But he had to tell her the truth. "We are on the rock,

Wendy," he said, "but it is growing smaller. Soon the water will be over it." She did not understand even now. "We must go," she said, almost brightly. "Yes," he answered faintly. "Shall we swim or fly, Peter?" He had to tell her. "Do you think you could swim or fly as far as the island, Wendy, without my help?" She had to admit that she was too tired. He moaned. "What is it?" she asked, anxious about him at once. "I can't help you, Wendy. Hook wounded me. I can neither fly nor swim." "Do you mean we shall both be drowned?" "Look how the water is rising." They put their hands over their eyes to shut out the sight. They thought they would soon be no more. As they sat thus something brushed against Peter as light as a kiss, and stayed there, as if saying timidly, "Can I be of any use?" It was the tail of a kite, which Michael had made some days before. It had torn itself out of his hand and floated away. "Michael's kite," Peter said without interest, but next moment he had seized the tail, and was pulling the kite toward him. "It lifted Michael off the ground," he cried; "why should it not carry you?" "Both of us!" "It can't lift two; Michael and Curly tried." "Let us draw lots," Wendy said bravely. "And you a lady; never." Already he had tied the tail round her. She clung to him; she refused to go without him; but with a "Good-bye, Wendy," he pushed her from the rock; and in a few minutes she was borne out of his sight. Peter was alone on the lagoon. The rock was very small now; soon it would be submerged. Pale rays of light tiptoed across the waters; and by and by there was to be heard a sound at once the most musical and the most melancholy in the world: the mermaids calling to the moon. Peter was not quite like other boys; but he was afraid at last. A tremor ran through him, like a shudder passing over the sea; but on the sea one shudder follows another till there are hundreds of them, and Peter felt just the one. Next moment he was standing erect on the rock again, with that smile on his face and a drum beating within him. It was saying, "To die will be an awfully big adventure." CHAPTER IX *The Never Bird* The last sounds Peter heard before he was quite alone were the mermaids retiring one by one to their bedchambers under the sea. He was too far away to hear their doors shut; but every door in the coral caves where they live rings a tiny bell when it opens or closes (as in all the nicest houses on the mainland), and he heard the bells. Steadily the waters rose till they were nibbling at his feet; and to pass the time until they made their final gulp, he watched the only thing moving on the lagoon. He thought it was a piece of floating paper, perhaps part of the kite, and wondered idly how long it would take to drift ashore. Presently he noticed as an odd thing that it was undoubtedly out upon the lagoon with some definite purpose, for it was fighting the tide, and sometimes winning; and when it won, Peter, always sympathetic to the weaker side, could not help clapping; it was such a gallant piece of paper. It was not really a piece of paper; it was the Never bird, making desperate efforts to reach Peter on her nest. By working her wings, in a way she had learned since the nest fell into the water, she was able to some extent to guide her strange craft, but by the time Peter recognised her she was very exhausted. She had come to save him, to give him her nest, though there were eggs in it. I rather wonder at the bird, for though he had been nice to her, he had also sometimes tormented her. I can suppose only that, like Mrs. Darling and the rest of them, she was melted because he had all his first teeth. She called out to him what she had come for, and he called out to her what was she doing there; but of course neither of them understood the other's language. In fanciful stories people can talk to the birds freely, and I wish for the moment I could pretend that this was such a story, and say that Peter replied intelligently to the Never bird; but truth is best, and I want to tell only what really happened. Well, not only could they not understand each other, but they forgot their manners. "I—want—you—to—get—into—the—nest," the bird called, speaking as slowly and distinctly as possible, "and—then—you—can—drift—ashore, but—I—am—too—tired—to—bring—it—any—nearer—so—you—must—try—to—swim—to—it." "What are you quacking about?" Peter answered. "Why don't you let the nest drift as usual?" "I—want—you—" the bird said, and repeated it all over. Then Peter tried slow and distinct. "What—are—you—quacking—about?" and so on. The Never bird became irritated; they have very short tempers. "You dunderheaded little jay," she screamed, "why don't you do as I tell you?" Peter felt that she was calling him names, and at a venture he retorted hotly: "So are you!" Then rather curiously they both snapped out the same remark: "Shut up!" "Shut up!" Nevertheless the bird was determined to save him if she could, and by one last mighty effort she propelled the nest against the rock. Then up she flew; deserting her eggs, so as to make her meaning clear. Then at last he understood, and clutched the nest and waved his thanks to the bird as she fluttered overhead. It was not to receive his thanks, however, that she hung there in the sky; it was not even to watch him get into the nest; it was to see what he did with her eggs. There were two large white eggs, and Peter lifted them up and reflected. The bird covered her face with her wings, so as not to see the last of her eggs; but she could not help peeping between the feathers. I forget whether I have told you that there was a stave on the rock, driven into it by some buccaneers of long ago to mark the site of buried treasure. The children had discovered the glittering hoard, and when in mischievous mood used to fling showers of moidores, diamonds, pearls and pieces of eight to the gulls, who pounced upon them for food, and then flew away, raging at the scurvy trick that had been played upon them. The stave was still there, and on it Starkey had hung his hat, a deep tarpaulin, watertight, with a broad brim. Peter put the eggs into this hat and set it on the lagoon. It floated beautifully. The Never bird saw at once what he was up to, and screamed her admiration of him; and, alas, Peter crowed his agreement with her. Then he got into the nest, reared the stave in it as a mast, and hung up his shirt for a sail. At the same moment the bird fluttered down upon the hat and once more sat snugly on her eggs. She drifted in one direction, and he was borne off in another, both cheering. Of course when Peter landed he beached his barque in a place where the bird would easily find it; but the hat was such a great success that she abandoned the nest. It drifted about till it went to pieces, and often Starkey came to the shore of the lagoon, and with many bitter feelings watched the bird sitting on his hat. As we shall not see her again, it may be worth mentioning here that all Never birds now build in that shape of nest, with a broad brim on which the youngsters take an airing. Great were the rejoicings when Peter reached the home under the ground almost as soon as Wendy, who had been carried hither and thither by the kite. Every boy had adventures to tell; but perhaps the biggest adventure of all was that they were several hours late for bed. This so inflated them that they did various dodgy things to get staying up still longer, such as demanding bandages; but Wendy, though glorying in having them all home again safe and sound, was scandalised by the lateness of the hour, and cried, "To bed, to bed," in a voice that had to be obeyed. Next day, however, she was awfully tender, and gave out bandages to every one; and they played till bed-time at limping about and carrying their arms in slings. CHAPTER X *The Happy Home* One important result of the brush on the lagoon was that it made the redskins their friends. Peter had saved Tiger Lily from a dreadful fate, and now there was nothing she and her braves would not do for him. All night they sat above, keeping watch over the home under the ground and awaiting the big attack by the pirates

which obviously could not be much longer delayed. Even by day they hung about, smoking the pipe of peace, and looking almost as if they wanted tit-bits to eat. They called

Peter the Great White Father, prostrating themselves before him; and he liked this tremendously, so that it was not really good for him. "The great white father," he would

say to them in a very lordly manner, as they grovelled at his feet, "is glad to see the Piccaninny warriors protecting his wigwam from the pirates." "Me Tiger Lily," that lovely

creature would reply. "Peter Pan save me, me his velly nice friend. Me no let pirates hurt him." She was far too pretty to cringe in this way, but Peter thought it his due, and

he would answer condescendingly, "It is good. Peter Pan has spoken." Always when he said, "Peter Pan has spoken," it meant that they must now shut up, and they accepted

it humbly in that spirit; but they were by no means so respectful to the other boys, whom they looked upon as just ordinary braves. They said "How-do?" to them, and things

like that; and what annoyed the boys was that Peter seemed to think this all right. Secretly Wendy sympathised with them a little, but she was far too loyal a housewife to

listen to any complaints against father. "Father knows best," she always said, whatever her private opinion must be. Her private opinion was that the redskins should not call

her a squaw. We have now reached the evening that was to be known among them as the Night of Nights, because of its adventures and their upshot. The day, as if quietly

gathering its forces, had been almost uneventful, and now the redskins in their blankets were at their posts above, while, below, the children were having their evening meal;

all except Peter, who had gone out to get the time. The way you got the time on the island was to find the crocodile, and then stay near him till the clock struck. This meal

happened to be a make-believe tea, and they sat round the board, guzzling in their greed; and really, what with their chatter and recriminations, the noise, as Wendy said, was

positively deafening. To be sure, she did not mind noise, but she simply would not have them grabbing things, and then excusing themselves by saying that Tootles had

pushed their elbow. There was a fixed rule that they must never hit back at meals, but should refer the matter of dispute to Wendy by raising the right arm politely and saying,

"I complain of so-and-so;" but what usually happened was that they forgot to do this or did it too much. "Silence," cried Wendy when for the twentieth time she had told

them that they were not all to speak at once. "Is your calabash empty, Slightly darling?" "Not quite empty, mummy," Slightly said, after looking into an imaginary mug. "He

hasn't even begun to drink his milk," Nibs interposed. This was telling, and Slightly seized his chance. "I complain of Nibs," he cried promptly. John, however, had held up

his hand first. "Well, John?" "May I sit in Peter's chair, as he is not here?" "Sit in father's chair, John!" Wendy was scandalised. "Certainly not." "He is not really our father,"

John answered. "He didn't even know how a father does till I showed him." This was grumbling. "We complain of John," cried the twins. Tootles held up his hand. He was

so much the humblest of them, indeed he was the only humble one, that Wendy was specially gentle with him. "I don't suppose," Tootles said diffidently, "that I could be

father." "No, Tootles." Once Tootles began, which was not very often, he had a silly way of going on. "As I can't be father," he said heavily, "I don't suppose, Michael, you

would let me be baby?" "No, I won't," Michael rapped out. He was already in his basket. "As I can't be baby," Tootles said, getting heavier and heavier, "do you think I could be a twin?" "No, indeed," replied the twins; "it's awfully difficult to be a twin." "As I can't be anything important," said Tootles, "would any of you like to see me do a trick?"

"No," they all replied. Then at last he stopped. "I hadn't really any hope," he said. The hateful telling broke out again. "Slightly is coughing on the table." "The twins began

with cheese-cakes." "Curly is taking both butter and honey." "Nibs is speaking with his mouth full." "I complain of the twins." "I complain of Curly." "I complain of Nibs."

"Oh dear, oh dear," cried Wendy, "I'm sure I sometimes think that spinsters are to be envied." She told them to clear away, and sat down to her work-basket: a heavy load

of stockings and every knee with a hole in it as usual. "Wendy," remonstrated Michael, "I'm too big for a cradle." "I must have somebody in a cradle," she said almost tartly,

"and you are the littlest. A cradle is such a nice homely thing to have about a house." While she sewed they played around her; such a group of happy faces and dancing limbs

lit up by that romantic fire. It had become a very familiar scene this in the home under the ground, but we are looking on it for the last time. There was a step above, and

Wendy, you may be sure, was the first to recognise it. "Children, I hear your father's step. He likes you to meet him at the door." Above, the redskins crouched before Peter.

"Watch well, braves. I have spoken." And then, as so often before, the gay children dragged him from his tree. As so often before, but never again. He had brought nuts for

the boys as well as the correct time for Wendy. "Peter, you just spoil them, you know," Wendy simpered. "Ah, old lady," said Peter, hanging up his gun. "It was me told him

mothers are called old lady," Michael whispered to Curly. "I complain of Michael," said Curly instantly. The first twin came to Peter. "Father, we want to dance." "Dance

away, my little man," said Peter, who was in high good humour. "But we want you to dance." Peter was really the best dancer among them, but he pretended to be

scandalised. "Me! My old bones would rattle." "And mummy too." "What," cried Wendy, "the mother of such an armful, dance!" "But on a Saturday night," Slightly

insinuated. It was not really Saturday night, at least it may have been, for they had long lost count of the days; but always if they wanted to do anything special they said this

was Saturday night, and then they did it. "Of course it is Saturday night, Peter," Wendy said, relenting. "People of our figure, Wendy." "But it is only among our own

progeny." "True, true." So they were told they could dance, but they must put on their nighties first. "Ah, old lady," Peter said aside to Wendy, warming himself by the fire

and looking down at her as she sat turning a heel, "there is nothing more pleasant of an evening for you and me when the day's toil is over than to rest by the fire with the

little ones near by." "It is sweet, Peter, isn't it?" Wendy said, frightfully gratified. "Peter, I think Curly has your nose." "Michael takes after you." She went to him and put

her hand on his shoulder. "Dear Peter," she said, "with such a large family, of course, I have now passed my best, but you don't want to change me, do you?" "No, Wendy."

Certainly he did not want a change, but he looked at her uncomfortably, blinking, you know, like one not sure whether he was awake or asleep. "Peter, what is it?" "I was just

thinking," he said, a little scared. "It is only make-believe, isn't it, that I am their father?" "Oh yes," Wendy said primly. "You see," he continued apologetically, "it would

make me seem so old to be their real father." "But they are ours, Peter, yours and mine." "But not really, Wendy?" he asked anxiously. "Not if you don't wish it," she replied;

and she distinctly heard his sigh of relief. "Peter," she asked, trying to speak firmly, "what are your exact feelings for me?" "Those of a devoted son, Wendy." "I thought so," she said, and went and sat by herself at the extreme end of the room. "You are so queer," he said, frankly puzzled, "and Tiger Lily is just the same. There is something she wants to be to me, but she says it is not my mother." "No, indeed, it is not," Wendy replied with frightful emphasis. Now we know why she was prejudiced against the redskins. "Then what is it?" "It isn't for a lady to tell." "Oh, very well," Peter said, a little nettled. "Perhaps Tinker Bell will tell me." "Oh yes, Tinker Bell will tell you," Wendy retorted scornfully. "She is an abandoned little creature." Here Tink, who was in her boudoir, eavesdropping, squeaked out something impudent. "She says she glories in being abandoned," Peter interpreted. He had a sudden idea. "Perhaps Tink wants to be my mother?" "You silly ass!" cried Tinker Bell in a passion. She had said it so often that Wendy needed no translation. "I almost agree with her," Wendy snapped. Fancy Wendy snapping. But she had been much tried, and she little knew what was to happen before the night was out. If she had known she would not have snapped. None of them knew. Perhaps it was best not to know. Their ignorance gave them one more glad hour; and as it was to be their last hour on the island, let us rejoice that there were sixty glad minutes in it. They sang and danced in their night-gowns. Such a deliciously creepy song it was, in which they pretended to be frightened at their own shadows; little witting that so soon shadows would close in upon them, from whom they would shrink in real fear. So uproariously gay was the dance, and how they buffeted each other on the bed and out of it! It was a pillow fight rather than a dance, and when it was finished, the pillows insisted on one bout more, like partners who know that they may never meet again. The stories they told, before it was time for Wendy's good-night story! Even Slightly tried to tell a story that night, but the beginning was so fearfully dull that it appalled not only the others, but himself, and he said happily: "Yes, it is a dull beginning. I say, let us pretend that it is the end." And then at last they all got into bed for Wendy's story, the story they loved best, the story Peter hated. Usually when she began to tell this story he left the room or put his hands over his ears; and possibly if he had done either of those things this time they might all still be on the island. But to-night he remained on his stool; and we shall see what happened. CHAPTER XI *Wendy's Story* Listen, then," said Wendy, settling down to her story, with Michael at her feet and seven boys in the bed. "There was once a gentleman—" "I had rather he had been a lady," Curly said. "I wish he had been a white rat," said Nibs. "Quiet," their mother admonished them. "There was a lady also, and—" "O mummy," cried the first twin, "you mean that there is a lady also, don't you? She is not dead, is she?" "Oh no." "I am awfully glad she isn't dead," said Tootles. "Are you glad, John?" "Of course I am." "Are you glad, Nibs?" "Rather." "Are you glad, Twins?" "We are just glad." "Oh dear," sighed Wendy. "Little less noise there," Peter called out, determined that she should have fair play, however beastly a story it might be in his opinion. "The gentleman's name," Wendy continued, "was Mr. Darling, and her name was Mrs. Darling." "I knew them," John said, to annoy the others. "I think I knew them," said Michael rather doubtfully. "They were married, you know," explained Wendy, "and what do you think they had?" "White rats," cried Nibs, inspired. "No." "It's awfully puzzling," said Tootles, who knew the story by heart. "Quiet, Tootles. They had three descendants." "What is descendants?" "Well, you are one, Twin." "Do you hear that, John? I am a descendant." "Descendants are only children," said John. "Oh dear, oh dear," sighed Wendy. "Now these three children had a faithful nurse called Nana; but

Mr. Darling was angry with her and chained her up in the yard; and so all the children flew away." "It's an awfully good story," said Nibs. "They flew away," Wendy continued, "to the Neverland, where the lost children are." "I just thought they did," Curly broke in excitedly, "I don't know how it is, but I just thought they did!" "O Wendy," cried Tootles, "was one of the lost children called Tootles?" "Yes, he was." "I am in a story. Hurrah, I am in a story, Nibs." "Hush. Now I want you to consider the feelings of the unhappy parents with all their children flown away." "Oo!" they all moaned, though they were not really considering the feelings of the unhappy parents one jot. "Think of the empty beds!" "It's awfully sad," the first twin said cheerfully. "I don't see how it can have a happy ending," said the second twin. "Do you, Nibs?" "I'm frightfully anxious." "If you knew how great is a mother's love," Wendy told them triumphantly, "you would have no fear." She had now come to the part that Peter hated.

"I do like a mother's love," said Tootles, hitting Nibs with a pillow. "Do you like a mother's love, Nibs?" "I do just," said Nibs, hitting back. "You see," Wendy said complacently, "our heroine knew that the mother would always leave the window open for her children to fly back by; so they stayed away for years and had a lovely time."

"Did they ever go back?" "Let us now," said Wendy, bracing herself for her finest effort, "take a peep into the future;" and they all gave themselves the twist that makes peeps into the future easier. "Years have rolled by; and who is this elegant lady of uncertain age alighting at London Station?" "O Wendy, who is she?" cried Nibs, every bit as excited as if he didn't know. "Can it be—yes—no—it is—the fair Wendy!" "Oh!" "And who are the two noble portly figures accompanying her, now grown to man's estate? Can they be John and Michael? They are!" "Oh!" "See, dear brothers," says Wendy, pointing upwards, "there is the window still standing open. Ah, now we are rewarded for our sublime faith in a mother's love." So up they flew to their mummy and daddy; and pen cannot describe the happy scene, over which we draw a veil." That was the story, and they were as pleased with it as the fair narrator herself. Everything just as it should be, you see. Off we skip like the most heartless things in the world, which is what children are, but so attractive; and we have an entirely selfish time; and then when we have need of special attention we nobly return for it, confident that we shall be embraced instead of smacked. So great indeed was their faith in a mother's love that they felt they could afford to be callous for a bit longer. But there was one there who knew better, and when Wendy finished he uttered a hollow groan. "What is it, Peter?" she cried, running to him, thinking he was ill. She felt him solicitously, lower down than his chest. "Where is it, Peter?" "It isn't that kind of pain," Peter replied darkly. "Then what kind is it?" "Wendy, you are wrong about mothers." They all gathered round him in affright, so alarming was his agitation; and with a fine candour he told them what he had hitherto concealed. "Long ago," he said, "I thought like you that my mother would always keep the window open for me; so I stayed away for moons and moons and moons, and then flew back; but the window was barred, for mother had forgotten all about me, and there was another little boy sleeping in my bed." I am not sure that this was true, but Peter thought it was true; and it scared them. "Are you sure mothers are like that?" "Yes." So this was the truth about mothers. The toads! Still it is best to be careful; and no one knows so quickly as a child when he should give in.

"Wendy, let us go home," cried John and Michael together. "Yes," she said, clutching them. "Not to-night?" asked the lost boys bewildered. They knew in what they called their hearts that one can get on quite well without a mother, and that it is only the mothers who think you can't. "At once," Wendy replied resolutely, for the horrible thought

had come to her: "Perhaps mother is in half mourning by this time." This dread made her forgetful of what must be Peter's feelings, and she said to him rather sharply, "Peter,

will you make the necessary arrangements?" "If you wish it," he replied, as coolly as if she had asked him to pass the nuts. Not so much as a sorry-to-lose-you between them!

If she did not mind the parting, he was going to show her, was Peter, that neither did he. But of course he cared very much; and he was so full of wrath against grown-ups,

who, as usual, were spoiling everything, that as soon as he got inside his tree he breathed intentionally quick short breaths at the rate of about five to a second. He did this

because there is a saying in the Neverland that, every time you breathe, a grown-up dies; and Peter was killing them off vindictively as fast as possible. Then having given

the necessary instructions to the redskins he returned to the home, where an unworthy scene had been enacted in his absence. Panic-stricken at the thought of losing Wendy,

the lost boys had advanced upon her threateningly. "It will be worse than before she came," they cried. "We shan't let her go." "Let's keep her prisoner." "Ay, chain her up."

In her extremity an instinct told her to which of them to turn. "Tootles," she cried, "I appeal to you." Was it not strange? she appealed to Tootles, quite the silliest one.

Grandly, however, did Tootles respond. For that one moment he dropped his silliness and spoke with dignity. "I am just Tootles," he said, "and nobody minds me. But the

first who does not behave to Wendy like an English gentleman I will blood him severely." He drew his hanger; and for that instant his sun was at noon. The others held back

uneasily. Then Peter returned, and they saw at once that they would get no support from him. He would keep no girl in the Neverland against her will. "Wendy," he said,

striding up and down, "I have asked the redskins to guide you through the wood, as flying tires you so." "Thank you, Peter." "Then," he continued, in the short sharp voice

of one accustomed to be obeyed, "Tinker Bell will take you across the sea. Wake her, Nibs." Nibs had to knock twice before he got an answer, though Tink had really been

sitting up in bed listening for some time. "Who are you? How dare you? Go away," she cried. "You are to get up, Tink," Nibs called, "and take Wendy on a journey." Of

course Tink had been delighted to hear that Wendy was going; but she was jolly well determined not to be her courier, and she said so in still more offensive language. Then

she pretended to be asleep again. "She says she won't," Nibs exclaimed, aghast at such insubordination, whereupon Peter went sternly toward the young lady's chamber.

"Tink," he rapped out, "if you don't get up and dress at once I will open the curtains, and then we shall all see you in your *négligée*." This made her leap to the floor. "Who

said I wasn't getting up?" she cried. In the meantime the boys were gazing very forlornly at Wendy, now equipped with John and Michael for the journey. By this time they

were dejected, not merely because they were about to lose her, but also because they felt that she was going off to something nice to which they had not been invited. Novelty

was beckoning to them as usual. Crediting them with a nobler feeling, Wendy melted. "Dear ones," she said, "if you will all come with me I feel almost sure I can get my

father and mother to adopt you." The invitation was meant specially for Peter, but each of the boys was thinking exclusively of himself, and at once they jumped with joy.

"But won't they think us rather a handful?" Nibs asked in the middle of his jump. "Oh no," said Wendy, rapidly thinking it out, "it will only mean having a few beds in the drawing-room; they can be hidden behind screens on first Thursdays." "Peter, can we go?" they all cried imploringly. They took it for granted that if they went he would

go also, but really they scarcely cared. Thus children are ever ready, when novelty knocks, to desert their dearest ones. "All right," Peter replied with a bitter smile; and

immediately they rushed to get their things. "And now, Peter," Wendy said, thinking she had put everything right, "I am going to give you your medicine before you go."

She loved to give them medicine, and undoubtedly gave them too much. Of course it was only water, but it was out of a bottle, and she always shook the bottle and counted

the drops, which gave it a certain medicinal quality. On this occasion, however, she did not give Peter his draught, for just as she had prepared it, she saw a look on his face

that made her heart sink. "Get your things, Peter," she cried, shaking. "No," he answered, pretending indifference, "I am not going with you, Wendy." "Yes, Peter." "No."

To show that her departure would leave him unmoved, he skipped up and down the room, playing gaily on his heartless pipes. She had to run about after him, though it was

rather undignified. "To find your mother," she coaxed. Now, if Peter had ever quite had a mother, he no longer missed her. He could do very well without one. He had

thought them out, and remembered only their bad points. "No, no," he told Wendy decisively; "perhaps she would say I was old, and I just want always to be a little boy and

to have fun." "But, Peter—" "No." And so the others had to be told. "Peter isn't coming." Peter not coming! They gazed blankly at him, their sticks over their backs, and

on each stick a bundle. Their first thought was that if Peter was not going he had probably changed his mind about letting them go. But he was far too proud for that. "If you

find your mothers," he said darkly, "I hope you will like them." The awful cynicism of this made an uncomfortable impression, and most of them began to look rather

doubtful. After all, their faces said, were they not noodles to want to go? "Now then," cried Peter, "no fuss, no blubbering; good-bye, Wendy;" and he held out his hand

cheerily, quite as if they must really go now, for he had something important to do. She had to take his hand, as there was no indication that he would prefer a thimble. "You

will remember about changing your flannels, Peter?" she said, lingering over him. She was always so particular about their flannels. "Yes." "And you will take your

medicine?" "Yes." That seemed to be everything; and an awkward pause followed. Peter, however, was not the kind that breaks down before people. "Are you ready, Tinker

Bell?" he called out. "Ay! ay!" "Then lead the way." Tink darted up the nearest tree; but no one followed her, for it was at this moment that the pirates made their dreadful

attack upon the redskins. Above, where all had been so still, the air was rent with shrieks and the clash of steel. Below, there was dead silence. Mouths opened and remained

open. Wendy fell on her knees, but her arms were extended toward Peter. All arms were extended to him, as if suddenly blown in his direction; they were beseeching him

mutely not to desert them. As for Peter, he seized his sword, the same he thought he had slain Barbecue with; and the lust of battle was in his eye. CHAPTER XII *The*

Children Are Carried Off The pirate attack had been a complete surprise: a sure proof that the unscrupulous Hook had conducted it improperly, for to surprise redskins fairly

is beyond the wit of the white man. By all the unwritten laws of savage warfare it is always the redskin who attacks, and with the wiliness of his race he does it just before the

dawn, at which time he knows the courage of the whites to be at its lowest ebb. The white men have in the meantime made a rude stockade on the summit of yonder undulating ground, at the foot of which a stream runs, for it is destruction to be too far from water. There they await the onslaught, the inexperienced ones clutching their revolvers and treading on twigs, but the old hands sleeping tranquilly until just before the dawn. Through the long black night the savage scouts wriggle, snake-like, among the grass without stirring a blade. The brushwood closes behind them as silently as sand into which a mole has dived. Not a sound is to be heard, save when they give vent to a wonderful imitation of the lonely call of the coyote. The cry is answered by other braves; and some of them do it even better than the coyotes, who are not very good at it. So the chill hours wear on, and the long suspense is horribly trying to the paleface who has to live through it for the first time; but to the trained hand those ghastly calls and still ghastlier silences are but an intimation of how the night is marching. That this was the usual procedure was so well known to Hook that in disregarding it he cannot be excused on the plea of ignorance. The Piccaninnies, on their part, trusted implicitly to his honour, and their whole action of the night stands out in marked contrast to his.

They left nothing undone that was consistent with the reputation of their tribe. With that alertness of the senses which is at once the marvel and despair of civilised peoples, they knew that the pirates were on the island from the moment one of them trod on a dry stick; and in an incredibly short space of time the coyote cries began. Every foot of ground between the spot where Hook had landed his forces and the home under the trees was stealthily examined by braves wearing their moccasins with the heels in front. They found only one hillock with a stream at its base, so that Hook had no choice; here he must establish himself and wait for just before the dawn. Everything being thus mapped out with almost diabolical cunning, the main body of the redskins folded their blankets around them, and in the phlegmatic manner that is to them the pearl of manhood squatted above the children's home, awaiting the cold moment when they should deal pale death. Here dreaming, though wide-awake, of the exquisite tortures to which they were to put him at break of day, those confiding savages were found by the treacherous Hook. From the accounts afterwards supplied by such of the scouts as escaped the carnage, he does not seem even to have paused at the rising ground, though it is certain that in that grey light he must have seen it: no thought of waiting to be attacked appears from first to last to have visited his subtle mind; he would not even hold off till the night was nearly spent; on he pounded with no policy but to fall to. What could the bewildered scouts do, masters as they were of every warlike artifice save this one, but trot helplessly after him, exposing themselves fatally to view, the while they gave pathetic utterance to the coyote cry. Around the brave Tiger Lily were a dozen of her stoutest warriors, and they suddenly saw the perfidious pirates bearing down upon them. Fell from their eyes then the film through which they had looked at victory. No more would they torture at the stake. For them the happy hunting-grounds now. They knew it; but as their fathers' sons they acquitted themselves. Even then they had time to gather in a phalanx that would have been hard to break had they risen quickly, but this they were forbidden to do by the traditions of their race. It is written that the noble savage must never express surprise in the presence of the white. Thus terrible as the sudden appearance of the pirates must have been to them, they remained stationary for a moment, not a muscle moving; as if the foe had come by invitation. Then, indeed, the tradition gallantly upheld, they seized their weapons, and the air was torn with the war-cry; but it was now too late. It is no part of ours to describe what was a massacre rather than a fight. Thus perished many of the flower of the Piccaninny tribe. Not all unavenged did they die, for with Lean Wolf fell Alf Mason, to disturb the Spanish Main no more, and among others who bit the dust were Geo. Scourie, Chas. Turley, and the Alsatian Foggerty. Turley fell to the tomahawk of the terrible Panther, who ultimately cut a way through the pirates with Tiger Lily and a small remnant of the tribe. To what extent Hook is to blame for his tactics on this occasion is for the historian to decide.

Had he waited on the rising ground till the proper hour he and his men would probably have been butchered; and in judging him it is only fair to take this into account. What he should perhaps have done was to acquaint his opponents that he proposed to follow a new method. On the other hand this, as destroying the element of surprise, would have made his strategy of no avail, so that the whole question is beset with difficulties. One cannot at least withhold a reluctant admiration for the wit that had conceived so bold a scheme, and the fell genius with which it was carried out. What were his own feelings about himself at that triumphant moment? Fain would his dogs have known, as breathing heavily and wiping their cutlasses, they gathered at a discreet distance from his hook, and squinted through their ferret eyes at this extraordinary man. Elation must have been in his heart, but his face did not reflect it: ever a dark and solitary enigma, he stood aloof from his followers in spirit as in substance. The night's work was not yet over, for it was not the redskins he had come out to destroy; they were but the bees to be smoked, so that he should get at the honey. It was Pan he wanted, Pan and Wendy and their band, but chiefly Pan. Peter was such a small boy that one tends to wonder at the man's hatred of him. True he had flung Hook's arm to the crocodile; but even this and the increased insecurity of life to which it led, owing to the crocodile's pertinacity, hardly account for a vindictiveness so relentless and malignant. The truth is that there was a something about Peter which goaded the pirate captain to frenzy. It was not his courage, it was not his engaging appearance, it was not—. There is no beating about the bush, for we know quite well what it was, and have got to tell. It was Peter's cockiness. This had got on Hook's nerves; it made his iron claw twitch, and at night it disturbed him like an insect. While Peter lived, the tortured man felt that he was a lion in a cage into which a sparrow had come. The question now was how to get down the trees, or how to get his dogs down? He ran his greedy eyes over them, searching for the thinnest ones. They wriggled uncomfortably, for they knew he would not scruple to ram them down with poles. In the meantime, what of the boys? We have seen them at the first clang of weapons, turned as it were into stone figures, open-mouthed, all appealing with outstretched arms to Peter; and we return to them as their mouths close, and their arms fall to their sides. The pandemonium above has ceased almost as suddenly as it arose, passed like a fierce gust of wind; but they know that in the passing it has determined their fate. Which side had won? The pirates, listening avidly at the mouths of the trees, heard the question put by every boy, and alas, they also heard Peter's answer. "If the redskins have won," he said, "they will beat the tom-tom; it is always their sign of victory." Now Smee had found the tom-tom, and was at that moment sitting on it. "You will never hear the tom-tom again," he muttered, but inaudibly of course, for strict silence had been enjoined. To his amazement Hook signed to him to beat the tom-tom, and slowly there came to Smee an understanding of the dreadful wickedness of the order. Never, probably, had this simple man admired Hook so much. Twice Smee beat upon the instrument, and then stopped to listen gleefully. "The tom-tom," the miscreants heard Peter cry; "an Indian victory!" The doomed children answered with a cheer that was music to the black hearts above, and almost immediately

they repeated their goodbyes to Peter. This puzzled the pirates, but all their other feelings were swallowed by a base delight that the enemy were about to come up the trees.

They smirked at each other and rubbed their hands. Rapidly and silently Hook gave his orders: one man to each tree, and the others to arrange themselves in a line two yards

apart. CHAPTER XIII *Do You Believe In Fairies?* The more quickly this horror is disposed of the better. The first to emerge from his tree was Curly. He rose out of it into

the arms of Cecco, who flung him to Smee, who flung him to Starkey, who flung him to Bill Jukes, who flung him to Noodler, and so he was tossed from one to another til

he fell at the feet of the black pirate. All the boys were plucked from their trees in this ruthless manner; and several of them were in the air at a time, like bales of goods flung

from hand to hand. A different treatment was accorded to Wendy, who came last. With ironical politeness Hook raised his hat to her, and, offering her his arm, escorted her

to the spot where the others were being gagged. He did it with such an air, he was so frightfully *distingué*, that she was too fascinated to cry out. She was only a little girl.

Perhaps it is tell-tale to divulge that for a moment Hook entranced her, and we tell on her only because her slip led to strange results. Had she haughtily unhanded him (and

we should have loved to write it of her), she would have been hurled through the air like the others, and then Hook would probably not have been present at the tying of the

children; and had he not been at the tying he would not have discovered Slightly's secret, and without the secret he could not presently have made his foul attempt on Peter's

life. They were tied to prevent their flying away, doubled up with their knees close to their ears; and for this job the black pirate had cut a rope into nine equal pieces. All were

well until Slightly's turn came, when he was found to be like those irritating parcels that use up all the string in going round and leave no tags with which to tie a knot. The

pirates kicked him in their rage, just as you kick the parcel (though in fairness you should kick the string); and strange to say it was Hook who told them to belay their

violence. His lip was curled with malicious triumph. While his dogs were merely sweating because every time they tried to pack the unhappy lad tight in one part he bulged

out in another, Hook's master mind had gone far beneath Slightly's surface, probing not for effects but for causes; and his exultation showed that he had found them. Slightly,

white to the gills, knew that Hook had surprised his secret, which was this, that no boy so blown out could use a tree wherein an average man need stick. Poor Slightly, most

wretched of all the children now, for he was in a panic about Peter, bitterly regretted what he had done. Madly addicted to the drinking of water when he was hot, he had

swelled in consequence to his present girth, and instead of reducing himself to fit his tree he had, unknown to the others, whittled his tree to make it fit him. Sufficient of this

Hook guessed to persuade him that Peter at last lay at his mercy, but no word of the dark design that now formed in the subterranean caverns of his mind crossed his lips; he

merely signed that the captives were to be conveyed to the ship, and that he would be alone. How to convey them? Hunched up in their ropes they might indeed be rolled

down hill like barrels, but most of the way lay through a morass. Again Hook's genius surmounted difficulties. He indicated that the little house must be used as a conveyance.

The children were flung into it, four stout pirates raised it on their shoulders, the others fell in behind, and singing the hateful pirate chorus the strange procession set off through the wood. I don't know whether any of the children were crying; if so, the singing drowned the sound; but as the little house disappeared in the forest, a brave though

tiny jet of smoke issued from its chimney as if defying Hook. Hook saw it, and it did Peter a bad service. It dried up any trickle of pity for him that may have remained in

the pirate's infuriated breast. The first thing he did on finding himself alone in the fast falling night was to tiptoe to Slightly's tree, and make sure that it provided him with

a passage. Then for long he remained brooding; his hat of ill omen on the sward, so that a gentle breeze which had arisen might play refreshingly through his hair. Dark as

were his thoughts his blue eyes were as soft as the periwinkle. Intently he listened for any sound from the nether world, but all was as silent below as above; the house under

the ground seemed to be but one more empty tenement in the void. Was that boy asleep, or did he stand waiting at the foot of Slightly's tree, with his dagger in his hand?

There was no way of knowing, save by going down. Hook let his cloak slip softly to the ground, and then biting his lips till a lewd blood stood on them, he stepped into the

tree. He was a brave man; but for a moment he had to stop there and wipe his brow, which was dripping like a candle. Then silently he let himself go into the unknown. He

arrived unmolested at the foot of the shaft, and stood still again, biting at his breath, which had almost left him. As his eyes became accustomed to the dim light various objects

in the home under the trees took shape; but the only one on which his greedy gaze rested, long sought for and found at last, was the great bed. On the bed lay Peter fast asleep.

Unaware of the tragedy being enacted above, Peter had continued, for a little time after the children left, to play gaily on his pipes: no doubt rather a forlorn attempt to prove

to himself that he did not care. Then he decided not to take his medicine, so as to grieve Wendy. Then he lay down on the bed outside the coverlet, to vex her still more; for

she had always tucked them inside it, because you never know that you may not grow chilly at the turn of the night. Then he nearly cried; but it struck him how indignant

she would be if he laughed instead; so he laughed a haughty laugh and fell asleep in the middle of it. Sometimes, though not often, he had dreams, and they were more painful

than the dreams of other boys. For hours he could not be separated from these dreams, though he wailed piteously in them. They had to do, I think, with the riddle of his

existence. At such times it had been Wendy's custom to take him out of bed and sit with him on her lap, soothing him in dear ways of her own invention, and when he grew

calmer to put him back to bed before he quite woke up, so that he should not know of the indignity to which she had subjected him. But on this occasion he had fallen at once

into a dreamless sleep. One arm dropped over the edge of the bed, one leg was arched, and the unfinished part of his laugh was stranded on his mouth, which was open,

showing the little pearls. Thus defenceless Hook found him. He stood silent at the foot of the tree looking across the chamber at his enemy. Did no feeling of compassion

disturb his sombre breast? The man was not wholly evil; he loved flowers (I have been told) and sweet music (he was himself no mean performer on the harpsichord); and,

let it be frankly admitted, the idyllic nature of the scene stirred him profoundly. Mastered by his better self he would have returned reluctantly up the tree, but for one thing.

What stayed him was Peter's impertinent appearance as he slept. The open mouth, the drooping arm, the arched knee: they were such a personification of cockiness as, taken

together, will never again one may hope be presented to eyes so sensitive to their offensiveness. They steeled Hook's heart. If his rage had broken him into a hundred pieces every one of them would have disregarded the incident, and leapt at the sleeper. Though a light from the one lamp shone dimly on the bed Hook stood in darkness himself, and at the first stealthy step forward he discovered an obstacle, the door of Slightly's tree. It did not entirely fill the aperture, and he had been looking over it. Feeling for the catch, he found to his fury that it was low down, beyond his reach. To his disordered brain it seemed then that the irritating quality in Peter's face and figure visibly increased, and he rattled the door and flung himself against it. Was his enemy to escape him after all? But what was that? The red in his eye had caught sight of Peter's medicine standing on a ledge within easy reach. He fathomed what it was straightway, and immediately he knew that the sleeper was in his power. Lest he should be taken alive, Hook always carried about his person a dreadful drug, blended by himself of all the death-dealing rings that had come into his possession. These he had boiled down into a yellow liquid quite unknown to science, which was probably the most virulent poison in existence. Five drops of this he now added to Peter's cup. His hand shook, but it was in exultation rather than in shame. As he did it he avoided glancing at the sleeper, but not lest pity should unnerve him; merely to avoid spilling. Then one long gloating look he cast upon his victim, and turning, wormed his way with difficulty up the tree. As he emerged at the top he looked the very spirit of evil breaking from its hole. Donning his hat at its most rakish angle, he wound his cloak around him, holding one end in front as if to conceal his person from the night, of which it was the blackest part, and muttering strangely to himself stole away through the trees. Peter slept on. The light guttered and went out, leaving the tenement in darkness; but still he slept. It must have been not less than ten o'clock by the crocodile, when he suddenly sat up in his bed, wakened by he knew not what. It was a soft cautious tapping on the door of his tree. Soft and cautious, but in that stillness it was sinister. Peter felt for his dagger till his hand gripped it. Then he spoke. "Who is that?" For long there was no answer: then again the knock. "Who are you?" No answer. He was thrilled, and he loved being thrilled. In two strides he reached his door. Unlike Slightly's door it filled the aperture, so that he could no see beyond it, nor could the one knocking see him. "I won't open unless you speak," Peter cried. Then at last the visitor spoke, in a lovely bell-like voice. "Let me in, Peter." It was Tink, and quickly he unbarred to her. She flew in excitedly, her face flushed and her dress stained with mud. "What is it?" "Oh, you could never guess," she cried, and offered him three guesses. "Out with it!" he shouted; and in one ungrammatical sentence, as long as the ribbons conjurers pull from their mouths, she told of the capture of Wendy and the boys. Peter's heart bobbed up and down as he listened. Wendy bound, and on the pirate ship; she who loved everything to be just so! "I'll rescue her," he cried, leaping at his weapons. As he leapt he thought of something he could do to please her. He could take his medicine. His hand closed on the fatal draught. "No!" shrieked Tinker Bell, who had heard Hook muttering about his deed as he sped through the forest. "Why not?" "It is poisoned." "Poisoned? Who could have poisoned it?" "Hook." "Don't be silly. How could Hook have got down here?" Alas, Tinker Bell could not explain this, for even she did not know the dark secret of Slightly's tree. Nevertheless Hook's words had left no room for doubt. The cup was poisoned. "Besides," said Peter, quite believing himself, "I never fell asleep." He raised the cup. No time for word now; time for deeds; and with one of her lightning movements Tink got between his lips and the draught, and drained it to the dregs. "Why, Tink, how dare you drink m medicine?" But she did not answer. Already she was reeling in the air. "What is the matter with you?" cried Peter, suddenly afraid. "It was poisoned, Peter," she told him

softly; "and now I am going to be dead." "O Tink, did you drink it to save me?" "Yes." "But why, Tink?" Her wings would scarcely carry her now, but in reply she alighted

on his shoulder and gave his chin a loving bite. She whispered in his ear "you silly ass," and then, tottering to her chamber, lay down on the bed. His head almost filled the

fourth wall of her little room as he knelt near her in distress. Every moment her light was growing fainter; and he knew that if it went out she would be no more. She liked

his tears so much that she put out her beautiful finger and let them run over it. Her voice was so low that at first he could not make out what she said. Then he made it out.

She was saying that she thought she could get well again if children believed in fairies. Peter flung out his arms. There were no children there, and it was night-time; but he

addressed all who might be dreaming of the Neverland, and who were therefore nearer to him than you think: boys and girls in their nighties, and naked papooses in their

baskets hung from trees. "Do you believe?" he cried. Tink sat up in bed almost briskly to listen to her fate. She fancied she heard answers in the affirmative, and then again

she wasn't sure. "What do you think?" she asked Peter. "If you believe," he shouted to them, "clap your hands; don't let Tink die." Many clapped. Some didn't. A few little

beasts hissed. The clapping stopped suddenly; as if countless mothers had rushed to their nurseries to see what on earth was happening; but already Tink was saved. First

her voice grew strong; then she popped out of bed; then she was flashing through the room more merry and impudent than ever. She never thought of thanking those who

believed, but she would have liked to get at the ones who had hissed. "And now to rescue Wendy." The moon was riding in a cloudy heaven when Peter rose from his tree,

begirt with weapons and wearing little else, to set out upon his perilous quest. It was not such a night as he would have chosen. He had hoped to fly, keeping not far from the

ground so that nothing unwonted should escape his eyes; but in that fitful light to have flown low would have meant trailing his shadow through the trees, thus disturbing the

birds and acquainting a watchful foe that he was astir. He regretted now that he had given the birds of the island such strange names that they are very wild and difficult of

approach. There was no other course but to press forward in redskin fashion, at which happily he was an adept. But in what direction, for he could not be sure that the children

had been taken to the ship? A slight fall of snow had obliterated all footmarks; and a deathly silence pervaded the island, as if for a space Nature stood still in horror of the

recent carnage. He had taught the children something of the forest lore that he had himself learned from Tiger Lily and Tinker Bell, and knew that in their dire hour they

were not likely to forget it. Slightly, if he had an opportunity, would blaze the trees, for instance, Curly would drop seeds, and Wendy would leave her handkerchief at some

important place. But morning was needed to search for such guidance, and he could not wait. The upper world had called him, but would give no help. The crocodile passed

him, but not another living thing, not a sound, not a movement; and yet he knew well that sudden death might be at the next tree, or stalking him from behind. He swore this

terrible oath: "Hook or me this time." Now he crawled forward like a snake; and again, erect, he darted across a space on which the moonlight played: one finger on his lip

and his dagger at the ready. He was frightfully happy. CHAPTER XIV *The Pirate Ship* One green light squinting over Kidd's Creek, which is near the mouth of the pirate river, marked where the brig, the *Jolly Roger*, lay, low in the water; a rakish-looking craft foul to the hull, every beam in her detestable like ground strewn with mangled

feathers. She was the cannibal of the seas, and scarce needed that watchful eye, for she floated immune in the horror of her name. She was wrapped in the blanket of night

through which no sound from her could have reached the shore. There was little sound, and none agreeable save the whir of the ship's sewing machine at which Smee sat

ever industrious and obliging, the essence of the commonplace, pathetic Smee. I know not why he was so infinitely pathetic, unless it were because he was so pathetically

unaware of it; but even strong men had to turn hastily from looking at him, and more than once on summer evenings he had touched the fount of Hook's tears and made it

flow. Of this, as of almost everything else, Smee was quite unconscious. A few of the pirates leant over the bulwarks drinking in the miasma of the night; others sprawled

by barrels over games of dice and cards; and the exhausted four who had carried the little house lay prone on the deck, where even in their sleep they rolled skilfully to this

side or that out of Hook's reach, lest he should claw them mechanically in passing. Hook trod the deck in thought. O man unfathomable. It was his hour of triumph. Peter

had been removed for ever from his path, and all the other boys were on the brig, about to walk the plank. It was his grimmest deed since the days when he had brought

Barbecue to heel; and knowing as we do how vain a tabernacle is man, could we be surprised had he now paced the deck unsteadily, bellied out by the winds of his success?

But there was no elation in his gait, which kept pace with the action of his sombre mind. Hook was profoundly dejected. He was often thus when communing with himself

on board ship in the quietude of the night. It was because he was so terribly alone. This inscrutable man never felt more alone than when surrounded by his dogs. They were

socially so inferior to him. Hook was not his true name. To reveal who he really was would even at this date set the country in a blaze; but as those who read between the lines

must already have guessed, he had been at a famous public school; and its traditions still clung to him like garments, with which indeed they are largely concerned. Thus it

was offensive to him even now to board a ship in the same dress in which he grappled her; and he still adhered in his walk to the school's distinguished slouch. But above all

he retained the passion for good form. Good form! However much he may have degenerated, he still knew that this is all that really matters. From far within him he heard

creaking as of rusty portals, and through them came a stern tap-tap-tap, like hammering in the night when one cannot sleep. "Have you been good form to-day?" was the

eternal question. "Fame, fame, that glittering bauble, it is mine," he cried. "Is it quite good form to be distinguished at anything?" the tap-tap from his school replied. "I am

the only man whom Barbecue feared," he urged; "and Flint himself feared Barbecue." "Barbecue, Flint—what house?" came the cutting retort. Most disquieting reflection

of all, was it not bad form to think about good form? His vitals were tortured by this problem. It was a claw within him sharper than the iron one; and as it tore him, the

perspiration dripped down his tallow countenance and streaked his doublet. Ofttimes he drew his sleeve across his face, but there was no damming that trickle. Ah, envy not

Hook. There came to him a presentiment of his early dissolution. It was as if Peter's terrible oath had boarded the ship. Hook felt a gloomy desire to make his dying speech,

lest presently there should be no time for it. "Better for Hook," he cried, "if he had had less ambition!" It was in his darkest hours only that he referred to himself in the third person. "No little children love me!" Strange that he should think of this, which had never troubled him before; perhaps the sewing machine brought it to his mind. For long

he muttered to himself, staring at Smee, who was hemming placidly, under the conviction that all children feared him. Feared him! Feared Smee! There was not a child on

board the brig that night who did not already love him. He had said horrid things to them and hit them with the palm of his hand, because he could not hit with his fist; but

they had only clung to him the more. Michael had tried on his spectacles. To tell poor Smee that they thought him lovable! Hook itched to do it, but it seemed too brutal.

Instead, he revolved this mystery in his mind: why do they find Smee lovable? He pursued the problem like the sleuth-hound that he was. If Smee was lovable, what was it

that made him so? A terrible answer suddenly presented itself: "Good form?" Had the bo'sun good form without knowing it, which is the best form of all? He remembered

that you have to prove you don't know you have it before you are eligible for Pop. With a cry of rage he raised his iron hand over Smee's head; but he did not tear. What

arrested him was this reflection: "To claw a man because he is good form, what would that be?" "Bad form!" The unhappy Hook was as impotent as he was damp, and he

fell forward like a cut flower. His dogs thinking him out of the way for a time, discipline instantly relaxed; and they broke into a bacchanalian dance, which brought him to

his feet at once; all traces of human weakness gone, as if a bucket of water had passed over him. "Quiet, you scugs," he cried, "or I'll cast anchor in you;" and at once the din

was hushed. "Are all the children chained, so that they cannot fly away?" "Ay, ay." "Then hoist them up." The wretched prisoners were dragged from the hold, all except

Wendy, and ranged in line in front of him. For a time he seemed unconscious of their presence. He lolled at his ease, humming, not unmelodiously, snatches of a rude song,

and fingering a pack of cards. Ever and anon the light from his cigar gave a touch of colour to his face. "Now then, bullies," he said briskly, "six of you walk the plank to-

night, but I have room for two cabin boys. Which of you is it to be?" "Don't irritate him unnecessarily," had been Wendy's instructions in the hold; so Tootles stepped

forward politely. Tootles hated the idea of signing under such a man, but an instinct told him that it would be prudent to lay the responsibility on an absent person; and though

a somewhat silly boy, he knew that mothers alone are always willing to be the buffer. All children know this about mothers, and despise them for it, but make constant use of

it. So Tootles explained prudently, "You see, sir, I don't think my mother would like me to be a pirate. Would your mother like you to be a pirate, Slightly?" He winked at

Slightly, who said mournfully, "I don't think so," as if he wished things had been otherwise. "Would your mother like you to be a pirate, Twin?" "I don't think so," said the

first twin, as clever as the others. "Nibs, would—" "Stow this gab," roared Hook, and the spokesmen were dragged back. "You, boy," he said, addressing John, "you look

as if you had a little pluck in you. Didst never want to be a pirate, my hearty?" Now John had sometimes experienced this hankering at maths. prep.; and he was struck by

Hook's picking him out. "I once thought of calling myself Red-handed Jack," he said diffidently. "And a good name too. We'll call you that here, bully, if you join." "What

do you think, Michael?" asked John. "What would you call me if I join?" Michael demanded. "Blackbeard Joe." Michael was naturally impressed. "What do you think,

John?" He wanted John to decide, and John wanted him to decide. "Shall we still be respectful subjects of the King?" John inquired. Through Hook's teeth came the answer:

"You would have to swear, 'Down with the King.'" Perhaps John had not behaved very well so far, but he shone out now. "Then I refuse!" he cried, banging the barrel in front of Hook. "And I refuse," cried Michael. "Rule Britannia!" squeaked Curly. The infuriated pirates buffeted them in the mouth; and Hook roared out, "That seals your doom. Bring up their mother. Get the plank ready." They were only boys, and they went white as they saw Jukes and Cecco preparing the fatal plank. But they tried to look brave when Wendy was brought up. No words of mine can tell you how Wendy despised those pirates. To the boys there was at least some glamour in the pirate calling; but all that she saw was that the ship had not been tidied for years. There was not a porthole on the grimy glass of which you might not have written with your finger "Dirty pig;" and she had already written it on several. But as the boys gathered round her she had no thought, of course, save for them. "So, my beauty," said Hook, as if he spoke in syrup, "you are to see your children walk the plank." Fine gentleman though he was, the intensity of his communings had soiled his ruff, and suddenly he knew that she was gazing at it. With a hasty gesture he tried to hide it, but he was too late. "Are they to die?" asked Wendy, with a look of such frightful contempt that he nearly fainted. "They are," he snarled. "Silence all," he called gloatingly, "for a mother's last words to her children." At this moment Wendy was grand. "These are my last words, dear boys," she said firmly. "I feel that I have a message to you from your real mothers, and it is this: 'We hope our sons will die like English gentlemen.'" Even the pirates were awed, and Tootles cried out hysterically, "I am going to do what my mother hopes. What are you to do, Nibs?" "What my mother hopes. What are you to do, Twin?" "What my mother hopes. John, what are—" But Hook had found his voice again. "Tie her up," he shouted. It was Smee who tied her to the mast. "See here, honey," he whispered, "I'll save you if you promise to be my mother." But not even for Smee would she make such a promise. "I would almost rather have no children at all," she said disdainfully. It is sad to know that not a boy was looking at her as Smee tied her to the mast; the eyes of all were on the plank: that last little walk they were about to take. They were no longer able to hope that they would walk it manfully, for the capacity to think had gone from them; they could stare and shiver only. Hook smiled on them with his teeth closed, and took a step toward Wendy. His intention was to turn her face so that she should see the boys walking the plank one by one. But he never reached her, he never heard the cry of anguish he hoped to wring from her. He heard something else instead. It was the terrible tick-tick of the crocodile. They all heard it—pirates, boys, Wendy—and immediately every head was blown in one direction; not to the water whence the sound proceeded, but toward Hook. All knew that what was about to happen concerned him alone, and that from being actors they were suddenly become spectators. Very frightful was it to see the change that came over him. It was as if he had been clipped at every joint. He fell in a little heap. The sound came steadily nearer; and in advance of it came this ghastly thought, "the crocodile is about to board the ship!" Even the iron claw hung inactive; as if knowing that it was no intrinsic part of what the attacking force wanted. Left so fearfully alone, any other man would have lain with his eyes shut where he fell: but the gigantic brain of Hook was still working, and under its guidance he crawled on his knees along the deck as far from the sound as he could go. The pirates respectfully cleared a passage for him, and it was only when he brought up against the bulwarks that he spoke. "Hide me," he cried hoarsely. They gathered round him; all eyes averted from the thing that was coming aboard. They had no thought of fighting it. It was Fate. Only when Hook was hidden from them did curiosity loosen

the limbs of the boys so that they could rush to the ship's side to see the crocodile climbing it. Then they got the strangest surprise of this Night of Nights; for it was no

crocodile that was coming to their aid. It was Peter. He signed to them not to give vent to any cry of admiration that might rouse suspicion. Then he went on ticking.

CHAPTER XV *"Hook Or Me This Time"* Odd things happen to all of us on our way through life without our noticing for a time that they have happened. Thus, to take an

instance, we suddenly discover that we have been deaf in one ear for we don't know how long, but, say, half an hour. Now such an experience had come that night to Peter.

When last we saw him he was stealing across the island with one finger to his lips and his dagger at the ready. He had seen the crocodile pass by without noticing anything

peculiar about it, but by and by he remembered that it had not been ticking. At first he thought this eerie, but soon he concluded rightly that the clock had run down. Without

giving a thought to what might be the feelings of a fellow-creature thus abruptly deprived of its closest companion, Peter at once considered how he could turn the

catastrophe to his own use; and he decided to tick, so that wild beasts should believe he was the crocodile and let him pass unmolested. He ticked superbly, but with one

unforeseen result. The crocodile was among those who heard the sound, and it followed him, though whether with the purpose of regaining what it had lost, or merely as a

friend under the belief that it was again ticking itself, will never be certainly known, for, like all slaves to a fixed idea, it was a stupid beast. Peter reached the shore without

mishap, and went straight on, his legs encountering the water as if quite unaware that they had entered a new element. Thus many animals pass from land to water, but no

other human of whom I know. As he swam he had but one thought: "Hook or me this time." He had ticked so long that he now went on ticking without knowing that he was

doing it. Had he known he would have stopped, for to board the brig by the help of the tick, though an ingenious idea, had not occurred to him. On the contrary, he thought

he had scaled her side as noiseless as a mouse; and he was amazed to see the pirates cowering from him, with Hook in their midst as abject as if he had heard the crocodile.

The crocodile! No sooner did Peter remember it than he heard the ticking. At first he thought the sound did come from the crocodile, and he looked behind him swiftly. Then

he realised that he was doing it himself, and in a flash he understood the situation. "How clever of me," he thought at once, and signed to the boys not to burst into applause.

It was at this moment that Ed Teynte the quartermaster emerged from the forecastle and came along the deck. Now, reader, time what happened by your watch. Peter struck

true and deep. John clapped his hands on the ill-fated pirate's mouth to stifle the dying groan. He fell forward. Four boys caught him to prevent the thud. Peter gave the

signal, and the carrion was cast overboard. There was a splash, and then silence. How long has it taken? "One!" (Slightly had begun to count.) None too soon, Peter, every

inch of him on tiptoe, vanished into the cabin; for more than one pirate was screwing up his courage to look round. They could hear each other's distressed breathing now,

which showed them that the more terrible sound had passed. "It's gone, captain," Smee said, wiping his spectacles. "All's still again." Slowly Hook let his head emerge from

his ruff, and listened so intently that he could have caught the echo of the tick. There was not a sound, and he drew himself up firmly to his full height. "Then here's to

Johnny Plank," he cried brazenly, hating the boys more than ever because they had seen him unbend. He broke into the villainous ditty: "Yo ho, yo ho, the frisky plank, You walks along it so, Till it goes down and you goes down To Davy Jones below!" To terrorise the prisoners the more, though with a certain loss of dignity, he danced along an imaginary plank, grimacing at them as he sang; and when he finished he cried, "Do you want a touch of the cat before you walk the plank?" At that they fell on their knees.

"No, no," they cried so piteously that every pirate smiled. "Fetch the cat, Jukes," said Hook; "it's in the cabin." The cabin! Peter was in the cabin! The children gazed at each other. "Ay, ay," said Jukes blithely, and he strode into the cabin. They followed him with their eyes; they scarce knew that Hook had resumed his song, his dogs joining in with him: "Yo ho, yo ho, the scratching cat, Its tails are nine, you know, And when they're writ upon your back—" What was the last line will never be known, for of a sudden the song was stayed by a dreadful screech from the cabin. It wailed through the ship, and died away. Then was heard a crowing sound which was well understood by the boys, but to the pirates was almost more eerie than the screech. "What was that?" cried Hook. "Two," said Slightly solemnly. The Italian Cecco hesitated for a moment and then swung into the cabin. He tottered out, haggard. "What's the matter with Bill Jukes, you dog?" hissed Hook, towering over him. "The matter wi' him is he's dead, stabbed," replied Cecco in a hollow voice. "Bill Jukes dead!" cried the startled pirates. "The cabin's as black as a pit," Cecco said, almost gibbering, "but there is something terrible in there: the thing you heard crowing." The exultation of the boys, the lowering looks of the pirates, both were seen by Hook. "Cecco," he said in his most steely voice, "go back and fetch me out that doodle-doo." Cecco, bravest of the brave, cowered before his captain, crying "No, no;" but Hook was purring to his claw. "Did you say you would go, Cecco?" he said musingly. Cecco went, first flinging up his arms despairingly. There was no more singing, all listened now; and again came a death-screech and again a crow. No one spoke except Slightly. "Three," he said. Hook rallied his dogs with a gesture. "S' death and odds fish," he thundered, "who is to bring me that doodle-doo?" "Wait till Cecco comes out," growled Starkey, and the others took up the cry. "I think I heard you volunteer, Starkey," said Hook, purring again. "No, by thunder!" Starkey cried. "My hook thinks you did," said Hook, crossing to him. "I wonder if it would not be advisable, Starkey, to humour the hook?" "I'll swing before I go in there," replied Starkey doggedly, and again he had the support of the crew. "Is it mutiny?" asked Hook more pleasantly than ever. "Starkey's ringleader!" "Captain, mercy," Starkey whimpered, all of a tremble now. "Shake hands, Starkey," said Hook, proffering his claw. Starkey looked round for help, but all deserted him. As he backed Hook advanced, and now the red spark was in his eye. With a despairing scream the pirate leapt upon Long Tom and precipitated himself into the sea. "Four," said Slightly. "And now," Hook asked courteously, "did any other gentleman say mutiny?" Seizing a lantern and raising his claw with a menacing gesture, "I'll bring out that doodle-doo myself," he said, and sped into the cabin. "Five." How Slightly longed to say it. He wetted his lips to be ready, but Hook came staggering out, without his lantern. "Something blew out the light," he said a little unsteadily. "Something!" echoed Mullins. "What of Cecco?" demanded Noodler. "He's as dead as Jukes," said Hook shortly. His reluctance to return to the cabin impressed them all unfavourably, and the mutinous sounds again broke forth. All pirates are superstitious; and Cookson cried, "They do say the surest sign ship's accurst is when there's one on board more than can be accounted for." "I've heard," muttered Mullins, "he always boards the pirate craft at last. Had he a tail, captain?"

"They say," said another, looking viciously at Hook, "that when he comes it's in the likeness of the wickedest man aboard." "Had he a hook, captain?" asked Cookson insolently; and one after another took up the cry, "The ship's doomed." At this the children could not resist raising a cheer. Hook had well-nigh forgotten his prisoners, but as he swung round on them now his face lit up again. "Lads," he cried to his crew, "here's a notion. Open the cabin door and drive them in. Let them fight the doodle-doo for their lives. If they kill him, we're so much the better; if he kills them, we're none the worse." For the last time his dogs admired Hook, and devotedly they did his bidding.

The boys, pretending to struggle, were pushed into the cabin and the door was closed on them. "Now, listen," cried Hook, and all listened. But not one dared to face the door. Yes, one, Wendy, who all this time had been bound to the mast. It was for neither a scream nor a crow that she was watching; it was for the reappearance of Peter. She had not long to wait. In the cabin he had found the thing for which he had gone in search: the key that would free the children of their manacles; and now they all stole forth, armed with such weapons as they could find. First signing to them to hide, Peter cut Wendy's bonds, and then nothing could have been easier than for them all to fly off together; but one thing barred the way, an oath, "Hook or me this time." So when he had freed Wendy, he whispered to her to conceal herself with the others, and himself took her place by the mast, her cloak around him so that she should pass for her. Then he took a great breath and crowed. To the pirates it was a voice crying that all the boys lay slain in the cabin; and they were panic-stricken. Hook tried to hearten them; but like the dogs he had made them they showed him their fangs, and he knew that if he took his eyes off them now they would leap at him. "Lads," he said, ready to cajole or strike as need be, but never quailing for an instant, "I've thought it out. There's a Jonah aboard." "Ay," they snarled, "a man wi' a hook." "No, lads, no, it's the girl. Never was luck on a pirate ship wi' a woman on board. We'll right the ship when she's gone." Some of them remembered that this had been a saying of Flint's. "It's worth trying," they said doubtfully. "Fling the girl overboard," cried Hook; and they made a rush at the figure in the cloak. "There's none can save you now, missy," Mullins hissed jeeringly. "There's one," replied the figure. "Who's that?" "Peter Pan the avenger!" came the terrible answer; and as he spoke Peter flung off his cloak. Then they all knew who 'twas that had been undoing them in the cabin, and twice Hook essayed to speak and twice he failed. In that frightful moment I think his fierce heart broke. At last he cried, "Cleave him to the brisket," but without conviction. "Down, boys, and at them," Peter's voice rang out; and in another moment the clash of arms was resounding through the ship. Had the pirates kept together it is certain that they would have won; but the onset came when they were all unstrung, and they ran hither and thither, striking wildly, each thinking himself the last survivor of the crew. Man to man they were the stronger; but they fought on the defensive only, which enabled the boys to hunt in pairs and choose their quarry. Some of the miscreants leapt into the sea; others hid in dark recesses, where they were found by Slightly, who did not fight, but ran about with a lantern which he flashed in their faces, so that they were half blinded and fell an easy prey to the reeking swords of the other boys. There was little sound to be heard but the clang of weapons, an occasional screech or splash, and Slightly monotonously counting—

five—six—seven—eight— nine—ten—eleven. I think all were gone when a group of savage boys surrounded Hook, who seemed to have a charmed life, as he kept them at bay in that circle of fire. They had done for his dogs, but this man alone seemed to be a match for them all. Again and again they closed upon him, and again and again he hewed a clear space. He had lifted up one boy with his hook, and was using him as a buckler, when another, who had just passed his sword through Mullins, sprang into the fray. "Put up your swords, boys," cried the newcomer, "this man is mine." Thus suddenly Hook found himself face to face with Peter. The others drew back and formed a ring round them. For long the two enemies looked at one another; Hook shuddering slightly, and Peter with the strange smile upon his face. "So, Pan," said Hook at last, "this is all your doing." "Ay, James Hook," came the stern answer, "it is all my doing." "Proud and insolent youth," said Hook, "prepare to meet thy doom." "Dark and sinister man," Peter answered, "have at thee." Without more words they fell to, and for a space there was no advantage to either blade. Peter was a superb swordsman, and parried with dazzling rapidity; ever and anon he followed up a feint with a lunge that got past his foe's defence, but his shorter reach stood him in ill stead, and he could not drive the steel home. Hook, scarcely his inferior in brilliancy, but not quite so nimble in wrist play, forced him back by the weight of his onset, hoping suddenly to end all with a favourite thrust, taught him long ago by Barbecue at Rio; but to his astonishment he found this thrust turned aside again and again. Then he sought to close and give the quietus with his iron hook, which all this time had been pawing the air; but Peter doubled under it and, lunging fiercely, pierced him in the ribs. At sight of his own blood whose peculiar colour, you remember, was offensive to him, the sword fell from Hook's hand, and he was at Peter's mercy. "Now!" cried all the boys, but with a magnificent gesture Peter invited his opponent to pick up his sword. Hook did so instantly, but with a tragic feeling that Peter was showing good form. Hitherto he had thought it was some fiend fighting him, but darker suspicions assailed him now. "Pan, who and what art thou?" he cried huskily. "I'm youth, I'm joy," Peter answered at a venture, "I'm a little bird that has broken out of the egg." This, of course, was nonsense; but it was proof to the unhappy Hook that Peter did not know in the least who or what he was, which is the very pinnacle of good form. "To't again," he cried despairingly. He fought now like a human flail, and every sweep of that terrible sword would have severed in twain any man or boy who obstructed it; but Peter fluttered round him as if the very wind it made blew him out of the danger zone. And again and again he darted in and pricked. Hook was fighting now without hope. That passionate breast no longer asked for life; but for one boon it craved: to see Peter's bad form before it was cold for ever. Abandoning the fight he rushed into the powder magazine and fired it. "In two minutes," he cried, "the ship will be blown to pieces." Now, now, he thought, true form will show. But Peter issued from the powder magazine with the shell in his hands, and calmly flung it overboard. What sort of form was Hook himself showing? Misguided man though he was, we may be glad, without sympathising with him, that in the end he was true to the traditions of his race. The other boys were flying around him now, flouting, scornful; and as he staggered about the deck striking up at them impotently, his mind was no longer with them; it was slouching in the playing fields of long ago, or being sent up for good, or watching the wall-game from a famous wall. And his shoes were right, and his waistcoat was right, and his tie was right, and his socks were right. Jame

Hook, thou not wholly unheroic figure, farewell. For we have come to his last moment. Seeing Peter slowly advancing upon him through the air with dagger poised, he sprang upon the bulwarks to cast himself into the sea. He did not know that the crocodile was waiting for him; for we purposely stopped the clock that this knowledge might be spared him: a little mark of respect from us at the end. He had one last triumph, which I think we need not grudge him. As he stood on the bulwark looking over his shoulder at Peter gliding through the air, he invited him with a gesture to use his foot. It made Peter kick instead of stab. At last Hook had got the boon for which he craved.

"Bad form," he cried jeeringly, and went content to the crocodile. Thus perished James Hook. "Seventeen," Slightly sang out; but he was not quite correct in his figures. Fifteen paid the penalty for their crimes that night; but two reached the shore: Starkey to be captured by the redskins, who made him nurse for all their papooses, a melancholy come-down for a pirate; and Smee, who henceforth wandered about the world in his spectacles, making a precarious living by saying he was the only man that Jas. Hook had feared. Wendy, of course, had stood by taking no part in the fight, though watching Peter with glistening eyes; but now that all was over she became prominent again. She praised them equally, and shuddered delightfully when Michael showed her the place where he had killed one; and then she took them into Hook's cabin and pointed to his watch which was hanging on a nail. It said "half-past one"! The lateness of the hour was almost the biggest thing of all. She got them to bed in the pirates' bunks pretty quickly, you may be sure; all but Peter, who strutted up and down on deck, until at last he fell asleep by the side of Long Tom. He had one of his dreams that night, and cried in his sleep for a long time, and Wendy held him tight. CHAPTER XVI *The Return Home* By three bells that morning they were all stirring their stumps; for there was a big sea running, and Tootles, the bo'sun, was among them, with a rope's end in his hand and chewing tobacco. They all donned pirate clothes cut off at the knee, shaved smartly, and tumbled up, with the true nautical roll and hitching their trousers. It need not be said who was the captain. Nibs and John were first and second mate. There was a woman aboard. The rest were tars before the mast, and lived in the fo'c'sle. Peter had already lashed himself to the wheel; but he piped all hands and delivered a short address to them; said he hoped they would do their duty like gallant hearties, but that he knew they were the scum of Rio and the Gold Coast, and if they snapped at him he would tear them. His bluff strident words struck the note sailors understand, and they cheered him lustily. Then a few sharp orders were given, and they turned the ship round, and nosed her for the mainland. Captain Pan calculated, after consulting the ship's chart, that if this weather lasted they should strike the Azores about the 21st of June, after which it would save time to fly. Some of them wanted it to be an honest ship and others were in favour of keeping it a pirate; but the captain treated them as dogs, and they dared not express their wishes to him even in a round robin. Instant obedience was the only safe thing. Slightly got a dozen for looking perplexed when told to take soundings. The general feeling was that Peter was honest just now to lull Wendy's suspicions, but that there might be a change when the new suit was ready, which, against her will, she was making for him out of some of Hook's wickedest garments. It was afterwards whispered among them that on the first night he wore this suit he sat long in the cabin with Hook's cigar-holder in his mouth and one hand clenched, all but the forefinger, which he bent and held threateningly aloft like a hook. Instead of watching the ship, however, we must now return to that desolate home from which three of our characters had taken heartless flight so long ago. It seems a shame to have neglected No. 14 all this time;

and yet we may be sure that Mrs. Darling does not blame us. If we had returned sooner to look with sorrowful sympathy at her, she would probably have cried, "Don't be

silly; what do I matter? Do go back and keep an eye on the children." So long as mothers are like this their children will take advantage of them; and they may lay to that.

Even now we venture into that familiar nursery only because its lawful occupants are on their way home; we are merely hurrying on in advance of them to see that their beds

are properly aired and that Mr. and Mrs. Darling do not go out for the evening. We are no more than servants. Why on earth should their beds be properly aired, seeing that

they left them in such a thankless hurry? Would it not serve them jolly well right if they came back and found that their parents were spending the week-end in the country?

It would be the moral lesson they have been in need of ever since we met them; but if we contrived things in this way Mrs. Darling would never forgive us. One thing I should

like to do immensely, and that is to tell her, in the way authors have, that the children are coming back, that indeed they will be here on Thursday week. This would spoil so

completely the surprise to which Wendy and John and Michael are looking forward. They have been planning it out on the ship: mother's rapture, father's shout of joy,

Nana's leap through the air to embrace them first, when what they ought to be preparing for is a good hiding. How delicious to spoil it all by breaking the news in advance;

so that when they enter grandly Mrs. Darling may not even offer Wendy her mouth, and Mr. Darling may exclaim pettishly, "Dash it all, here are those boys again."

However, we should get no thanks even for this. We are beginning to know Mrs. Darling by this time, and may be sure that she would upbraid us for depriving the children

of their little pleasure. "But, my dear madam, it is ten days till Thursday week; so that by telling you what's what, we can save you ten days of unhappiness." "Yes, but at

what a cost! By depriving the children of ten minutes of delight." "Oh, if you look at it in that way." "What other way is there in which to look at it?" You see, the woman

had no proper spirit. I had meant to say extraordinarily nice things about her; but I despise her, and not one of them will I say now. She does not really need to be told to have

things ready, for they are ready. All the beds are aired, and she never leaves the house, and observe, the window is open. For all the use we are to her, we might go back to

the ship. However, as we are here we may as well stay and look on. That is all we are, lookers-on. Nobody really wants us. So let us watch and say jaggy things, in the hope

that some of them will hurt. The only change to be seen in the night-nursery is that between nine and six the kennel is no longer there. **When the children flew away, Mr.**

Darling felt in his bones that all the blame was his for having chained Nana up, and that from first to last she had been wiser than he. Of course, as we have seen, he was quite

a simple man; indeed he might have passed for a boy again if he had been able to take his baldness off; but he had also a noble sense of justice and a lion courage to do what

seemed right to him; and having thought the matter out with anxious care after the flight of the children, he went down on all fours and crawled into the kennel. To all Mrs.

Darling's dear invitations to him to come out he replied sadly but firmly: "No, my own one, this is the place for me." In the bitterness of his remorse he swore that he would

never leave the kennel until his children came back. Of course this was a pity; but whatever Mr. Darling did he had to do in excess; otherwise he soon gave up doing it. And there never was a more humble man than the once proud George Darling, as he sat in the kennel of an evening talking with his wife of their children and all their pretty ways.

Very touching was his deference to Nana. He would not let her come into the kennel, but on all other matters he followed her wishes implicitly. Every morning the kennel was carried with Mr. Darling in it to a cab, which conveyed him to his office, and he returned home in the same way at six. Something of the strength of character of the man will be seen if we remember how sensitive he was to the opinion of neighbours: this man whose every movement now attracted surprised attention. Inwardly he must have suffered torture; but he preserved a calm exterior even when the young criticised his little home, and he always lifted his hat courteously to any lady who looked inside. It may have been quixotic, but it was magnificent. Soon the inward meaning of it leaked out, and the great heart of the public was touched. Crowds followed the cab, cheering it lustily; charming girls scaled it to get his autograph; interviews appeared in the better class of papers, and society invited him to dinner and added, "Do come in the kennel."

On that eventful Thursday week Mrs. Darling was in the night-nursery awaiting George's return home: a very sad-eyed woman. Now that we look at her closely and remember the gaiety of her in the old days, all gone now just because she has lost her babes, I find I won't be able to say nasty things about her after all. If she was too fond of her rubbishy children she couldn't help it. Look at her in her chair, where she has fallen asleep. The corner of her mouth, where one looks first, is almost withered up. Her hand moves restlessly on her breast as if she had a pain there. Some like Peter best and some like Wendy best, but I like her best. Suppose, to make her happy, we whisper to her in her sleep that the brats are coming back. They are really within two miles of the window now, and flying strong, but all we need whisper is that they are on the way. Let's. It is a pity we did it, for she has started up, calling their names; and there is no one in the room but Nana. "O Nana, I dreamt my dear ones had come back." Nana had filmy eyes, but all she could do was to put her paw gently on her mistress's lap; and they were sitting together thus when the kennel was brought back. As Mr. Darling puts his head out at it to kiss his wife, we see that his face is more worn than of yore, but has a softer expression. He gave his hat to Liza, who took it scornfully; for she had no imagination, and was quite incapable of understanding the motives of such a man. Outside, the crowd who had accompanied the cab home were still cheering, and he was naturally not unmoved. "Listen to them," he said; "it is very gratifying." "Lot of little boys," sneered Liza. "There were several adults to-day," he assured her with a faint flush; but when she tossed her head he had not a word of reproof for her. Social success had not spoilt him; it had made him sweeter. For some time he sat half out of the kennel, talking with Mrs. Darling of this success, and pressing her hand reassuringly when she said she hoped his head would not be turned by it. "But if I had been a weak man," he said. "Good heavens, if I had been a weak man!" "And, George," she said timidly, "you are as full of remorse as ever, aren't you?" "Full of remorse as ever, dearest! See my punishment: living in a kennel." "But it is punishment, isn't it, George? You are sure you are not enjoying it?" "My love!" You may be sure she begged his pardon; and then, feeling drowsy, he curled round in the kennel. "Won't you play me to sleep," he asked, "on the nursery piano?" and as she was crossing to the day nursery he added thoughtlessly, "And shut that window. I feel a draught." "O George, never ask me to do that. The window must always be left open for them, always, always." Now it was his turn to beg her pardon; and she went into the day nursery and played, and soon he was asleep; and while he slept, Wendy and John and Michael flew into the room. Oh

no. We have written it so, because that was the charming arrangement planned by them before we left the ship; but something must have happened since then, for it is not

they who have flown in, it is Peter and Tinker Bell. Peter's first words tell all. "Quick, Tink," he whispered, "close the window; bar it. That's right. Now you and I must ge

away by the door; and when Wendy comes she will think her mother has barred her out; and she will have to go back with me." Now I understand what had hitherto puzzled

me, why when Peter had exterminated the pirates he did not return to the island and leave Tink to escort the children to the mainland. This trick had been in his head all the

time. Instead of feeling that he was behaving badly he danced with glee; then he peeped into the day-nursery to see who was playing. He whispered to Tink, "It's Wendy's

mother. She is a pretty lady, but not so pretty as my mother. Her mouth is full of thimbles, but not so full as my mother's was." Of course he knew nothing whatever abou

his mother; but he sometimes bragged about her. He did not know the tune, which was "Home, Sweet Home," but he knew it was saying, "Come back, Wendy, Wendy

Wendy;" and he cried exultantly, "You will never see Wendy again, lady, for the window is barred." He peeped in again to see why the music had stopped; and now he saw

that Mrs. Darling had laid her head on the box, and that two tears were sitting on her eyes. "She wants me to unbar the window," thought Peter, "but I won't, not I." He

peeped again, and the tears were still there, or another two had taken their place. "She's awfully fond of Wendy," he said to himself. He was angry with her now for not seeing

why she could not have Wendy. The reason was so simple: "I'm fond of her too. We can't both have her, lady." But the lady would not make the best of it, and he was

unhappy. He ceased to look at her, but even then she would not let go of him. He skipped about and made funny faces, but when he stopped it was just as if she were inside

him, knocking. "Oh, all right," he said at last, and gulped. Then he unbarred the window. "Come on, Tink," he cried, with a frightful sneer at the laws of nature; "we don

want any silly mothers;" and he flew away. Thus Wendy and John and Michael found the window open for them after all, which of course was more than they deserved

They alighted on the floor, quite unashamed of themselves, and the youngest one had already forgotten his home. "John," he said, looking around him doubtfully, "I thin

I have been here before." "Of course you have, you silly. There is your old bed." "So it is," Michael said, but not with much conviction. "I say," cried John, "the kennel

and he dashed across to look into it. "Perhaps Nana is inside it," Wendy said. But John whistled. "Hullo," he said, "there's a man inside it." "It's father!" exclaimed Wend

"Let me see father," Michael begged eagerly, and he took a good look. "He is not so big as the pirate I killed," he said with such frank disappointment that I am glad M

Darling was asleep; it would have been sad if those had been the first words he heard his little Michael say. Wendy and John had been taken aback somewhat at finding the

father in the kennel. "Surely," said John, like one who had lost faith in his memory, "he used not to sleep in the kennel?" "John," Wendy said falteringly, "perhaps we do

remember the old life as well as we thought we did." A chill fell upon them; and serve them right. "It is very careless of mother," said that young scoundrel John, "not to

here when we come back." It was then that Mrs. Darling began playing again. "It's mother!" cried Wendy, peeping. "So it is!" said John. "Then are you not really our moth

Wendy?" asked Michael, who was surely sleepy. "Oh dear!" exclaimed Wendy, with her first real twinge of remorse, "it was quite time we came back." "Let us creep in," John suggested, "and put our hands over her eyes." But Wendy, who saw that they must break the joyous news more gently, had a better plan. "Let us all slip into our beds, and be there when she comes in, just as if we had never been away." And so when Mrs. Darling went back to the night-nursery to see if her husband was asleep, all the beds were occupied. The children waited for her cry of joy, but it did not come. She saw them, but she did not believe they were there. You see, she saw them in their beds so often in her dreams that she thought this was just the dream hanging around her still. She sat down in the chair by the fire, where in the old days she had nursed them. They could not understand this, and a cold fear fell upon all the three of them. "Mother!" Wendy cried. "That's Wendy," she said, but still she was sure it was the dream. "Mother!" "That's John," she said. "Mother!" cried Michael. He knew her now. "That's Michael," she said, and she stretched out her arms for the three little selfish children they would never envelop again. Yes, they did, they went round Wendy and John and Michael, who had slipped out of bed and run to her. "George, George," she cried when she could speak; and Mr. Darling woke to share her bliss, and Nana came rushing in. There could not have been a lovelier sight; but there was none to see it except a strange boy who was staring in at the window. He had ecstasies innumerable that other children can never know; but he was looking through the window at the one joy from which he must be for ever barred. CHAPTER XVII *When Wendy Grew Up* I hope you want to know what became of the other boys. They were waiting below to give Wendy time to explain about them, and when they had counted five hundred they went up. They went up by the stair, because they thought this would make a better impression. They stood in a row in front of Mrs. Darling, with their hats off, and wishing they were not wearing their pirate clothes. They said nothing, but their eyes asked her to have them. They ought to have looked at Mr. Darling also, but they forgot about him. Of course Mrs. Darling said at once that she would have them; but Mr. Darling was curiously depressed, and they saw that he considered six a rather large number. "I must say," he said to Wendy, "that you don't do things by halves," a grudging remark which the twins thought was pointed at them. The first twin was the proud one, and he asked, flushing, "Do you think we should be too much of a handful, sir? Because if so we can go away." "Father!" Wendy cried, shocked; but still the cloud was on him. He knew he was behaving unworthily, but he could not help it. "We could lie doubled up," said Nibs. "I always cut their hair myself," said Wendy. "George!" Mrs. Darling exclaimed, pained to see her dear one showing himself in such an unfavourable light. Then he burst into tears, and the truth came out. He was as glad to have them as she was, he said, but he thought they should have asked his consent as well as hers, instead of treating him as a cypher in his own house. "I don't think he is a cypher," Tootles cried instantly. "Do you think he is a cypher, Curly?" "No, I don't. Do you think he is a cypher, Slightly?" "Rather not. Twin, what do you think?" It turned out that not one of them thought him a cypher; and he was absurdly gratified, and said he would find space for them all in the drawing-room if they fitted in. "We'll fit in, sir," they assured him. "Then follow the leader," he cried gaily. "Mind you, I am not sure that we have a drawing-room, but we pretend we have, and it's all the same. Hoop la!" He went off dancing through the house, and they all cried "Hoop la!" and danced after him, searching for the drawing-room; and I forget whether they found it, but at any rate they found corners, and they all fitted in. As for Peter, he saw Wendy once again before he flew away. He did not

exactly come to the window, but he brushed against it in passing, so that she could open it if she liked and call to him. That was what she did. "Hullo, Wendy, good-bye," he

said. "Oh dear, are you going away?" "Yes." "You don't feel, Peter," she said falteringly, "that you would like to say anything to my parents about a very sweet subject?"

"No." "About me, Peter?" "No." Mrs. Darling came to the window, for at present she was keeping a sharp eye on Wendy. She told Peter that she had adopted all the other

boys, and would like to adopt him also. "Would you send me to school?" he inquired craftily. "Yes." "And then to an office?" "I suppose so." "Soon I should be a man?"

"Very soon." "I don't want to go to school and learn solemn things," he told her passionately. "I don't want to be a man. O Wendy's mother, if I was to wake up and feel

there was a beard!" "Peter," said Wendy the comforter, "I should love you in a beard;" and Mrs. Darling stretched out her arms to him, but he repulsed her. "Keep back, lady,

no one is going to catch me and make me a man." "But where are you going to live?" "With Tink in the house we built for Wendy. The fairies are to put it high up among

the tree tops where they sleep at nights." "How lovely," cried Wendy so longingly that Mrs. Darling tightened her grip. "I thought all the fairies were dead," Mrs. Darling

said. "There are always a lot of young ones," explained Wendy, who was now quite an authority, "because you see when a new baby laughs for the first time a new fairy is

born, and as there are always new babies there are always new fairies. They live in nests on the tops of trees; and the mauve ones are boys and the white ones are girls, and

the blue ones are just little sillies who are not sure what they are." "I shall have such fun," said Peter, with one eye on Wendy. "It will be rather lonely in the evening," she

said, "sitting by the fire." "I shall have Tink." "Tink can't go a twentieth part of the way round," she reminded him a little tartly. "Sneaky tell-tale!" Tink called out from

somewhere round the corner. "It doesn't matter," Peter said. "O Peter, you know it matters." "Well, then, come with me to the little house." "May I, mummy?" "Certainly

not. I have got you home again, and I mean to keep you." "But he does so need a mother." "So do you, my love." "Oh, all right," Peter said, as if he had asked her from

politeness merely; but Mrs. Darling saw his mouth twitch, and she made this handsome offer: to let Wendy go to him for a week every year to do his spring cleaning. Wendy

would have preferred a more permanent arrangement; and it seemed to her that spring would be long in coming, but this promise sent Peter away quite gay again. He had

no sense of time, and was so full of adventures that all I have told you about him is only a halfpenny-worth of them. I suppose it was because Wendy knew this that her last

words to him were these rather plaintive ones: "You won't forget me, Peter, will you, before spring-cleaning time comes?" Of course Peter promised; and then he flew away.

He took Mrs. Darling's kiss with him. The kiss that had been for no one else Peter took quite easily. Funny. But she seemed satisfied. Of course all the boys went to school;

and most of them got into Class III., but Slightly was put first into Class IV. and then into Class V. Class I. is the top class. Before they had attended school a week they saw

what goats they had been not to remain on the island; but it was too late now, and soon they settled down to being as ordinary as you or me or Jenkins minor. It is sad to have

to say that the power to fly gradually left them. At first Nana tied their feet to the bed-posts so that they should not fly away in the night; and one of their diversions by day was to pretend to fall off buses; but by and by they ceased to tug at their bonds in bed, and found that they hurt themselves when they let go of the bus. In time they could not even fly after their hats. Want of practice, they called it; but what it really meant was that they no longer believed. Michael believed longer than the other boys, though they jeered at him; so he was with Wendy when Peter came for her at the end of the first year. She flew away with Peter in the frock she had woven from leaves and berries in the Neverland, and her one fear was that he might notice how short it had become, but he never noticed, he had so much to say about himself. She had looked forward to thrilling talks with him about old times, but new adventures had crowded the old ones from his mind. "Who is Captain Hook?" he asked with interest when she spoke of the arch enemy. "Don't you remember," she asked, amazed, "how you killed him and saved all our lives?" "I forget them after I kill them," he replied carelessly. When she expressed a doubtful hope that Tinker Bell would be glad to see her he said, "Who is Tinker Bell?" "O Peter," she said, shocked; but even when she explained he could not remember. "There are such a lot of them," he said. "I expect she is no more." I expect he was right, for fairies don't live long, but they are so little that a short time seems a good while to them. Wendy was pained too to find that the past year was but as yesterday to Peter; it had seemed such a long year of waiting to her. But he was exactly as fascinating as ever, and they had a lovely spring cleaning in the little house on the tree tops. Next year he did not come for her. She waited in a new frock because the old one simply would not meet; but he never came. "Perhaps he is ill," Michael said. "You know he is never ill." Michael came close to her and whispered, with a shiver, "Perhaps there is no such person, Wendy!" and then Wendy would have cried if Michael had not been crying. Peter came next spring cleaning; and the strange thing was that he never knew he had missed a year. That was the last time the girl Wendy ever saw him. For a little longer she tried for his sake not to have growing pains; and she felt she was untrue to him when she got a prize for general knowledge. But the years came and went without bringing the careless boy; and when they met again Wendy was a married woman, and Peter was no more to her than a little dust in the box in which she had kept her toys. Wendy was grown up. You need not be sorry for her. She was one of the kind that likes to grow up. In the end she grew up of her own free will a day quicker than other girls. All the boys were grown up and done for by this time; so it is scarcely worth while saying anything more about them. You may see the twins and Nibs and Curly any day going to an office, each carrying a little bag and an umbrella. Michael is an engine-driver. Slightly married a lady of title, and so he became a lord. You see that judge in a wig coming out at the iron door? That used to be Tootles. The bearded man who doesn't know any story to tell his children was once John. Wendy was married in white with a pink sash. It is strange to think that Peter did not alight in the church and forbid the banns. Years rolled on again, and Wendy had a daughter. This ought not to be written in ink but in a golden splash. She was called Jane, and always had an odd inquiring look, as if from the moment she arrived on the mainland she wanted to ask questions. When she was old enough to ask them they were mostly about Peter Pan. She loved to hear of Peter, and Wendy told her all she could remember in the very nursery from which the famous flight had taken place. It was Jane's nursery now, for her father had bought it at the three per cents. from Wendy's father, who was no longer fond of stairs. Mrs. Darling was now dead and forgotten. There were only two beds in the nursery now, Jane's and her nurse's; and there was no kennel, for Nana also had passed away. She died of old age, and at the end she had been rather difficult to get on with, being very firmly convinced that no one knew how to look after children except herself. Once a week Jane's nurse had her evening off, and then it was Wendy's part to put Jane to bed. That was the time for stories. It was Jane's invention to raise the sheet over her mother's head and her own, thus making a tent, and in the awful darkness to whisper:—

"What do we see now?" "I don't think I see anything to-night," says Wendy, with a feeling that if Nana were here she would object to further conversation. "Yes, you do," says Jane, "you see when you were a little girl." "That is a long time ago, sweetheart," says Wendy. "Ah me, how time flies!" "Does it fly," asks the artful child, "the way you flew when you were a little girl?" "The way I flew! Do you know, Jane, I sometimes wonder whether I ever did really fly." "Yes, you did." "The dear old days when I could fly!" "Why can't you fly now, mother?" "Because I am grown up, dearest. When people grow up they forget the way." "Why do they forget the way?" "Because they are no longer gay and innocent and heartless. It is only the gay and innocent and heartless who can fly." "What is gay and innocent and heartless? I do wish I was gay and innocent and heartless." Or perhaps Wendy admits that she does see something. "I do believe," she says, "that it is this nursery!" "I do believe it is!" says Jane. "Go on."

They are now embarked on the great adventure of the night when Peter flew in looking for his shadow. "The foolish fellow," says Wendy, "tried to stick it on with soap, and when he could not he cried, and that woke me, and I sewed it on for him." "You have missed a bit," interrupts Jane, who now knows the story better than her mother. "When you saw him sitting on the floor crying what did you say?" "I sat up in bed and I said, 'Boy, why are you crying?'" "Yes, that was it," says Jane, with a big breath. "And then he flew us all away to the Neverland and the fairies and the pirates and the redskins and the mermaids' lagoon, and the home under the ground, and the little house." "Yes! Which did you like best of all?" "I think I liked the home under the ground best of all." "Yes, so do I. What was the last thing Peter ever said to you?" "The last thing he ever said to me was, 'Just always be waiting for me, and then some night you will hear me crowing.'" "Yes." "But, alas, he forgot all about me." Wendy said it with a smile. She was as grown up as that. "What did his crow sound like?" Jane asked one evening. "It was like this," Wendy said, trying to imitate Peter's crow. "No, it wasn't," Jane said gravely, "it was like this;" and she did it ever so much better than her mother. Wendy was a little startled. "My darling, how can you know?" "I often hear it when I am sleeping," Jane said. "Ah yes, many girls hear it when they are sleeping, but I was the only one who heard it awake." "Lucky you!" said Jane. And then one night came the tragedy. It was the spring of the year, and the story had been told for the night, and Jane was now asleep in her bed. Wendy was sitting on the floor, very close to the fire, so as to see to darn, for there was no other light in the nursery; and while she sat darning she heard a crow. Then the window blew open as of old, and Peter dropped on the floor. He was exactly the same as ever, and Wendy saw at once that he still had all his first teeth. He was a little boy, and she was grown up. She huddled by the fire not daring to move, helpless and guilty, a big woman. "Hullo, Wendy," he said, not noticing any difference, for he was thinking chiefly of himself; and in the dim light her white dress might have been the nightgown in which he had seen her first. "Hullo, Peter," she replied faintly, squeezing herself as small as possible. Something inside her was crying

"Woman, woman, let go of me." "Hullo, where is John?" he asked, suddenly missing the third bed. "John is not here now," she gasped. "Is Michael asleep?" he asked, with

a careless glance at Jane. "Yes," she answered; and now she felt that she was untrue to Jane as well as to Peter. "That is not Michael," she said quickly, lest a judgment should

fall on her. Peter looked. "Hullo, is it a new one?" "Yes." "Boy or girl?" "Girl." Now surely he would understand; but not a bit of it. "Peter," she said, faltering, "are you

expecting me to fly away with you?" "Of course; that is why I have come." He added a little sternly, "Have you forgotten that this is spring-cleaning time?" She knew it was

useless to say that he had let many spring-cleaning times pass. "I can't come," she said apologetically, "I have forgotten how to fly." "I'll soon teach you again." "O Peter,

don't waste the fairy dust on me." She had risen; and now at last a fear assailed him. "What is it?" he cried, shrinking. "I will turn up the light," she said, "and then you can

see for yourself." For almost the only time in his life that I know of, Peter was afraid. "Don't turn up the light," he cried. She let her hands play in the hair of the tragic boy.

She was not a little girl heart-broken about him; she was a grown woman smiling at it all, but they were wet smiles. Then she turned up the light, and Peter saw. He gave a

cry of pain; and when the tall beautiful creature stooped to lift him in her arms he drew back sharply. "What is it?" he cried again. She had to tell him. "I am old, Peter. I am

ever so much more than twenty. I grew up long ago." "You promised not to!" "I couldn't help it. I am a married woman, Peter." "No, you're not." "Yes, and the little girl in

the bed is my baby." "No, she's not." But he supposed she was; and he took a step towards the sleeping child with his fist upraised. Of course he did not strike her. He sat

down on the floor and sobbed, and Wendy did not know how to comfort him, though she could have done it so easily once. She was only a woman now, and she ran out of

the room to try to think. Peter continued to cry, and soon his sobs woke Jane. She sat up in bed, and was interested at once. "Boy," she said, "why are you crying?" Peter rose

and bowed to her, and she bowed to him from the bed. "Hullo," he said. "Hullo," said Jane. "My name is Peter Pan," he told her. "Yes, I know." "I came back for my mother,"

he explained, "to take her to the Neverland." "Yes, I know," Jane said, "I've been waiting for you." When Wendy returned diffidently she found Peter sitting on the bed-post

crowing gloriously, while Jane in her nighty was flying round the room in solemn ecstasy. "She is my mother," Peter explained; and Jane descended and stood by his side,

with the look on her face that he liked to see on ladies when they gazed at him. "He does so need a mother," Jane said. "Yes, I know," Wendy admitted rather forlornly; "no

one knows it so well as I." "Good-bye," said Peter to Wendy; and he rose in the air, and the shameless Jane rose with him; it was already her easiest way of moving about.

Wendy rushed to the window. "No, no!" she cried. "It is just for spring-cleaning time," Jane said, "he wants me always to do his spring cleaning." "If only I could go with

you!" Wendy sighed. "You see you can't fly," said Jane. Of course in the end Wendy let them fly away together. Our last glimpse of her shows her at the window, watching

them receding into the sky until they were as small as stars. As you look at Wendy you may see her hair becoming white, and her figure little again, for all this happened long

ago. Jane is now a common grown-up, with a daughter called Margaret; and every spring-cleaning time, except when he forgets, Peter comes for Margaret and takes her to

he Neverland, where she tells him stories about himself, to which he listens eagerly. When Margaret grows up she will have a daughter, who is to be Peter's mother in turn;

and thus it will go on, so long as children are gay and innocent and heartless. THE END. PETER PAN IN KENSINGTON GARDENS | Chapter I *The Grand Tour Of The*

Gardens You must see for yourselves that it will be difficult to follow Peter Pan's adventures unless you are familiar with the Kensington Gardens. They are in London, wher

the King lives, and I used to take David there nearly every day unless he was looking decidedly flushed. No child has ever been in the whole of the Gardens, because it is so

soon time to turn back. The reason it is soon time to turn back is that, if you are as small as David, you sleep from twelve to one. If your mother was not so sure that you

sleep from twelve to one, you could most likely see the whole of them. The Gardens are bounded on one side by a never-ending line of omnibuses, over which your nurse

has such authority that if she holds up her finger to any one of them it stops immediately. She then crosses with you in safety to the other side. There are more gates to the

Gardens than one gate, but that is the one you go in at, and before you go in you speak to the lady with the balloons, who sits just outside. This is as near to being inside as

she may venture, because, if she were to let go her hold of the railings for one moment, the balloons would lift her up, and she would be flown away. She sits very squat, for

the balloons are always tugging at her, and the strain has given her quite a red face. Once she was a new one, because the old had let go, and David was very sorry for

the old one, but as she did let go, he wished he had been there to see. The Gardens are a tremendous big place, with millions and hundreds of trees; and first you come to the

Figs, but you scorn to loiter there, for the Figs is the resort of superior little persons, who are forbidden to mix with the commonalty, and is so named, according to legend,

because they dress in full fig. These dainty ones are themselves contemptuously called Figs by David and other heroes, and you have a key to the manners and customs of

this dandiacal section of the Gardens when I tell you that cricket is called crickers here. Occasionally a rebel Fig climbs over the fence into the world, and such a one was Miss

Mabel Grey, of whom I shall tell you when we come to Miss Mabel Grey's gate. She was the only really celebrated Fig. We are now in the Broad Walk, and it is as much

bigger than the other walks as your father is bigger than you. David wondered if it began little, and grew and grew, until it was quite grown up, and whether the other walks

are its babies, and he drew a picture, which diverted him very much, of the Broad Walk giving a tiny walk an airing in a perambulator. In the Broad Walk you meet all the

people who are worth knowing, and there is usually a grown-up with them to prevent them going on the damp grass, and to make them stand disgraced at the corner of a

seat if they have been mad-dog or Mary-Annish. To be Mary-Annish is to behave like a girl, whimpering because nurse won't carry you, or simpering with your thumb in

your mouth, and it is a hateful quality; but to be mad-dog is to kick out at everything, and there is some satisfaction in that. If I were to point out all the notable places as we

pass up the Broad Walk, it would be time to turn back before we reach them, and I simply wave my stick at Cecco Hewlett's Tree, that memorable spot where a boy called

Cecco lost his penny, and, looking for it, found twopence. There has been a good deal of excavation going on there ever since. Farther up the walk is the little wooden house

in which Marmaduke Perry hid. There is no more awful story of the Gardens than this of Marmaduke Perry, who had been Mary-Annish three days in succession, and was

sentenced to appear in the Broad Walk dressed in his sister's clothes. He hid in the little wooden house, and refused to emerge until they brought him knickerbockers with pockets. You now try to go to the Round Pond, but nurses hate it, because they are not really manly, and they make you look the other way, at the Big Penny and the Baby's

Palace. She was the most celebrated baby of the Gardens, and lived in the palace all alone, with ever so many dolls, so people rang the bell, and up she got out of her bed,

though it was past six o'clock, and she lighted a candle and opened the door in her nighty, and then they all cried with great rejoicings, "Hail, Queen of England!" What

puzzled David most was how she knew where the matches were kept. The Big Penny is a statue about her. Next we come to the Hump, which is the part of the Broad Walk

where all the big races are run; and even though you had no intention of running you do run when you come to the Hump, it is such a fascinating, slide-down kind of place.

Often you stop when you have run about half-way down it, and then you are lost; but there is another little wooden house near here, called the Lost House, and so you tell

the man that you are lost and then he finds you. It is glorious fun racing down the Hump, but you can't do it on windy days because then you are not there, but the fallen

leaves do it instead of you. There is almost nothing that has such a keen sense of fun as a fallen leaf. From the Hump we can see the gate that is called after Miss Mabel Grey,

the Fig I promised to tell you about. There were always two nurses with her, or else one mother and one nurse, and for a long time she was a pattern-child who always

coughed off the table and said, "How do you do?" to the other Figs, and the only game she played at was flinging a ball gracefully and letting the nurse bring it back to her.

Then one day she tired of it all and went mad-dog, and, first, to show that she really was mad-dog, she unloosened both her boot-laces and put out her tongue east, west,

north, and south. She then flung her sash into a puddle and danced on it till dirty water was squirted over her frock, after which she climbed the fence and had a series of

incredible adventures, one of the least of which was that she kicked off both her boots. At last she came to the gate that is now called after her, out of which she ran into streets

David and I have never been in though we have heard them roaring, and still she ran on and would never again have been heard of had not her mother jumped into a 'bus

and thus overtaken her. It all happened, I should say, long ago, and this is not the Mabel Grey whom David knows. Returning up the Broad Walk we have on our right the

Baby Walk, which is so full of perambulators that you could cross from side to side stepping on babies, but the nurses won't let you do it. From this walk a passage called

Bunting's Thumb, because it is that length, leads into Picnic Street, where there are real kettles, and chestnut-blossom falls into your mug as you are drinking. Quite common

children picnic here also, and the blossom falls into their mugs just the same. Next comes St. Govor's Well, which was full of water when Malcolm the Bold fell into it. He

was his mother's favourite, and he let her put her arm round his neck in public because she was a widow; but he was also partial to adventures, and liked to play with a

chimney-sweep who had killed a good many bears. The sweep's name was Sooty, and one day, when they were playing near the well, Malcolm fell in and would have been

drowned had not Sooty dived in and rescued him; and the water had washed Sooty clean, and he now stood revealed as Malcolm's long-lost father. So Malcolm would not

let his mother put her arm round his neck any more. Between the well and the Round Pond are the cricket pitches, and frequently the choosing of sides exhausts so much

time that there is scarcely any cricket. Everybody wants to bat first, and as soon as he is out he bowls unless you are the better wrestler, and while you are wrestling with him the fielders have scattered to play at something else. The Gardens are noted for two kinds of cricket: boy cricket, which is real cricket with a bat, and girl cricket, which is

with a racquet and the governess. Girls can't really play cricket, and when you are watching their futile efforts you make funny sounds at them. Nevertheless, there was a very

disagreeable incident one day when some forward girls challenged David's team, and a disturbing creature called Angela Clare sent down so many yorkers that—However,

instead of telling you the result of that regrettable match I shall pass on hurriedly to the Round Pond, which is the wheel that keeps all the Gardens going. It is round because

it is in the very middle of the Gardens, and when you are come to it you never want to go any farther. You can't be good all the time at the Round Pond, however much you

try. You can be good in the Broad Walk all the time, but not at the Round Pond, and the reason is that you forget, and, when you remember, you are so wet that you may as

well be wetter. There are men who sail boats on the Round Pond, such big boats that they bring them in barrows, and sometimes in perambulators, and then the baby has to

walk. The bow-legged children in the Gardens are those who had to walk too soon because their father needed the perambulator. You always want to have a yacht to sail on

the Round Pond, and in the end your uncle gives you one; and to carry it to the pond the first day is splendid, also to talk about it to boys who have no uncle is splendid, but

soon you like to leave it at home. For the sweetest craft that slips her moorings in the Round Pond is what is called a stick-boat, because she is rather like a stick until she is in

the water and you are holding the string. Then as you walk round, pulling her, you see little men running about her deck, and sails rise magically and catch the breeze, and

you put in on dirty nights at snug harbours which are unknown to the lordly yachts. Night passes in a twink, and again your rakish craft noses for the wind, whales spout,

you glide over buried cities, and have brushes with pirates, and cast anchor on coral isles. You are a solitary boy while all this is taking place, for two boys together cannot

adventure far upon the Round Pond, and though you may talk to yourself throughout the voyage, giving orders and executing them with despatch, you know not, when it

is time to go home, where you have been or what swelled your sails; your treasure-trove is all locked away in your hold, so to speak, which will be opened, perhaps, by another

little boy many years afterwards. But those yachts have nothing in their hold. Does any one return to this haunt of his youth because of the yachts that used to sail it? Oh no.

It is the stick-boat that is freighted with memories. The yachts are toys, their owner a fresh-water mariner; they can cross and re-cross a pond only while the stick-boat goes

to sea. You yachtsmen with your wands, who think we are all there to gaze on you, your ships are only accidents of this place, and were they all to be boarded and sunk by

the ducks, the real business of the Round Pond would be carried on as usual. Paths from everywhere crowd like children to the pond. Some of them are ordinary paths, which

have a rail on each side, and are made by men with their coats off, but others are vagrants, wide at one spot, and at another so narrow that you can stand astride them. They

are called Paths that have Made Themselves, and David did wish he could see them doing it. But, like all the most wonderful things that happen in the Gardens, it is done

we concluded, at night after the gates are closed. We have also decided that the paths make themselves because it is their only chance of getting to the Round Pond. One of

these gypsy paths comes from the place where the sheep get their hair cut. When David shed his curls at the hair-dresser's, I am told, he said good-bye to them without tremor, though his mother has never been quite the same bright creature since; so he despises the sheep as they run from their shearer, and calls out tauntingly, "Cowardy,

cowardy custard!" But when the man grips them between his legs David shakes a fist at him for using such big scissors. Another startling moment is when the man turns back

the grimy wool from the sheeps' shoulders and they look suddenly like ladies in the stalls of a theatre. The sheep are so frightened by the shearing that it makes them quite

white and thin, and as soon as they are set free they begin to nibble the grass at once, quite anxiously, as if they feared that they would never be worth eating. David wonders

whether they know each other, now that they are so different, and if it makes them fight with the wrong ones. They are great fighters, and thus so unlike country sheep that

every year they give my St. Bernard dog, Porthos, a shock. He can make a field of country sheep fly by merely announcing his approach, but these town sheep come toward

him with no promise of gentle entertainment, and then a light from last year breaks upon Porthos. He cannot with dignity retreat, but he stops and looks about him as if lost

in admiration of the scenery, and presently he strolls away with a fine indifference and a glint at me from the corner of his eye. The Serpentine begins near here. It is a lovely

lake, and there is a drowned forest at the bottom of it. If you peer over the edge you can see the trees all growing upside down, and they say that at night there are also

drowned stars in it. If so, Peter Pan sees them when he is sailing across the lake in the Thrush's Nest. A small part only of the Serpentine is in the Gardens, for soon it passes

beneath a bridge to far away where the island is on which all the birds are born that become baby boys and girls. No one who is human, except Peter Pan (and he is only half

human), can land on the island, but you may write what you want (boy or girl, dark or fair) on a piece of paper, and then twist it into the shape of a boat and slip it into the

water, and it reaches Peter Pan's island after dark. We are on the way home now, though of course, it is all pretence that we can go to so many of the places in one day. I

should have had to be carrying David long ago, and resting on every seat like old Mr. Salford. That was what we called him, because he always talked to us of a lovely place

called Salford where he had been born. He was a crab-apple of an old gentleman who wandered all day in the Gardens from seat to seat trying to fall in with somebody who

was acquainted with the town of Salford, and when we had known him for a year or more we actually did meet another aged solitary who had once spent Saturday to Monday

in Salford. He was meek and timid, and carried his address inside his hat, and whatever part of London he was in search of he always went to Westminster Abbey first as a

starting-point. Him we carried in triumph to our other friend, with the story of that Saturday to Monday, and never shall I forget the gloating joy with which Mr. Salford

leapt at him. They have been cronies ever since, and I noticed that Mr. Salford, who naturally does most of the talking, keeps tight grip of the other old man's coat. The two

last places before you come to our gate are the Dog's Cemetery and the chaffinch's nest, but we pretend not to know what the Dog's Cemetery is, as Porthos is always with

us. The nest is very sad. It is quite white, and the way we found it was wonderful. We were having another look among the bushes for David's lost worsted ball, and instead

of the ball we found a lovely nest made of the worsted, and containing four eggs, with scratches on them very like David's handwriting, so we think they must have been the

mother's love-letters to the little ones inside. Every day we were in the Gardens we paid a call at the nest, taking care that no cruel boy should see us, and we dropped crumbs, and soon the bird knew us as friends, and sat in the nest looking at us kindly with her shoulders hunched up. But one day when we went there were only two eggs in the nest,

and the next time there were none. The saddest part of it was that the poor little chaffinch fluttered about the bushes, looking so reproachfully at us that we knew she thought

we had done it; and though David tried to explain to her, it was so long since he had spoken the bird language that I fear she did not understand. He and I left the Gardens

that day with our knuckles in our eyes. CHAPTER II *Peter Pan* If you ask your mother whether she knew about Peter Pan when she was a little girl, she will say, "Why, of

course I did, child;" and if you ask her whether he rode on a goat in those days, she will say, "What a foolish question to ask; certainly he did." Then if you ask your

grandmother whether she knew about Peter Pan when she was a girl, she also says, "Why, of course I did, child," but if you ask her whether he rode on a goat in those days,

she says she never heard of his having a goat. Perhaps she has forgotten, just as she sometimes forgets your name and calls you Mildred, which is your mother's name. Still,

she could hardly forget such an important thing as the goat. Therefore there was no goat when your grandmother was a little girl. This shows that, in telling the story of Peter

Pan, to begin with the goat (as most people do) is as silly as to put on your jacket before your vest. Of course, it also shows that Peter is ever so old, but he is really always

the same age, so that does not matter in the least. His age is one week, and though he was born so long ago he has never had a birthday, nor is there the slightest chance of

his ever having one. The reason is that he escaped from being a human when he was seven days old; he escaped by the window and flew back to the Kensington Gardens. If

you think he was the only baby who ever wanted to escape, it shows how completely you have forgotten your own young days. When David heard this story first he was

quite certain that he had never tried to escape, but I told him to think back hard, pressing his hands to his temples, and when he had done this hard, and even harder, he

distinctly remembered a youthful desire to return to the tree-tops, and with that memory came others, as that he had lain in bed planning to escape as soon as his mother was

asleep, and how she had once caught him half-way up the chimney. All children could have such recollections if they would press their hands hard to their temples, for, having

been birds before they were human, they are naturally a little wild during the first few weeks, and very itchy at the shoulders, where their wings used to be. So David tells

me. I ought to mention here that the following is our way with a story: First I tell it to him, and then he tells it to me, the understanding being that it is quite a different story;

and then I retell it with his additions, and so we go on until no one could say whether it is more his story or mine. In this story of Peter Pan, for instance, the bald narrative

and most of the moral reflections are mine, though not all, for this boy can be a stern moralist; but the interesting bits about the ways and customs of babies in the bird-stage

are mostly reminiscences of David's, recalled by pressing his hands to his temples and thinking hard. Well, Peter Pan got out by the window, which had no bars. Standing on

the ledge he could see trees far away, which were doubtless the Kensington Gardens, and the moment he saw them he entirely forgot that he was now a little boy in a

nightgown, and away he flew, right over the houses to the Gardens. It is wonderful that he could fly without wings, but the place itched tremendously, and—and—perhaps

we could all fly if we were as dead-confident-sure of our capacity to do it as was bold Peter Pan that evening. He alighted gaily on the open sward, between the Baby's Palace and the Serpentine, and the first thing he did was to lie on his back and kick. He was quite unaware already that he had ever been human, and thought he was a bird, even in appearance, just the same as in his early days, and when he tried to catch a fly he did not understand that the reason he missed it was because he had attempted to seize it with his hand, which, of course, a bird never does. He saw, however, that it must be past Lock-out Time, for there were a good many fairies about, all too busy to notice him; they were getting breakfast ready, milking their cows, drawing water, and so on, and the sight of the water-pails made him thirsty, so he flew over to the Round Pond to have a drink. He stooped and dipped his beak in the pond; he thought it was his beak, but, of course, it was only his nose, and therefore, very little water came up, and that not so refreshing as usual, so next he tried a puddle, and he fell flop into it. When a real bird falls in flop, he spreads out his feathers and pecks them dry, but Peter could not remember what was the thing to do, and he decided rather sulkily to go to sleep on the weeping-beech in the Baby Walk. At first he found some difficulty in balancing himself on a branch, but presently he remembered the way, and fell asleep. He awoke long before morning, shivering, and saying to himself, "I never was out on such a cold night;" he had really been out on colder nights when he was a bird, but, of course, as everybody knows, what seems a warm night to a bird is a cold night to a boy in a nightgown. Peter also felt strangely uncomfortable, as if his head was stuffy; he heard loud noises that made him look round sharply, though they were really himself sneezing. There was something he wanted very much, but, though he knew he wanted it, he could not think what it was. What he wanted so much was his mother to blow his nose, but that never struck him, so he decided to appeal to the fairies for enlightenment. They are reputed to know a good deal. There were two of them strolling along the Baby Walk, with their arms round each other's waists, and he hopped down to address them. The fairies have their tiffs with the birds, but they usually give a civil answer to a civil question, and he was quite angry when these two ran away the moment they saw him. Another was lolling on a garden chair, reading a postage-stamp which some human had let fall, and when he heard Peter's voice he popped in alarm behind a tulip. To Peter's bewilderment he discovered that every fairy he met fled from him. A band of workmen, who were sawing down a toadstool, rushed away, leaving their tools behind them. A milkmaid turned her pail upside down and hid in it. Soon the Gardens were in an uproar. Crowds of fairies were running this way and that, asking each other stoutly who was afraid; lights were extinguished, doors barricaded, and from the grounds of Queen Mab's palace came the rub-a-dub of drums, showing that the royal guard had been called out. A regiment of Lancers came charging down the Broad Walk, armed with holly-leaves, with which they jag the enemy horribly in passing. Peter heard the little people crying everywhere that there was a human in the Gardens after Lock-out Time, but he never thought for a moment that he was the human. He was feeling stuffier and stuffier, and more and more wistful to learn what he wanted done to his nose, but he pursued them with the vital question in vain; the timid creatures ran from him, and even the Lancers, when he approached them up the Hump, turned swiftly into a side-walk, on the pretence that they saw him there. Despairing of the fairies, he resolved to consult the birds, but now he remembered, as an odd thing, that all the birds on the weeping-beech had flown away when he alighted on it, and though this had not troubled him at the time, he saw its meaning now. Every living thing was shunning him. Poor little Peter Pan!

He sat down and cried, and even then he did not know that, for a bird, he was sitting on his wrong part. It is a blessing that he did not know, for otherwise he would have lost

faith in his power to fly, and the moment you doubt whether you can fly, you cease for ever to be able to do it. The reason birds can fly and we can't is simply that they have

perfect faith, for to have faith is to have wings. Now, except by flying, no one can reach the island in the Serpentine, for the boats of humans are forbidden to land there, and

there are stakes round it, standing up in the water, on each of which a bird-sentinel sits by day and night. It was to the island that Peter now flew to put his strange case before

old Solomon Caw, and he alighted on it with relief, much heartened to find himself at last at home, as the birds call the island. All of them were asleep, including the sentinels,

except Solomon, who was wide awake on one side, and he listened quietly to Peter's adventures, and then told him their true meaning. "Look at your nightgown, if you don't

believe me," Solomon said; and with staring eyes Peter looked at his nightgown, and then at the sleeping birds. Not one of them wore anything. "How many of your toes

are thumbs?" said Solomon a little cruelly, and Peter saw to his consternation, that all his toes were fingers. The shock was so great that it drove away his cold. "Ruffle your

feathers," said that grim old Solomon, and Peter tried most desperately hard to ruffle his feathers, but he had none. Then he rose up, quaking, and for the first time since he

stood on the window ledge, he remembered a lady who had been very fond of him. "I think I shall go back to mother," he said timidly. "Good-bye," replied Solomon Caw

with a queer look. But Peter hesitated. "Why don't you go?" the old one asked politely. "I suppose," said Peter huskily, "I suppose I can still fly." You see he had lost faith.

"Poor little half-and-half!" said Solomon, who was not really hard-hearted, "You will never be able to fly again, not even on windy days. You must live here on the island

always." "And never even go to the Kensington Gardens?" Peter asked tragically. "How could you get across?" said Solomon. He promised very kindly, however, to teach

Peter as many of the bird ways as could be learned by one of such an awkward shape. "Then I shan't be exactly a human?" Peter asked. "No." "Nor exactly a bird?" "No."

"What shall I be?" "You will be a Betwixt-and-Between," Solomon said, and certainly he was a wise old fellow, for that is exactly how it turned out. The birds on the island

never got used to him. His oddities tickled them every day, as if they were quite new, though it was really the birds that were new. They came out of the eggs daily, and

laughed at him at once; then off they soon flew to be humans, and other birds came out of other eggs; and so it went on for ever. The crafty mother-birds, when they tired

of sitting on their eggs, used to get the young ones to break their shells a day before the right time by whispering to them that now was their chance to see Peter washing or

drinking or eating. Thousands gathered round him daily to watch him do these things, just as you watch the peacocks, and they screamed with delight when he lifted the

crusts they flung him with his hands instead of in the usual way with the mouth. All his food was brought to him from the Gardens at Solomon's orders by the birds. He

would not eat worms or insects (which they thought very silly of him), so they brought him bread in their beaks. Thus, when you cry out, "Greedy! Greedy!" to the bird

that flies away with the big crust, you know now that you ought not to do this, for he is very likely taking it to Peter Pan. Peter wore no nightgown now. You see, the birds

were always begging him for bits of it to line their nests with, and, being very good-natured, he could not refuse, so by Solomon's advice he had hidden what was left of it

But, though he was now quite naked, you must not think that he was cold or unhappy. He was usually very happy and gay, and the reason was that Solomon had kept his

promise and taught him many of the bird ways. To be easily pleased, for instance, and always to be really doing something, and to think that whatever he was doing was a

thing of vast importance. Peter became very clever at helping the birds to build their nests; soon he could build better than a wood-pigeon, and nearly as well as a blackbird,

though never did he satisfy the finches, and he made nice little water-troughs near the nests and dug up worms for the young ones with his fingers. He also became very

learned in bird-lore, and knew an east wind from a west wind by its smell, and he could see the grass growing and hear the insects walking about inside the tree-trunks. But

the best thing Solomon had done was to teach him to have a glad heart. All birds have glad hearts unless you rob their nests, and so as they were the only kind of heart

Solomon knew about, it was easy to him to teach Peter how to have one. Peter's heart was so glad that he felt he must sing all day long, just as the birds sing for joy, but, being

partly human, he needed an instrument, so he made a pipe of reeds, and he used to sit by the shore of the island of an evening, practising the sough of the wind and the ripple

of the water, and catching handfuls of the shine of the moon, and he put them all in his pipe and played them so beautifully that even the birds were deceived, and they would

say to each other, "Was that a fish leaping in the water or was it Peter playing leaping fish on his pipe?" And sometimes he played the birth of birds, and then the mothers

would turn round in their nests to see whether they had laid an egg. If you are a child of the Gardens you must know the chestnut-tree near the bridge, which comes out in

flower first of all the chestnuts, but perhaps you have not heard why this tree leads the way. It is because Peter wearies for summer and plays that it has come, and the chestnut

being so near, hears him and is cheated. But as Peter sat by the shore tootling divinely on his pipe he sometimes fell into sad thoughts, and then the music became sad also,

and the reason of all this sadness was that he could not reach the Gardens, though he could see them through the arch of the bridge. He knew he could never be a real human

again, and scarcely wanted to be one, but oh! how he longed to play as other children play, and of course there is no such lovely place to play in as the Gardens. The birds

brought him news of how boys and girls play, and wistful tears started in Peter's eyes. Perhaps you wonder why he did not swim across. The reason was that he could not

swim. He wanted to know how to swim, but no one on the island knew the way except the ducks, and they are so stupid. They were quite willing to teach him, but all they

could say about it was, "You sit down on the top of the water in this way, and then you kick out like that." Peter tried it often, but always before he could kick out he sank.

What he really needed to know was how you sit on the water without sinking, and they said it was quite impossible to explain such an easy thing as that. Occasionally swans

touched on the island, and he would give them all his day's food and then ask them how they sat on the water, but as soon as he had no more to give them the hateful things

hissed at him and sailed away. Once he really thought he had discovered a way of reaching the Gardens. A wonderful white thing, like a runaway newspaper, floated high

over the island and then tumbled, rolling over and over after the manner of a bird that has broken its wing. Peter was so frightened that he hid, but the birds told him it was

only a kite, and what a kite is, and that it must have tugged its string out of a boy's hand, and soared away. After that they laughed at Peter for being so fond of the kite; he loved it so much that he even slept with one hand on it, and I think this was pathetic and pretty, for the reason he loved it was because it had belonged to a real boy. To the

birds this was a very poor reason, but the older ones felt grateful to him at this time because he had nursed a number of fledglings through the German measles, and they

offered to show him how birds fly a kite. So six of them took the end of the string in their beaks and flew away with it; and to his amazement it flew after them and went even

higher than they. Peter screamed out, "Do it again!" and with great good-nature they did it several times, and always instead of thanking them he cried, "Do it again!" which

shows that even now he had not quite forgotten what it was to be a boy. At last, with a grand design burning within his brave heart, he begged them to do it once more with

him clinging to the tail, and now a hundred flew off with the string, and Peter clung to the tail, meaning to drop off when he was over the Gardens. But the kite broke to

pieces in the air, and he would have been drowned in the Serpentine had he not caught hold of two indignant swans and made them carry him to the island. After this the

birds said that they would help him no more in his mad enterprise. Nevertheless, Peter did reach the Gardens at last by the help of Shelley's boat, as I am now to tell you.

CHAPTER III *The Thrush's Nest* Shelley was a young gentleman and as grown-up as he need ever expect to be. He was a poet; and they are never exactly grown-up. They

are people who despise money except what you need for to-day, and he had all that and five pounds over. So, when he was walking in the Kensington Gardens, he made a

paper boat of his bank-note, and sent it sailing on the Serpentine. It reached the island at night; and the look-out brought it to Solomon Caw, who thought at first that it was

the usual thing, a message from a lady, saying she would be obliged if he could let her have a good one. They always ask for the best one he has, and if he likes the letter he

sends one from Class A, but if it ruffles him he sends very funny ones indeed. Sometimes he sends none at all, and at another time he sends a nestful; it all depends on the

mood you catch him in. He likes you to leave it all to him, and if you mention particularly that you hope he will see his way to making it *a boy this time*, he is almost sure to

send another girl. And whether you are a lady or only a little boy who wants a baby-sister, always take pains to write your address clearly. You can't think what a lot of babies

Solomon has sent to the wrong house. Shelley's boat, when opened, completely puzzled Solomon, and he took counsel of his assistants, who having walked over it twice,

first with their toes pointed out, and then with their toes pointed in, decided that it came from some greedy person who wanted five. They thought this because there was a

large five printed on it. "Preposterous!" cried Solomon in a rage, and he presented it to Peter; anything useless which drifted upon the island was usually given to Peter as a

plaything. But he did not play with his precious bank-note, for he knew what it was at once, having been very observant during the week when he was an ordinary boy. With

so much money, he reflected, he could surely at last contrive to reach the Gardens, and he considered all the possible ways, and decided (wisely, I think) to choose the best

way. But, first, he had to tell the birds of the value of Shelley's boat; and though they were too honest to demand it back, he saw that they were galled, and they cast such

black looks at Solomon, who was rather vain of his cleverness, that he flew away to the end of the island, and sat there very depressed with his head buried in his wings. Now

Peter knew that unless Solomon was on your side, you never got anything done for you in the island, so he followed him and tried to hearten him. Nor was this all that Pete did to gain the powerful old fellow's good-will. You must know that Solomon had no intention of remaining in office all his life. He looked forward to retiring by and by, and devoting his green old age to a life of pleasure on a certain yew-stump in the Figs which had taken his fancy, and for years he had been quietly filling his stocking. It was a stocking belonging to some bathing person which had been cast upon the island, and at the time I speak of it contained a hundred and eighty crumbs, thirty-four nuts, sixteen crusts, a pen-wiper, and a boot-lace. When his stocking was full, Solomon calculated that he would be able to retire on a competency. Peter now gave him a pound. He cut it off his bank-note with a sharp stick. This made Solomon his friend for ever, and after the two had consulted together they called a meeting of the thrushes. You will see presently why thrushes only were invited. The scheme to be put before them was really Peter's, but Solomon did most of the talking, because he soon became irritable if other people talked. He began by saying that he had been much impressed by the superior ingenuity shown by the thrushes in nest-building, and this put them into good-humour at once, as it was meant to do; for all the quarrels between birds are about the best way of building nests. Other birds, said Solomon, omitted to line their nests with mud, and as a result they did not hold water. Here he cocked his head as if he had used an unanswerable argument; but, unfortunately, a Mrs. Finch had come to the meeting uninvited, and she squeaked out, "We don't build nests to hold water, but to hold eggs," and then the thrushes stopped cheering, and Solomon was so perplexed that he took several sips of water. "Consider," he said at last, "how warm the mud makes the nest." "Consider," cried Mrs. Finch, "that when water gets into the nest it remains there and your little ones are drowned." The thrushes begged Solomon with a look to say something crushing in reply to this, but again he was perplexed. "Try another drink," suggested Mrs. Finch pertly. Kate was her name, and all Kates are saucy. Solomon did try another drink, and it inspired him. "If," said he, "a finch's nest is placed on the Serpentine it fills and breaks to pieces, but a thrush's nest is still as dry as the cup of a swan's back." How the thrushes applauded! Now they knew why they lined their nests with mud, and when Mrs. Finch called out, "We don't place our nests on the Serpentine," they did what they should have done at first—chased her from the meeting. After this it was most orderly. What they had been brought together to hear, said Solomon, was this: their young friend, Peter Pan, as they well knew, wanted very much to be able to cross to the Gardens, and he now proposed, with their help, to build a boat. At this the thrushes began to fidget, which made Peter tremble for his scheme. Solomon explained hastily that what he meant was not one of the cumbrous boats that humans use; the proposed boat was to be simply a thrush's nest large enough to hold Peter. But still, to Peter's agony, the thrushes were sulky. "We are very busy people," they grumbled, "and this would be a big job." "Quite so," said Solomon, "and, of course, Peter would not allow you to work for nothing. You must remember that he is now in comfortable circumstances, and he will pay you such wages as you have never been paid before. Peter Pan authorises me to say that you shall all be paid sixpence a day." Then all the thrushes hopped for joy, and that very day was begun the celebrated Building of the Boat. All their ordinary business fell into arrears. It was the time of the year when they should have been pairing, but not a thrush's nest was built except this big one, and so Solomon soon ran short of thrushes with which to supply the demand from the mainland. The stout, rather greedy children, who look so well in perambulators but get puffed easily when they walk, were all young thrushes once, and ladies often ask specially for them. What do you think Solomon did? He sent over to the house-tops for

a lot of sparrows and ordered them to lay their eggs in old thrushes' nests, and sent their young to the ladies and swore they were all thrushes! It was known afterwards on

the island as the Sparrow's Year; and so, when you meet grown-up people in the Gardens who puff and blow as if they thought themselves bigger than they are, very likely

they belong to that year. You ask them. Peter was a just master, and paid his workpeople every evening. They stood in rows on the branches, waiting politely while he cut

the paper sixpences out of his bank-note, and presently he called the roll, and then each bird, as the names were mentioned, flew down and got sixpence. It must have been a

fine sight. And at last, after months of labour, the boat was finished. O the glory of Peter as he saw it growing more and more like a great thrush's nest! From the very

beginning of the building of it he slept by its side, and often woke up to say sweet things to it, and after it was lined with mud and the mud had dried he always slept in it. He

sleeps in his nest still, and has a fascinating way of curling round in it, for it is just large enough to hold him comfortably when he curls round like a kitten. It is brown inside,

of course, but outside it is mostly green, being woven of grass and twigs, and when these wither or snap the walls are thatched afresh. There are also a few feathers here and

there, which came off the thrushes while they were building. The other birds were extremely jealous, and said that the boat would not balance on the water, but it lay most

beautifully steady; they said the water would come into it, but no water came into it. Next they said that Peter had no oars, and this caused the thrushes to look at each other

in dismay; but Peter replied that he had no need of oars, for he had a sail, and with such a proud, happy face he produced a sail which he had fashioned out of his nightgown,

and though it was still rather like a nightgown it made a lovely sail. And that night, the moon being full, and all the birds asleep, he did enter his coracle (as Master Francis

Pretty would have said) and depart out of the island. And first, he knew not why, he looked upward, with his hands clasped, and from that moment his eyes were pinned to

the west. He had promised the thrushes to begin by making short voyages, with them as his guides, but far away he saw the Kensington Gardens beckoning to him beneath

the bridge, and he could not wait. His face was flushed, but he never looked back; there was an exultation in his little breast that drove out fear. Was Peter the least gallant of

the English mariners who have sailed westward to meet the Unknown? At first, his boat turned round and round, and he was driven back to the place of his starting,

whereupon he shortened sail, by removing one of the sleeves, and was forthwith carried backwards by a contrary breeze, to his no small peril. He now let go the sail, with

the result that he was drifted towards the far shore, where are black shadows he knew not the dangers of, but suspected them, and so once more hoisted his nightgown and

went roomer of the shadows until he caught a favouring wind, which bore him westward, but at so great a speed that he was like to be broke against the bridge. Which, having

avoided, he passed under the bridge and came, to his great rejoicing, within full sight of the delectable Gardens. But having tried to cast anchor, which was a stone at the end

of a piece of the kite-string, he found no bottom, and was fain to hold off, seeking for moorage; and, feeling his way, he buffeted against a sunken reef that cast him overboard

by the greatness of the shock, and he was near to being drowned, but clambered back into the vessel. There now arose a mighty storm, accompanied by roaring of waters, such as he had never heard the like, and he was tossed this way and that, and his hands so numbed with the cold that he could not close them. Having escaped the danger of

which, he was mercifully carried into a small bay, where his boat rode at peace. Nevertheless, he was not yet in safety; for, on pretending to disembark, he found a multitude

of small people drawn up on the shore to contest his landing, and shouting shrilly to him to be off, for it was long past Lock-out Time. This, with much brandishing of their

holly-leaves, and also a company of them carried an arrow which some boy had left in the Gardens, and this they were prepared to use as a battering-ram. Then Peter, who

knew them for the fairies, called out that he was not an ordinary human and had no desire to do them displeasure, but to be their friend; nevertheless, having found a jolly

harbour, he was in no temper to draw off therefrom, and he warned them if they sought to mischief him to stand to their harms. So saying, he boldly leapt ashore, and they

gathered around him with intent to slay him, but there then arose a great cry among the women, and it was because they had now observed that his sail was a baby's

nightgown. Whereupon, they straightway loved him, and grieved that their laps were too small, the which I cannot explain, except by saying that such is the way of women.

The men-fairies now sheathed their weapons on observing the behaviour of their women, on whose intelligence they set great store, and they led him civilly to their queen,

who conferred upon him the courtesy of the Gardens after Lock-out Time, and henceforth Peter could go whither he chose, and the fairies had orders to put him in comfort.

Such was his first voyage to the Gardens, and you may gather from the antiquity of the language that it took place a long time ago. But Peter never grows any older, and if

we could be watching for him under the bridge to-night (but, of course, we can't), I dare say we should see him hoisting his nightgown and sailing or paddling towards us

in the Thrushes Nest. When he sails, he sits down, but he stands up to paddle. I shall tell you presently how he got his paddle. Long before the time for the opening of the

gates comes he steals back to the island, for people must not see him (he is not so human as all that), but this gives him hours for play, and he plays exactly as real children

play. At least he thinks so, and it is one of the pathetic things about him that he often plays quite wrongly. You see, he had no one to tell him how children really play, for the

fairies are all more or less in hiding until dusk, and so know nothing, and though the birds pretended that they could tell him a great deal, when the time for telling came, it

was wonderful how little they really knew. They told him the truth about hide-and-seek, and he often plays it by himself, but even the ducks on the Round Pond could not

explain to him what it is that makes the pond so fascinating to boys. Every night the ducks have forgotten all the events of the day, except the number of pieces of cake thrown

to them. They are gloomy creatures, and say that cake is not what it was in their young days. So Peter had to find out many things for himself. He often played ships at the

Round Pond, but his ship was only a hoop which he had found on the grass. Of course, he had never seen a hoop, and he wondered what you play at with them, and decided

that you play at pretending they are boats. This hoop always sank at once, but he waded in for it, and sometimes he dragged it gleefully round the rim of the pond, and he

was quite proud to think that he had discovered what boys do with hoops. Another time, when he found a child's pail, he thought it was for sitting in, and he sat so hard in it

that he could scarcely get out of it. Also he found a balloon. It was bobbing about on the Hump, quite as if it was having a game by itself, and he caught it after an exciting chase. But he thought it was a ball, and Jenny Wren had told him that boys kick balls, so he kicked it; and after that he could not find it anywhere. Perhaps the most surprising

thing he found was a perambulator. It was under a lime-tree, near the entrance to the Fairy Queen's Winter Palace (which is within the circle of the seven Spanish chestnuts)

and Peter approached it warily, for the birds had never mentioned such things to him. Lest it was alive, he addressed it politely, and then, as it gave no answer, he went nearer

and felt it cautiously. He gave it a little push, and it ran from him, which made him think it must be alive after all; but, as it had run from him, he was not afraid. So he stretched

out his hand to pull it to him, but this time it ran at him, and he was so alarmed that he leapt the railing and scudded away to his boat. You must not think, however, that he

was a coward, for he came back next night with a crust in one hand and a stick in the other, but the perambulator had gone, and he never saw any other one. I have promised

to tell you also about his paddle. It was a child's spade which he had found near St. Govor's Well, and he thought it was a paddle. Do you pity Peter Pan for making these

mistakes? If so, I think it rather silly of you. What I mean is that, of course, one must pity him now and then, but to pity him all the time would be impertinence. He thought

he had the most splendid time in the Gardens, and to think you have it is almost quite as good as really to have it. He played without ceasing, while you often waste time

being mad-dog or Mary-Annish. He could be neither of these things, for he had never heard of them, but do you think he is to be pitied for that? Oh, he was merry! He was

as much merrier than you, for instance, as you are merrier than your father. Sometimes he fell, like a spinning-top, and from sheer merriment. Have you seen a greyhound

leaping the fences of the Gardens? That is how Peter leaps them. And think of the music of his pipe. Gentlemen who walk home at night write to the papers to say they heard

a nightingale in the Gardens, but it is really Peter's pipe they hear. Of course, he had no mother—at least, what use was she to him! You can be sorry for him for that, but

don't be too sorry, for the next thing I mean to tell you is how he revisited her. It was the fairies who gave him the chance. CHAPTER IV *Lock-Out Time* It is frightfully

difficult to know much about the fairies, and almost the only thing known for certain is that there are fairies wherever there are children. Long ago children were forbidden

the Gardens, and at that time there was not a fairy in the place; then the children were admitted, and the fairies came trooping in that very evening. They can't resist following

the children, but you seldom see them, partly because they live in the daytime behind the railings, where you are not allowed to go, and also partly because they are

cunning. They are not a bit cunning after Lock-out, but until Lock-out, my word! When you were a bird you knew the fairies pretty well, and you remember a good deal

about them in your babyhood, which it is a great pity you can't write down, for gradually you forget, and I have heard of children who declared that they had never once

seen a fairy. Very likely if they said this in the Kensington Gardens, they were standing looking at a fairy all the time. The reason they were cheated was that she pretended

to be something else. This is one of their best tricks. They usually pretend to be flowers, because the court sits in the Fairies' Basin, and there are so many flowers there,

all along the Baby Walk, that a flower is the thing least likely to attract attention. They dress exactly like flowers, and change with the seasons, putting on white when lilies

are in and blue for bluebells, and so on. They like crocus and hyacinth time best of all, as they are partial to a bit of colour, but tulips (except white ones, which are the fairy cradles) they consider garish, and they sometimes put off dressing like tulips for days, so that the beginning of the tulip weeks is almost the best time to catch them. When they think you are not looking they skip along pretty lively, but if you look, and they fear there is no time to hide, they stand quite still pretending to be flowers. Then, after you have passed without knowing that they were fairies, they rush home and tell their mothers they have had such an adventure. The Fairy Basin, you remember, is all covered with ground-ivy (from which they make their castor oil!), with flowers growing in it here and there. Most of them really are flowers, but some of them are fairies. You never can be sure of them, but a good plan is to walk by looking the other way, and then turn round sharply. Another good plan, which David and I sometimes follow, is to stare them down. After a long time they can't help winking, and then you know for certain that they are fairies. There are also numbers of them along the Baby Walk, which is a famous gentle place, as spots frequented by fairies are called. Once twenty-four of them had an extraordinary adventure. They were a girls' school out for a walk with the governess, and all wearing hyacinth gowns, when she suddenly put her finger to her mouth, and then they all stood still on an empty bed and pretended to be hyacinths. Unfortunately what the governess had heard was two gardeners coming to plant new flowers in that very bed. They were wheeling a hand-cart with the flowers in it, and were quite surprised to find the bed occupied. "Pity to lift them hyacinths," said the one man. "Duke's orders," replied the other, and, having emptied the cart, they dug up the boarding school and put the poor, terrified things in it in five rows. Of course, neither the governess nor the girls dare let on that they were fairies, so they were carted far away to a potting-shed, out of which they escaped in the night without their shoes, but there was a great row about it among the parents, and the school was ruined.

As for their houses, it is no use looking for them, because they are the exact opposite of our houses. You can see our houses by day but you can't see them by dark. Well, you can see their houses by dark, but you can't see them by day, for they are the colour of night, and I never heard of any one yet who could see night in the daytime. This does not mean that they are black, for night has its colours just as day has, but ever so much brighter. Their blues and reds and greens are like ours with a light behind them. The palace is entirely built of many-coloured glasses, and it is quite the loveliest of all royal residences, but the queen sometimes complains because the common people will peep in to see what she is doing. They are very inquisitive folk, and press quite hard against the glass, and that is why their noses are mostly snubby. The streets are miles long and very twisty, and have paths on each side made of bright worsted. The birds used to steal the worsted for their nests, but a policeman has been appointed to hold on at the other end. One of the great differences between the fairies and us is that they never do anything useful. When the first baby laughed for the first time, his laugh broke into a million pieces, and they all went skipping about. That was the beginning of fairies. They look tremendously busy, you know, as if they had not a moment to spare, but if you were to ask them what they are doing, they could not tell you in the least. They are frightfully ignorant, and everything they do is make-believe. They have a postman, but he never calls except at Christmas with his little box, and though they have beautiful schools, nothing is taught in them; the youngest child being chief person is always elected mistress, and when she has called the roll, they all go out for a walk and never come back. It is a very noticeable thing that, in fairy families, the youngest is always chief person, and usually becomes a prince or princess; and children remember this, and think it must be so among humans also; and that is why they are often made uneasy when

they come upon their mother furtively putting new frills on the basinette. You have probably observed that your baby-sister wants to do all sorts of things that your mother

and her nurse want her not to do—to stand up at sitting-down time, and to sit down at stand-up time, for instance, or to wake up when she should fall asleep, or to crawl on

the floor when she is wearing her best frock, and so on, and perhaps you put this down to naughtiness. But it is not; it simply means that she is doing as she has seen the fairies

do; she begins by following their ways, and it takes about two years to get her into the human ways. Her fits of passion, which are awful to behold, and are usually called

teething, are no such thing; they are her natural exasperation, because we don't understand her, though she is talking an intelligible language. She is talking fairy. The reason

mothers and nurses know what her remarks mean, before other people know, as that "Guch" means "Give it to me at once," while "Wa" is "Why do you wear such a funny

hat?" is because, mixing so much with babies, they have picked up a little of the fairy language. Of late David has been thinking back hard about the fairy tongue, with his

hands clutching his temples, and he has remembered a number of their phrases which I shall tell you some day if I don't forget. He had heard them in the days when he was

a thrush, and though I suggested to him that perhaps it is really bird language he is remembering, he says not, for these phrases are about fun and adventures, and the birds

talked of nothing but nest-building. He distinctly remembers that the birds used to go from spot to spot like ladies at shop windows, looking at the different nests and saying

"Not my colour, my dear," and "How would that do with a soft lining?" and "But will it wear?" and "What hideous trimming!" and so on. The fairies are exquisite dancers,

and that is why one of the first things the baby does is to sign to you to dance to him and then to cry when you do it. They hold their great balls in the open air, in what

called a fairy ring. For weeks afterwards you can see the ring on the grass. It is not there when they begin, but they make it by waltzing round and round. Sometimes you will

find mushrooms inside the ring, and these are fairy chairs that the servants have forgotten to clear away. The chairs and the rings are the only telltale marks these little people

leave behind them, and they would remove even these were they not so fond of dancing that they toe it till the very moment of the opening of the gates. David and I once

found a fairy ring quite warm. But there is also a way of finding out about the ball before it takes place. You know the boards which tell at what time the Gardens are to close

to-day. Well, these tricky fairies sometimes slyly change the board on a ball night, so that it says the Gardens are to close at six-thirty, for instance, instead of at seven. This

enables them to get begun half an hour earlier. If on such a night we could remain behind in the Gardens, as the famous Maimie Mannering did, we might see delicious sights,

hundreds of lovely fairies hastening to the ball, the married ones wearing their wedding rings round their waists; the gentlemen, all in uniform, holding up the ladies' trains,

and linkmen running in front carrying winter cherries, which are the fairy-lanterns, the cloakroom where they put on their silver slippers and get a ticket for their wraps, the

flowers streaming up from the Baby Walk to look on, and always welcome because they can lend a pin, the supper-table, with Queen Mab at the head of it, and behind her

chair the Lord Chamberlain, who carries a dandelion on which he blows when her Majesty wants to know the time. The table-cloth varies according to the seasons, and

May it is made of chestnut blossom. The way the fairy servants do is this: The men, scores of them, climb up the trees and shake the branches, and the blossom falls like snow.

Then the lady servants sweep it together by whisking their skirts until it is exactly like a tablecloth, and that is how they get their tablecloth. They have real glasses and real

wine of three kinds, namely, blackthorn wine, berberris wine, and cowslip wine, and the Queen pours out, but the bottles are so heavy that she just pretends to pour out.

There is bread-and-butter to begin with, of the size of a threepenny bit; and cakes to end with, and they are so small that they have no crumbs. The fairies sit round on

mushrooms, and at first they are well-behaved and always cough off the table, and so on, but after a bit they are not so well-behaved and stick their fingers into the butter,

which is got from the roots of old trees, and the really horrid ones crawl over the tablecloth chasing sugar or other delicacies with their tongues. When the Queen sees them

doing this she signs to the servants to wash up and put away, and then everybody adjourns to the dance, the Queen walking in front while the Lord Chamberlain walks behind

her, carrying two little pots, one of which contains the juice of wallflower and the other the juice of Solomon's seals. Wallflower juice is good for reviving dancers who fall

to the ground in a fit, and Solomon's seals juice is for bruises. They bruise very easily, and when Peter plays faster and faster they foot it till they fall down in fits. For, as you

know without my telling you, Peter Pan is the fairies' orchestra. He sits in the middle of the ring, and they would never dream of having a smart dance nowadays without

him. "P. P." is written on the corner of the invitation-cards sent out by all really good families. They are grateful little people, too, and at the princesses coming-of-age ball

(they come of age on their second birthday and have a birthday every month) they gave him the wish of his heart. The way it was done was this. The Queen ordered him to

kneel, and then said that for playing so beautifully she would give him the wish of his heart. Then they all gathered round Peter to hear what was the wish of his heart, but

for a long time he hesitated, not being certain what it was himself. "If I chose to go back to mother," he asked at last, "could you give me that wish?" Now this question vexed

them, for were he to return to his mother they should lose his music, so the Queen tilted her nose contemptuously and said, "Pooh! ask for a much bigger wish than that."

"Is that quite a little wish?" he inquired. "As little as this," the Queen answered, putting her hands near each other. "What size is a big wish?" he asked. She measured it off

on her skirt and it was a very handsome length. Then Peter reflected and said, "Well, then, I think I shall have two little wishes instead of one big one." Of course, the fairies

had to agree, though his cleverness rather shocked them, and he said that his first wish was to go to his mother, but with the right to return to the Gardens if he found her

disappointing. His second wish he would hold in reserve. They tried to dissuade him, and even put obstacles in the way. "I can give you the power to fly to her house," the

Queen said, "but I can't open the door for you." "The window I flew out at will be open," Peter said confidently. "Mother always keeps it open in the hope that I may fly

back." "How do you know?" they asked, quite surprised, and, really, Peter could not explain how he knew. "I just do know," he said. So as he persisted in his wish, they had

to grant it. The way they gave him power to fly was this: They all tickled him on the shoulder, and soon he felt a funny itching in that part, and then up he rose higher and

higher, and flew away out of the Gardens and over the housetops. It was so delicious that instead of flying straight to his own home he skimmed away over St. Paul's to the

Crystal Palace and back by the river and Regent's Park, and by the time he reached his mother's window he had quite made up his mind that his second wish should be to

become a bird. The window was wide open, just as he knew it would be, and in he fluttered, and there was his mother lying asleep. Peter alighted softly on the wooden rail

at the foot of the bed and had a good look at her. She lay with her head on her hand, and the hollow in the pillow was like a nest lined with her brown wavy hair. He

remembered, though he had long forgotten it, that she always gave her hair a holiday at night. How sweet the frills of her nightgown were! He was very glad she was such a

pretty mother. But she looked sad, and he knew why she looked sad. One of her arms moved as if it wanted to go round something, and he knew what it wanted to go round.

"O mother!" said Peter to himself, "if you just knew who is sitting on the rail at the foot of the bed." Very gently he patted the little mound that her feet made, and he could

see by her face that she liked it. He knew he had but to say "Mother" ever so softly, and she would wake up. They always wake up at once if it is you that says their name.

Then she would give such a joyous cry and squeeze him tight. How nice that would be to him, but oh! how exquisitely delicious it would be to her. That, I am afraid, is how

Peter regarded it. In returning to his mother he never doubted that he was giving her the greatest treat a woman can have. Nothing can be more splendid, he thought, than

to have a little boy of your own. How proud of him they are! and very right and proper, too. But why does Peter sit so long on the rail; why does he not tell his mother that

he has come back? I quite shrink from the truth, which is that he sat there in two minds. Sometimes he looked longingly at his mother, and sometimes he looked longingly at

the window. Certainly it would be pleasant to be her boy again, but on the other hand, what times those had been in the Gardens! Was he so sure that he should enjoy wearing

clothes again? He popped off the bed and opened some drawers to have a look at his old garments. They were still there, but he could not remember how you put them on.

The socks, for instance, were they worn on the hands or on the feet? He was about to try one of them on his hand, when he had a great adventure. Perhaps the drawer had

creaked; at any rate, his mother woke up, for he heard her say "Peter," as if it was the most lovely word in the language. He remained sitting on the floor and held his breath,

wondering how she knew that he had come back. If she said "Peter" again, he meant to cry "Mother" and run to her. But she spoke no more, she made little moans only, and

when he next peeped at her she was once more asleep, with tears on her face. It made Peter very miserable, and what do you think was the first thing he did? Sitting on the

rail at the foot of the bed, he played a beautiful lullaby to his mother on his pipe. He had made it up himself out of the way she said "Peter," and he never stopped playing

until she looked happy. He thought this so clever of him that he could scarcely resist wakening her to hear her say, "O Peter, how exquisitely you play!" However, as she now

seemed comfortable, he again cast looks at the window. You must not think that he meditated flying away and never coming back. He had quite decided to be his mother's

boy, but hesitated about beginning to-night. It was the second wish which troubled him. He no longer meant to make it a wish to be a bird, but not to ask for a second wish

seemed wasteful, and, of course, he could not ask for it without returning to the fairies. Also, if he put off asking for his wish too long it might go bad. He asked himself if

he had not been hard-hearted to fly away without saying good-bye to Solomon. "I should like awfully to sail in my boat just once more," he said wistfully to his sleeping mother. He quite argued with her as if she could hear him. "It would be so splendid to tell the birds of this adventure," he said coaxingly. "I promise to come back," he said solemnly, and meant it, too. And in the end, you know, he flew away. Twice he came back from the window, wanting to kiss his mother, but he feared the delight of it might waken her, so at last he played her a lovely kiss on his pipe, and then he flew back to the Gardens. Many nights, and even months, passed before he asked the fairies for his second wish; and I am not sure that I quite know why he delayed so long. One reason was that he had so many good-byes to say, not only to his particular friends, but to a hundred favourite spots. Then he had his last sail, and his very last sail, and his last sail of all, and so on. Again, a number of farewell feasts were given in his honour; and another comfortable reason was that, after all, there was no hurry, for his mother would never weary of waiting for him. This last reason displeased old Solomon, for it was an encouragement to the birds to procrastinate. Solomon had several excellent mottoes for keeping them at their work, such as "Never put off laying to-day because you can lay to-morrow," and "In this world there are no second chances," and yet here was Peter gaily putting off and none the worse for it. The birds pointed this out to each other, and fell into lazy habits. But, mind you, though Peter was so slow in going back to his mother, he was quite decided to go back. The best proof of this was his caution with the fairies. They were most anxious that he should remain in the Gardens to play to them, and to bring this to pass they tried to trick him into making such a remark as "I wish the grass was not so wet," and some of them danced out of time in the hope that he might cry, "I do wish you would keep time!" Then they would have said that this was his second wish. But he smoked their design, and though on occasions he began, "I wish—" he always stopped in time. So when at last he said to them bravely, "I wish now to go back to mother for ever and always," they had to tickle his shoulders and let him go. He went in a hurry in the end, because he had dreamt that his mother was crying, and he knew what was the great thing she cried for, and that a hug from her splendid Peter would quickly make her to smile. Oh! he felt sure of it, and so eager was he to be nestling in her arms that this time he flew straight to the window, which was always to be open for him. But the window was closed, and there were iron bars on it, and peering inside he saw his mother sleeping peacefully with her arm around another little boy. Peter called, "Mother! mother!" but she heard him not; in vain he beat his little limbs against the iron bars. He had to fly back, sobbing, to the Gardens, and he never saw his dear again. What a glorious boy he had meant to be to her! Ah, Peter! we who have made the great mistake, how differently we should all act at the second chance. But Solomon was right—there is no second chance, not for most of us. When we reach the window it is Lock-out Time. The iron bars are up for life. CHAPTER V *The Little House* Everybody has heard of the Little House in the Kensington Gardens, which is the only house in the whole world that the fairies have built for humans. But no one has really seen it, except just three or four, and they have not only seen it but slept in it, and unless you sleep in it you never see it. This is because it is not there when you lie down, but it is there when you wake up and step outside. In a kind of way every one may see it, but what you see is not really it, but only the light in the windows. You see the light after Lock-out Time. David, for instance, saw it quite distinctly far away among the trees as we were going home from the pantomime, and Oliver Bailey saw it the night he stayed so late at the Temple, which is the name of his father's office.

Angela Clare, who loves to have a tooth extracted because then she is treated to tea in a shop, saw more than one light, she saw hundreds of them all together; and this must

have been the fairies building the house, for they build it every night, and always in a different part of the Gardens. She thought one of the lights was bigger than the others,

though she was not quite sure, for they jumped about so, and it might have been another one that was bigger. But if it was the same one, it was Peter Pan's light. Heaps of

children have seen the light, so that is nothing. But Maimie Mannering was the famous one for whom the house was first built. Maimie was always rather a strange girl, and

it was at night that she was strange. She was four years of age, and in the daytime she was the ordinary kind. She was pleased when her brother Tony, who was a magnificent

fellow of six, took notice of her, and she looked up to him in the right way, and tried in vain to imitate him, and was flattered rather than annoyed when he shoved her about.

Also, when she was batting, she would pause though the ball was in the air to point out to you that she was wearing new shoes. She was quite the ordinary kind in the daytime.

But as the shades of night fell, Tony, the swaggerer, lost his contempt for Maimie and eyed her fearfully; and no wonder, for with dark there came into her face a look that I

can describe only as a leary look. It was also a serene look that contrasted grandly with Tony's uneasy glances. Then he would make her presents of his favourite toys (which

he always took away from her next morning), and she accepted them with a disturbing smile. The reason he was now become so wheedling and she so mysterious was (in

brief) that they knew they were about to be sent to bed. It was then that Maimie was terrible. Tony entreated her not to do it to-night, and the mother and their coloured

nurse threatened her, but Maimie merely smiled her agitating smile. And by and by when they were alone with their night-light she would start up in bed crying "Hsh! what

was that?" Tony beseeches her, "It was nothing—don't, Maimie, don't!" and pulls the sheet over his head. "It is coming nearer!" she cries. "Oh, look at it, Tony! It is feeling

your bed with its horns—it is boring for you, O Tony, oh!" and she desists not until he rushes downstairs in his combinations, screeching. When they came up to whip Maimie

they usually found her sleeping tranquilly—not shamming, you know, but really sleeping, and looking like the sweetest little angel, which seems to me to make it almost

worse. But of course it was daytime when they were in the Gardens, and then Tony did most of the talking. You could gather from his talk that he was a very brave boy, and

no one was so proud of it as Maimie. She would have loved to have a ticket on her saying that she was his sister. And at no time did she admire him more than when he told

her, as he often did with splendid firmness, that one day he meant to remain behind in the Gardens after the gates were closed. "O Tony," she would say with awful respect,

"but the fairies will be so angry!" "I dare say," replied Tony carelessly. "Perhaps," she said, thrilling, "Peter Pan will give you a sail in his boat!" "I shall make him," replied

Tony; no wonder she was proud of him. But they should not have talked so loudly, for one day they were overheard by a fairy who had been gathering skeleton leaves, from

which the little people weave their summer curtains, and after that Tony was a marked boy. They loosened the rails before he sat on them, so that down he came on the back

of his head; they tripped him up by catching his bootlace, and bribed the ducks to sink his boat. Nearly all the nasty accidents you meet with in the Gardens occur because

the fairies have taken an ill-will to you, and so it behooves you to be careful what you say about them. Maimie was one of the kind who like to fix a day for doing things, bu

Tony was not that kind, and when she asked him which day he was to remain behind in the Gardens after Lock-out he merely replied, "Just some day;" he was quite vague about which day except when she asked, "Will it be to-day?" and then he could always say for certain that it would not be to-day. So she saw that he was waiting for a real good chance. This brings us to an afternoon when the Gardens were white with snow; and there was ice on the Round Pond; not thick enough to skate on, but at least you could spoil it for to-morrow by flinging stones, and many bright little boys and girls were doing that. When Tony and his sister arrived they wanted to go straight to the pond, but their ayah said they must take a sharp walk first, and as she said this she glanced at the time-board to see when the Gardens closed that night. It read half-past five. Poor ayah! She is the one who laughs continuously because there are so many white children in the world, but she was not to laugh much more that day. Well, they went up the Baby Walk and back, and when they returned to the time-board she was surprised to see that it now read five o'clock for closing-time. But she was unacquainted with the tricky ways of the fairies, and so did not see (as Maimie and Tony saw at once) that they had changed the hour because there was to be a ball to-night. She said there was only time now to walk to the top of the Hump and back, and as they trotted along with her she little guessed what was thrilling their little breasts. You see the chance had come of seeing a fairy ball. Never, Tony felt, could he hope for a better chance. He had to feel this for Maimie so plainly felt it for him. Her eager eyes asked the question, "Is it to-day?" and he gasped and then nodded. Maimie slipped her hand into Tony's, and hers was hot, but his was cold. She did a very kind thing; she took off her scarf and gave it to him. "In case you should feel cold," she whispered. Her face was aglow, but Tony's was very gloomy. As they turned on the top of the Hump he whispered to her, "I'm afraid nurse would see me, so I shan't be able to do it." Maimie admired him more than ever for being afraid of nothing but their ayah, when there were so many unknown terrors to fear, and she said aloud, "Tony, I shall race you to the gate," and in a whisper, "then you can hide," and off they ran. Tony could always outdistance her easily, but never had she known him speed away so quickly as now, and she was sure he hurried that he might have more time to hide. "Brave, brave!" her doting eyes were crying when she got a dreadful shock; instead of hiding, her hero had run out at the gate! At this bitter sight Maimie stopped blankly, as if all her lapful of darling treasures were suddenly spilled, and then for very disdain she could not sob; in a swell of protest against all puling cowards she ran to St. Govor's Well and hid in Tony's stead. When the ayah reached the gate and saw Tony far in front she thought her other charge was with him and passed out. Twilight crept over the Gardens, and hundreds of people passed out, including the last one, who always has to run for it, but Maimie saw them not. She had shut her eyes tight and glued them with passionate tears. When she opened them something very cold ran up her legs and up her arms and dropped into her heart. It was the stillness of the Gardens. Then she heard *clang*, then from another part *clang*, then *clang*, *clang* far away. It was the Closing of the Gates. Immediately the last clang had died away Maimie distinctly heard a voice say, "So that's all right." It had a wooden sound and seemed to come from above, and she looked up in time to see an elm-tree stretching out its arms and yawning. She was about to say, "I never knew you could speak!" when a metallic voice that seemed to come from the ladle at the well remarked to the elm, "I suppose it is a bit coldish up there?" and the elm replied, "Not particularly, but you do get numb standing so long on one leg," and he flapped his arms vigorously just as the cab-men do before they drive off. Maimie was quite surprised to see that a number of other tall trees were doing the same sort of thing, and she stole away to the Baby Walk and crouched observantly under a Minorca holly which shrugged its shoulders but did not seem to mind her. She was not in the least cold. She was wearing a russet-coloured pelisse and had the hood over her head, so that nothing of her showed except her dear little face and her curls. The rest of her real self was hidden far away inside so many warm garments that in shape she seemed rather like a ball. She was about forty round the waist.

There was a good deal going on in the Baby Walk, where Maimie arrived in time to see a magnolia and a Persian lilac step over the railing and set off for a smart walk. They moved in a jerky sort of way certainly, but that was because they used crutches. An elderberry hobbled across the walk, and stood chatting with some young quinces, and they all had crutches. The crutches were the sticks that are tied to young trees and shrubs. They were quite familiar objects to Maimie, but she had never known what they were for until to-night. She peeped up the walk and saw her first fairy. He was a street boy fairy who was running up the walk closing the weeping trees. The way he did it was this: he pressed a spring in the trunks and they shut like umbrellas, deluging the little plants beneath with snow. "O you naughty, naughty child!" Maimie cried indignantly, for she knew what it was to have a dripping umbrella about your ears. Fortunately the mischievous fellow was out of earshot, but a chrysanthemum heard her, and said so pointedly, "Hoity-toity, what is this?" that she had to come out and show herself. Then the whole vegetable kingdom was rather puzzled what to do. "Of course it is no affair of ours," a spindle-tree said after they had whispered together, "but you know quite well you ought not to be here, and perhaps our duty is to report you to the fairies; what do you think yourself?" "I think you should not," Maimie replied, which so perplexed them that they said petulantly there was no arguing with her. "I wouldn't ask it of you," she assured them, "if I thought it was wrong," and of course after this they could not well carry tales. They then said, "Well-a-day," and "Such is life," for they can be frightfully sarcastic; but she felt sorry for those of them who had no crutches, and she said good-naturedly, "Before I go to the fairies' ball, I should like to take you for a walk one at a time; you can lean on me, you know." At this they clapped their hands, and she escorted them up the Baby Walk and back again, one at a time, putting an arm or a finger round the very frail, setting their leg right when it got too ridiculous, and treating the foreign ones quite as courteously as the English, though she could not understand a word they said. They behaved well on the whole, though some whimpered that she had not taken them as far as she took Nancy or Grace or Dorothy, and others jagged her, but it was quite unintentional, and she was too much of a lady to cry out. So much walking tired her, and she was anxious to be off to the ball, but she no longer felt afraid. The reason she felt no more fear was that it was now night-time, and in the dark, you remember, Maimie was always rather strange. They were now loth to let her go, for, "If the fairies see you," they warned her, "they will mischief you—stab you to death, or compel you to nurse their children, or turn you into something tedious, like an evergreen oak." As they said this they looked with affected pity at an evergreen oak, for in winter they are very envious of the evergreens. "Oh, la!" replied the oak bitingly, "how deliciously cosy it is to stand here buttoned to the neck and watch you poor naked creatures shivering." This made them sulky, though they had really brought it on themselves, and they drew for Maimie a very gloomy picture of the perils that would face her if she insisted on going to the ball. She learned from a purple

filbert that the court was not in its usual good temper at present, the cause being the tantalising heart of the Duke of Christmas Daisies. He was an Oriental fairy, very poorly

of a dreadful complaint, namely, inability to love, and though he had tried many ladies in many lands he could not fall in love with one of them. Queen Mab, who rules in

the Gardens, had been confident that her girls would bewitch him, but alas! his heart, the doctor said, remained cold. This rather irritating doctor, who was his private

physician, felt the Duke's heart immediately after any lady was presented, and then always shook his bald head and murmured, "Cold, quite cold." Naturally Queen Mab

felt disgraced, and first she tried the effect of ordering the court into tears for nine minutes, and then she blamed the Cupids and decreed that they should wear fools' caps

until they thawed the Duke's frozen heart. "How I should love to see the Cupids in their dear little fools' caps!" Maimie cried, and away she ran to look for them very

recklessly, for the Cupids hate to be laughed at. It is always easy to discover where a fairies' ball is being held, as ribbons are stretched between it and all the populous parts

of the Gardens, on which those invited may walk to the dance without wetting their pumps. This night the ribbons were red, and looked very pretty on the snow. Maimie

walked alongside one of them for some distance without meeting anybody, but at last she saw a fairy cavalcade approaching. To her surprise they seemed to be returning

from the ball, and she had just time to hide from them by bending her knees and holding out her arms and pretending to be a garden chair. There were six horsemen in front

and six behind; in the middle walked a prim lady wearing a long train held up by two pages, and on the train, as if it were a couch, reclined a lovely girl, for in this way do

aristocratic fairies travel about. She was dressed in golden rain, but the most enviable part of her was her neck, which was blue in colour and of a velvet texture, and of course

showed off her diamond necklace as no white throat could have glorified it. The high-born fairies obtain this admired effect by pricking their skin, which lets the blue blood

come through and dye them, and you cannot imagine anything so dazzling unless you have seen the ladies' busts in the jewellers' windows. Maimie also noticed that the whole

cavalcade seemed to be in a passion, tilting their noses higher than it can be safe for even fairies to tilt them, and she concluded that this must be another case in which the

doctor had said "Cold, quite cold." Well, she followed the ribbon to a place where it became a bridge over a dry puddle into which another fairy had fallen and been unable

to climb out. At first this little damsel was afraid of Maimie, who most kindly went to her aid, but soon she sat in her hand chatting gaily and explaining that her name was

Brownie, and that though only a poor street singer she was on her way to the ball to see if the Duke would have her. "Of course," she said, "I am rather plain," and this made

Maimie uncomfortable, for indeed the simple little creature was almost quite plain for a fairy. It was difficult to know what to reply. "I see you think I have no chance,"

Brownie said falteringly. "I don't say that," Maimie answered politely; "of course your face is just a tiny bit homely, but—" Really it was quite awkward for her. Fortunately

she remembered about her father and the bazaar. He had gone to a fashionable bazaar where all the most beautiful ladies in London were on view for half a crown the second

day, but on his return home, instead of being dissatisfied with Maimie's mother, he had said, "You can't think, my dear, what a relief it is to see a homely face again." Maimie repeated this story, and it fortified Brownie tremendously, indeed she had no longer the slightest doubt that the Duke would choose her. So she scudded away up the ribbon,

calling out to Maimie not to follow lest the Queen should mischief her. But Maimie's curiosity tugged her forward, and presently at the seven Spanish chestnuts she saw a

wonderful light. She crept forward until she was quite near it, and then she peeped from behind a tree. The light, which was as high as your head above the ground, was

composed of myriads of glow-worms all holding on to each other, and so forming a dazzling canopy over the fairy ring. There were thousands of little people looking on,

but they were in shadow and drab in colour compared to the glorious creatures within that luminous circle, who were so bewilderingly bright that Maimie had to wink hard

all the time she looked at them. It was amazing and even irritating to her that the Duke of Christmas Daisies should be able to keep out of love for a moment: yet out of love

his dusky grace still was: you could see it by the shamed looks of the Queen and court (though they pretended not to care), by the way darling ladies brought forward for his

approval burst into tears as they were told to pass on, and by his own most dreary face. Maimie could also see the pompous doctor feeling the Duke's heart and hear him give

utterance to his parrot cry, and she was particularly sorry for the Cupids, who stood in their fools' caps in obscure places and, every time they heard that "Cold, quite cold,"

bowed their disgraced little heads. She was disappointed not to see Peter Pan, and I may as well tell you now why he was so late that night. It was because his boat had got

wedged on the Serpentine between fields of floating ice, through which he had to break a perilous passage with his trusty paddle. The fairies had as yet scarcely missed him,

for they could not dance, so heavy were their hearts. They forget all the steps when they are sad, and remember them again when they are merry. David tells me that fairies

never say, "We feel happy": what they say is, "We feel *dancey*." Well, they were looking very undancey indeed, when sudden laughter broke out among the onlookers, caused

by Brownie, who had just arrived and was insisting on her right to be presented to the Duke. Maimie craned forward eagerly to see how her friend fared, though she had

really no hope; no one seemed to have the least hope except Brownie herself, who, however, was absolutely confident. She was led before his grace, and the doctor putting a

finger carelessly on the ducal heart, which for convenience' sake was reached by a little trap-door in his diamond shirt, had begun to say mechanically, "Cold, qui——," when

he stopped abruptly. "What's this," he cried, and first he shook the heart like a watch, and then he put his ear to it. "Bless my soul!" cried the doctor, and by this time of course

the excitement among the spectators was tremendous, fairies fainting right and left. Everybody stared breathlessly at the Duke, who was very much startled, and looked as

if he would like to run away. "Good gracious me!" the doctor was heard muttering, and now the heart was evidently on fire, for he had to jerk his fingers away from it and

put them in his mouth. The suspense was awful. Then in a loud voice, and bowing low, "My Lord Duke," said the physician elatedly, "I have the honour to inform your

excellency that your grace is in love." You can't conceive the effect of it. Brownie held out her arms to the Duke and he flung himself into them, the Queen leapt into the

arms of the Lord Chamberlain, and the ladies of the court leapt into the arms of her gentlemen, for it is etiquette to follow her example in everything. Thus in a single

moment about fifty marriages took place, for if you leap into each other's arms it is a fairy wedding. Of course a clergyman has to be present. How the crowd cheered and leapt! Trumpets brayed, the moon came out, and immediately a thousand couples seized hold of its rays as if they were ribbons in a May dance and waltzed in wild abandon round the fairy ring. Most gladsome sight of all, the Cupids plucked the hated fools' caps from their heads and cast them high in the air. And then Maimie went and spoiled everything. She couldn't help it. She was crazy with delight over her little friend's good fortune, so she took several steps forward and cried in an ecstasy, "O Brownie, how splendid!" Everybody stood still, the music ceased, the lights went out, and all in the time you may take to say, "Oh dear!" An awful sense of her peril came upon Maimie; too late she remembered that she was a lost child in a place where no human must be between the locking and the opening of the gates; she heard the murmur of an angry multitude; she saw a thousand swords flashing for her blood, and she uttered a cry of terror and fled. How she ran! And all the time her eyes were starting out of her head. Many times she lay down, and then quickly jumped up and ran on again. Her little mind was so entangled in terrors that she no longer knew she was in the Gardens. The one thing she was sure of was that she must never cease to run, and she thought she was still running long after she had dropped in the Figs and gone to sleep. She thought the snowflakes falling on her face were her mother kissing her good-night. She thought her coverlet of snow was a warm blanket, and tried to pull it over her head. And when she heard talking through her dreams she thought it was mother bringing father to the nursery door to look at her as she slept. But it was the fairies. I am very glad to be able to say that they no longer desired to mischief her. When she rushed away they had rent the air with such cries as "Slay her!" "Turn her into something extremely unpleasant!" and so on, but the pursuit was delayed while they discussed who should march in front, and this gave Duchess Brownie time to cast herself before the Queen and demand a boon. Every bride has a right to a boon, and what she asked for was Maimie's life. "Anything except that," replied Queen Mab sternly, and all the fairies echoed, "Anything except that." But when they learned how Maimie had befriended Brownie and so enabled her to attend the ball to their great glory and renown, they gave three huzzas for the little human, and set off, like an army, to thank her, the court advancing in front and the canopy keeping step with it. They traced Maimie easily by her footprints in the snow. But though they found her deep in snow in the Figs, it seemed impossible to thank Maimie, for they could not waken her. They went through the form of thanking her—that is to say, the new King stood on her body and read her a long address of welcome, but she heard not a word of it. They also cleared the snow off her, but soon she was covered again, and they saw she was in danger of perishing of cold. "Turn her into something that does not mind the cold," seemed a good suggestion of the doctors, but the only thing they could think of that does not mind cold was a snowflake. "And it might melt," the Queen pointed out, so that idea had to be given up. A magnificent attempt was made to carry her to a sheltered spot, but though there were so many of them she was too heavy. By this time all the ladies were crying in their handkerchiefs, but presently the Cupids had a lovely idea. "Build a house round her," they cried, and at once everybody perceived that this was the thing to do; in a moment a hundred fairy sawyers were among the branches, architects were running round Maimie, measuring her; a bricklayer's yard sprang up at her feet, seventy-five masons rushed up with the foundation-stone, and the Queen laid it, overseers were appointed to keep the boys off, scaffoldings were run up, the whole place rang with hammers and chisels and turning-lathes, and by this time the roof was on and the glaziers were putting in the windows. The house was exactly the size of Maimie, and perfectly lovely. One of her arms was extended, and this had bothered them for a second, but they built a verandah round it leading to the front door. The windows were the size of a coloured picture-book and the door rather smaller, but it would be easy for her to get out by taking off the roof. The fairies, as is their custom, clapped their hands with delight over their cleverness, and they were so madly in love with the little house that they could not bear to think they had finished it. So they gave it ever so many little extra touches, and even then they added more extra touches. For instance, two of them ran up a ladder and put on a chimney. "Now we fear it is quite finished," they sighed. But no, for another two ran up the ladder, and tied some smoke to the chimney. "That certainly finishes it," they said reluctantly. "Not at all," cried a glow-worm; "if she were to wake without seeing a night-light she might be frightened, so I shall be her night-light." "Wait one moment," said a china merchant, "and I shall make you a saucer." Now, alas! it was absolutely finished. Oh, dear no! "Gracious me!" cried a brass manufacturer, "There's no handle on the door," and he put one on. An ironmonger added a scraper, and an old lady ran up with a door-mat. Carpenters arrived with a water-butt, and the painters insisted on painting it. Finished at last! "Finished! How can it be finished," the plumber demanded scornfully, "before hot and cold are put in," and he put in hot and cold. Then an army of gardeners arrived with fairy carts and spades and seeds and bulbs and forcing-houses, and soon they had a flower-garden to the right of the verandah, and a vegetable garden to the left, and roses and clematis on the walls of the house, and in less time than five minutes all these dear things were in full bloom. Oh, how beautiful the little house was now! But it was at last finished true as true, and they had to leave it and return to the dance. They all kissed their hands to it as they went away, and the last to go was Brownie. She stayed a moment behind the others to drop a pleasant dream down the chimney. All through the night the exquisite little house stood there in the Figs taking care of Maimie, and she never knew. She slept until the dream was quite finished, and woke feeling deliciously cosy just as morning was breaking from its egg, and then she almost fell asleep again, and then she called out, "Tony," for she thought she was at home in the nursery. As Tony made no answer she sat up, whereupon her head hit the roof, and it opened like the lid of a box, and to her bewilderment she saw all around her the Kensington Gardens lying deep in snow. As she was not in the nursery she wondered whether this was really herself, so she pinched her cheeks, and then she knew was herself, and this reminded her that she was in the middle of a great adventure. She remembered now everything that had happened to her from the closing of the gate up to her running away from the fairies, but however, she asked herself, had she got into this funny place? She stepped out by the roof, right over the garden, and then she saw the dear house in which she had passed the night. It so entranced her that she could think of nothing else. "O you darling! O you sweet! O you love!" she cried. Perhaps a human voice frightened the little house, or maybe it now knew that its work was done, for no sooner had Maimie spoken than it began to grow smaller; it shrank so slowly that she could scarce believe it was shrinking, yet she soon knew that it could not contain her now. It always remained as complete as ever, but it became smaller and smaller, and the garden dwindled at the same time, and the snow crept closer, lapping house and garden up. Now the house was the size of a little dog's kennel, and now of a Noah's

Ark, but still you could see the smoke and the door-handle and the roses on the wall, every one complete. The glow-worm light was waning too, but it was still there.

"Darling, loveliest, don't go!" Maimie cried, falling on her knees, for the little house was now the size of a reel of thread, but still quite complete. But as she stretched out her arms imploringly the snow crept up on all sides until it met itself, and where the little house had been was now one unbroken expanse of snow. Maimie stamped her foot naughtily, and was putting her fingers to her eyes, when she heard a kind voice say, "Don't cry, pretty human, don't cry," and then she turned round and saw a beautiful little naked boy regarding her wistfully. She knew at once that he must be Peter Pan. CHAPTER VI *Peter's Goat* Maimie felt quite shy, but Peter knew not what shy was. "I hope you have had a good night," he said earnestly. "Thank you," she replied, "I was so cosy and warm. But you"—and she looked at his nakedness awkwardly—"don't you feel the least bit cold?" Now cold was another word Peter had forgotten, so he answered, "I think not, but I may be wrong: you see I am rather ignorant. I am not exactly a boy; Solomon says I am a Betwixt-and-Between." "So that is what it is called," said Maimie thoughtfully. "That's not my name," he explained, "my name is Peter Pan." "Yes, of course," she said, "I know, everybody knows." You can't think how pleased Peter was to learn that all the people outside the gates knew about him. He begged Maimie to tell him what they knew and what they said, and she did so. They were sitting by this time on a fallen tree; Peter had cleared off the snow for Maimie, but he sat on a snowy bit himself. "Squeeze closer," Maimie said. "What is that?" he asked, and she showed him, and then he did it. They talked together and he found that people knew a great deal about him, but not everything, not that he had gone back to his mother and been barred out, for instance, and he said nothing of this to Maimie, for it still humiliated him. "Do they know that I play games exactly like real boys?" he asked very proudly. "O Maimie, please tell them!" But when he revealed how he played, by sailing his hoop on the Round Pond, and so on, she was simply horrified. "All your ways of playing," she said with her big eyes on him, "are quite, quite wrong, and not in the least like how boys play." Poor Peter uttered a little moan at this, and he cried for the first time for I know not how long. Maimie was extremely sorry for him, and lent him her handkerchief, but he didn't know in the least what to do with it, so she showed him, that is to say, she wiped her eyes, and then gave it back to him, saying, "Now you do it," but instead of wiping his own eyes he wiped hers, and she thought it best to pretend that this was what she had meant. She said out of pity for him, "I shall give you a kiss if you like," but though he once knew, he had long forgotten what kisses are, and he replied, "Thank you," and held out his hand, thinking she had offered to put something into it. This was a great shock to her, but she felt she could not explain without shaming him, so with charming delicacy she gave Peter a thimble which happened to be in her pocket, and pretended that it was a kiss. Poor little boy! He quite believed her, and to this day he wears it on his finger, though there can be scarcely any one who needs a thimble so little.

You see, though still a tiny child, it was really years and years since he had seen his mother, and I dare say the baby who had supplanted him was now a man with whiskers.

But you must not think that Peter Pan was a boy to pity rather than to admire; if Maimie began by thinking this, she soon found she was very much mistaken. Her eyes glistened with admiration when he told her of his adventures, especially of how he went to and fro between the island and the Gardens in the Thrush's Nest. "How romantic!" Maimie exclaimed, but this was another unknown word, and he hung his head thinking she was despising him. "I suppose Tony would not have done that?" he

said very humbly. "Never, never!" she answered with conviction, "He would have been afraid." "What is afraid?" asked Peter longingly. He thought it must be some splendid

thing. "I do wish you would teach me how to be afraid, Maimie," he said. "I believe no one could teach that to you," she answered adoringly, but Peter thought she meant

that he was stupid. She had told him about Tony and of the wicked thing he did in the dark to frighten him (she knew quite well that it was wicked), but Peter misunderstood

her meaning and said, "Oh, how I wish I was as brave as Tony!" It quite irritated her. "You are twenty thousand times braver than Tony," she said; "you are ever so much

the bravest boy I ever knew." He could scarcely believe she meant it, but when he did believe he screamed with joy. "And if you want very much to give me a kiss," Maimie

said, "you can do it." Very reluctantly Peter began to take the thimble off his finger. He thought she wanted it back. "I don't mean a kiss," she said hurriedly, "I mean a

thimble." "What's that?" Peter asked. "It's like this," she said, and kissed him. "I should love to give you a thimble," Peter said gravely, so he gave her one. He gave her quite

a number of thimbles, and then a delightful idea came into his head. "Maimie," he said, "will you marry me?" Now, strange to tell, the same idea had come at exactly the

same time into Maimie's head. "I should like to," she answered, "but will there be room in your boat for two?" "If you squeeze close," he said eagerly. "Perhaps the birds

would be angry?" He assured her that the birds would love to have her, though I am not so certain of it myself. Also that there were very few birds in winter. "Of course

they might want your clothes," he had to admit rather falteringly. She was somewhat indignant at this. "They are always thinking of their nests," he said apologetically, "and

there are some bits of you"—he stroked the fur on her pelisse—"that would excite them very much." "They shan't have my fur," she said sharply. "No," he said, still

fondling it, however, "No. O Maimie," he said rapturously, "do you know why I love you? It is because you are like a beautiful nest." Somehow this made her uneasy. "I

think you are speaking more like a bird than a boy now," she said, holding back, and indeed he was even looking rather like a bird. "After all," she said, "you are only

Betwixt-and-Between." But it hurt him so much that she immediately added, "It must be a delicious thing to be." "Come and be one, then, dear Maimie," he implored her,

and they set off for the boat, for it was now very near Open-Gate time. "And you are not a bit like a nest," he whispered to please her. "But I think it is rather nice to be like

one," she said in a woman's contradictory way. "And, Peter, dear, though I can't give them my fur, I wouldn't mind their building in it. Fancy a nest in my neck with little

spotty eggs in it! O Peter, how perfectly lovely!" But as they drew near the Serpentine, she shivered a little, and said, "Of course I shall go and see mother often, quite often.

It is not as if I was saying good-bye for ever to mother, it is not in the least like that." "Oh no," answered Peter, but in his heart he knew it was very like that, and he would

have told her so had he not been in a quaking fear of losing her. He was so fond of her, he felt he could not live without her. "She will forget her mother in time, and be happy

with me," he kept saying to himself, and he hurried her on, giving her thimbles by the way. But even when she had seen the boat and exclaimed ecstatically over its loveliness

she still talked tremblingly about her mother. "You know quite well, Peter, don't you," she said, "that I wouldn't come unless I knew for certain I could go back to mother whenever I want to? Peter, say it." He said it, but he could no longer look her in the face. "If you are sure your mother will always want you," he added rather sourly. "The

idea of mother's not always wanting me!" Maimie cried, and her face glistened. "If she doesn't bar you out," said Peter huskily. "The door," replied Maimie, "will always,

always be open, and mother will always be waiting at it for me." "Then," said Peter, not without grimness, "step in, if you feel so sure of her," and he helped Maimie into

the Thrush's Nest. "But why don't you look at me?" she asked, taking him by the arm. Peter tried hard not to look, he tried to push off, then he gave a great gulp and jumped

ashore and sat down miserably in the snow. She went to him. "What is it, dear, dear Peter?" she said, wondering. "O Maimie," he cried, "it isn't fair to take you with me if

you think you can go back! Your mother"—he gulped again—"you don't know them as well as I do." And then he told her the woeful story of how he had been barred out,

and she gasped all the time. "But my mother," she said, "*my* mother—" "Yes, she would;" said Peter, "they are all the same. I dare say she is looking for another one already."

Maimie said aghast, "I can't believe it. You see, when you went away your mother had none, but my mother has Tony, and surely they are satisfied when they have one."

Peter replied bitterly, "You should see the letters Solomon gets from ladies who have six." Just then they heard a grating *creak*, followed by *creak, creak*, all round the Gardens.

It was the Opening of the Gates, and Peter jumped nervously into his boat. He knew Maimie would not come with him now, and he was trying bravely not to cry. But Maimie

was sobbing painfully. "If I should be too late," she said in agony, "O Peter, if she has got another one already!" Again he sprang ashore as if she had called him back. "I

shall come and look for you to-night," he said, squeezing close, "but if you hurry away I think you will be in time." Then he pressed a last thimble on her sweet little mouth,

and covered his face with his hands so that he might not see her go. "Dear Peter!" she cried. "Dear Maimie!" cried the tragic boy. She leapt into his arms, so that it was a sort

of fairy wedding, and then she hurried away. Oh, how she hastened to the gates! Peter, you may be sure, was back in the Gardens that night as soon as Lock-out sounded,

but he found no Maimie, and so he knew she had been in time. For long he hoped that some night she would come back to him; often he thought he saw her waiting for him

by the shore of the Serpentine as his bark drew to land, but Maimie never went back. She wanted to, but she was afraid that if she saw her dear Betwixt-and-Between again

she would linger with him too long, and besides the ayah now kept a sharp eye on her. But she often talked lovingly of Peter, and she knitted a kettle-holder for him, and one

day when she was wondering what Easter present he would like, her mother made a suggestion. "Nothing," she said thoughtfully, "would be so useful to him as a goat." "He

could ride on it," cried Maimie, "and play on his pipe at the same time." "Then," her mother asked, "won't you give him your goat, the one you frighten Tony with at night?"

"But it isn't a real goat," Maimie said. "It seems very real to Tony," replied her mother. "It seems frightfully real to me too," Maimie admitted, "but how could I give it to

Peter?" Her mother knew a way, and next day, accompanied by Tony (who was really quite a nice boy, though of course he could not compare), they went to the Gardens,

and Maimie stood alone within a fairy ring, and then her mother, who was a rather gifted lady, said— My daughter, tell me, if you can, What have you got for Peter Pan? To

which Maimie replied— I have a goat for him to ride, Observe me cast it far and wide. She then flung her arms about as if she were sowing seed, and turned round three times. Next Tony said— If P. doth find it waiting here, Wilt ne'er again make me to fear? And Maimie answered— By dark or light I fondly swear Never to see goat

anywhere. She also left a letter to Peter in a likely place, explaining what she had done, and begging him to ask the fairies to turn the goat into one convenient for riding or

Well, it all happened just as she hoped, for Peter found the letter, and of course nothing could be easier for the fairies than to turn the goat into a real one, and so that is how

Peter got the goat on which he now rides round the Gardens every night playing sublimely on his pipe. And Maimie kept her promise, and never frightened Tony with a goat

again, though I have heard that she created another animal. Until she was quite a big girl she continued to leave presents for Peter in the Gardens (with letters explaining how

humans play with them), and she is not the only one who has done this. David does it, for instance, and he and I know the likeliest place for leaving them in, and we shall tell

you if you like, but for mercy's sake don't ask us before Porthos, for he is so fond of toys that, were he to find out the place, he would take every one of them. Though Peter

still remembers Maimie he is become as gay as ever, and often in sheer happiness he jumps off his goat and lies kicking merrily on the grass. Oh, he has a joyful time! But he

has still a vague memory that he was a human once, and it makes him especially kind to the house-swallows when they visit the island, for house-swallows are the spirits of

little children who have died. They always build in the eaves of the houses where they lived when they were humans, and sometimes they try to fly in at a nursery window,

and perhaps that is why Peter loves them best of all the birds. And the little house? Every lawful night (that is to say, every night except ball nights) the fairies now build the

little house lest there should be a human child lost in the Gardens, and Peter rides the marches looking for lost ones, and if he finds them he carries them on his goat to the

little house, and when they wake up they are in it, and when they step out they see it. The fairies build the house merely because it is so pretty, but Peter rides round in memory

of Maimie, and because he still loves to do just as he believes real boys would do. But you must not think that, because somewhere among the trees the little house is twinkling,

it is a safe thing to remain in the Gardens after Lock-out time. If the bad ones among the fairies happen to be out that night they will certainly mischief you, and even though

they are not, you may perish of cold and dark before Peter Pan comes round. He has been too late several times, and when he sees he is too late he runs back to the Thrush's

Nest for his paddle, of which Maimie had told him the true use, and he digs a grave for the child and erects a little tombstone, and carves the poor thing's initials on it. He

does this at once because he thinks it is what real boys would do, and you must have noticed the little stones, and that there are always two together. He puts them in twos

because they seem less lonely. I think that quite the most touching sight in the Gardens is the two tombstones of Walter Stephen Matthews and Phoebe Phelps. They stand

together at the spot where the parish of Westminster St. Mary's is said to meet the Parish of Paddington. Here Peter found the two babes, who had fallen unnoticed from

their perambulators, Phoebe aged thirteen months and Walter probably still younger, for Peter seems to have felt a delicacy about putting any age on his stone. They lie side

by side, and the simple inscriptions read W. St. M. 13a P.P. 1841. David sometimes places white flowers on these two innocent graves. But how strange for parents, when they

hurry into the Gardens at the opening of the gates looking for their lost one, to find the sweetest little tombstone instead. I do hope that Peter is not too ready with his spade.

It is all rather sad. THE END. PETER AND WENDY | Chapter I *Peter Breaks Through* **All children, except one, grow up.** They soon know that they will grow up, and the way Wendy knew was this. One day when she was two years old she was playing in a garden, and she plucked another flower and ran with it to her mother. I suppose she must have looked rather delightful, for Mrs. Darling put her hand to her heart and cried, "Oh, why can't you remain like this for ever!" This was all that passed between them on the subject, but henceforth Wendy knew that she must grow up. You always know after you are two. Two is the beginning of the end. Of course they lived at 14, and until Wendy came her mother was the chief one. She was a lovely lady, with a romantic mind and such a sweet mocking mouth. Her romantic mind was like the tiny boxes, one within the other, that come from the puzzling East, however many you discover there is always one more; and her sweet mocking mouth had one kiss on it that Wendy could never get, though there it was, perfectly conspicuous in the right-hand corner. The way Mr. Darling won her was this: the many gentlemen who had been boys when she was a girl discovered simultaneously that they loved her, and they all ran to her house to propose to her except Mr. Darling, who took a cab and nipped in first, and so he got her. He got all of her, except the innermost box and the kiss. He never knew about the box, and in time he gave up trying for the kiss. Wendy thought Napoleon could have got it, but I can picture him trying, and then going off in a passion, slamming the door. Mr. Darling used to boast to Wendy that her mother not only loved him but respected him. He was one of those deep ones who know about stocks and shares. Of course no one really knows, but he quite seemed to know, and he often said stocks were up and shares were down in a way that would have made any woman respect him. Mrs. Darling was married in white, and at first she kept the books perfectly, almost gleefully, as if it were a game, not so much as a Brussels sprout was missing; but by and by whole cauliflowers dropped out, and instead of them there were pictures of babies without faces. She drew them when she should have been totting up. They were Mrs. Darling's guesses. Wendy came first, then John, then Michael. For a week or two after Wendy came it was doubtful whether they would be able to keep her, as she was another mouth to feed. Mr. Darling was frightfully proud of her, but he was very honourable, and he sat on the edge of Mrs. Darling's bed, holding her hand and calculating expenses, while she looked at him imploringly. She wanted to risk it, come what might, but that was not his way; his way was with a pencil and a piece of paper, and if she confused him with suggestions he had to begin at the beginning again. "Now don't interrupt," he would beg of her. "I have one pound seventeen here, and two and six at the office; I can cut off my coffee at the office, say ten shillings, making two nine and six, with your eighteen and three makes three nine seven, with five naught naught in my cheque-book makes eight nine seven—who is that moving?—eight nine seven, dot and carry seven—don't speak, my own—and the pound you lent to that man who came to the door—quiet, child—dot and carry child—there, you've done it!—did I say nine nine seven? yes, I said nine nine seven; the question is, can we try it for a year on nine nine seven?" "Of course we can, George," she cried. But she was prejudiced in Wendy's favour, and he was really the grander character of the two. "Remember mumps," he warned her almost threateningly, and off he went again. "Mumps one pound, that is what I have put down, but I daresay it will be more like thirty shillings—don't speak—measles one five, German measles half a guinea, makes two fifteen six—don't waggle your finger—

whooping-cough, say fifteen shillings"—and so on it went, and it added up differently each time; but at last Wendy just got through, with mumps reduced to twelve six, and

the two kinds of measles treated as one. There was the same excitement over John, and Michael had even a narrower squeak; but both were kept, and soon you might have

seen the three of them going in a row to Miss Fulsom's Kindergarten school, accompanied by their nurse. Mrs. Darling loved to have everything just so, and Mr. Darling had

a passion for being exactly like his neighbours; so, of course, they had a nurse. As they were poor, owing to the amount of milk the children drank, this nurse was a prim

Newfoundland dog, called Nana, who had belonged to no one in particular until the Darlings engaged her. She had always thought children important, however, and the

Darlings had become acquainted with her in Kensington Gardens, where she spent most of her spare time peeping into perambulators, and was much hated by careless

nursemaids, whom she followed to their homes and complained of to their mistresses. She proved to be quite a treasure of a nurse. How thorough she was at bath-time; and

up at any moment of the night if one of her charges made the slightest cry. Of course her kennel was in the nursery. She had a genius for knowing when a cough is a thing

to have no patience with and when it needs stocking round your throat. She believed to her last day in old-fashioned remedies like rhubarb leaf, and made sounds of contempt

over all this new-fangled talk about germs, and so on. It was a lesson in propriety to see her escorting the children to school, walking sedately by their side when they were

well behaved, and butting them back into line if they strayed. On John's footer days she never once forgot his sweater, and she usually carried an umbrella in her mouth in

case of rain. There is a room in the basement of Miss Fulsom's school where the nurses wait. They sat on forms, while Nana lay on the floor, but that was the only difference.

They affected to ignore her as of an inferior social status to themselves, and she despised their light talk. She resented visits to the nursery from Mrs. Darling's friends, but

if they did come she first whipped off Michael's pinafore and put him into the one with blue braiding, and smoothed out Wendy and made a dash at John's hair. No nursery

could possibly have been conducted more correctly, and Mr. Darling knew it, yet he sometimes wondered uneasily whether the neighbours talked. He had his position in the

city to consider. Nana also troubled him in another way. He had sometimes a feeling that she did not admire him. "I know she admires you tremendously, George," Mrs.

Darling would assure him, and then she would sign to the children to be specially nice to father. Lovely dances followed, in which the only other servant, Liza, was sometimes

allowed to join. Such a midget she looked in her long skirt and maid's cap, though she had sworn, when engaged, that she would never see ten again. The gaiety of those

romps! And gayest of all was Mrs. Darling, who would pirouette so wildly that all you could see of her was the kiss, and then if you had dashed at her you might have got

There never was a simpler happier family until the coming of Peter Pan. Mrs. Darling first heard of Peter when she was tidying up her children's minds. It is the nightly

custom of every good mother after her children are asleep to rummage in their minds and put things straight for next morning, repacking into their proper places the many

articles that have wandered during the day. If you could keep awake (but of course you can't) you would see your own mother doing this, and you would find it very

interesting to watch her. It is quite like tidying up drawers. You would see her on her knees, I expect, lingering humorously over some of your contents, wondering where on earth you had picked this thing up, making discoveries sweet and not so sweet, pressing this to her cheek as if it were as nice as a kitten, and hurriedly stowing that out of sight. When you wake in the morning, the naughtinesses and evil passions with which you went to bed have been folded up small and placed at the bottom of your mind, and on the top, beautifully aired, are spread out your prettier thoughts, ready for you to put on. I don't know whether you have ever seen a map of a person's mind. Doctors sometimes draw maps of other parts of you, and your own map can become intensely interesting, but catch them trying to draw a map of a child's mind, which is not only confused, but keeps going round all the time. There are zigzag lines on it, just like your temperature on a card, and these are probably roads in the island; for the Neverland is always more or less an island, with astonishing splashes of colour here and there, and coral reefs and rakish-looking craft in the offing, and savages and lonely lairs, and gnomes who are mostly tailors, and caves through which a river runs, and princes with six elder brothers, and a hut fast going to decay, and one very small old lady with a hooked nose. It would be an easy map if that were all; but there is also first day at school, religion, fathers, the round pond, needlework, murders, hangings, verbs that take the dative, chocolate pudding day, getting into braces, say ninety-nine, three-pence for pulling out your tooth yourself, and so on, and either these are part of the island or they are another map showing through, and it is all rather confusing, especially as nothing will stand still. Of course the Neverlands vary a good deal. John's, for instance, had a lagoon with flamingoes flying over it at which John was shooting, while Michael, who was very small, had a flamingo with lagoons flying over it. John lived in a boat turned upside down on the sands, Michael in a wigwam, Wendy in a house of leaves deftly sewn together. John had no friends, Michael had friends at night, Wendy had a pet wolf forsaken by its parents, but on the whole the Neverlands have a family resemblance, and if they stood still in a row you could say of them that they have each other's nose, and so forth. On these magic shores children at play are for ever beaching their coracles. We too have been there; we can still hear the sound of the surf, though we shall land no more. Of all delectable islands the Neverland is the snuggest and most compact, not large and sprawly, you know, with tedious distances between one adventure and another, but nicely crammed. When you play at it by day with the chairs and table-cloth, it is not in the least alarming, but in the two minutes before you go to sleep it becomes very nearly real. That is why there are night-lights. Occasionally in her travels through her children's minds Mrs. Darling found things she could not understand, and of these quite the most perplexing was the word *Peter*. She knew of no Peter, and yet he was here and there in John and Michael's minds, while Wendy's began to be scrawled all over with him. The name stood out in bolder letters than any of the other words, and as Mrs. Darling gazed she felt that it had an oddly cocky appearance. "Yes, he is rather cocky," Wendy admitted with regret. Her mother had been questioning her. "But who is he, my pet?" "He is Peter Pan, you know, mother." At first Mrs. Darling did not know, but after thinking back into her childhood she just remembered a Peter Pan who was said to live with the fairies. There were odd stories about him, as that when children died he went part of the way with them, so that they should not be frightened. She had believed in him at the time, but now that she was married and full of sense she quite doubted whether there was any such person. "Besides," she said to Wendy, "he would be grown up by this time." "Oh no, he isn't grown up," Wendy assured her confidently, "and he is just my size." She meant that he was her size in both mind and body; she didn't know how she knew it, she just knew it. Mrs. Darling consulted

Mr. Darling, but he smiled pooh-pooh. "Mark my words," he said, "it is some nonsense Nana has been putting into their heads; just the sort of idea a dog would have. Leave

it alone, and it will blow over." But it would not blow over; and soon the troublesome boy gave Mrs. Darling quite a shock. Children have the strangest adventures without

being troubled by them. For instance, they may remember to mention, a week after the event happened, that when they were in the wood they met their dead father and had

a game with him. It was in this casual way that Wendy one morning made a disquieting revelation. Some leaves of a tree had been found on the nursery floor, which certainly

were not there when the children went to bed, and Mrs. Darling was puzzling over them when Wendy said with a tolerant smile: "I do believe it is that Peter again!"

"Whatever do you mean, Wendy?" "It is so naughty of him not to wipe," Wendy said, sighing. She was a tidy child. She explained in quite a matter-of-fact way that she

thought Peter sometimes came to the nursery in the night and sat on the foot of her bed and played on his pipes to her. Unfortunately she never woke, so she didn't know

how she knew, she just knew. "What nonsense you talk, precious. No one can get into the house without knocking." "I think he comes in by the window," she said. "My love

it is three floors up." "Were not the leaves at the foot of the window, mother?" It was quite true; the leaves had been found very near the window. Mrs. Darling did not know

what to think, for it all seemed so natural to Wendy that you could not dismiss it by saying she had been dreaming. "My child," the mother cried, "why did you not tell me

of this before?" "I forgot," said Wendy lightly. She was in a hurry to get her breakfast. Oh, surely she must have been dreaming. But, on the other hand, there were the leaves.

Mrs. Darling examined them carefully; they were skeleton leaves, but she was sure they did not come from any tree that grew in England. She crawled about the floor, peering

at it with a candle for marks of a strange foot. She rattled the poker up the chimney and tapped the walls. She let down a tape from the window to the pavement, and it was

sheer drop of thirty feet, without so much as a spout to climb up by. Certainly Wendy had been dreaming. But Wendy had not been dreaming, as the very next night showed,

the night on which the extraordinary adventures of these children may be said to have begun. On the night we speak of all the children were once more in bed. It happened

to be Nana's evening off, and Mrs. Darling had bathed them and sung to them till one by one they had let go her hand and slid away into the land of sleep. All were looking

so safe and cosy that she smiled at her fears now and sat down tranquilly by the fire to sew. It was something for Michael, who on his birthday was getting into shirts. The fire

was warm, however, and the nursery dimly lit by three night-lights, and presently the sewing lay on Mrs. Darling's lap. Then her head nodded, oh, so gracefully. She was

asleep. Look at the four of them, Wendy and Michael over there, John here, and Mrs. Darling by the fire. There should have been a fourth night-light. While she slept she

had a dream. She dreamt that the Neverland had come too near and that a strange boy had broken through from it. He did not alarm her, for she thought she had seen him

before in the faces of many women who have no children. Perhaps he is to be found in the faces of some mothers also. But in her dream he had rent the film that obscures the

Neverland, and she saw Wendy and John and Michael peeping through the gap. The dream by itself would have been a trifle, but while she was dreaming the window of nursery blew open, and a boy did drop on the floor. He was accompanied by a strange light, no bigger than your fist, which darted about the room like a living thing; and I think it must have been this light that wakened Mrs. Darling. She started up with a cry, and saw the boy, and somehow she knew at once that he was Peter Pan. If you or I or Wendy had been there we should have seen that he was very like Mrs. Darling's kiss. He was a lovely boy, clad in skeleton leaves and the juices that ooze out of trees; but the most entrancing thing about him was that he had all his first teeth. When he saw she was a grown-up, he gnashed the little pearls at her. CHAPTER II *The Shadow* Mrs. Darling screamed, and, as if in answer to a bell, the door opened, and Nana entered, returned from her evening out. She growled and sprang at the boy, who leapt lightly through the window. Again Mrs. Darling screamed, this time in distress for him, for she thought he was killed, and she ran down into the street to look for his little body, but it was not there; and she looked up, and in the black night she could see nothing but what she thought was a shooting star. She returned to the nursery, and found Nana with something in her mouth, which proved to be the boy's shadow. As he leapt at the window Nana had closed it quickly, too late to catch him, but his shadow had not had time to get out; slam went the window and snapped it off. You may be sure Mrs. Darling examined the shadow carefully, but it was quite the ordinary kind. Nana had no doubt of what was the best thing to do with this shadow. She hung it out at the window, meaning "He is sure to come back for it; let us put it where he can get it easily without disturbing the children." But unfortunately Mrs. Darling could not leave it hanging out at the window; it looked so like the washing and lowered the whole tone of the house. She thought of showing it to Mr. Darling, but he was totting up winter greatcoats for John and Michael, with a wet towel round his head to keep his brain clear, and it seemed a shame to trouble him; besides, she knew exactly what he would say: "It all comes of having a dog for a nurse." She decided to roll the shadow up and put it away carefully in a drawer, until a fitting opportunity came for telling her husband. Ah me! The opportunity came a week later, on that never-to-be-forgotten Friday. Of course it was a Friday. "I ought to have been specially careful on a Friday," she used to say afterwards to her husband, while perhaps Nana was on the other side of her, holding her hand. "No, no," Mr. Darling always said, "I am responsible for it all. I, George Darling, did it. *Mea culpa, mea culpa.*" He had had a classical education. They sat thus night after night recalling that fatal Friday, till every detail of it was stamped on their brains and came through on the other side like the faces on a bad coinage. "If only I had not accepted that invitation to dine at 27," Mrs. Darling said. "If only I had not poured my medicine into Nana's bowl," said Mr. Darling. "If only I had pretended to like the medicine," was what Nana's wet eyes said. "My liking for parties, George." "My fatal gift of humour, dearest." "My touchiness about trifles, dear master and mistress." Then one or more of them would break down altogether; Nana at the thought, "It's true, it's true, they ought not to have had a dog for a nurse." Many a time it was Mr. Darling who put the handkerchief to Nana's eyes. "That fiend!" Mr. Darling would cry, and Nana's bark was the echo of it, but Mrs. Darling never upbraided Peter; there was something in the right-hand corner of her mouth that wanted her not to call Peter names. They would sit there in the empty nursery, recalling fondly every smallest detail of that dreadful evening. It had begun so uneventfully, so precisely like a hundred other evenings, with Nana putting on the water for Michael's bath and carrying him to it on her back. "I won't go to bed," he had shouted, like one who still believed that he had the last word on the subject, "I won't, I won't. Nana, it isn't six o'clock yet. Oh dear,

oh dear, I shan't love you any more, Nana. I tell you I won't be bathed, I won't, I won't!" Then Mrs. Darling had come in, wearing her white evening-gown. She had dressed

early because Wendy so loved to see her in her evening-gown, with the necklace George had given her. She was wearing Wendy's bracelet on her arm; she had asked for the

loan of it. Wendy so loved to lend her bracelet to her mother. She had found her two older children playing at being herself and father on the occasion of Wendy's birth, and

John was saying: "I am happy to inform you, Mrs. Darling, that you are now a mother," in just such a tone as Mr. Darling himself may have used on the real occasion. Wendy

had danced with joy, just as the real Mrs. Darling must have done. Then John was born, with the extra pomp that he conceived due to the birth of a male, and Michael came

from his bath to ask to be born also, but John said brutally that they did not want any more. Michael had nearly cried. "Nobody wants me," he said, and of course the lady

in evening-dress could not stand that. "I do," she said, "I so want a third child." "Boy or girl?" asked Michael, not too hopefully. "Boy." Then he had leapt into her arms.

Such a little thing for Mr. and Mrs. Darling and Nana to recall now, but not so little if that was to be Michael's last night in the nursery. They go on with their recollections.

"It was then that I rushed in like a tornado, wasn't it?" Mr. Darling would say, scorning himself; and indeed he had been like a tornado. Perhaps there was some excuse for

him. He, too, had been dressing for the party, and all had gone well with him until he came to his tie. It is an astounding thing to have to tell, but this man, though he knew

about stocks and shares, had no real mastery of his tie. Sometimes the thing yielded to him without a contest, but there were occasions when it would have been better for

the house if he had swallowed his pride and used a made-up tie. This was such an occasion. He came rushing into the nursery with the crumpled little brute of a tie in his

hand. "Why, what is the matter, father dear?" "Matter!" he yelled; he really yelled. "This tie, it will not tie." He became dangerously sarcastic. "Not round my neck! Round

the bed-post! Oh yes, twenty times have I made it up round the bed-post, but round my neck, no! Oh dear no! begs to be excused!" He thought Mrs. Darling was not

sufficiently impressed, and he went on sternly, "I warn you of this, mother, that unless this tie is round my neck we don't go out to dinner to-night, and if I don't go out to

dinner to-night, I never go to the office again, and if I don't go to the office again, you and I starve, and our children will be flung into the streets." Even then Mrs. Darling

was placid. "Let me try, dear," she said, and indeed that was what he had come to ask her to do, and with her nice cool hands she tied his tie for him, while the children stood

around to see their fate decided. Some men would have resented her being able to do it so easily, but Mr. Darling was far too fine a nature for that; he thanked her carelessly,

at once forgot his rage, and in another moment was dancing round the room with Michael on his back. "How wildly we romped!" says Mrs. Darling now, recalling it. "Our

last romp!" Mr. Darling groaned. "O George, do you remember Michael suddenly said to me, "How did you get to know me, mother?" "I remember!" "They were rather

sweet, don't you think, George?" "And they were ours, ours! and now they are gone." The romp had ended with the appearance of Nana, and most unluckily Mr. Darling

collided against her, covering his trousers with hairs. They were not only new trousers, but they were the first he had ever had with braid on them, and he had to bite his to prevent the tears coming. Of course Mrs. Darling brushed him, but he began to talk again about its being a mistake to have a dog for a nurse. "George, Nana is a treasure."

"No doubt, but I have an uneasy feeling at times that she looks upon the children as puppies." "Oh no, dear one, I feel sure she knows they have souls." "I wonder," Mr.

Darling said thoughtfully, "I wonder." It was an opportunity, his wife felt, for telling him about the boy. At first he pooh-poohed the story, but he became thoughtful when

she showed him the shadow. "It is nobody I know," he said, examining it carefully, "but he does look a scoundrel." "We were still discussing it, you remember," says Mr.

Darling, "when Nana came in with Michael's medicine. You will never carry the bottle in your mouth again, Nana, and it is all my fault. Strong man though he was, there is

no doubt that he had behaved rather foolishly over the medicine. If he had a weakness, it was for thinking that all his life he had taken medicine boldly; and so now, when

Michael dodged the spoon in Nana's mouth, he had said reprovingly, "Be a man, Michael." "Won't; won't," Michael cried naughtily. Mrs. Darling left the room to get a

chocolate for him, and Mr. Darling thought this showed want of firmness. "Mother, don't pamper him," he called after her. "Michael, when I was your age I took medicine

without a murmur. I said "Thank you, kind parents, for giving me bottles to make me well." He really thought this was true, and Wendy, who was now in her night-gown,

believed it also, and she said, to encourage Michael, "That medicine you sometimes take, father, is much nastier, isn't it?" "Ever so much nastier," Mr. Darling said bravely,

"and I would take it now as an example to you, Michael, if I hadn't lost the bottle. **He had not exactly lost it; he had climbed in the dead of night to the top of the wardrobe**

and hidden it there. What he did not know was that the faithful Liza had found it, and put it back on his wash-stand. "I know where it is, father," Wendy cried, always glad

to be of service. "I'll bring it," and she was off before he could stop her. Immediately his spirits sank in the strangest way. "John," he said, shuddering, "it's most beastly

stuff. It's that nasty, sticky, sweet kind." "It will soon be over, father," John said cheerily, and then in rushed Wendy with the medicine in a glass. "I have been as quick as I

could," she panted. "You have been wonderfully quick," her father retorted, with a vindictive politeness that was quite thrown away upon her. "Michael first," he said

doggedly. "Father first," said Michael, who was of a suspicious nature. "I shall be sick, you know," Mr. Darling said threateningly. "Come on, father," said John. "Hold your

tongue, John," his father rapped out. Wendy was quite puzzled. "I thought you took it quite easily, father." "That is not the point," he retorted. "The point is, that there is

more in my glass than in Michael's spoon." His proud heart was nearly bursting. "And it isn't fair; I would say it though it were with my last breath; it isn't fair." "Father, I

am waiting," said Michael coldly. "It's all very well to say you are waiting; so am I waiting." "Father's a cowardy custard." "So are you a cowardy custard." "I'm not

frightened." "Neither am I frightened." "Well, then, take it." "Well, then, you take it." Wendy had a splendid idea. "Why not both take it at the same time?" "Certainly,"

said Mr. Darling. "Are you ready, Michael?" Wendy gave the words, one, two, three, and Michael took his medicine, but Mr. Darling slipped his behind his back. There was

a yell of rage from Michael, and "O father!" Wendy exclaimed. "What do you mean by 'O father?'" Mr. Darling demanded. "Stop that row, Michael. I meant to take mine,

but I—I missed it." It was dreadful the way all the three were looking at him, just as if they did not admire him. "Look here, all of you," he said entreatingly, as soon as Nana had gone into the bathroom, "I have just thought of a splendid joke. I shall pour my medicine into Nana's bowl, and she will drink it, thinking it is milk!" It was the colour

of milk; but the children did not have their father's sense of humour, and they looked at him reproachfully as he poured the medicine into Nana's bowl. "What fun," he said

doubtfully, and they did not dare expose him when Mrs. Darling and Nana returned. "Nana, good dog," he said, patting her, "I have put a little milk into your bowl, Nana."

Nana wagged her tail, ran to the medicine, and began lapping it. Then she gave Mr. Darling such a look, not an angry look: she showed him the great red tear that makes us

so sorry for noble dogs, and crept into her kennel. Mr. Darling was frightfully ashamed of himself, but he would not give in. In a horrid silence Mrs. Darling smelt the bowl.

"O George," she said, "it's your medicine!" "It was only a joke," he roared, while she comforted her boys, and Wendy hugged Nana. "Much good," he said bitterly, "my

wearing myself to the bone trying to be funny in this house." And still Wendy hugged Nana. "That's right," he shouted. "Coddle her! Nobody coddles me. Oh dear no! I

am only the breadwinner, why should I be coddled, why, why, why!" "George," Mrs. Darling entreated him, "not so loud; the servants will hear you." Somehow they had

got into the way of calling Liza the servants. "Let them," he answered recklessly. "Bring in the whole world. But I refuse to allow that dog to lord it in my nursery for an

hour longer." The children wept, and Nana ran to him beseechingly, but he waved her back. He felt he was a strong man again. "In vain, in vain," he cried; "the proper place

for you is the yard, and there you go to be tied up this instant." "George, George," Mrs. Darling whispered, "remember what I told you about that boy." Alas, he would not

listen. He was determined to show who was master in that house, and when commands would not draw Nana from the kennel, he lured her out of it with honeyed words,

and seizing her roughly, dragged her from the nursery. He was ashamed of himself, and yet he did it. It was all owing to his too affectionate nature, which craved for

admiration. When he had tied her up in the back-yard, the wretched father went and sat in the passage, with his knuckles to his eyes. In the meantime Mrs. Darling had put

the children to bed in unwonted silence and lit their night-lights. They could hear Nana barking, and John whimpered, "It is because he is chaining her up in the yard," but

Wendy was wiser. "That is not Nana's unhappy bark," she said, little guessing what was about to happen; "that is her bark when she smells danger." Danger! "Are you sure,

Wendy?" "Oh yes." Mrs. Darling quivered and went to the window. It was securely fastened. She looked out, and the night was peppered with stars. They were crowding

round the house, as if curious to see what was to take place there, but she did not notice this, nor that one or two of the smaller ones winked at her. Yet a nameless fear clutched

at her heart and made her cry, "Oh, how I wish that I wasn't going to a party to-night!" Even Michael, already half asleep, knew that she was perturbed, and he asked, "Can

anything harm us, mother, after the night-lights are lit?" "Nothing, precious," she said; "they are the eyes a mother leaves behind her to guard her children." She went from

bed to bed singing enchantments over them, and little Michael flung his arms round her. "Mother," he cried, "I'm glad of you." They were the last words she was to hear

from him for a long time. No. 27 was only a few yards distant, but there had been a slight fall of snow, and Father and Mother Darling picked their way over it deftly not to

soil their shoes. They were already the only persons in the street, and all the stars were watching them. Stars are beautiful, but they may not take an active part in anything, they must just look on for ever. It is a punishment put on them for something they did so long ago that no star now knows what it was. So the older ones have become glassy-eyed and seldom speak (winking is the star language), but the little ones still wonder. They are not really friendly to Peter, who has a mischievous way of stealing up behind them and trying to blow them out; but they are so fond of fun that they were on his side to-night, and anxious to get the grown-ups out of the way. So as soon as the door of 27 closed on Mr. and Mrs. Darling there was a commotion in the firmament, and the smallest of all the stars in the Milky Way screamed out: "Now, Peter!" CHAPTER III

Come Away, Come Away! For a moment after Mr. and Mrs. Darling left the house the night-lights by the beds of the three children continued to burn clearly. They were awfully nice little night-lights, and one cannot help wishing that they could have kept awake to see Peter; but Wendy's light blinked and gave such a yawn that the other two yawned also, and before they could close their mouths all the three went out. There was another light in the room now, a thousand times brighter than the night-lights, and in the time we have taken to say this, it has been in all the drawers in the nursery, looking for Peter's shadow, rummaged the wardrobe and turned every pocket inside out. It was not really a light; it made this light by flashing about so quickly, but when it came to rest for a second you saw it was a fairy, no longer than your hand, but still growing. It was a girl called Tinker Bell exquisitely gowned in a skeleton leaf, cut low and square, through which her figure could be seen to the best advantage. She was slightly inclined to *embonpoint*. A moment after the fairy's entrance the window was blown open by the breathing of the little stars, and Peter dropped in. He had carried Tinker Bell part of the way, and his hand was still messy with the fairy dust. "Tinker Bell," he called softly, after making sure that the children were asleep, "Tink, where are you?" She was in a jug for the moment, and liking it extremely; she had never been in a jug before. "Oh, do come out of that jug, and tell me, do you know where they put my shadow?" The loveliest tinkle as of golden bells answered him. It is the fairy language. You ordinary children can never hear it, but if you were to hear it you would know that you had heard it once before. Tink said that the shadow was in the big box. She meant the chest of drawers, and Peter jumped at the drawers, scattering their contents to the floor with both hands, as kings toss ha'pence to the crowd. In a moment he had recovered his shadow, and in his delight he forgot that he had shut Tinker Bell up in the drawer. If he thought at all, but I don't believe he ever thought, it was that he and his shadow, when brought near each other, would join like drops of water; and when they did not he was appalled. He tried to stick it on with soap from the bathroom, but that also failed. A shudder passed through Peter, and he sat on the floor and cried. His sobs woke Wendy, and she sat up in bed. She was not alarmed to see a stranger crying on the nursery floor; she was only pleasantly interested. "Boy," she said courteously, "why are you crying?" Peter could be exceedingly polite also, having learned the grand manner at fairy ceremonies, and he rose and bowed to her beautifully. She was much pleased, and bowed beautifully to him from the bed. "What's your name?" he asked. "Wendy Moira Angela Darling," she replied with some satisfaction. "What is your name?" "Peter Pan." She was already sure that he must be Peter, but it did seem a comparatively short name. "Is that all?" "Yes," he said rather sharply. He felt for the first time that it was a shortish name. "I'm so sorry," said Wendy Moira Angela. "It doesn't matter," Peter gulped. She asked where he lived. "Second to the right," said Peter, "and then straight on till morning." "What a funny address!" Peter had a sinking. For the first time he felt that perhaps it was a funny address. "No, it isn't," he said. "I mean," Wendy said nicely, remembering that she was hostess, "is that what they put on the letters?" He wished she had not mentioned letters. "Don't get any letters," he said contemptuously. "But your mother gets letters?" "Don't have a mother," he said. Not only had he no mother, but he had not the slightest desire to have one. He thought them very overrated persons. Wendy, however, felt at once that she was in the presence of a tragedy. "O Peter, no wonder you were crying," she said, and got out of bed and ran to him. "I wasn't crying about mothers," he said rather indignantly. "I was crying because I can't get my shadow to stick on. Besides, I wasn't crying." "It has come off?" "Yes." Then Wendy saw the shadow on the floor, looking so draggled, and she was frightfully sorry for Peter. "How awful!" she said, but she could not help smiling when she saw that he had been trying to stick it on with soap. How exactly like a boy! Fortunately she knew at once what to do. "It must be sewn on," she said, just a little patronisingly. "What's sewn?" he asked. "You're dreadfully ignorant." "No, I'm not." But she was exulting in his ignorance. "I shall sew it on for you, my little man," she said, though he was as tall as herself; and she got out her housewife, and sewed the shadow on to Peter's foot. "I daresay it will hurt a little," she warned him. **"Oh, I shan't cry," said Peter, who was already of opinion that he had never cried in his life.** And he clenched his teeth and did not cry; and soon his shadow was behaving properly, though still a little creased.

"Perhaps I should have ironed it," Wendy said thoughtfully; but Peter, boylike, was indifferent to appearances, and he was now jumping about in the wildest glee. Alas, he had already forgotten that he owed his bliss to Wendy. He thought he had attached the shadow himself. "How clever I am," he crowed rapturously, "oh, the cleverness of me!" It is humiliating to have to confess that this conceit of Peter was one of his most fascinating qualities. To put it with brutal frankness, there never was a cockier boy. But for the moment Wendy was shocked. "You conceit," she exclaimed, with frightful sarcasm; "of course I did nothing!" "You did a little," Peter said carelessly, and continued to dance. "A little!" she replied with hauteur. "If I am no use I can at least withdraw;" and she sprang in the most dignified way into bed and covered her face with the blankets. To induce her to look up he pretended to be going away, and when this failed he sat on the end of the bed and tapped her gently with his foot. "Wendy," he said, "don't withdraw. I can't help crowing, Wendy, when I'm pleased with myself." Still she would not look up, though she was listening eagerly. "Wendy," he continued, in a voice that no woman has ever yet been able to resist, "Wendy, one girl is more use than twenty boys." Now Wendy was every inch a woman, though there were not very many inches, and she peeped out of the bed-clothes. "Do you really think so, Peter?" "Yes, I do." "I think it's perfectly sweet of you," she declared, "and I'll get up again," and she sat with him on the side of the bed. She also said she would give him a kiss if he liked, but Peter did not know what she meant, and he held out his hand expectantly. "Surely you know what a kiss is?" she asked, aghast. "I shall know when you give it to me," he replied stiffly; and not to hurt his feelings she gave him a thimble. "Now," said he, "shall I give you a kiss?" and she replied with a slight primness, "If you please." She made herself rather cheap by inclining her face toward him, but he merely dropped an acorn button into her hand, so she slowly returned her face to where it had been before, and said nicely that she would wear his kiss on the chain round her neck. It was lucky that she did put it on that chain, for it was afterwards to save her life. When people in our set are introduced, it is customary for them to ask each other's age, and so Wendy, who always liked to do the correct thing, asked Peter how old he was. It was not really a happy question to ask him; it was like an examination paper that asks grammar, when what you want to be asked is Kings of England. "I don't know," he replied uneasily, "but I am quite young." He really knew nothing about it; he had merely suspicions, but he said at a venture, "Wendy, I ran away the day I was born." Wendy was quite surprised, but interested; and she indicated in the charming drawing-room manner, by a touch on her night-gown, that he could sit nearer her. "It was because I heard father and mother," he explained in a low voice, "talking about what I was to be when I became a man." He was extraordinarily agitated now. "I don't want ever to be a man," he said with passion. "I want always to be a little boy and to have fun. So I ran away to Kensington Gardens and lived a long, long time among the fairies." She gave him a look of the most intense admiration, and he thought it was because he had run away, but it was really because he knew fairies. Wendy had lived such a home life that to know fairies struck her as quite delightful. She poured out questions about them, to his surprise, for they were rather a nuisance to him, getting in his way and so on, and indeed he sometimes had to give them a hiding. Still, he liked them on the whole, and he told her about the beginning of fairies. "You see, Wendy, when the first baby laughed for the first time, its laugh broke into a thousand pieces, and they all went skipping about, and that was the beginning of fairies." Tedious talk this, but being a stay-at-home she liked it. "And so," he went on good-naturedly, "there ought to be one fairy for every boy and girl." "Ought to be? Isn't there?" "No. You see children know such a lot now, they soon don't believe in fairies, and every time a child says, 'I don't believe in fairies,' there is a fairy somewhere that falls down dead." Really, he thought they had now talked enough about fairies, and it struck him that Tinker Bell was keeping very quiet. "I can't think where she has gone to," he said, rising, and he called Tink by name. Wendy's heart went flutter with a sudden thrill. "Peter," she cried, clutching him, "you don't mean to tell me that there is a fairy in this room!" "She was here just now," he said a little impatiently. "You don't hear her, do you?" and they both listened. "The only sound I hear," said Wendy, "is like a tinkle of bells." "Well, that's Tink, that's the fairy language. I think I hear her too." The sound came from the chest of drawers, and Peter made a merry face. No one could ever look quite so merry as Peter, and the loveliest of gurgles was his laugh. He had his first laugh still. "Wendy," he whispered gleefully, "I do believe I shut her up in the drawer!" He let poor Tink out of the drawer, and she flew about the nursery screaming with fury. "You shouldn't say such things," Peter retorted. "Of course I'm very sorry, but how could I know you were in the drawer?" Wendy was not listening to him. "O Peter," she cried, "if she would only stand still and let me see her!" "They hardly ever stand still," he said, but for one moment Wendy saw the romantic figure come to rest on the cuckoo clock. "O the lovely!" she cried, though Tink's face was still distorted with passion. "Tink," said Peter amiably, "this lady says she wishes you were her fairy." Tinker Bell answered insolently. "What does she say, Peter?" He had to translate. "She is not very polite. She says you are a great ugly girl, and that she is my fairy." He tried to argue with Tink. "You know you can't be my fairy, Tink, because I am a gentleman and you are a lady." To this Tink replied in these words, "You silly ass," and disappeared into the bathroom. "She is quite a common fairy," Peter explained apologetically, "she is called Tinker Bell because she mends the pots and kettles." They were together in the armchair by this time, and Wendy plied

him with more questions. "If you don't live in Kensington Gardens now—" "Sometimes I do still." "But where do you live mostly now?" "With the lost boys." "Who are

they?" "They are the children who fall out of their perambulators when the nurse is looking the other way. If they are not claimed in seven days they are sent far away to

the Neverland to defray expenses. I'm captain." "What fun it must be!" "Yes," said cunning Peter, "but we are rather lonely. You see we have no female companionship."

"Are none of the others girls?" "Oh no; girls, you know, are much too clever to fall out of their prams." This flattered Wendy immensely. "I think," she said, "it is perfectly

lovely the way you talk about girls; John there just despises us." For reply Peter rose and kicked John out of bed, blankets and all; one kick. This seemed to Wendy rather

forward for a first meeting, and she told him with spirit that he was not captain in her house. However, John continued to sleep so placidly on the floor that she allowed him

to remain there. "And I know you meant to be kind," she said, relenting, "so you may give me a kiss." For the moment she had forgotten his ignorance about kisses. "I thought

you would want it back," he said a little bitterly, and offered to return her the thimble. "Oh dear," said the nice Wendy, "I don't mean a kiss, I mean a thimble." "What's

that?" "It's like this." She kissed him. "Funny!" said Peter gravely. "Now shall I give you a thimble?" "If you wish to," said Wendy, keeping her head erect this time. Peter

thimbled her, and almost immediately she screeched. "What is it, Wendy?" "It was exactly as if some one were pulling my hair." "That must have been Tink. I never knew

her so naughty before." And indeed Tink was darting about again, using offensive language. "She says she will do that to you, Wendy, every time I give you a thimble." "But

why?" "Why, Tink?" Again Tink replied, "You silly ass." Peter could not understand why, but Wendy understood; and she was just slightly disappointed when he admitted

that he came to the nursery window not to see her but to listen to stories. "You see I don't know any stories. None of the lost boys know any stories." "How perfectly awful,"

Wendy said. "Do you know," Peter asked, "why swallows build in the eaves of houses? It is to listen to the stories. O Wendy, your mother was telling you such a lovely

story." "Which story was it?" "About the prince who couldn't find the lady who wore the glass slipper." "Peter," said Wendy excitedly, "that was Cinderella, and he found

her, and they lived happy ever after." Peter was so glad that he rose from the floor, where they had been sitting, and hurried to the window. "Where are you going?" she cried

with misgiving. "To tell the other boys." "Don't go, Peter," she entreated, "I know such lots of stories." Those were her precise words, so there can be no denying that it

was she who first tempted him. He came back, and there was a greedy look in his eyes now which ought to have alarmed her, but did not. "Oh, the stories I could tell to the

boys!" she cried, and then Peter gripped her and began to draw her toward the window. "Let me go!" she ordered him. "Wendy, do come with me and tell the other boys."

Of course she was very pleased to be asked, but she said, "Oh dear, I can't. Think of mummy! Besides, I can't fly." "I'll teach you." "Oh, how lovely to fly." "I'll teach you

how to jump on the wind's back, and then away we go." "Oo!" she exclaimed rapturously. "Wendy, Wendy, when you are sleeping in your silly bed you might be flying about

with me saying funny things to the stars." "Oo!" "And, Wendy, there are mermaids." "Mermaids! With tails?" "Such long tails." "Oh," cried Wendy, "to see a mermaid!"

He had become frightfully cunning. "Wendy," he said, "how we should all respect you." She was wriggling her body in distress. It was quite as if she were trying to remain on the nursery floor. But he had no pity for her. "Wendy," he said, the sly one, "you could tuck us in at night." "Oo!" "None of us has ever been tucked in at night." "Oo," and her arms went out to him. "And you could darn our clothes, and make pockets for us. None of us has any pockets." How could she resist. "Of course it's awfully fascinating!" she cried. "Peter, would you teach John and Michael to fly too?" "If you like," he said indifferently, and she ran to John and Michael and shook them. "Wake up," she cried, "Peter Pan has come and he is to teach us to fly." John rubbed his eyes. "Then I shall get up," he said. Of course he was on the floor already. "Hallo," he said, "I am up!" Michael was up by this time also, looking as sharp as a knife with six blades and a saw, but Peter suddenly signed silence. Their faces assumed the awful craftiness of children listening for sounds from the grown-up world. All was as still as salt. Then everything was right. No, stop! Everything was wrong. Nana, who had been barking distressfully all the evening, was quiet now. It was her silence they had heard! "Out with the light! Hide! Quick!" cried John, taking command for the only time throughout the whole adventure. And thus when Liza entered, holding Nana, the nursery seemed quite its old self, very dark; and you could have sworn you heard its three wicked inmates breathing angelically as they slept. They were really doing it artfully from behind the window curtains. Liza was in a bad temper, for she was mixing the Christmas puddings in the kitchen, and had been drawn away from them, with a raisin still on her cheek, by Nana's absurd suspicions. She thought the best way of getting a little quiet was to take Nana to the nursery for a moment, but in custody of course. "There, you suspicious brute," she said, not sorry that Nana was in disgrace. "They are perfectly safe, aren't they? Every one of the little angels sound asleep in bed. Listen to their gentle breathing." Here Michael, encouraged by his success, breathed so loudly that they were nearly detected. Nana knew that kind of breathing, and she tried to drag herself out of Liza's clutches. But Liza was dense. "No more of it, Nana," she said sternly, pulling her out of the room. "I warn you if you bark again I shall go straight for master and missus and bring them home from the party, and then, oh, won't master whip you, just." She tied the unhappy dog up again, but do you think Nana ceased to bark? Bring master and missus home from the party! Why, that was just what she wanted. Do you think she cared whether she was whipped so long as her charges were safe? Unfortunately Liza returned to her puddings, and Nana, seeing that no help would come from her, strained and strained at the chain until at last she broke it. In another moment she had burst into the dining-room of 27 and flung up her paws to heaven, her most expressive way of making a communication. Mr. and Mrs. Darling knew at once that something terrible was happening in their nursery, and without a good-bye to their hostess they rushed into the street. But it was now ten minutes since three scoundrels had been breathing behind the curtains; and Peter Pan can do a great deal in ten minutes. We now return to the nursery. "It's all right," John announced, emerging from his hiding-place. "I say, Peter, can you really fly?" Instead of troubling to answer him Peter flew round the room, taking the mantelpiece on the way. "How topping!" said John and Michael. "How sweet!" cried Wendy. "Yes, I'm sweet, oh, I am sweet!" said Peter, forgetting his manners again. It looked delightfully easy, and they tried it first from the floor and then from the beds, but they always went down instead of up. "I say, how do you do it?" asked John, rubbing his knee. He was quite a practical boy. **"You just think lovely wonderful thoughts,"** Peter explained, **"and they lift you up in the air."** He

showed them again. "You're so nippy at it," John said; "couldn't you do it very slowly once?" Peter did it both slowly and quickly. "I've got it now, Wendy!" cried John, but

soon he found he had not. Not one of them could fly an inch, though even Michael was in words of two syllables, and Peter did not know A from Z. Of course Peter had

been trifling with them, for no one can fly unless the fairy dust has been blown on him. Fortunately, as we have mentioned, one of his hands was messy with it, and he blew

some on each of them, with the most superb results. "Now just wriggle your shoulders this way," he said, "and let go." They were all on their beds, and gallant Michael let

go first. He did not quite mean to let go, but he did it, and immediately he was borne across the room. "I flewed!" he screamed while still in mid-air. John let go and met

Wendy near the bathroom. "Oh, lovely!" "Oh, ripping!" "Look at me!" "Look at me!" "Look at me!" They were not nearly so elegant as Peter, they could not help kicking

a little, but their heads were bobbing against the ceiling, and there is almost nothing so delicious as that. Peter gave Wendy a hand at first, but had to desist, Tink was so

indignant. Up and down they went, and round and round. Heavenly was Wendy's word. "I say," cried John, "why shouldn't we all go out!" Of course it was to this that

Peter had been luring them. Michael was ready: he wanted to see how long it took him to do a billion miles. But Wendy hesitated. "Mermaids!" said Peter again. "Oo!" "An

there are pirates." "Pirates," cried John, seizing his Sunday hat, "let us go at once." It was just at this moment that Mr. and Mrs. Darling hurried with Nana out of 27. The

ran into the middle of the street to look up at the nursery window; and, yes, it was still shut, but the room was ablaze with light, and most heart-gripping sight of all, the

could see in shadow on the curtain three little figures in night attire circling round and round, not on the floor but in the air. Not three figures, four! In a tremble they opene

the street door. Mr. Darling would have rushed upstairs, but Mrs. Darling signed to him to go softly. She even tried to make her heart go softly. Will they reach the nurser

in time? If so, how delightful for them, and we shall all breathe a sigh of relief, but there will be no story. On the other hand, if they are not in time, I solemnly promise th

it will all come right in the end. They would have reached the nursery in time had it not been that the little stars were watching them. Once again the stars blew the windo

open, and that smallest star of all called out: "Cave, Peter!" Then Peter knew that there was not a moment to lose. "Come," he cried imperiously, and soared out at once in

the night, followed by John and Michael and Wendy. Mr. and Mrs. Darling and Nana rushed into the nursery too late. The birds were flown. CHAPTER IV *The Flig*

Second to the right, and straight on till morning." That, Peter had told Wendy, was the way to the Neverland; but even birds, carrying maps and consulting them at wind

corners, could not have sighted it with these instructions. Peter, you see, just said anything that came into his head. At first his companions trusted him implicitly, and so gre

were the delights of flying that they wasted time circling round church spires or any other tall objects on the way that took their fancy. John and Michael raced, Micha

getting a start. They recalled with contempt that not so long ago they had thought themselves fine fellows for being able to fly round a room. Not so long ago. But how lo

ago? They were flying over the sea before this thought began to disturb Wendy seriously. John thought it was their second sea and their third night. Sometimes it was da and sometimes light, and now they were very cold and again too warm. Did they really feel hungry at times, or were they merely pretending, because Peter had such a jolly new way of feeding them? His way was to pursue birds who had food in their mouths suitable for humans and snatch it from them; then the birds would follow and snatch it back; and they would all go chasing each other gaily for miles, parting at last with mutual expressions of good-will. But Wendy noticed with gentle concern that Peter did not seem to know that this was rather an odd way of getting your bread and butter, nor even that there are other ways. Certainly they did not pretend to be sleepy, they were sleepy; and that was a danger, for the moment they popped off, down they fell. The awful thing was that Peter thought this funny. "There he goes again!" he would cry gleefully, as Michael suddenly dropped like a stone. "Save him, save him!" cried Wendy, looking with horror at the cruel sea far below. Eventually Peter would dive through the air, and catch Michael just before he could strike the sea, and it was lovely the way he did it; but he always waited till the last moment, and you felt it was his cleverness that interested him and not the saving of human life. Also he was fond of variety, and the sport that engrossed him one moment would suddenly cease to engage him, so there was always the possibility that the next time you fell he would let you go. He could sleep in the air without falling, by merely lying on his back and floating, but this was, partly at least, because he was so light that if you got behind him and blew he went faster. "Do be more polite to him," Wendy whispered to John, when they were playing "Follow my Leader." "Then tell him to stop showing off," said John. When playing Follow my Leader, Peter would fly close to the water and touch each shark's tail in passing, just as in the street you may run your finger along an iron railing. They could not follow him in this with much success, so perhaps it was rather like showing off, especially as he kept looking behind to see how many tails they missed. "You must be nice to him," Wendy impressed on her brothers. "What could we do if he were to leave us?" "We could go back," Michael said. "How could we ever find our way back without him?" "Well, then, we could go on," said John. "That is the awful thing, John. We should have to go on, for we don't know how to stop." This was true; Peter had forgotten to show them how to stop. John said that if the worst came to the worst, all they had to do was to go straight on, for the world was round, and so in time they must come back to their own window. "And who is to get food for us, John?" "I nipped a bit out of that eagle's mouth pretty neatly, Wendy." "After the twentieth try," Wendy reminded him. "And even though we became good at picking up food, see how we bump against clouds and things if he is not near to give us a hand." Indeed they were constantly bumping. They could now fly strongly, though they still kicked far too much; but if they saw a cloud in front of them, the more they tried to avoid it, the more certainly did they bump into it. If Nana had been with them, she would have had a bandage round Michael's forehead by this time. Peter was not with them for the moment, and they felt rather lonely up there by themselves. He could go so much faster than they that he would suddenly shoot out of sight, to have some adventure in which they had no share. He would come down laughing over something fearfully funny he had been saying to a star, but he had already forgotten what it was, or he would come up with mermaid scales still sticking to him, and yet not be able to say for certain what had been happening. It was really rather irritating to children who had never seen a mermaid. "And if he forgets them, so quickly," Wendy argued, "how can we expect that he will go on remembering us?" Indeed, sometimes when he returned he did not remember them, at least not well. Wendy was sure of it. She saw recognition come into his eyes as he was

about to pass them the time of day and go on; once even she had to tell him her name. "I'm Wendy," she said agitatedly. He was very sorry. "I say, Wendy," he whispered to

her, "always if you see me forgetting you, just keep on saying 'I'm Wendy,' and then I'll remember." Of course this was rather unsatisfactory. However, to make amends he

showed them how to lie out flat on a strong wind that was going their way, and this was such a pleasant change that they tried it several times and found they could sleep thus

with security. Indeed they would have slept longer, but Peter tired quickly of sleeping, and soon he would cry in his captain voice, "We get off here." So with occasional tiffs,

but on the whole rollicking, they drew near the Neverland; for after many moons they did reach it, and, what is more, they had been going pretty straight all the time, not

perhaps so much owing to the guidance of Peter or Tink as because the island was out looking for them. It is only thus that any one may sight those magic shores. "There it

is," said Peter calmly. "Where, where?" "Where all the arrows are pointing." Indeed a million golden arrows were pointing out the island to the children, all directed by their

friend the sun, who wanted them to be sure of their way before leaving them for the night. Wendy and John and Michael stood on tiptoe in the air to get their first sight of

the island. Strange to say, they all recognised it at once, and until fear fell upon them they hailed it, not as something long dreamt of and seen at last, but as a familiar friend

to whom they were returning home for the holidays. "John, there's the lagoon!" "Wendy, look at the turtles burying their eggs in the sand." "I say, John, I see your flamingo

with the broken leg!" "Look, Michael, there's your cave!" "John, what's that in the brushwood?" "It's a wolf with her whelps. Wendy, I do believe that's your little whelp!"

"There's my boat, John, with her sides stove in!" "No, it isn't! Why, we burned your boat." "That's her, at any rate. I say, John, I see the smoke of the redskin camp!"

"Where? Show me, and I'll tell you by the way the smoke curls whether they are on the war-path." "There, just across the Mysterious River." "I see now. Yes, they are

on the war-path right enough." Peter was a little annoyed with them for knowing so much, but if he wanted to lord it over them his triumph was at hand, for have I not told you

that anon fear fell upon them? It came as the arrows went, leaving the island in gloom. In the old days at home the Neverland had always begun to look a little dark and

threatening by bedtime. Then unexplored patches arose in it and spread, black shadows moved about in them, the roar of the beasts of prey was quite different now, and,

above all, you lost the certainty that you would win. You were quite glad that the night-lights were in. You even liked Nana to say that this was just the mantelpiece over here,

and that the Neverland was all make-believe. Of course the Neverland had been make-believe in those days, but it was real now, and there were no night-lights, and it was

getting darker every moment, and where was Nana? They had been flying apart, but they huddled close to Peter now. His careless manner had gone at last, his eyes were

sparkling, and a tingle went through them every time they touched his body. They were now over the fearsome island, flying so low that sometimes a tree grazed their feet.

Nothing horrid was visible in the air, yet their progress had become slow and laboured, exactly as if they were pushing their way through hostile forces. Sometimes they

hung in the air until Peter had beaten on it with his fists. "They don't want us to land," he explained. "Who are they?" Wendy whispered, shuddering. But he could not would not say. Tinker Bell had been asleep on his shoulder, but now he wakened her and sent her on in front. Sometimes he poised himself in the air, listening intently, with his hand to his ear, and again he would stare down with eyes so bright that they seemed to bore two holes to earth. Having done these things, he went on again. His courage was almost appalling. "Would you like an adventure now," he said casually to John, "or would you like to have your tea first?" Wendy said "tea first" quickly, and Michael pressed her hand in gratitude, but the braver John hesitated. "What kind of adventure?" he asked cautiously. "There's a pirate asleep in the pampas just beneath us," Peter told him. "If you like, we'll go down and kill him." "I don't see him," John said after a long pause. "I do." "Suppose," John said a little huskily, "he were to wake up." Peter spoke indignantly. "You don't think I would kill him while he was sleeping! I would wake him first, and then kill him. That's the way I always do." "I say! Do you kill many?"

"Tons." John said "how ripping," but decided to have tea first. He asked if there were many pirates on the island just now, and Peter said he had never known so many. "Who is captain now?" "Hook," answered Peter; and his face became very stern as he said that hated word. "Jas. Hook?" "Ay." Then indeed Michael began to cry, and even John could speak in gulps only, for they knew Hook's reputation. "He was Blackbeard's bo'sun," John whispered huskily. "He is the worst of them all. He is the only man of whom Barbecue was afraid." "That's him," said Peter. "What is he like? Is he big?" "He is not so big as he was." "How do you mean?" "I cut off a bit of him." "You!" "Yes, me," said Peter sharply. "I wasn't meaning to be disrespectful." "Oh, all right." "But, I say, what bit?" "His right hand." "Then he can't fight now?" "Oh, can't he just!" "Left-hander?" "He has an iron hook instead of a right hand, and he claws with it." "Claws!" "I say, John," said Peter. "Yes." "Say, 'Ay, ay, sir.'" "Ay, ay, sir." "There is one thing," Peter continued, "that every boy who serves under me has to promise, and so must you." John paled. "It is this, if we meet Hook in open fight, you must leave him to me."

"I promise," John said loyally. For the moment they were feeling less eerie because Tink was flying with them, and in her light they could distinguish each other. Unfortunately she could not fly so slowly as they, and so she had to go round and round them in a circle in which they moved as in a halo. Wendy quite liked it, until Peter pointed out the drawback. "She tells me," he said, "that the pirates sighted us before the darkness came, and got Long Tom out." "The big gun?" "Yes. And of course they must see her light, and if they guess we are near it they are sure to let fly." "Wendy!" "John!" "Michael!" "Tell her to go away at once, Peter," the three cried simultaneously, but he refused. "She thinks we have lost the way," he replied stiffly, "and she is rather frightened. You don't think I would send her away all by herself when she is frightened!"

For a moment the circle of light was broken, and something gave Peter a loving little pinch. "Then tell her," Wendy begged, "to put out her light." "She can't put it out. That is about the only thing fairies can't do. It just goes out of itself when she falls asleep, same as the stars." "Then tell her to sleep at once," John almost ordered. "She can't sleep except when she's sleepy. It is the only other thing fairies can't do." "Seems to me," growled John, "these are the only two things worth doing." Here he got a pinch, but not a loving one. "If only one of us had a pocket," Peter said, "we could carry her in it." However, they had set off in such a hurry that there was not a pocket between the four of them. He had a happy idea. John's hat! Tink agreed to travel by hat if it was carried in the hand. John carried it, though she had hoped to be carried by Peter. Presently

Wendy took the hat, because John said it struck against his knee as he flew; and this, as we shall see, led to mischief, for Tinker Bell hated to be under an obligation to Wendy.

In the black topper the light was completely hidden, and they flew on in silence. It was the stillest silence they had ever known, broken once by a distant lapping, which Peter explained was the wild beasts drinking at the ford, and again by a rasping sound that might have been the branches of trees rubbing together, but he said it was the redskins sharpening their knives. Even these noises ceased. To Michael the loneliness was dreadful. "If only something would make a sound!" he cried. As if in answer to his request, the air was rent by the most tremendous crash he had ever heard. The pirates had fired Long Tom at them. The roar of it echoed through the mountains, and the echoes seemed to cry savagely, "Where are they, where are they, where are they?" Thus sharply did the terrified three learn the difference between an island of make-believe and the same island come true. When at last the heavens were steady again, John and Michael found themselves alone in the darkness. John was treading the air mechanically, and Michael without knowing how to float was floating. "Are you shot?" John whispered tremulously. "I haven't tried yet," Michael whispered back. We know now that no one had been hit. Peter, however, had been carried by the wind of the shot far out to sea, while Wendy was blown upwards with no companion but Tinker Bell. It would have been well for Wendy if at that moment she had dropped the hat. I don't know whether the idea came suddenly to Tink, or whether she had planned it on the way, but she at once popped out of the hat and began to lure Wendy to her destruction. Tink was not all bad: or, rather, she was all bad just now, but, on the other hand, sometimes she was all good. Fairies have to be one thing or the other, because being so small they unfortunately have room for one feeling only at a time. They are, however, allowed to change, only it must be a complete change. At present she was full of jealousy of Wendy. What she said in her lovely tinkle Wendy could not of course understand, and I believe some of it was bad words, but it sounded kind, and she flew back and forward, plainly meaning "Follow me, and all will be well." What else could poor Wendy do? She called to Peter and John and Michael, and got only mocking echoes in reply. She did not yet know that Tink hated her with the fierce hatred of a very woman. And so, bewildered, and now staggering in her flight, she followed Tink to her doom. CHAPTER V *The Island Come True* Feeling that Peter was on his way back, the Neverland had again woke into life. We ought to use the pluperfect and say wakened, but woke is better and was always used by Peter. In his absence things are usually quiet on the island. The fairies take an hour longer in the morning, the beasts attend to their young, the redskins feed heavily for six days and nights, and when pirates and lost boys meet they merely bite their thumbs at each other. But with the coming of Peter, who hates lethargy, they are all under way again: if you put your ear to the ground now, you would hear the whole island seething with life. On this evening the chief forces of the island were disposed as follows. The lost boys were out looking for Peter, the pirates were out looking for the lost boys, the redskins were out looking for the pirates, and the beasts were out looking for the redskins. They were going round and round the island, but they did not meet because all were going at the same rate. All wanted blood except the boys, who liked it as a rule, but to-night were out to greet their captain. The boys on the island vary, of course, in numbers, according as they get killed and so on; and when they seem to be growing up, which is against the rules, Peter thins them out; but at this time there were six of them, counting the twins as two. Let us pretend to lie here among the sugar-cane and watch them as they steal by in single file, each with his hand on his dagger.

They are forbidden by Peter to look in the least like him, and they wear the skins of bears slain by themselves, in which they are so round and furry that when they fall they

roll. They have therefore become very sure-footed. The first to pass is Tootles, not the least brave but the most unfortunate of all that gallant band. He had been in fewer

adventures than any of them because the big things constantly happened just when he had stepped round the corner; all would be quiet, he would take the opportunity of

going off to gather a few sticks for firewood, and then when he returned the others would be sweeping up the blood. This ill-luck had given a gentle melancholy to his

countenance, but instead of souring his nature had sweetened it, so that he was quite the humblest of the boys. Poor kind Tootles, there is danger in the air for you to-night.

Take care lest an adventure is now offered you, which, if accepted, will plunge you in deepest woe. Tootles, the fairy Tink who is bent on mischief this night is looking for

a tool, and she thinks you the most easily tricked of the boys. 'Ware Tinker Bell. Would that he could hear us, but we are not really on the island, and he passes by, biting his

knuckles. Next comes Nibs, the gay and debonair, followed by Slightly, who cuts whistles out of the trees and dances ecstatically to his own tunes. Slightly is the most

conceited of the boys. He thinks he remembers the days before he was lost, with their manners and customs, and this has given his nose an offensive tilt. Curly is fourth; he

is a pickle, and so often has he had to deliver up his person when Peter said sternly, "Stand forth the one who did this thing," that now at the command he stands forth

automatically whether he has done it or not. Last come the Twins, who cannot be described because we should be sure to be describing the wrong one. Peter never quite knew

what twins were, and his band were not allowed to know anything he did not know, so these two were always vague about themselves, and did their best to give satisfaction

by keeping close together in an apologetic sort of way. The boys vanish in the gloom, and after a pause, but not a long pause, for things go briskly on the island, come the

pirates on their track. We hear them before they are seen, and it is always the same dreadful song: "Avast belay, yo ho, heave to, A-pirating we go, And if we're parted by a

shot We're sure to meet below!" A more villainous-looking lot never hung in a row on Execution dock. Here, a little in advance, ever and again with his head to the ground

listening, his great arms bare, pieces of eight in his ears as ornaments, is the handsome Italian Cecco, who cut his name in letters of blood on the back of the governor of the

prison at Gao. That gigantic black behind him has had many names since he dropped the one with which dusky mothers still terrify their children on the banks of the Guadjo-

mo. Here is Bill Jukes, every inch of him tattooed, the same Bill Jukes who got six dozen on the *Walrus* from Flint before he would drop the bag of moidores; and Cookson,

said to be Black Murphy's brother (but this was never proved); and Gentleman Starkey, once an usher in a public school and still dainty in his ways of killing; and Skylights

(Morgan's Skylights); and the Irish bo'sun Smee, an oddly genial man who stabbed, so to speak, without offence, and was the only Nonconformist in Hook's crew; and

Noodler, whose hands were fixed on backwards; and Robt. Mullins and Alf Mason and many another ruffian long known and feared on the Spanish Main. In the midst of

them, the blackest and largest jewel in that dark setting, reclined James Hook, or as he wrote himself, Jas. Hook, of whom it is said he was the only man that the Sea-Cook feared. He lay at his ease in a rough chariot drawn and propelled by his men, and instead of a right hand he had the iron hook with which ever and anon he encouraged them

to increase their pace. As dogs this terrible man treated and addressed them, and as dogs they obeyed him. In person he was cadaverous and blackavized, and his hair was

dressed in long curls, which at a little distance looked like black candles, and gave a singularly threatening expression to his handsome countenance. His eyes were of the blue

of the forget-me-not, and of a profound melancholy, save when he was plunging his hook into you, at which time two red spots appeared in them and lit them up horribly.

In manner, something of the grand seigneur still clung to him, so that he even ripped you up with an air, and I have been told that he was a *raconteur* of repute. He was never

more sinister than when he was most polite, which is probably the truest test of breeding; and the elegance of his diction, even when he was swearing, no less than the

distinction of his demeanour, showed him one of a different caste from his crew. A man of indomitable courage, it was said of him that the only thing he shied at was the

sight of his own blood, which was thick and of an unusual colour. In dress he somewhat aped the attire associated with the name of Charles II, having heard it said in some

earlier period of his career that he bore a strange resemblance to the ill-fated Stuarts; and in his mouth he had a holder of his own contrivance which enabled him to smoke

two cigars at once. But doubtedly the grimmest part of him was his iron claw. Let us now kill a pirate, to show Hook's method. Skylights will do. As they pass, Skylights

lurches clumsily against him, ruffling his lace collar; the hook shoots forth, there is a tearing sound and one screech, then the body is kicked aside, and the pirates pass on. He

has not even taken the cigars from his mouth. Such is the terrible man against whom Peter Pan is pitted. Which will win? On the trail of the pirates, stealing noiselessly down

the war-path, which is not visible to inexperienced eyes, come the redskins, every one of them with his eyes peeled. They carry tomahawks and knives, and their naked bodies

gleam with paint and oil. Strung around them are scalps, of boys as well as of pirates, for these are the Piccaninny tribe, and not to be confused with the softer-hearted

Delawares or the Hurons. In the van, on all fours, is Great Big Little Panther, a brave of so many scalps that in his present position they somewhat impede his progress.

Bringing up the rear, the place of greatest danger, comes Tiger Lily, proudly erect, a princess in her own right. She is the most beautiful of dusky Dianas and the belle of the

Piccaninnies, coquettish, cold and amorous by turns; there is not a brave who would not have the wayward thing to wife, but she staves off the altar with a hatchet. Observe

how they pass over fallen twigs without making the slightest noise. The only sound to be heard is their somewhat heavy breathing. The fact is that they are all a little fat just

now after the heavy gorging, but in time they will work this off. For the moment, however, it constitutes their chief danger. The redskins disappear as they have come like

shadows, and soon their place is taken by the beasts, a great and motley procession: lions, tigers, bears, and the innumerable smaller savage things that flee from them, of

every kind of beast, and, more particularly, all the man-eaters, live cheek by jowl on the favoured island. Their tongues are hanging out, they are hungry to-night. When

they have passed, comes the last figure of all, a gigantic crocodile. We shall see for whom she is looking presently. The crocodile passes, but soon the boys appear again,

the procession must continue indefinitely until one of the parties stops or changes its pace. Then quickly they will be on top of each other. All are keeping a sharp look-out in front, but none suspects that the danger may be creeping up from behind. This shows how real the island was. The first to fall out of the moving circle was the boys. They flung themselves down on the sward, close to their underground home. "I do wish Peter would come back," every one of them said nervously, though in height and still more in breadth they were all larger than their captain. "I am the only one who is not afraid of the pirates," Slightly said, in the tone that prevented his being a general favourite; but perhaps some distant sound disturbed him, for he added hastily, "but I wish he would come back, and tell us whether he has heard anything more about Cinderella." They talked of Cinderella, and Tootles was confident that his mother must have been very like her. It was only in Peter's absence that they could speak of mothers, the subject being forbidden by him as silly. "All I remember about my mother," Nibs told them, "is that she often said to father, 'Oh, how I wish I had a cheque-book of my own.'" I don't know what a cheque-book is, but I should just love to give my mother one." While they talked they heard a distant sound. You or I, not being wild things of the woods, would have heard nothing, but they heard it, and it was the grim song: "Yo ho, yo ho, the pirate life, The flag o' skull and bones, A merry hour, a hempen rope, And hey for Davy Jones." At once the lost boys—but where are they? They are no longer there. Rabbits could not have disappeared more quickly. I will tell you where they are. With the exception of Nibs, who has darted away to reconnoitre, they are already in their home under the ground, a very delightful residence of which we shall see a good deal presently. But how have they reached it? for there is no entrance to be seen, not so much as a large stone, which if rolled away would disclose the mouth of a cave. Look closely, however, and you may note that there are here seven large trees, each with a hole in its hollow trunk as large as a boy. **These are the seven entrances to the home under the ground, for which Hook has been searching in vain these many moons.** Will he find it to-night? As the pirates advanced, the quick eye of Starkey sighted Nibs disappearing through the wood, and at once his pistol flashed out. But an iron claw gripped his shoulder. "Captain, let go," he cried, writhing. Now for the first time we hear the voice of Hook. It was a black voice. "Put back that pistol first," it said threateningly. "It was one of those boys you hate. I could have shot him dead." "Ay, and the sound would have brought Tiger Lily's redskins upon us. Do you want to lose your scalp?" "Shall I after him, captain," asked pathetic Smee, "and tickle him with Johnny Corkscrew?" Smee had pleasant names for everything, and his cutlass was Johnny Corkscrew, because he wriggled it in the wound. One could mention many lovable traits in Smee. For instance, after killing, it was his spectacles he wiped instead of his weapon. "Johnny's a silent fellow," he reminded Hook. "Not now, Smee," Hook said darkly. "He is only one, and I want to mischief all the seven. Scatter and look for them." The pirates disappeared among the trees, and in a moment their captain and Smee were alone. Hook heaved a heavy sigh; and I know not why it was, perhaps it was because of the soft beauty of the evening, but there came over him a desire to confide to his faithful bo'sun the story of his life. He spoke long and earnestly, but what it was all about Smee, who was rather stupid, did not know in the least. Anon he caught the word Peter. "Most of all," Hook was saying passionately, "I want their captain, Peter Pan. 'Twas he cut off my arm." He brandished the hook threateningly. "I've waited long to shake his hand with this. Oh, I'll tear him!" "And yet," said Smee, "I have often heard you say that hook was worth a score of hands, for combing the hair and other homely uses." "Ay," the captain answered, "if I was a mother I would pray to have my children born with this instead of that," and he cast a look of pride upon his iron hand and

one of scorn upon the other. Then again he frowned. "Peter flung my arm," he said, wincing, "to a crocodile that happened to be passing by." "I have often," said Smee,

"noticed your strange dread of crocodiles." "Not of crocodiles," Hook corrected him, "but of that one crocodile." He lowered his voice. "It liked my arm so much, Smee,

that it has followed me ever since, from sea to sea and from land to land, licking its lips for the rest of me." "In a way," said Smee, "it's a sort of compliment." "I want no

such compliments," Hook barked petulantly. "I want Peter Pan, who first gave the brute its taste for me." He sat down on a large mushroom, and now there was a quiver in

his voice. "Smee," he said huskily, "that crocodile would have had me before this, but by a lucky chance it swallowed a clock which goes tick tick inside it, and so before it

can reach me I hear the tick and bolt." He laughed, but in a hollow way. "Some day," said Smee, "the clock will run down, and then he'll get you." Hook wetted his dry lips.

"Ay," he said, "that's the fear that haunts me." Since sitting down he had felt curiously warm. "Smee," he said, "this seat is hot." He jumped up. "Odds bobs, hammer and

tongs I'm burning." They examined the mushroom, which was of a size and solidity unknown on the mainland; they tried to pull it up, and it came away at once in their

hands, for it had no root. Stranger still, smoke began at once to ascend. The pirates looked at each other. "A chimney!" they both exclaimed. They had indeed discovered the

chimney of the home under the ground. It was the custom of the boys to stop it with a mushroom when enemies were in the neighbourhood. Not only smoke came out of

it. There came also children's voices, for so safe did the boys feel in their hiding-place that they were gaily chattering. The pirates listened grimly, and then replaced the

mushroom. They looked around them and noted the holes in the seven trees. "Did you hear them say Peter Pan's from home?" Smee whispered, fidgeting with Johnny

Corkscrew. Hook nodded. He stood for a long time lost in thought, and at last a curdling smile lit up his swarthy face. Smee had been waiting for it. "Unrip your plan

captain," he cried eagerly. "To return to the ship," Hook replied slowly through his teeth, "and cook a large rich cake of a jolly thickness with green sugar on it. There can

be but one room below, for there is but one chimney. The silly moles had not the sense to see that they did not need a door apiece. That shows they have no mother. We will

leave the cake on the shore of the mermaids' lagoon. These boys are always swimming about there, playing with the mermaids. They will find the cake and they will gobble

it up, because, having no mother, they don't know how dangerous 'tis to eat rich damp cake." He burst into laughter, not hollow laughter now, but honest laughter. "Aha,

they will die. Smee had listened with growing admiration. "It's the wickedest, prettiest policy ever I heard of," he cried, and in their exultation they danced and sang: "Avast

belay, when I appear, By fear they're overtook; Nought's left upon your bones when you Have shaken claws with Cook." They began the verse, but they never finished

for another sound broke in and stilled them. It was at first such a tiny sound that a leaf might have fallen on it and smothered it, but as it came nearer it was more distinct. *Tick*

tick tick! Hook stood shuddering, one foot in the air. "The crocodile," he gasped, and bounded away, followed by his bo'sun. It was indeed the crocodile. It had passed

the redskins, who were now on the trail of the other pirates. It oozed on after Hook. Once more the boys emerged into the open; but the dangers of the night were not yet over, for presently Nibs rushed breathless into their midst, pursued by a pack of wolves. The tongues of the pursuers were hanging out; the baying of them was horrible.

"Save me, save me!" cried Nibs, falling on the ground. "But what can we do, what can we do?" It was a high compliment to Peter that at that dire moment their thoughts turned to him. "What would Peter do?" they cried simultaneously. Almost in the same breath they added, "Peter would look at them through his legs." And then, "Let us do what Peter would do." It is quite the most successful way of defying wolves, and as one boy they bent and looked through their legs. The next moment is the long one; but victory came quickly, for as the boys advanced upon them in this terrible attitude, the wolves dropped their tails and fled. Now Nibs rose from the ground, and the others thought that his staring eyes still saw the wolves. But it was not wolves he saw. "I have seen a wonderfuller thing," he cried, as they gathered round him eagerly. "A great white bird. It is flying this way." "What kind of a bird, do you think?" "I don't know," Nibs said, awestruck, "but it looks so weary, and as it flies it moans, 'Poor Wendy.'"

"Poor Wendy?" "I remember," said Slightly instantly, "there are birds called Wendies." "See, it comes," cried Curly, pointing to Wendy in the heavens. Wendy was now almost overhead, and they could hear her plaintive cry. But more distinct came the shrill voice of Tinker Bell. The jealous fairy had now cast off all disguise of friendship, and was darting at her victim from every direction, pinching savagely each time she touched. "Hullo, Tink," cried the wondering boys. Tink's reply rang out: "Peter wants you to shoot the Wendy." It was not in their nature to question when Peter ordered. "Let us do what Peter wishes," cried the simple boys. "Quick, bows and arrows." All but Tootles popped down their trees. He had a bow and arrow with him, and Tink noted it, and rubbed her little hands. "Quick, Tootles, quick," she screamed. "Peter will be so pleased." Tootles excitedly fitted the arrow to his bow. "Out of the way, Tink," he shouted; and then he fired, and Wendy fluttered to the ground with an arrow in her breast.

CHAPTER VI *The Little House* Foolish Tootles was standing like a conqueror over Wendy's body when the other boys sprang, armed, from their trees. "You are too late," he cried proudly, "I have shot the Wendy. Peter will be so pleased with me." Overhead Tinker Bell shouted "Silly ass!" and darted into hiding. The others did not hear her. They had crowded round Wendy, and as they looked a terrible silence fell upon the wood. If Wendy's heart had been beating they would all have heard it. Slightly was the first to speak. "This is no bird," he said in a scared voice. "I think it must be a lady." "A lady?" said Tootles, and fell a-trembling. "And we have killed her," Nibs said hoarsely. They all whipped off their caps. "Now I see," Curly said; "Peter was bringing her to us." He threw himself sorrowfully on the ground. "A lady to take care of us at last," said one of the twins, "and you have killed her." They were sorry for him, but sorrier for themselves, and when he took a step nearer them they turned from him. Tootles' face was very white, but there was a dignity about him now that had never been there before. "I did it," he said, reflecting. "When ladies used to come to me in dreams, I said, 'Pretty mother, pretty mother.' But when at last she really came, I shot her." He moved slowly away. "Don't go," they called in pity. "I must," he answered, shaking; "I am so afraid of Peter." It was at this tragic moment that they heard a sound which made the heart of every one of them rise to his mouth. They heard Peter crow. "Peter!" they cried, for it was always thus that he signalled his return. "Hide her," they whispered, and gathered hastily around Wendy. But Tootles stood aloof. Again came that ringing crow, and Peter dropped in front of them. "Greeting, boys," he cried, and mechanically they saluted, and then again was silence. He frowned. "I am back," he said hotly,

"why do you not cheer?" They opened their mouths, but the cheers would not come. He overlooked it in his haste to tell the glorious tidings. "Great news, boys," he cried,

"I have brought at last a mother for you all." Still no sound, except a little thud from Tootles as he dropped on his knees. "Have you not seen her?" asked Peter, becoming

troubled. "She flew this way." "Ah me," one voice said, and another said, "Oh, mournful day." Tootles rose. "Peter," he said quietly, "I will show her to you," and when the

others would still have hidden her he said, "Back, twins, let Peter see." So they all stood back, and let him see, and after he had looked for a little time he did not know what

to do next. "She is dead," he said uncomfortably. "Perhaps she is frightened at being dead." He thought of hopping off in a comic sort of way till he was out of sight of her,

and then never going near the spot any more. They would all have been glad to follow if he had done this. But there was the arrow. He took it from her heart and faced his

band. "Whose arrow?" he demanded sternly. "Mine, Peter," said Tootles on his knees. "Oh, dastard hand," Peter said, and he raised the arrow to use it as a dagger. Tootles

did not flinch. He bared his breast. "Strike, Peter," he said firmly, "strike true." Twice did Peter raise the arrow, and twice did his hand fall. "I cannot strike," he said with

awe, "there is something stays my hand." All looked at him in wonder, save Nibs, who fortunately looked at Wendy. "It is she," he cried, "the Wendy lady; see, her arm.

Wonderful to relate, Wendy had raised her arm. Nibs bent over her and listened reverently. "I think she said 'Poor Tootles,'" he whispered. "She lives," Peter said briefly

Slightly cried instantly, "The Wendy lady lives." Then Peter knelt beside her and found his button. You remember she had put it on a chain that she wore round her neck

"See," he said, "the arrow struck against this. It is the kiss I gave her. It has saved her life." "I remember kisses," Slightly interposed quickly, "let me see it. Ay, that's a kiss.

Peter did not hear him. He was begging Wendy to get better quickly, so that he could show her the mermaids. Of course she could not answer yet, being still in a frightf

faint; but from overhead came a wailing note. "Listen to Tink," said Curly, "she is crying because the Wendy lives." Then they had to tell Peter of Tink's crime, and almo

never had they seen him look so stern. "Listen, Tinker Bell," he cried, "I am your friend no more. Begone from me for ever." She flew on to his shoulder and pleaded, b

he brushed her off. Not until Wendy again raised her arm did he relent sufficiently to say, "Well, not for ever, but for a whole week." Do you think Tinker Bell was gratef

to Wendy for raising her arm? Oh dear no, never wanted to pinch her so much. Fairies indeed are strange, and Peter, who understood them best, often cuffed them. But wh

to do with Wendy in her present delicate state of health? "Let us carry her down into the house," Curly suggested. "Ay," said Slightly, "that is what one does with ladie

"No, no," Peter said, "you must not touch her. It would not be sufficiently respectful." "That," said Slightly, "is what I was thinking." "But if she lies there," Tootles sa

"she will die." "Ay, she will die," Slightly admitted, "but there is no way out." "Yes, there is," cried Peter. "Let us build a little house round her." They were all delight

"Quick," he ordered them, "bring me each of you the best of what we have. Gut our house. Be sharp." In a moment they were as busy as tailors the night before a weddi

They scurried this way and that, down for bedding, up for firewood, and while they were at it, who should appear but John and Michael. As they dragged along the grou they fell asleep standing, stopped, woke up, moved another step and slept again. "John, John," Michael would cry, "wake up. Where is Nana, John, and mother?" And then

John would rub his eyes and mutter, "It is true, we did fly." You may be sure they were very relieved to find Peter. "Hullo, Peter," they said. "Hullo," replied Peter amicably,

though he had quite forgotten them. **He was very busy at the moment measuring Wendy with his feet to see how large a house she would need.** Of course he meant to leave

room for chairs and a table. John and Michael watched him. "Is Wendy asleep?" they asked. "Yes." "John," Michael proposed, "let us wake her and get her to make supper

for us," but as he said it some of the other boys rushed on carrying branches for the building of the house. "Look at them!" he cried. "Curly," said Peter in his most captainy

voice, "see that these boys help in the building of the house." "Ay, ay, sir." "Build a house?" exclaimed John. "For the Wendy," said Curly. "For Wendy?" John said, aghast.

"Why, she is only a girl." "That," explained Curly, "is why we are her servants." "You? Wendy's servants!" "Yes," said Peter, "and you also. Away with them." The

astounded brothers were dragged away to hack and hew and carry. "Chairs and a fender first," Peter ordered. "Then we shall build the house round them." "Ay," said

Slightly, "that is how a house is built; it all comes back to me." Peter thought of everything. "Slightly," he ordered, "fetch a doctor." "Ay, ay," said Slightly at once, and

disappeared, scratching his head. But he knew Peter must be obeyed, and he returned in a moment, wearing John's hat and looking solemn. "Please, sir," said Peter, going

to him, "are you a doctor?" The difference between him and the other boys at such a time was that they knew it was make-believe, while to him make-believe and true were

exactly the same thing. This sometimes troubled them, as when they had to make-believe that they had had their dinners. If they broke down in their make-believe he rapped

them on the knuckles. "Yes, my little man," anxiously replied Slightly, who had chapped knuckles. "Please, sir," Peter explained, "a lady lies very ill." She was lying at their

feet, but Slightly had the sense not to see her. "Tut, tut, tut," he said, "where does she lie?" "In yonder glade." "I will put a glass thing in her mouth," said Slightly; and he

made-believe to do it, while Peter waited. It was an anxious moment when the glass thing was withdrawn. "How is she?" inquired Peter. "Tut, tut, tut," said Slightly, "this

has cured her." "I am glad," Peter cried. "I will call again in the evening," Slightly said; "give her beef tea out of a cup with a spout to it;" but after he had returned the hat

to John he blew big breaths, which was his habit on escaping from a difficulty. In the meantime the wood had been alive with the sound of axes; almost everything needed

for a cosy dwelling already lay at Wendy's feet. "If only we knew," said one, "the kind of house she likes best." "Peter," shouted another, "she is moving in her sleep." "Her

mouth opens," cried a third, looking respectfully into it. "Oh, lovely!" "Perhaps she is going to sing in her sleep," said Peter. "Wendy, sing the kind of house you would like

to have." Immediately, without opening her eyes, Wendy began to sing: "I wish I had a pretty house, The littlest ever seen, With funny little red walls And roof of mossy

green." They gurgled with joy at this, for by the greatest good luck the branches they had brought were sticky with red sap, and all the ground was carpeted with moss. As

they rattled up the little house they broke into song themselves: "We've built the little walls and roof And made a lovely door, So tell us, mother Wendy, What are you

wanting more?" To this she answered rather greedily: "Oh, really next I think I'll have Gay windows all about, With roses peeping in, you know, And babies peeping out."

With a blow of their fists they made windows, and large yellow leaves were the blinds. But roses——? "Roses," cried Peter sternly. Quickly they made-believe to grow the

loveliest roses up the walls. Babies? To prevent Peter ordering babies they hurried into song again: "We've made the roses peeping out, The babes are at the door, We cannot

make ourselves, you know, 'Cos we've been made before." Peter, seeing this to be a good idea, at once pretended that it was his own. The house was quite beautiful, and no

doubt Wendy was very cosy within, though, of course, they could no longer see her. Peter strode up and down, ordering finishing touches. Nothing escaped his eagle eye.

Just when it seemed absolutely finished, "There's no knocker on the door," he said. They were very ashamed, but Tootles gave the sole of his shoe, and it made an excellent

knocker. Absolutely finished now, they thought. Not a bit of it. "There's no chimney," Peter said; "we must have a chimney." "It certainly does need a chimney," said John

importantly. This gave Peter an idea. He snatched the hat off John's head, knocked out the bottom, and put the hat on the roof. The little house was so pleased to have such

a capital chimney that, as if to say thank you, smoke immediately began to come out of the hat. Now really and truly it was finished. Nothing remained to do but to knock.

"All look your best," Peter warned them; "first impressions are awfully important." He was glad no one asked him what first impressions are; they were all too busy looking

their best. He knocked politely; and now the wood was as still as the children, not a sound to be heard except from Tinker Bell, who was watching from a branch and openly

sneering. What the boys were wondering was, would any one answer the knock? If a lady, what would she be like? The door opened and a lady came out. It was Wendy.

They all whipped off their hats. She looked properly surprised, and this was just how they had hoped she would look. "Where am I?" she said. Of course Slightly was the

first to get his word in. "Wendy lady," he said rapidly, "for you we built this house." "Oh, say you're pleased," cried Nibs. "Lovely, darling house," Wendy said, and they

were the very words they had hoped she would say. "And we are your children," cried the twins. Then all went on their knees, and holding out their arms cried, "O Wendy

lady, be our mother." "Ought I?" Wendy said, all shining. "Of course it's frightfully fascinating, but you see I am only a little girl. I have no real experience." "That doesn't

matter," said Peter, as if he were the only person present who knew all about it, though he was really the one who knew least. "What we need is just a nice motherly person."

"Oh dear!" Wendy said, "you see I feel that is exactly what I am." "It is, it is," they all cried; "we saw it at once." "Very well," she said, "I will do my best. Come inside at

once, you naughty children; I am sure your feet are damp. And before I put you to bed I have just time to finish the story of Cinderella." In they went; I don't know how

there was room for them, but you can squeeze very tight in the Neverland. And that was the first of the many joyous evenings they had with Wendy. By and by she tucked

them up in the great bed in the home under the trees, but she herself slept that night in the little house, and Peter kept watch outside with drawn sword, for the pirates could

be heard carousing far away and the wolves were on the prowl. The little house looked so cosy and safe in the darkness, with a bright light showing through its blinds, and

the chimney smoking beautifully, and Peter standing on guard. After a time he fell asleep, and some unsteady fairies had to climb over him on their way home from an orgy.

Any of the other boys obstructing the fairy path at night they would have mischiefed, but they just tweaked Peter's nose and passed on. CHAPTER VII *The Home Under*

The Ground One of the first things Peter did next day was to measure Wendy and John and Michael for hollow trees. Hook, you remember, had sneered at the boys for thinking they needed a tree apiece, but this was ignorance, for unless your tree fitted you it was difficult to go up and down, and no two of the boys were quite the same size.

Once you fitted, you drew in your breath at the top, and down you went at exactly the right speed, while to ascend you drew in and let out alternately, and so wriggled up.

Of course, when you have mastered the action you are able to do these things without thinking of them, and then nothing can be more graceful. But you simply must fit, and Peter measures you for your tree as carefully as for a suit of clothes: the only difference being that the clothes are made to fit you, while you have to be made to fit the tree.

Usually it is done quite easily, as by your wearing too many garments or too few; but if you are bumpy in awkward places or the only available tree is an odd shape, Peter does some things to you, and after that you fit. Once you fit, great care must be taken to go on fitting, and this, as Wendy was to discover to her delight, keeps a whole family in perfect condition. Wendy and Michael fitted their trees at the first try, but John had to be altered a little. After a few days' practice they could go up and down as gaily as buckets in a well. And how ardently they grew to love their home under the ground; especially Wendy. It consisted of one large room, as all houses should do, with a floor in which you could dig if you wanted to go fishing, and in this floor grew stout mushrooms of a charming colour, which were used as stools. A Never tree tried hard to grow in the centre of the room, but every morning they sawed the trunk through, level with the floor. By tea-time it was always about two feet high, and then they put a door on top of it, the whole thus becoming a table; as soon as they cleared away, they sawed off the trunk again, and thus there was more room to play. There was an enormous fireplace which was in almost any part of the room where you cared to light it, and across this Wendy stretched strings, made of fibre, from which she suspended her washing.

The bed was tilted against the wall by day, and let down at 6.30, when it filled nearly half the room; and all the boys except Michael slept in it, lying like sardines in a tin. There was a strict rule against turning round until one gave the signal, when all turned at once. Michael should have used it also; but Wendy would have a baby, and he was the littlest, and you know what women are, and the short and the long of it is that he was hung up in a basket. It was rough and simple, and not unlike what baby bears would have made of an underground house in the same circumstances. But there was one recess in the wall, no larger than a bird-cage, which was the private apartment of Tinker Bell. It could be shut off from the rest of the home by a tiny curtain, which Tink, who was most fastidious, always kept drawn when dressing or undressing. No woman, however large, could have had a more exquisite boudoir and bed-chamber combined. The couch, as she always called it, was a genuine Queen Mab, with club legs; and she varied the bedspreads according to what fruit-blossom was in season. Her mirror was a Puss-in-boots, of which there are now only three, unchipped, known to the fairy dealers; the wash-stand was Pie-crust and reversible, the chest of drawers an authentic Charming the Sixth, and the carpet and rugs of the best (the early) period of Margery and Robin. There was a chandelier from Tiddly winks for the look of the thing, but of course she lit the residence herself. Tink was very contemptuous of the rest of the house, as indeed was perhaps inevitable, and her chamber, though beautiful, looked rather conceited, having the appearance of a nose permanently turned up. I suppose it was all especially entrancing to Wendy, because those rampagious boys of hers gave her so much to do. Really there were whole weeks when, except perhaps with a stocking

in the evening, she was never above ground. The cooking, I can tell you, kept her nose to the pot, and even if there was nothing in it, even though there was no pot, she had

to keep watching that it came aboil just the same. You never exactly knew whether there would be a real meal or just a make-believe, it all depended upon Peter's whim: he

could eat, really eat, if it was part of a game, but he could not stodge just to feel stodgy, which is what most children like better than anything else; the next best thing being

to talk about it. Make-believe was so real to him that during a meal of it you could see him getting rounder. Of course it was trying, but you simply had to follow his lead,

and if you could prove to him that you were getting loose for your tree he let you stodge. Wendy's favourite time for sewing and darning was after they had all gone to bed.

Then, as she expressed it, she had a breathing time for herself; and she occupied it in making new things for them, and putting double pieces on the knees, for they were all

most frightfully hard on their knees. When she sat down to a basketful of their stockings, every heel with a hole in it, she would fling up her arms and exclaim, "Oh dear, I

am sure I sometimes think spinsters are to be envied." Her face beamed when she exclaimed this. You remember about her pet wolf. Well, it very soon discovered that she

had come to the island and it found her out, and they just ran into each other's arms. After that it followed her about everywhere. As time wore on did she think much about

the beloved parents she had left behind her? This is a difficult question, because it is quite impossible to say how time does wear on in the Neverland, where it is calculated

by moons and suns, and there are ever so many more of them than on the mainland. But I am afraid that Wendy did not really worry about her father and mother; she was

absolutely confident that they would always keep the window open for her to fly back by, and this gave her complete ease of mind. What did disturb her at times was that

John remembered his parents vaguely only, as people he had once known, while Michael was quite willing to believe that she was really his mother. These things scared her

a little, and nobly anxious to do her duty, she tried to fix the old life in their minds by setting them examination papers on it, as like as possible to the ones she used to do at

school. The other boys thought this awfully interesting, and insisted on joining, and they made slates for themselves, and sat round the table, writing and thinking hard about

the questions she had written on another slate and passed round. They were the most ordinary questions—"What was the colour of Mother's eyes? Which was taller, Father

or Mother? Was Mother blonde or brunette? Answer all three questions if possible." "(A) Write an essay of not less than 40 words on How I spent my last Holidays, or The

Carakters of Father and Mother compared. Only one of these to be attempted." Or "(1) Describe Mother's laugh; (2) Describe Father's laugh; (3) Describe Mother's Party

Dress; (4) Describe the Kennel and its Inmate." They were just everyday questions like these, and when you could not answer them you were told to make a cross; and it was

really dreadful what a number of crosses even John made. Of course the only boy who replied to every question was Slightly, and no one could have been more hopeful of

coming out first, but his answers were perfectly ridiculous, and he really came out last: a melancholy thing. Peter did not compete. For one thing he despised all mothers

except Wendy, and for another he was the only boy on the island who could neither write nor spell; not the smallest word. He was above all that sort of thing. By the way the questions were all written in the past tense. What was the colour of Mother's eyes, and so on. Wendy, you see, had been forgetting too. Adventures, of course, as we shall

see, were of daily occurrence; but about this time Peter invented, with Wendy's help, a new game that fascinated him enormously, until he suddenly had no more interest in

it, which, as you have been told, was what always happened with his games. It consisted in pretending not to have adventures, in doing the sort of thing John and Michael

had been doing all their lives: sitting on stools flinging balls in the air, pushing each other, going out for walks and coming back without having killed so much as a grizzly.

To see Peter doing nothing on a stool was a great sight; he could not help looking solemn at such times, to sit still seemed to him such a comic thing to do. He boasted that he

had gone a walk for the good of his health. For several suns these were the most novel of all adventures to him; and John and Michael had to pretend to be delighted also;

otherwise he would have treated them severely. He often went out alone, and when he came back you were never absolutely certain whether he had had an adventure or not.

He might have forgotten it so completely that he said nothing about it; and then when you went out you found the body; and, on the other hand, he might say a great deal

about it, and yet you could not find the body. Sometimes he came home with his head bandaged, and then Wendy cooed over him and bathed it in lukewarm water, while he

told a dazzling tale. But she was never quite sure, you know. There were, however, many adventures which she knew to be true because she was in them herself, and there

were still more that were at least partly true, for the other boys were in them and said they were wholly true. To describe them all would require a book as large as an English-

Latin, Latin-English Dictionary, and the most we can do is to give one as a specimen of an average hour on the island. The difficulty is which one to choose. Should we take

the brush with the redskins at Slightly Gulch? It was a sanguinary affair, and especially interesting as showing one of Peter's peculiarities, which was that in the middle of a

fight he would suddenly change sides. At the Gulch, when victory was still in the balance, sometimes leaning this way and sometimes that, he called out, "I'm redskin to-day;

what are you, Tootles?" And Tootles answered, "Redskin; what are you, Nibs?" and Nibs said, "Redskin; what are you, Twin?" and so on; and they were all redskin; and of

course this would have ended the fight had not the real redskins, fascinated by Peter's methods, agreed to be lost boys for that once, and so at it they all went again, more

fiercely than ever. The extraordinary upshot of this adventure was—but we have not decided yet that this is the adventure we are to narrate. Perhaps a better one would be

the night attack by the redskins on the house under the ground, when several of them stuck in the hollow trees and had to be pulled out like corks. Or we might tell how Peter

saved Tiger Lily's life in the Mermaids' Lagoon, and so made her his ally. Or we could tell of that cake the pirates cooked so that the boys might eat it and perish; and how

they placed it in one cunning spot after another; but always Wendy snatched it from the hands of her children, so that in time it lost its succulence, and became as hard as a

stone, and was used as a missile, and Hook fell over it in the dark. Or suppose we tell of the birds that were Peter's friends, particularly of the Never bird that built in a tree

overhanging the lagoon, and how the nest fell into the water, and still the bird sat on her eggs, and Peter gave orders that she was not to be disturbed. That is a pretty story,

and the end shows how grateful a bird can be; but if we tell it we must also tell the whole adventure of the lagoon, which would of course be telling two adventures rather than just one. A shorter adventure, and quite as exciting, was Tinker Bell's attempt, with the help of some street fairies, to have the sleeping Wendy conveyed on a great

floating leaf to the mainland. Fortunately the leaf gave way and Wendy woke, thinking it was bath-time, and swam back. Or again, we might choose Peter's defiance of the

lions, when he drew a circle round him on the ground with an arrow and defied them to cross it; and though he waited for hours, with the other boys and Wendy looking on

breathlessly from trees, not one of them dared to accept his challenge. Which of these adventures shall we choose? The best way will be to toss for it. I have tossed, and the

lagoon has won. This almost makes one wish that the gulch or the cake or Tink's leaf had won. Of course I could do it again, and make it best out of three; however, perhaps

fairest to stick to the lagoon. CHAPTER VIII *The Mermaids' Lagoon* If you shut your eyes and are a lucky one, you may see at times a shapeless pool of lovely pale colours

suspended in the darkness; then if you squeeze your eyes tighter, the pool begins to take shape, and the colours become so vivid that with another squeeze they must go on

fire. But just before they go on fire you see the lagoon. This is the nearest you ever get to it on the mainland, just one heavenly moment; if there could be two moments you

might see the surf and hear the mermaids singing. The children often spent long summer days on this lagoon, swimming or floating most of the time, playing the mermaid

games in the water, and so forth. You must not think from this that the mermaids were on friendly terms with them; on the contrary, it was among Wendy's lasting regrets

that all the time she was on the island she never had a civil word from one of them. When she stole softly to the edge of the lagoon she might see them by the score, especially

on Marooners' Rock, where they loved to bask, combing out their hair in a lazy way that quite irritated her; or she might even swim, on tiptoe as it were, to within a yard of

them, but then they saw her and dived, probably splashing her with their tails, not by accident, but intentionally. They treated all the boys in the same way, except of course

Peter, who chatted with them on Marooners' Rock by the hour, and sat on their tails when they got cheeky. He gave Wendy one of their combs. The most haunting time at

which to see them is at the turn of the moon, when they utter strange wailing cries; but the lagoon is dangerous for mortals then, and until the evening of which we have now

to tell, Wendy had never seen the lagoon by moonlight, less from fear, for of course Peter would have accompanied her, than because she had strict rules about every one

being in bed by seven. She was often at the lagoon, however, on sunny days after rain, when the mermaids come up in extraordinary numbers to play with their bubbles. The

bubbles of many colours made in rainbow water they treat as balls, hitting them gaily from one to another with their tails, and trying to keep them in the rainbow till they

burst. The goals are at each end of the rainbow, and the keepers only are allowed to use their hands. Sometimes a dozen of these games will be going on in the lagoon at a

time, and it is quite a pretty sight. But the moment the children tried to join in they had to play by themselves, for the mermaids immediately disappeared. Nevertheless we

have proof that they secretly watched the interlopers, and were not above taking an idea from them; for John introduced a new way of hitting the bubble, with the head

instead of the hand, and the mermaids adopted it. This is the one mark that John has left on the Neverland. It must also have been rather pretty to see the children resting on

a rock for half an hour after their midday meal. Wendy insisted on their doing this, and it had to be a real rest even though the meal was make-believe. So they lay there the sun, and their bodies glistened in it, while she sat beside them and looked important. It was one such day, and they were all on Marooners' Rock. The rock was not much larger than their great bed, but of course they all knew how not to take up much room, and they were dozing or at least lying with their eyes shut, and pinching occasionally when they thought Wendy was not looking. She was very busy, stitching. While she stitched a change came to the lagoon. Little shivers ran over it, and the sun went away and shadows stole across the water, turning it cold. Wendy could no longer see to thread her needle, and when she looked up, the lagoon that had always hitherto been such a laughing place seemed formidable and unfriendly. It was not, she knew, that night had come, but something as dark as night had come. No, worse than that. It had not come, but it had sent that shiver through the sea to say that it was coming. What was it? There crowded upon her all the stories she had been told of Marooners' Rock, so called because evil captains put sailors on it and leave them there to drown. They drown when the tide rises, for then it is submerged. Of course she should have roused the children at once; not merely because of the unknown that was stalking toward them, but because it was no longer good for them to sleep on a rock grown chilly. But she was a young mother and she did not know this; she thought you simply must stick to your rule about half an hour after the midday meal. So, though fear was upon her, and she longed to hear male voices, she would not waken them. Even when she heard the sound of muffled oars, though her heart was in her mouth, she did not waken them. She stood over them to let them have their sleep out. Was it not brave of Wendy? It was well for those boys then that there was one among them who could sniff danger even in his sleep. Peter sprang erect, as wide awake at once as a dog, and with one warning cry he roused the others. He stood motionless, one hand to his ear. "Pirates!" he cried. The others came closer to him. A strange smile was playing about his face, and Wendy saw it and shuddered. While that smile was on his face no one dared address him; all they could do was to stand ready to obey. The order came sharp and incisive. "Dive!" There was a gleam of legs, and instantly the lagoon seemed deserted. Marooners' Rock stood alone in the forbidding waters, as if it were itself marooned. The boat drew nearer. It was the pirate dinghy, with three figures in her, Smee and Starkey, and the third a captive, no other than Tiger Lily. Her hands and ankles were tied, and she knew what was to be her fate. She was to be left on the rock to perish, an end to one of her race more terrible than death by fire or torture, for is it not written in the book of the tribe that there is no path through water to the happy hunting-ground? Yet her face was impassive; she was the daughter of a chief, she must die as a chief's daughter, it is enough. They had caught her boarding the pirate ship with a knife in her mouth. No watch was kept on the ship, it being Hook's boast that the wind of his name guarded the ship for a mile around. Now her fate would help to guard it also. One more wail would go the round in that wind by night. In the gloom that they brought with them the two pirates did not see the rock till they crashed into it. "Luff, you lubber," cried an Irish voice that was Smee's; "here's the rock. Now, then, what we have to do is to hoist the redskin on to it and leave her there to drown." It was the work of one brutal moment to land the beautiful girl on the rock; she was too proud to offer a vain resistance. Quite near the rock, but out of sight, two heads were bobbing up and down, Peter's and Wendy's. Wendy was crying, for it was the first tragedy she had seen. Peter had seen many tragedies, but he had forgotten them all. He was less sorry than Wendy for Tiger Lily: it was two against one that angered him, and he meant to save her. An easy way would have been to wait until the pirates had gone, but he was never one to choose the easy way. There was almost nothing he could not do, and he now imitated the voice of Hook. "Ahoy there, you lubbers," he called. It was a marvellous imitation. "The captain," said the pirates, staring at each other in surprise. "He must be swimming out to us," Starkey said, when they had looked for him in vain. "We are putting the redskin on the rock," Smee called out. "Set her free," came the astonishing answer. "Free!" "Yes, cut her bonds and let her go." "But, captain—" "At once, d'ye hear," cried Peter, "or I'll plunge my hook in you." "This is queer," Smee gasped. "Better do what the captain orders," said Starkey nervously. "Ay, ay," Smee said, and he cut Tiger Lily's cords. At once like an eel she slid between Starkey's legs into the water. Of course Wendy was very elated over Peter's cleverness; but she knew that he would be elated also and very likely crow and thus betray himself, so at once her hand went out to cover his mouth. But it was stayed even in the act, for "Boat ahoy!" rang over the lagoon in Hook's voice, and this time it was not Peter who had spoken. Peter may have been about to crow, but his face puckered in a whistle of surprise instead. "Boat ahoy!" again came the cry.

Now Wendy understood. The real Hook was also in the water. He was swimming to the boat, and as his men showed a light to guide him he had soon reached them. In the light of the lantern Wendy saw his hook grip the boat's side; she saw his evil swarthy face as he rose dripping from the water, and, quaking, she would have liked to swim away, but Peter would not budge. He was tingling with life and also top-heavy with conceit. "Am I not a wonder, oh, I am a wonder!" he whispered to her, and though she thought so also, she was really glad for the sake of his reputation that no one heard him except herself. He signed to her to listen. The two pirates were very curious to know what had brought their captain to them, but he sat with his head on his hook in a position of profound melancholy. "Captain, is all well?" they asked timidly, but he answered with a hollow moan. "He sighs," said Smee. "He sighs again," said Starkey. "And yet a third time he sighs," said Smee. "What's up, captain?" Then at last he spoke passionately. "The game's up," he cried, "those boys have found a mother." Affrighted though she was, Wendy swelled with pride. "O evil day," cried Starkey. "What's a mother?" asked the ignorant Smee. Wendy was so shocked that she exclaimed, "He doesn't know!" and always after this she felt that if you could have a pet pirate Smee would be her one. Peter pulled her beneath the water, for Hook had started up, crying, "What was that?" "I heard nothing," said Starkey, raising the lantern over the water, and as the pirates looked they saw a strange sight. It was the nest I have told you of, floating on the lagoon, and the Never bird was sitting on it. "See," said Hook in answer to Smee's question, "that is a mother. What a lesson. The nest must have fallen into the water, but would the mother desert her eggs? No." There was a break in his voice, as if for a moment he recalled innocent days when—but he brushed away this weakness with his hook. Smee, much impressed, gazed at the bird as the nest was borne past, but the more suspicious Starkey said, "If she is a mother, perhaps she is hanging about here to help Peter." Hook winced. "Ay," he said, "that is the fear that haunts me."

He was roused from this dejection by Smee's eager voice. "Captain," said Smee, "could we not kidnap these boys' mother and make her our mother?" "It is a princely scheme," cried Hook, and at once it took practical shape in his great brain. "We will seize the children and carry them to the boat: the boys we will make walk the plank, and Wendy shall be our mother." Again Wendy forgot herself. "Never!" she cried, and bobbed. "What was that?" But they could see nothing. They thought it must have been but a leaf

in the wind. "Do you agree, my bullies?" asked Hook. "There is my hand on it," they both said. "And there is my hook. Swear." They all swore. By this time they were on

the rock, and suddenly Hook remembered Tiger Lily. "Where is the redskin?" he demanded abruptly. He had a playful humour at moments, and they thought this was one

of the moments. "That is all right, captain," Smee answered complacently; "we let her go." "Let her go!" cried Hook. "'Twas your own orders," the bo'sun faltered. "You

called over the water to us to let her go," said Starkey. "Brimstone and gall," thundered Hook, "what cozening is here?" His face had gone black with rage, but he saw that

they believed their words, and he was startled. "Lads," he said, shaking a little, "I gave no such order." "It is passing queer," Smee said, and they all fidgeted uncomfortably.

Hook raised his voice, but there was a quiver in it. "Spirit that haunts this dark lagoon to-night," he cried, "dost hear me?" Of course Peter should have kept quiet, but of

course he did not. He immediately answered in Hook's voice: "Odds, bobs, hammer and tongs, I hear you." In that supreme moment Hook did not blanch, even at the gills,

but Smee and Starkey clung to each other in terror. "Who are you, stranger, speak?" Hook demanded. "I am James Hook," replied the voice, "captain of the *Jolly Roger*."

"You are not; you are not," Hook cried hoarsely. "Brimstone and gall," the voice retorted, "say that again, and I'll cast anchor in you." Hook tried a more ingratiating

manner. "If you are Hook," he said almost humbly, "come tell me, who am I?" "A codfish," replied the voice, "only a codfish." "A codfish!" Hook echoed blankly; and it

was then, but not till then, that his proud spirit broke. He saw his men draw back from him. "Have we been captained all this time by a codfish!" they muttered. "It is lowering

to our pride." They were his dogs snapping at him, but, tragic figure though he had become, he scarcely heeded them. Against such fearful evidence it was not their belief

in him that he needed, it was his own. He felt his ego slipping from him. "Don't desert me, bully," he whispered hoarsely to it. In his dark nature there was a touch of the

feminine, as in all the great pirates, and it sometimes gave him intuitions. Suddenly he tried the guessing game. "Hook," he called, "have you another voice?" Now Peter

could never resist a game, and he answered blithely in his own voice, "I have." "And another name?" "Ay, ay." "Vegetable?" asked Hook. "No." "Mineral?" "No."

"Animal?" "Yes." "Man?" "No!" This answer rang out scornfully. "Boy?" "Yes." "Ordinary boy?" "No!" "Wonderful boy?" To Wendy's pain the answer that rang out

this time was "Yes." "Are you in England?" "No." "Are you here?" "Yes." Hook was completely puzzled. "You ask him some questions," he said to the others, wiping his

damp brow. Smee reflected. "I can't think of a thing," he said regretfully. "Can't guess, can't guess," crowed Peter. "Do you give it up?" Of course in his pride he was

carrying the game too far, and the miscreants saw their chance. "Yes, yes," they answered eagerly. "Well, then," he cried, "I am Peter Pan." Pan! In a moment Hook was

himself again, and Smee and Starkey were his faithful henchmen. "Now we have him," Hook shouted. "Into the water, Smee. Starkey, mind the boat. Take him dead or

alive." He leaped as he spoke, and simultaneously came the gay voice of Peter. "Are you ready, boys?" "Ay, ay," from various parts of the lagoon. "Then lam into the

pirates." The fight was short and sharp. First to draw blood was John, who gallantly climbed into the boat and held Starkey. There was a fierce struggle, in which the cutlass was torn from the pirate's grasp. He wriggled overboard and John leapt after him. The dinghy drifted away. Here and there a head bobbed up in the water, and there was a flash of steel followed by a cry or a whoop. In the confusion some struck at their own side. The corkscrew of Smee got Tootles in the fourth rib, but he was himself pinked in turn by Curly. Farther from the rock Starkey was pressing Slightly and the twins hard. Where all this time was Peter? He was seeking bigger game. The others were all brave boys, and they must not be blamed for backing from the pirate captain. His iron claw made a circle of dead water round him, from which they fled like affrighted fishes.

But there was one who did not fear him: there was one prepared to enter that circle. Strangely, it was not in the water that they met. Hook rose to the rock to breathe, and at the same moment Peter scaled it on the opposite side. The rock was slippery as a ball, and they had to crawl rather than climb. Neither knew that the other was coming. Each feeling for a grip met the other's arm: in surprise they raised their heads; their faces were almost touching; so they met. Some of the greatest heroes have confessed that just before they fell to they had a sinking. Had it been so with Peter at that moment I would admit it. After all, this was the only man that the Sea-Cook had feared. But Peter had no sinking, he had one feeling only, gladness; and he gnashed his pretty teeth with joy. Quick as thought he snatched a knife from Hook's belt and was about to drive it home, when he saw that he was higher up the rock than his foe. It would not have been fighting fair. He gave the pirate a hand to help him up. It was then that Hook bit him. Not the pain of this but its unfairness was what dazed Peter. It made him quite helpless. He could only stare, horrified. Every child is affected thus the first time he is treated unfairly. All he thinks he has a right to when he comes to you to be yours is fairness. After you have been unfair to him he will love you again, but he will never afterwards be quite the same boy. No one ever gets over the first unfairness; no one except Peter. He often met it, but he always forgot it. I suppose that was the real difference between him and all the rest. So when he met it now it was like the first time; and he could just stare, helpless. Twice the iron hand clawed him. A few minutes afterwards the other boys saw Hook in the water striking wildly for the ship; no elation on his pestilent face now, only white fear, for the crocodile was in dogged pursuit of him. On ordinary occasions the boys would have swum alongside cheering; but now they were uneasy, for they had lost both Peter and Wendy, and were scouring the lagoon for them, calling them by name. They found the dinghy and went home in it, shouting "Peter, Wendy" as they went, but no answer came save mocking laughter from the mermaids. "They must be swimming back or flying," the boys concluded. They were not very anxious, they had such faith in Peter. They chuckled, boylike, because they would be late for bed; and it was all mother Wendy's fault! When their voices died away there came cold silence over the lagoon, and then a feeble cry. "Help, help!" Two small figures were beating against the rock; the girl had fainted and lay on the boy's arm. With a last effort Peter pulled her up the rock and then lay down beside her. Even as he also fainted saw that the water was rising. He knew that they would soon be drowned, but he could do no more. As they lay side by side a mermaid caught Wendy by the feet, and began pulling her softly into the water. Peter, feeling her slip from him, woke with a start, and was just in time to draw her back. But he had to tell her the truth. "We are on the rock, Wendy," he said, "but it is growing smaller. Soon the water will be over it." She did not understand even now. "We must go," she said, almost brightly. "Yes," he answered faintly. "Shall we swim or fly, Peter?" He had to tell her. "Do you think you could swim or fly as far as the island, Wendy, without my help?" She had to admit that she was

too tired. He moaned. "What is it?" she asked, anxious about him at once. "I can't help you, Wendy. Hook wounded me. I can neither fly nor swim." "Do you mean we shall

both be drowned?" "Look how the water is rising." They put their hands over their eyes to shut out the sight. They thought they would soon be no more. As they sat thus

something brushed against Peter as light as a kiss, and stayed there, as if saying timidly, "Can I be of any use?" It was the tail of a kite, which Michael had made some days

before. It had torn itself out of his hand and floated away. "Michael's kite," Peter said without interest, but next moment he had seized the tail, and was pulling the kite toward

him. "It lifted Michael off the ground," he cried; "why should it not carry you?" "Both of us!" "It can't lift two; Michael and Curly tried." "Let us draw lots," Wendy said

bravely. "And you a lady; never." Already he had tied the tail round her. She clung to him; she refused to go without him; but with a "Good-bye, Wendy," he pushed her

from the rock; and in a few minutes she was borne out of his sight. Peter was alone on the lagoon. The rock was very small now; soon it would be submerged. Pale rays of

light tiptoed across the waters; and by and by there was to be heard a sound at once the most musical and the most melancholy in the world: the mermaids calling to the moon.

Peter was not quite like other boys; but he was afraid at last. A tremor ran through him, like a shudder passing over the sea; but on the sea one shudder follows another till

there are hundreds of them, and Peter felt just the one. Next moment he was standing erect on the rock again, with that smile on his face and a drum beating within him. It

was saying, "To die will be an awfully big adventure." CHAPTER IX *The Never Bird* The last sounds Peter heard before he was quite alone were the mermaids retiring one

by one to their bedchambers under the sea. He was too far away to hear their doors shut; but every door in the coral caves where they live rings a tiny bell when it opens or

closes (as in all the nicest houses on the mainland), and he heard the bells. Steadily the waters rose till they were nibbling at his feet; and to pass the time until they made their

final gulp, he watched the only thing moving on the lagoon. He thought it was a piece of floating paper, perhaps part of the kite, and wondered idly how long it would take

to drift ashore. Presently he noticed as an odd thing that it was undoubtedly out upon the lagoon with some definite purpose, for it was fighting the tide, and sometimes

winning; and when it won, Peter, always sympathetic to the weaker side, could not help clapping; it was such a gallant piece of paper. It was not really a piece of paper; it

was the Never bird, making desperate efforts to reach Peter on her nest. By working her wings, in a way she had learned since the nest fell into the water, she was able to some

extent to guide her strange craft, but by the time Peter recognised her she was very exhausted. She had come to save him, to give him her nest, though there were eggs in it.

I rather wonder at the bird, for though he had been nice to her, he had also sometimes tormented her. I can suppose only that, like Mrs. Darling and the rest of them, she was

melted because he had all his first teeth. She called out to him what she had come for, and he called out to her what was she doing there; but of course neither of them

understood the other's language. In fanciful stories people can talk to the birds freely, and I wish for the moment I could pretend that this was such a story, and say that Peter

replied intelligently to the Never bird; but truth is best, and I want to tell only what really happened. Well, not only could they not understand each other, but they forgot their manners. "I—want—you—to—get—into—the—nest," the bird called, speaking as slowly and distinctly as possible, "and—then—you—can—drift—

ashore, but—I—am—too—tired—to—bring—it—any—nearer—so—you—must— try—to—swim—to—it." "What are you quacking about?" Peter answered.

"Why don't you let the nest drift as usual?" "I—want—you—" the bird said, and repeated it all over. Then Peter tried slow and distinct. "What—are—you—quacking—

about?" and so on. The Never bird became irritated; they have very short tempers. "You dunderheaded little jay," she screamed, "why don't you do as I tell you?" Peter felt

that she was calling him names, and at a venture he retorted hotly: "So are you!" Then rather curiously they both snapped out the same remark: "Shut up!" "Shut up!"

Nevertheless the bird was determined to save him if she could, and by one last mighty effort she propelled the nest against the rock. Then up she flew; deserting her eggs, so

as to make her meaning clear. Then at last he understood, and clutched the nest and waved his thanks to the bird as she fluttered overhead. It was not to receive his thanks,

however, that she hung there in the sky; it was not even to watch him get into the nest; it was to see what he did with her eggs. There were two large white eggs, and Peter

lifted them up and reflected. The bird covered her face with her wings, so as not to see the last of her eggs; but she could not help peeping between the feathers. I forget

whether I have told you that there was a stave on the rock, driven into it by some buccaneers of long ago to mark the site of buried treasure. The children had discovered the

glittering hoard, and when in mischievous mood used to fling showers of moidores, diamonds, pearls and pieces of eight to the gulls, who pounced upon them for food, and

then flew away, raging at the scurvy trick that had been played upon them. The stave was still there, and on it Starkey had hung his hat, a deep tarpaulin, watertight, with

broad brim. Peter put the eggs into this hat and set it on the lagoon. It floated beautifully. The Never bird saw at once what he was up to, and screamed her admiration of his

and, alas, Peter crowed his agreement with her. Then he got into the nest, reared the stave in it as a mast, and hung up his shirt for a sail. At the same moment the bird flutter

down upon the hat and once more sat snugly on her eggs. She drifted in one direction, and he was borne off in another, both cheering. Of course when Peter landed

beached his barque in a place where the bird would easily find it; but the hat was such a great success that she abandoned the nest. It drifted about till it went to pieces, an

often Starkey came to the shore of the lagoon, and with many bitter feelings watched the bird sitting on his hat. As we shall not see her again, it may be worth mentioni

here that all Never birds now build in that shape of nest, with a broad brim on which the youngsters take an airing. Great were the rejoicings when Peter reached the ho

under the ground almost as soon as Wendy, who had been carried hither and thither by the kite. Every boy had adventures to tell; but perhaps the biggest adventure of

was that they were several hours late for bed. This so inflated them that they did various dodgy things to get staying up still longer, such as demanding bandages; but Wer

though glorying in having them all home again safe and sound, was scandalised by the lateness of the hour, and cried, "To bed, to bed," in a voice that had to be obey

Next day, however, she was awfully tender, and gave out bandages to every one; and they played till bed-time at limping about and carrying their arms in slings. CHAPT

X. *The Happy Home* One important result of the brush on the lagoon was that it made the redskins their friends. Peter had saved Tiger Lily from a dreadful fate, and n there was nothing she and her braves would not do for him. All night they sat above, keeping watch over the home under the ground and awaiting the big attack by the pirates which obviously could not be much longer delayed. Even by day they hung about, smoking the pipe of peace, and looking almost as if they wanted tit-bits to eat. They called Peter the Great White Father, prostrating themselves before him; and he liked this tremendously, so that it was not really good for him. "The great white father," he would say to them in a very lordly manner, as they grovelled at his feet, "is glad to see the Piccaninny warriors protecting his wigwam from the pirates." "Me Tiger Lily," that lovely creature would reply. "Peter Pan save me, me his velly nice friend. Me no let pirates hurt him." She was far too pretty to cringe in this way, but Peter thought it his due, and he would answer condescendingly, "It is good. Peter Pan has spoken." Always when he said, "Peter Pan has spoken," it meant that they must now shut up, and they accepted it humbly in that spirit; but they were by no means so respectful to the other boys, whom they looked upon as just ordinary braves. They said "How-do?" to them, and things like that; and what annoyed the boys was that Peter seemed to think this all right. Secretly Wendy sympathised with them a little, but she was far too loyal a housewife to listen to any complaints against father. "Father knows best," she always said, whatever her private opinion must be. Her private opinion was that the redskins should not call her a squaw. We have now reached the evening that was to be known among them as the Night of Nights, because of its adventures and their upshot. The day, as if quietly gathering its forces, had been almost uneventful, and now the redskins in their blankets were at their posts above, while, below, the children were having their evening meal; all except Peter, who had gone out to get the time. The way you got the time on the island was to find the crocodile, and then stay near him till the clock struck. This meal happened to be a make-believe tea, and they sat round the board, guzzling in their greed; and really, what with their chatter and recriminations, the noise, as Wendy said, was positively deafening. To be sure, she did not mind noise, but she simply would not have them grabbing things, and then excusing themselves by saying that Tootles had pushed their elbow. There was a fixed rule that they must never hit back at meals, but should refer the matter of dispute to Wendy by raising the right arm politely and saying, "I complain of so-and-so;" but what usually happened was that they forgot to do this or did it too much. "Silence," cried Wendy when for the twentieth time she had told them that they were not all to speak at once. "Is your calabash empty, Slightly darling?" "Not quite empty, mummy," Slightly said, after looking into an imaginary mug. "He hasn't even begun to drink his milk," Nibs interposed. This was telling, and Slightly seized his chance. "I complain of Nibs," he cried promptly. John, however, had held up his hand first. "Well, John?" "May I sit in Peter's chair, as he is not here?" "Sit in father's chair, John!" Wendy was scandalised. "Certainly not." "He is not really our father," John answered. "He didn't even know how a father does till I showed him." This was grumbling. "We complain of John," cried the twins. Tootles held up his hand. He was so much the humblest of them, indeed he was the only humble one, that Wendy was specially gentle with him. "I don't suppose," Tootles said diffidently, "that I could be father." "No, Tootles." Once Tootles began, which was not very often, he had a silly way of going on. "As I can't be father," he said heavily, "I don't suppose, Michael, you would let me be baby?" "No, I won't," Michael rapped out. He was already in his basket. "As I can't be baby," Tootles said, getting heavier and heavier, "do you think I could be a twin?" "No, indeed," replied the twins; "it's awfully difficult to be a twin." "As I can't be anything important," said Tootles, "would any of you like to see me do a trick?"

"No," they all replied. Then at last he stopped. "I hadn't really any hope," he said. The hateful telling broke out again. "Slightly is coughing on the table." "The twins began

with cheese-cakes." "Curly is taking both butter and honey." "Nibs is speaking with his mouth full." "I complain of the twins." "I complain of Curly." "I complain of Nibs."

"Oh dear, oh dear," cried Wendy, "I'm sure I sometimes think that spinsters are to be envied." She told them to clear away, and sat down to her work-basket: a heavy load

of stockings and every knee with a hole in it as usual. "Wendy," remonstrated Michael, "I'm too big for a cradle." "I must have somebody in a cradle," she said almost tartly,

"and you are the littlest. A cradle is such a nice homely thing to have about a house." While she sewed they played around her; such a group of happy faces and dancing limbs

lit up by that romantic fire. It had become a very familiar scene this in the home under the ground, but we are looking on it for the last time. There was a step above, and

Wendy, you may be sure, was the first to recognise it. "Children, I hear your father's step. He likes you to meet him at the door." Above, the redskins crouched before Peter.

"Watch well, braves. I have spoken." And then, as so often before, the gay children dragged him from his tree. As so often before, but never again. He had brought nuts for

the boys as well as the correct time for Wendy. "Peter, you just spoil them, you know," Wendy simpered. "Ah, old lady," said Peter, hanging up his gun. "It was me told him

mothers are called old lady," Michael whispered to Curly. "I complain of Michael," said Curly instantly. The first twin came to Peter. "Father, we want to dance." "Dance

away, my little man," said Peter, who was in high good humour. "But we want you to dance." Peter was really the best dancer among them, but he pretended to be

scandalised. "Me! My old bones would rattle." "And mummy too." "What," cried Wendy, "the mother of such an armful, dance!" "But on a Saturday night," Slightly

insinuated. It was not really Saturday night, at least it may have been, for they had long lost count of the days; but always if they wanted to do anything special they said this

was Saturday night, and then they did it. "Of course it is Saturday night, Peter," Wendy said, relenting. "People of our figure, Wendy." "But it is only among our own

progeny." "True, true." So they were told they could dance, but they must put on their nighties first. "Ah, old lady," Peter said aside to Wendy, warming himself by the fire

and looking down at her as she sat turning a heel, "there is nothing more pleasant of an evening for you and me when the day's toil is over than to rest by the fire with the

little ones near by." "It is sweet, Peter, isn't it?" Wendy said, frightfully gratified. "Peter, I think Curly has your nose." "Michael takes after you." She went to him and put

her hand on his shoulder. "Dear Peter," she said, "with such a large family, of course, I have now passed my best, but you don't want to change me, do you?" "No, Wendy."

Certainly he did not want a change, but he looked at her uncomfortably, blinking, you know, like one not sure whether he was awake or asleep. "Peter, what is it?" "I was just

thinking," he said, a little scared. "It is only make-believe, isn't it, that I am their father?" "Oh yes," Wendy said primly. "You see," he continued apologetically, "it would

make me seem so old to be their real father." "But they are ours, Peter, yours and mine." "But not really, Wendy?" he asked anxiously. "Not if you don't wish it," she replied;

and she distinctly heard his sigh of relief. "Peter," she asked, trying to speak firmly, "what are your exact feelings for me?" "Those of a devoted son, Wendy." "I thought so," she said, and went and sat by herself at the extreme end of the room. "You are so queer," he said, frankly puzzled, "and Tiger Lily is just the same. There is something she wants to be to me, but she says it is not my mother." "No, indeed, it is not," Wendy replied with frightful emphasis. Now we know why she was prejudiced against the redskins. "Then what is it?" "It isn't for a lady to tell." "Oh, very well," Peter said, a little nettled. "Perhaps Tinker Bell will tell me." "Oh yes, Tinker Bell will tell you," Wendy retorted scornfully. "She is an abandoned little creature." Here Tink, who was in her boudoir, eavesdropping, squeaked out something impudent. "She says she glories in being abandoned," Peter interpreted. He had a sudden idea. "Perhaps Tink wants to be my mother?" "You silly ass!" cried Tinker Bell in a passion. She had said it so often that Wendy needed no translation. "I almost agree with her," Wendy snapped. Fancy Wendy snapping. But she had been much tried, and she little knew what was to happen before the night was out. If she had known she would not have snapped. None of them knew. Perhaps it was best not to know. Their ignorance gave them one more glad hour; and as it was to be their last hour on the island, let us rejoice that there were sixty glad minutes in it. They sang and danced in their night-gowns. Such a deliciously creepy song it was, in which they pretended to be frightened at their own shadows; little witting that so soon shadows would close in upon them, from whom they would shrink in real fear. So uproariously gay was the dance, and how they buffeted each other on the bed and out of it! It was a pillow fight rather than a dance, and when it was finished, the pillows insisted on one bout more, like partners who know that they may never meet again. The stories they told, before it was time for Wendy's good-night story! Even Slightly tried to tell a story that night, but the beginning was so fearfully dull that it appalled not only the others, but himself, and he said happily: "Yes, it is a dull beginning. I say, let us pretend that it is the end." And then at last they all got into bed for Wendy's story, the story they loved best, the story Peter hated. Usually when she began to tell this story he left the room or put his hands over his ears; and possibly if he had done either of those things this time they might all still be on the island. But to-night he remained on his stool; and we shall see what happened. CHAPTER XI *Wendy's Story* Listen, then," said Wendy, settling down to her story, with Michael at her feet and seven boys in the bed. "There was once a gentleman—" "I had rather he had been a lady," Curly said. "I wish he had been a white rat," said Nibs. "Quiet," their mother admonished them. "There was a lady also, and—" "O mummy," cried the first twin, "you mean that there is a lady also, don't you? She is not dead, is she?" "Oh no." "I am awfully glad she isn't dead," said Tootles. "Are you glad, John?" "Of course I am." "Are you glad, Nibs?" "Rather." "Are you glad, Twins?" "We are just glad." "Oh dear," sighed Wendy. "Little less noise there," Peter called out, determined that she should have fair play, however beastly a story it might be in his opinion. "The gentleman's name," Wendy continued, "was Mr. Darling, and her name was Mrs. Darling." "I knew them," John said, to annoy the others. "I think I knew them," said Michael rather doubtfully. "They were married, you know," explained Wendy, "and what do you think they had?" "White rats," cried Nibs, inspired. "No." "It's awfully puzzling," said Tootles, who knew the story by heart. "Quiet, Tootles. They had three descendants." "What is descendants?" "Well, you are one, Twin." "Do you hear that, John? I am a descendant." "Descendants are only children," said John. "Oh dear, oh dear," sighed Wendy. "Now these three children had a faithful nurse called Nana; but

Mr. Darling was angry with her and chained her up in the yard; and so all the children flew away." "It's an awfully good story," said Nibs. "They flew away," Wendy continued, "to the Neverland, where the lost children are." "I just thought they did," Curly broke in excitedly. "I don't know how it is, but I just thought they did!" "O Wendy," cried Tootles, "was one of the lost children called Tootles?" "Yes, he was." "I am in a story. Hurrah, I am in a story, Nibs." "Hush. Now I want you to consider the feelings of the unhappy parents with all their children flown away." "Oo!" they all moaned, though they were not really considering the feelings of the unhappy parents one jot. "Think of the empty beds!" "It's awfully sad," the first twin said cheerfully. "I don't see how it can have a happy ending," said the second twin. "Do you, Nibs?" "I'm frightfully anxious." "If you knew how great is a mother's love," Wendy told them triumphantly, "you would have no fear." She had now come to the part that Peter hated.

"I do like a mother's love," said Tootles, hitting Nibs with a pillow. "Do you like a mother's love, Nibs?" "I do just," said Nibs, hitting back. "You see," Wendy said complacently, "our heroine knew that the mother would always leave the window open for her children to fly back by; so they stayed away for years and had a lovely time."

"Did they ever go back?" "Let us now," said Wendy, bracing herself for her finest effort, "take a peep into the future;" and they all gave themselves the twist that makes peeps into the future easier. "Years have rolled by; and who is this elegant lady of uncertain age alighting at London Station?" "O Wendy, who is she?" cried Nibs, every bit as excited as if he didn't know. "Can it be—yes—no—it is—the fair Wendy!" "Oh!" "And who are the two noble portly figures accompanying her, now grown to man's estate? Can they be John and Michael? They are!" "Oh!" "See, dear brothers," says Wendy, pointing upwards, "there is the window still standing open. Ah, now we are rewarded for our sublime faith in a mother's love." So up they flew to their mummy and daddy; and pen cannot describe the happy scene, over which we draw a veil." That was the story, and they were as pleased with it as the fair narrator herself. Everything just as it should be, you see. Off we skip like the most heartless things in the world, which is what children are, but so attractive; and we have an entirely selfish time; and then when we have need of special attention we nobly return for it, confident that we shall be embraced instead of smacked. So great indeed was their faith in a mother's love that they felt they could afford to be callous for a bit longer. But there was one there who knew better, and when Wendy finished he uttered a hollow groan. "What is it, Peter?" she cried, running to him, thinking he was ill. She felt him solicitously, lower down than his chest. "Where is it, Peter?" "It isn't that kind of pain," Peter replied darkly. "Then what kind is it?" "Wendy, you are wrong about mothers." They all gathered round him in affright, so alarming was his agitation; and with a fine candour he told them what he had hitherto concealed. "Long ago," he said, "I thought like you that my mother would always keep the window open for me; so I stayed away for moons and moons and moons, and then flew back; but the window was barred, for mother had forgotten all about me, and there was another little boy sleeping in my bed." I am not sure that this was true, but Peter thought it was true; and it scared them. "Are you sure mothers are like that?" "Yes." So this was the truth about mothers. The toads! Still it is best to be careful; and no one knows so quickly as a child when he should give in.

"Wendy, let us go home," cried John and Michael together. "Yes," she said, clutching them. "Not to-night?" asked the lost boys bewildered. They knew in what they called their hearts that one can get on quite well without a mother, and that it is only the mothers who think you can't. "At once," Wendy replied resolutely, for the horrible thought

had come to her: "Perhaps mother is in half mourning by this time." This dread made her forgetful of what must be Peter's feelings, and she said to him rather sharply, "Peter,

will you make the necessary arrangements?" "If you wish it," he replied, as coolly as if she had asked him to pass the nuts. Not so much as a sorry-to-lose-you between them!

If she did not mind the parting, he was going to show her, was Peter, that neither did he. But of course he cared very much; and he was so full of wrath against grown-ups,

who, as usual, were spoiling everything, that as soon as he got inside his tree he breathed intentionally quick short breaths at the rate of about five to a second. He did this

because there is a saying in the Neverland that, every time you breathe, a grown-up dies; and Peter was killing them off vindictively as fast as possible. Then having given

the necessary instructions to the redskins he returned to the home, where an unworthy scene had been enacted in his absence. Panic-stricken at the thought of losing Wendy,

the lost boys had advanced upon her threateningly. "It will be worse than before she came," they cried. "We shan't let her go." "Let's keep her prisoner." "Ay, chain her up."

In her extremity an instinct told her to which of them to turn. "Tootles," she cried, "I appeal to you." Was it not strange? she appealed to Tootles, quite the silliest one.

Grandly, however, did Tootles respond. For that one moment he dropped his silliness and spoke with dignity. "I am just Tootles," he said, "and nobody minds me. But the

first who does not behave to Wendy like an English gentleman I will blood him severely." He drew his hanger; and for that instant his sun was at noon. The others held back

uneasily. Then Peter returned, and they saw at once that they would get no support from him. He would keep no girl in the Neverland against her will. "Wendy," he said,

striding up and down, "I have asked the redskins to guide you through the wood, as flying tires you so." "Thank you, Peter." "Then," he continued, in the short sharp voice

of one accustomed to be obeyed, "Tinker Bell will take you across the sea. Wake her, Nibs." Nibs had to knock twice before he got an answer, though Tink had really been

sitting up in bed listening for some time. "Who are you? How dare you? Go away," she cried. "You are to get up, Tink," Nibs called, "and take Wendy on a journey." Of

course Tink had been delighted to hear that Wendy was going; but she was jolly well determined not to be her courier, and she said so in still more offensive language. Then

she pretended to be asleep again. "She says she won't," Nibs exclaimed, aghast at such insubordination, whereupon Peter went sternly toward the young lady's chamber.

"Tink," he rapped out, "if you don't get up and dress at once I will open the curtains, and then we shall all see you in your *negligée*." This made her leap to the floor. "Who

said I wasn't getting up?" she cried. In the meantime the boys were gazing very forlornly at Wendy, now equipped with John and Michael for the journey. By this time they

were dejected, not merely because they were about to lose her, but also because they felt that she was going off to something nice to which they had not been invited. Novelty

was beckoning to them as usual. Crediting them with a nobler feeling, Wendy melted. "Dear ones," she said, "if you will all come with me I feel almost sure I can get my

father and mother to adopt you." The invitation was meant specially for Peter, but each of the boys was thinking exclusively of himself, and at once they jumped with joy.

"But won't they think us rather a handful?" Nibs asked in the middle of his jump. "Oh no," said Wendy, rapidly thinking it out, "it will only mean having a few beds in the drawing-room; they can be hidden behind screens on first Thursdays." "Peter, can we go?" they all cried imploringly. They took it for granted that if they went he would

go also, but really they scarcely cared. Thus children are ever ready, when novelty knocks, to desert their dearest ones. "All right," Peter replied with a bitter smile; and

immediately they rushed to get their things. "And now, Peter," Wendy said, thinking she had put everything right, "I am going to give you your medicine before you go."

She loved to give them medicine, and undoubtedly gave them too much. Of course it was only water, but it was out of a bottle, and she always shook the bottle and counted

the drops, which gave it a certain medicinal quality. On this occasion, however, she did not give Peter his draught, for just as she had prepared it, she saw a look on his face

that made her heart sink. "Get your things, Peter," she cried, shaking. "No," he answered, pretending indifference, "I am not going with you, Wendy." "Yes, Peter." "No."

To show that her departure would leave him unmoved, he skipped up and down the room, playing gaily on his heartless pipes. She had to run about after him, though it was

rather undignified. "To find your mother," she coaxed. Now, if Peter had ever quite had a mother, he no longer missed her. He could do very well without one. He had

thought them out, and remembered only their bad points. "No, no," he told Wendy decisively; "perhaps she would say I was old, and I just want always to be a little boy and

to have fun." "But, Peter—" "No." And so the others had to be told. "Peter isn't coming." Peter not coming! They gazed blankly at him, their sticks over their backs, and

on each stick a bundle. Their first thought was that if Peter was not going he had probably changed his mind about letting them go. But he was far too proud for that. "If you

find your mothers," he said darkly, "I hope you will like them." The awful cynicism of this made an uncomfortable impression, and most of them began to look rather

doubtful. After all, their faces said, were they not noodles to want to go? "Now then," cried Peter, "no fuss, no blubbering; good-bye, Wendy;" and he held out his hand

cheerily, quite as if they must really go now, for he had something important to do. She had to take his hand, as there was no indication that he would prefer a thimble. "You

will remember about changing your flannels, Peter?" she said, lingering over him. She was always so particular about their flannels. "Yes." "And you will take your

medicine?" "Yes." That seemed to be everything; and an awkward pause followed. Peter, however, was not the kind that breaks down before people. "Are you ready, Tinker

Bell?" he called out. "Ay, ay!" "Then lead the way." Tink darted up the nearest tree; but no one followed her, for it was at this moment that the pirates made their dreadful

attack upon the redskins. Above, where all had been so still, the air was rent with shrieks and the clash of steel. Below, there was dead silence. Mouths opened and remained

open. Wendy fell on her knees, but her arms were extended toward Peter. All arms were extended to him, as if suddenly blown in his direction; they were beseeching him

mutely not to desert them. As for Peter, he seized his sword, the same he thought he had slain Barbecue with; and the lust of battle was in his eye. CHAPTER XII *The*

Children Are Carried Off The pirate attack had been a complete surprise: a sure proof that the unscrupulous Hook had conducted it improperly, for to surprise redskins fairly

is beyond the wit of the white man. By all the unwritten laws of savage warfare it is always the redskin who attacks, and with the wiliness of his race he does it just before the

dawn, at which time he knows the courage of the whites to be at its lowest ebb. The white men have in the meantime made a rude stockade on the summit of yonder undulating ground, at the foot of which a stream runs, for it is destruction to be too far from water. There they await the onslaught, the inexperienced ones clutching their revolvers and treading on twigs, but the old hands sleeping tranquilly until just before the dawn. Through the long black night the savage scouts wriggle, snake-like, among the grass without stirring a blade. The brushwood closes behind them as silently as sand into which a mole has dived. Not a sound is to be heard, save when they give vent to a wonderful imitation of the lonely call of the coyote. The cry is answered by other braves; and some of them do it even better than the coyotes, who are not very good at it. So the chill hours wear on, and the long suspense is horribly trying to the paleface who has to live through it for the first time; but to the trained hand those ghastly calls and still ghastlier silences are but an intimation of how the night is marching. That this was the usual procedure was so well known to Hook that in disregarding it he cannot be excused on the plea of ignorance. The Piccaninnies, on their part, trusted implicitly to his honour, and their whole action of the night stands out in marked contrast to his.

They left nothing undone that was consistent with the reputation of their tribe. With that alertness of the senses which is at once the marvel and despair of civilised peoples, they knew that the pirates were on the island from the moment one of them trod on a dry stick; and in an incredibly short space of time the coyote cries began. Every foot of ground between the spot where Hook had landed his forces and the home under the trees was stealthily examined by braves wearing their moccasins with the heels in front. They found only one hillock with a stream at its base, so that Hook had no choice; here he must establish himself and wait for just before the dawn. Everything being thus mapped out with almost diabolical cunning, the main body of the redskins folded their blankets around them, and in the phlegmatic manner that is to them the pearl of manhood squatted above the children's home, awaiting the cold moment when they should deal pale death. Here dreaming, though wide-awake, of the exquisite tortures to which they were to put him at break of day, those confiding savages were found by the treacherous Hook. From the accounts afterwards supplied by such of the scouts as escaped the carnage, he does not seem even to have paused at the rising ground, though it is certain that in that grey light he must have seen it: no thought of waiting to be attacked appears from first to last to have visited his subtle mind; he would not even hold off till the night was nearly spent; on he pounded with no policy but to fall to. What could the bewildered scouts do, masters as they were of every warlike artifice save this one, but trot helplessly after him, exposing themselves fatally to view, the while they gave pathetic utterance to the coyote cry. Around the brave Tiger Lily were a dozen of her stoutest warriors, and they suddenly saw the perfidious pirates bearing down upon them. Fell from their eyes then the film through which they had looked at victory. No more would they torture at the stake. For them the happy hunting-grounds now. They knew it; but as their fathers' sons they acquitted themselves. Even then they had time to gather in a phalanx that would have been hard to break had they risen quickly, but this they were forbidden to do by the traditions of their race. It is written that the noble savage must never express surprise in the presence of the white. Thus terrible as the sudden appearance of the pirates must have been to them, they remained stationary for a moment, not a muscle moving; as if the foe had come by invitation. Then, indeed, the tradition gallantly upheld, they seized their weapons, and the air was torn with the war-cry; but it was now too late. It is no part of ours to describe what was a massacre rather than a fight. Thus perished many of the flower of the Piccaninny tribe. Not all unavenged did they die, for with Lean Wolf fell Alf Mason, to disturb the Spanish Main

no more, and among others who bit the dust were Geo. Scourie, Chas. Turley, and the Alsatian Foggerty. Turley fell to the tomahawk of the terrible Panther, who ultimately

cut a way through the pirates with Tiger Lily and a small remnant of the tribe. To what extent Hook is to blame for his tactics on this occasion is for the historian to decide.

Had he waited on the rising ground till the proper hour he and his men would probably have been butchered; and in judging him it is only fair to take this into account. What

he should perhaps have done was to acquaint his opponents that he proposed to follow a new method. On the other hand this, as destroying the element of surprise, would

have made his strategy of no avail, so that the whole question is beset with difficulties. One cannot at least withhold a reluctant admiration for the wit that had conceived so

bold a scheme, and the fell genius with which it was carried out. What were his own feelings about himself at that triumphant moment? Fain would his dogs have known, as

breathing heavily and wiping their cutlasses, they gathered at a discreet distance from his hook, and squinted through their ferret eyes at this extraordinary man. Elation must

have been in his heart, but his face did not reflect it: ever a dark and solitary enigma, he stood aloof from his followers in spirit as in substance. The night's work was not yet

over, for it was not the redskins he had come out to destroy; they were but the bees to be smoked, so that he should get at the honey. It was Pan he wanted, Pan and Wendy

and their band, but chiefly Pan. Peter was such a small boy that one tends to wonder at the man's hatred of him. True he had flung Hook's arm to the crocodile; but even this

and the increased insecurity of life to which it led, owing to the crocodile's pertinacity, hardly account for a vindictiveness so relentless and malignant. The truth is that there

was a something about Peter which goaded the pirate captain to frenzy. It was not his courage, it was not his engaging appearance, it was not——. There is no beating about

the bush, for we know quite well what it was, and have got to tell. It was Peter's cockiness. This had got on Hook's nerves; it made his iron claw twitch, and at night it

disturbed him like an insect. While Peter lived, the tortured man felt that he was a lion in a cage into which a sparrow had come. The question now was how to get down the

trees, or how to get his dogs down? He ran his greedy eyes over them, searching for the thinnest ones. They wriggled uncomfortably, for they knew he would not scruple to

ram them down with poles. In the meantime, what of the boys? We have seen them at the first clang of weapons, turned as it were into stone figures, open-mouthed, all

appealing with outstretched arms to Peter; and we return to them as their mouths close, and their arms fall to their sides. The pandemonium above has ceased almost as

suddenly as it arose, passed like a fierce gust of wind; but they know that in the passing it has determined their fate. Which side had won? The pirates, listening avidly at the

mouths of the trees, heard the question put by every boy, and alas, they also heard Peter's answer. "If the redskins have won," he said, "they will beat the tom-tom; it is always

their sign of victory." Now Smee had found the tom-tom, and was at that moment sitting on it. "You will never hear the tom-tom again," he muttered, but inaudibly of

course, for strict silence had been enjoined. To his amazement Hook signed to him to beat the tom-tom, and slowly there came to Smee an understanding of the dreadful

wickedness of the order. Never, probably, had this simple man admired Hook so much. Twice Smee beat upon the instrument, and then stopped to listen gleefully. "The tom-tom," the miscreants heard Peter cry; "an Indian victory!" The doomed children answered with a cheer that was music to the black hearts above, and almost immediately

they repeated their goodbyes to Peter. This puzzled the pirates, but all their other feelings were swallowed by a base delight that the enemy were about to come up the trees.

They smirked at each other and rubbed their hands. Rapidly and silently Hook gave his orders: one man to each tree, and the others to arrange themselves in a line two yards

apart. CHAPTER XIII *Do You Believe In Fairies?* The more quickly this horror is disposed of the better. The first to emerge from his tree was Curly. He rose out of it into

the arms of Cecco, who flung him to Smee, who flung him to Starkey, who flung him to Bill Jukes, who flung him to Noodler, and so he was tossed from one to another till

he fell at the feet of the black pirate. All the boys were plucked from their trees in this ruthless manner; and several of them were in the air at a time, like bales of goods flung

from hand to hand. A different treatment was accorded to Wendy, who came last. With ironical politeness Hook raised his hat to her, and, offering her his arm, escorted her

to the spot where the others were being gagged. He did it with such an air, he was so frightfully *distingué*, that she was too fascinated to cry out. She was only a little girl.

Perhaps it is tell-tale to divulge that for a moment Hook entranced her, and we tell on her only because her slip led to strange results. Had she haughtily unhanded him (and

we should have loved to write it of her), she would have been hurled through the air like the others, and then Hook would probably not have been present at the tying of the

children; and had he not been at the tying he would not have discovered Slightly's secret, and without the secret he could not presently have made his foul attempt on Peter's

life. They were tied to prevent their flying away, doubled up with their knees close to their ears; and for this job the black pirate had cut a rope into nine equal pieces. All went

well until Slightly's turn came, when he was found to be like those irritating parcels that use up all the string in going round and leave no tags with which to tie a knot. The

pirates kicked him in their rage, just as you kick the parcel (though in fairness you should kick the string); and strange to say it was Hook who told them to belay their

violence. His lip was curled with malicious triumph. While his dogs were merely sweating because every time they tried to pack the unhappy lad tight in one part he bulged

out in another, Hook's master mind had gone far beneath Slightly's surface, probing not for effects but for causes; and his exultation showed that he had found them. Slightly,

white to the gills, knew that Hook had surprised his secret, which was this, that no boy so blown out could use a tree wherein an average man need stick. Poor Slightly, most

wretched of all the children now, for he was in a panic about Peter, bitterly regretted what he had done. Madly addicted to the drinking of water when he was hot, he had

swelled in consequence to his present girth, and instead of reducing himself to fit his tree he had, unknown to the others, whittled his tree to make it fit him. Sufficient of this

Hook guessed to persuade him that Peter at last lay at his mercy, but no word of the dark design that now formed in the subterranean caverns of his mind crossed his lips; he

merely signed that the captives were to be conveyed to the ship, and that he would be alone. How to convey them? Hunched up in their ropes they might indeed be rolled

down hill like barrels, but most of the way lay through a morass. Again Hook's genius surmounted difficulties. He indicated that the little house must be used as a conveyance.

The children were flung into it, four stout pirates raised it on their shoulders, the others fell in behind, and singing the hateful pirate chorus the strange procession set off through the wood. I don't know whether any of the children were crying; if so, the singing drowned the sound; but as the little house disappeared in the forest, a brave though

tiny jet of smoke issued from its chimney as if defying Hook. Hook saw it, and it did Peter a bad service. It dried up any trickle of pity for him that may have remained in

the pirate's infuriated breast. The first thing he did on finding himself alone in the fast falling night was to tiptoe to Slightly's tree, and make sure that it provided him with

a passage. Then for long he remained brooding; his hat of ill omen on the sward, so that a gentle breeze which had arisen might play refreshingly through his hair. Dark as

were his thoughts his blue eyes were as soft as the periwinkle. Intently he listened for any sound from the nether world, but all was as silent below as above; the house under

the ground seemed to be but one more empty tenement in the void. Was that boy asleep, or did he stand waiting at the foot of Slightly's tree, with his dagger in his hand?

There was no way of knowing, save by going down. Hook let his cloak slip softly to the ground, and then biting his lips till a lewd blood stood on them, he stepped into the

tree. He was a brave man; but for a moment he had to stop there and wipe his brow, which was dripping like a candle. Then silently he let himself go into the unknown. He

arrived unmolested at the foot of the shaft, and stood still again, biting at his breath, which had almost left him. As his eyes became accustomed to the dim light various objects

in the home under the trees took shape; but the only one on which his greedy gaze rested, long sought for and found at last, was the great bed. On the bed lay Peter fast asleep.

Unaware of the tragedy being enacted above, Peter had continued, for a little time after the children left, to play gaily on his pipes: no doubt rather a forlorn attempt to prove

to himself that he did not care. Then he decided not to take his medicine, so as to grieve Wendy. Then he lay down on the bed outside the coverlet, to vex her still more; for

she had always tucked them inside it, because you never know that you may not grow chilly at the turn of the night. Then he nearly cried; but it struck him how indignant

she would be if he laughed instead; so he laughed a haughty laugh and fell asleep in the middle of it. Sometimes, though not often, he had dreams, and they were more painful

than the dreams of other boys. For hours he could not be separated from these dreams, though he wailed piteously in them. They had to do, I think, with the riddle of his

existence. At such times it had been Wendy's custom to take him out of bed and sit with him on her lap, soothing him in dear ways of her own invention, and when he grew

calmer to put him back to bed before he quite woke up, so that he should not know of the indignity to which she had subjected him. But on this occasion he had fallen at once

into a dreamless sleep. One arm dropped over the edge of the bed, one leg was arched, and the unfinished part of his laugh was stranded on his mouth, which was open,

showing the little pearls. Thus defenceless Hook found him. He stood silent at the foot of the tree looking across the chamber at his enemy. Did no feeling of compassion

disturb his sombre breast? The man was not wholly evil; he loved flowers (I have been told) and sweet music (he was himself no mean performer on the harpsichord); and,

let it be frankly admitted, the idyllic nature of the scene stirred him profoundly. Mastered by his better self he would have returned reluctantly up the tree, but for one thing.

What stayed him was Peter's impertinent appearance as he slept. The open mouth, the drooping arm, the arched knee: they were such a personification of cockiness as, taken

together, will never again one may hope be presented to eyes so sensitive to their offensiveness. They steeled Hook's heart. If his rage had broken him into a hundred pieces, every one of them would have disregarded the incident, and leapt at the sleeper. Though a light from the one lamp shone dimly on the bed Hook stood in darkness himself,

and at the first stealthy step forward he discovered an obstacle, the door of Slightly's tree. It did not entirely fill the aperture, and he had been looking over it. Feeling for the

catch, he found to his fury that it was low down, beyond his reach. To his disordered brain it seemed then that the irritating quality in Peter's face and figure visibly increased,

and he rattled the door and flung himself against it. Was his enemy to escape him after all? But what was that? The red in his eye had caught sight of Peter's medicine standing

on a ledge within easy reach. He fathomed what it was straightway, and immediately he knew that the sleeper was in his power. Lest he should be taken alive, Hook always

carried about his person a dreadful drug, blended by himself of all the death-dealing rings that had come into his possession. These he had boiled down into a yellow liquid

quite unknown to science, which was probably the most virulent poison in existence. Five drops of this he now added to Peter's cup. His hand shook, but it was in exultation

rather than in shame. As he did it he avoided glancing at the sleeper, but not lest pity should unnerve him; merely to avoid spilling. Then one long gloating look he cast upon

his victim, and turning, wormed his way with difficulty up the tree. As he emerged at the top he looked the very spirit of evil breaking from its hole. Donning his hat at its

most rakish angle, he wound his cloak around him, holding one end in front as if to conceal his person from the night, of which it was the blackest part, and muttering

strangely to himself stole away through the trees. Peter slept on. The light guttered and went out, leaving the tenement in darkness; but still he slept. It must have been not

less than ten o'clock by the crocodile, when he suddenly sat up in his bed, wakened by he knew not what. It was a soft cautious tapping on the door of his tree. Soft and

cautious, but in that stillness it was sinister. Peter felt for his dagger till his hand gripped it. Then he spoke. "Who is that?" For long there was no answer: then again the knock.

"Who are you?" No answer. He was thrilled, and he loved being thrilled. In two strides he reached his door. Unlike Slightly's door it filled the aperture, so that he could not

see beyond it, nor could the one knocking see him. "I won't open unless you speak," Peter cried. Then at last the visitor spoke, in a lovely bell-like voice. "Let me in, Peter."

It was Tink, and quickly he unbarred to her. She flew in excitedly, her face flushed and her dress stained with mud. "What is it?" "Oh, you could never guess," she cried, and

offered him three guesses. "Out with it!" he shouted; and in one ungrammatical sentence, as long as the ribbons conjurers pull from their mouths, she told of the capture of

Wendy and the boys. Peter's heart bobbed up and down as he listened. Wendy bound, and on the pirate ship; she who loved everything to be just so! "I'll rescue her," he

cried, leaping at his weapons. As he leapt he thought of something he could do to please her. He could take his medicine. His hand closed on the fatal draught. "No!" shrieked

Tinker Bell, who had heard Hook muttering about his deed as he sped through the forest. "Why not?" "It is poisoned." "Poisoned? Who could have poisoned it?" "Hook."

"Don't be silly. How could Hook have got down here?" Alas, Tinker Bell could not explain this, for even she did not know the dark secret of Slightly's tree. Nevertheless

Hook's words had left no room for doubt. The cup was poisoned. "Besides," said Peter, quite believing himself, "I never fell asleep." He raised the cup. No time for words

now; time for deeds; and with one of her lightning movements Tink got between his lips and the draught, and drained it to the dregs. "Why, Tink, how dare you drink my medicine?" But she did not answer. Already she was reeling in the air. "What is the matter with you?" cried Peter, suddenly afraid. "It was poisoned, Peter," she told him

softly; "and now I am going to be dead." "O Tink, did you drink it to save me?" "Yes." "But why, Tink?" Her wings would scarcely carry her now, but in reply she alighted

on his shoulder and gave his chin a loving bite. She whispered in his ear "you silly ass," and then, tottering to her chamber, lay down on the bed. His head almost filled the

fourth wall of her little room as he knelt near her in distress. Every moment her light was growing fainter; and he knew that if it went out she would be no more. She liked

his tears so much that she put out her beautiful finger and let them run over it. Her voice was so low that at first he could not make out what she said. Then he made it out.

She was saying that she thought she could get well again if children believed in fairies. Peter flung out his arms. There were no children there, and it was night-time; but he

addressed all who might be dreaming of the Neverland, and who were therefore nearer to him than you think: boys and girls in their nighties, and naked papooses in their

baskets hung from trees. "Do you believe?" he cried. Tink sat up in bed almost briskly to listen to her fate. She fancied she heard answers in the affirmative, and then again

she wasn't sure. "What do you think?" she asked Peter. "If you believe," he shouted to them, "clap your hands; don't let Tink die." Many clapped. Some didn't. A few little

beasts hissed. The clapping stopped suddenly; as if countless mothers had rushed to their nurseries to see what on earth was happening; but already Tink was saved. First

her voice grew strong; then she popped out of bed; then she was flashing through the room more merry and impudent than ever. She never thought of thanking those who

believed, but she would have liked to get at the ones who had hissed. "And now to rescue Wendy." The moon was riding in a cloudy heaven when Peter rose from his tree

begirt with weapons and wearing little else, to set out upon his perilous quest. It was not such a night as he would have chosen. He had hoped to fly, keeping not far from the

ground so that nothing unwonted should escape his eyes; but in that fitful light to have flown low would have meant trailing his shadow through the trees, thus disturbing the

birds and acquainting a watchful foe that he was astir. He regretted now that he had given the birds of the island such strange names that they are very wild and difficult of

approach. There was no other course but to press forward in redskin fashion, at which happily he was an adept. But in what direction, for he could not be sure that the children

had been taken to the ship? A slight fall of snow had obliterated all footmarks; and a deathly silence pervaded the island, as if for a space Nature stood still in horror of the

recent carnage. He had taught the children something of the forest lore that he had himself learned from Tiger Lily and Tinker Bell, and knew that in their dire hour they

were not likely to forget it. Slightly, if he had an opportunity, would blaze the trees, for instance, Curly would drop seeds, and Wendy would leave her handkerchief at some

important place. But morning was needed to search for such guidance, and he could not wait. The upper world had called him, but would give no help. The crocodile passed

him, but not another living thing, not a sound, not a movement; and yet he knew well that sudden death might be at the next tree, or stalking him from behind. He swore this

terrible oath: "Hook or me this time." Now he crawled forward like a snake; and again, erect, he darted across a space on which the moonlight played: one finger on his

and his dagger at the ready. He was frightfully happy. CHAPTER XIV *The Pirate Ship* One green light squinting over Kidd's Creek, which is near the mouth of the pir river, marked where the brig, the *Jolly Roger*, lay, low in the water; a rakish-looking craft foul to the hull, every beam in her detestable like ground strewn with mangled

feathers. She was the cannibal of the seas, and scarce needed that watchful eye, for she floated immune in the horror of her name. She was wrapped in the blanket of night,

through which no sound from her could have reached the shore. There was little sound, and none agreeable save the whir of the ship's sewing machine at which Smee sat,

ever industrious and obliging, the essence of the commonplace, pathetic Smee. I know not why he was so infinitely pathetic, unless it were because he was so pathetically

unaware of it; but even strong men had to turn hastily from looking at him, and more than once on summer evenings he had touched the fount of Hook's tears and made it

flow. Of this, as of almost everything else, Smee was quite unconscious. A few of the pirates leant over the bulwarks drinking in the miasma of the night; others sprawled

by barrels over games of dice and cards; and the exhausted four who had carried the little house lay prone on the deck, where even in their sleep they rolled skilfully to this

side or that out of Hook's reach, lest he should claw them mechanically in passing. Hook trod the deck in thought. O man unfathomable. It was his hour of triumph. Peter

had been removed for ever from his path, and all the other boys were on the brig, about to walk the plank. It was his grimmest deed since the days when he had brought

Barbecue to heel; and knowing as we do how vain a tabernacle is man, could we be surprised had he now paced the deck unsteadily, bellied out by the winds of his success?

But there was no elation in his gait, which kept pace with the action of his sombre mind. Hook was profoundly dejected. He was often thus when communing with himself

on board ship in the quietude of the night. It was because he was so terribly alone. This inscrutable man never felt more alone than when surrounded by his dogs. They were

socially so inferior to him. Hook was not his true name. To reveal who he really was would even at this date set the country in a blaze; but as those who read between the lines

must already have guessed, he had been at a famous public school; and its traditions still clung to him like garments, with which indeed they are largely concerned. Thus it

was offensive to him even now to board a ship in the same dress in which he grappled her; and he still adhered in his walk to the school's distinguished slouch. But above all

he retained the passion for good form. Good form! However much he may have degenerated, he still knew that this is all that really matters. From far within him he heard a

creaking as of rusty portals, and through them came a stern tap-tap-tap, like hammering in the night when one cannot sleep. "Have you been good form to-day?" was their

eternal question. "Fame, fame, that glittering bauble, it is mine," he cried. "Is it quite good form to be distinguished at anything?" the tap-tap from his school replied. "I am

the only man whom Barbecue feared," he urged; "and Flint himself feared Barbecue." "Barbecue, Flint—what house?" came the cutting retort. Most disquieting reflection

of all, was it not bad form to think about good form? His vitals were tortured by this problem. It was a claw within him sharper than the iron one; and as it tore him, the

perspiration dripped down his tallow countenance and streaked his doublet. Ofttimes he drew his sleeve across his face, but there was no damming that trickle. Ah, envy not

Hook. There came to him a presentiment of his early dissolution. It was as if Peter's terrible oath had boarded the ship. Hook felt a gloomy desire to make his dying speech,

lest presently there should be no time for it. "Better for Hook," he cried, "if he had had less ambition!" It was in his darkest hours only that he referred to himself in the third person. "No little children love me!" Strange that he should think of this, which had never troubled him before; perhaps the sewing machine brought it to his mind. For long

he muttered to himself, staring at Smee, who was hemming placidly, under the conviction that all children feared him. Feared him! Feared Smee! There was not a child on

board the brig that night who did not already love him. He had said horrid things to them and hit them with the palm of his hand, because he could not hit them with his fist; but

they had only clung to him the more. Michael had tried on his spectacles. To tell poor Smee that they thought him lovable! Hook itched to do it, but it seemed too brutal.

Instead, he revolved this mystery in his mind: why do they find Smee lovable? He pursued the problem like the sleuth-hound that he was. If Smee was lovable, what was it

that made him so? A terrible answer suddenly presented itself: "Good form?" Had the bo'sun good form without knowing it, which is the best form of all? He remembered

that you have to prove you don't know you have it before you are eligible for Pop. With a cry of rage he raised his iron hand over Smee's head; but he did not tear. What

arrested him was this reflection: "To claw a man because he is good form, what would that be?" "Bad form!" The unhappy Hook was as impotent as he was damp, and he

fell forward like a cut flower. His dogs thinking him out of the way for a time, discipline instantly relaxed; and they broke into a bacchanalian dance, which brought him to

his feet at once; all traces of human weakness gone, as if a bucket of water had passed over him. "Quiet, you scugs," he cried, "or I'll cast anchor in you;" and at once the din

was hushed. "Are all the children chained, so that they cannot fly away?" "Ay, ay." "Then hoist them up." The wretched prisoners were dragged from the hold, all except

Wendy, and ranged in line in front of him. For a time he seemed unconscious of their presence. He lolled at his ease, humming, not unmelodiously, snatches of a rude song,

and fingering a pack of cards. Ever and anon the light from his cigar gave a touch of colour to his face. "Now then, bullies," he said briskly, "six of you walk the plank to-

night, but I have room for two cabin boys. Which of you is it to be?" "Don't irritate him unnecessarily," had been Wendy's instructions in the hold; so Tootles stepped

forward politely. Tootles hated the idea of signing under such a man, but an instinct told him that it would be prudent to lay the responsibility on an absent person; and though

a somewhat silly boy, he knew that mothers alone are always willing to be the buffer. All children know this about mothers, and despise them for it, but make constant use of

it. So Tootles explained prudently, "You see, sir, I don't think my mother would like me to be a pirate. Would your mother like you to be a pirate, Slightly?" He winked at

Slightly, who said mournfully, "I don't think so," as if he wished things had been otherwise. "Would your mother like you to be a pirate, Twin?" "I don't think so," said the

first twin, as clever as the others. "Nibs, would—" "Stow this gab," roared Hook, and the spokesmen were dragged back. "You, boy," he said, addressing John, "you look

as if you had a little pluck in you. Didst never want to be a pirate, my hearty?" Now John had sometimes experienced this hankering at maths. prep.; and he was struck by

Hook's picking him out. "I once thought of calling myself Red-handed Jack," he said diffidently. "And a good name too. We'll call you that here, bully, if you join." "Wha-

do you think, Michael?" asked John. "What would you call me if I join?" Michael demanded. "Blackbeard Joe." Michael was naturally impressed. "What do you think

John?" He wanted John to decide, and John wanted him to decide. "Shall we still be respectful subjects of the King?" John inquired. Through Hook's teeth came the answer

"You would have to swear, 'Down with the King.'" Perhaps John had not behaved very well so far, but he shone out now. "Then I refuse!" he cried, banging the barrel in front of Hook. "And I refuse," cried Michael. "Rule Britannia!" squeaked Curly. The infuriated pirates buffeted them in the mouth; and Hook roared out, "That seals your doom. Bring up their mother. Get the plank ready." They were only boys, and they went white as they saw Jukes and Cecco preparing the fatal plank. But they tried to look brave when Wendy was brought up. No words of mine can tell you how Wendy despised those pirates. To the boys there was at least some glamour in the pirate calling; but all that she saw was that the ship had not been tidied for years. There was not a porthole on the grimy glass of which you might not have written with your finger "Dirty pig;" and she had already written it on several. But as the boys gathered round her she had no thought, of course, save for them. "So, my beauty," said Hook, as if he spoke in syrup, "you are to see your children walk the plank." Fine gentleman though he was, the intensity of his communings had soiled his ruff, and suddenly he knew that she was gazing at it. With a hasty gesture he tried to hide it, but he was too late. "Are they to die?" asked Wendy, with a look of such frightful contempt that he nearly fainted. "They are," he snarled. "Silence all," he called gloatingly, "for a mother's last words to her children." At this moment Wendy was grand. "These are my last words, dear boys," she said firmly. "I feel that I have a message to you from your real mothers, and it is this: 'We hope our sons will die like English gentlemen.'" Even the pirates were awed, and Tootles cried out hysterically, "I am going to do what my mother hopes. What are you to do, Nibs?" "What my mother hopes. What are you to do, Twin?" "What my mother hopes. John, what are——" But Hook had found his voice again. "Tie her up," he shouted. It was Smee who tied her to the mast. "See here, honey," he whispered, "I'll save you if you promise to be my mother." But not even for Smee would she make such a promise. "I would almost rather have no children at all," she said disdainfully. It is sad to know that not a boy was looking at her as Smee tied her to the mast; the eyes of all were on the plank: that last little walk they were about to take. They were no longer able to hope that they would walk it manfully, for the capacity to think had gone from them; they could stare and shiver only. Hook smiled on them with his teeth closed, and took a step toward Wendy. His intention was to turn her face so that she should see the boys walking the plank one by one. But he never reached her, he never heard the cry of anguish he hoped to wring from her. He heard something else instead. It was the terrible tick-tick of the crocodile. They all heard it—pirates, boys, Wendy—and immediately every head was blown in one direction; not to the water whence the sound proceeded, but toward Hook. All knew that what was about to happen concerned him alone, and that from being actors they were suddenly become spectators. Very frightful was it to see the change that came over him. It was as if he had been clipped at every joint. He fell in a little heap. The sound came steadily nearer; and in advance of it came this ghastly thought, "the crocodile is about to board the ship!" Even the iron claw hung inactive; as if knowing that it was no intrinsic part of what the attacking force wanted. Left so fearfully alone, any other man would have lain with his eyes shut where he fell: but the gigantic brain of Hook was still working, and under its guidance he crawled on his knees along the deck as far from the sound as he could go. The pirates respectfully cleared a passage for him, and it was only when he brought up against the bulwarks that he spoke. "Hide me," he cried hoarsely. They gathered round him; all eyes averted from the thing that was coming aboard. They had no thought of fighting it. It was Fate. Only when Hook was hidden from them did curiosity loosen the limbs of the boys so that they could rush to the ship's side to see the crocodile climbing it. Then they got the strangest surprise of this Night of Nights; for it was no crocodile that was coming to their aid. It was Peter. He signed to them not to give vent to any cry of admiration that might rouse suspicion. Then he went on ticking.

CHAPTER XV *"Hook Or Me This Time"* Odd things happen to all of us on our way through life without our noticing for a time that they have happened. Thus, to take an instance, we suddenly discover that we have been deaf in one ear for we don't know how long, but, say, half an hour. Now such an experience had come that night to Peter. When last we saw him he was stealing across the island with one finger to his lips and his dagger at the ready. He had seen the crocodile pass by without noticing anything peculiar about it, but by and by he remembered that it had not been ticking. At first he thought this eerie, but soon he concluded rightly that the clock had run down. Without giving a thought to what might be the feelings of a fellow-creature thus abruptly deprived of its closest companion, Peter at once considered how he could turn the catastrophe to his own use; and he decided to tick, so that wild beasts should believe he was the crocodile and let him pass unmolested. He ticked superbly, but with one unforeseen result. The crocodile was among those who heard the sound, and it followed him, though whether with the purpose of regaining what it had lost, or merely as a friend under the belief that it was again ticking itself, will never be certainly known, for, like all slaves to a fixed idea, it was a stupid beast. Peter reached the shore without mishap, and went straight on, his legs encountering the water as if quite unaware that they had entered a new element. Thus many animals pass from land to water, but no other human of whom I know. As he swam he had but one thought: "Hook or me this time." He had ticked so long that he now went on ticking without knowing that he was doing it. Had he known he would have stopped, for to board the brig by the help of the tick, though an ingenious idea, had not occurred to him. On the contrary, he thought he had scaled her side as noiseless as a mouse; and he was amazed to see the pirates cowering from him, with Hook in their midst as abject as if he had heard the crocodile.

The crocodile! No sooner did Peter remember it than he heard the ticking. At first he thought the sound did come from the crocodile, and he looked behind him swiftly. Then he realised that he was doing it himself, and in a flash he understood the situation. "How clever of me," he thought at once, and signed to the boys not to burst into applause.

It was at this moment that Ed Teynte the quartermaster emerged from the forecastle and came along the deck. Now, reader, time what happened by your watch. Peter struck true and deep. John clapped his hands on the ill-fated pirate's mouth to stifle the dying groan. He fell forward. Four boys caught him to prevent the thud. Peter gave the signal, and the carrion was cast overboard. There was a splash, and then silence. How long has it taken? "One!" (Slightly had begun to count.) None too soon, Peter, every inch of him on tiptoe, vanished into the cabin; for more than one pirate was screwing up his courage to look round. They could hear each other's distressed breathing now, which showed them that the more terrible sound had passed. "It's gone, captain," Smee said, wiping his spectacles. "All's still again." Slowly Hook let his head emerge from his ruff, and listened so intently that he could have caught the echo of the tick. There was not a sound, and he drew himself up firmly to his full height. "Then here's

Johnny Plank," he cried brazenly, hating the boys more than ever because they had seen him unbend. He broke into the villainous ditty: "Yo ho, yo ho, the frisky plank, You walks along it so, Till it goes down and you goes down To Davy Jones below!" To terrorise the prisoners the more, though with a certain loss of dignity, he danced along an imaginary plank, grimacing at them as he sang; and when he finished he cried, "Do you want a touch of the cat before you walk the plank?" At that they fell on their knees. "No, no," they cried so piteously that every pirate smiled. "Fetch the cat, Jukes," said Hook; "it's in the cabin." The cabin! Peter was in the cabin! The children gazed at each other. "Ay, ay," said Jukes blithely, and he strode into the cabin. They followed him with their eyes; they scarce knew that Hook had resumed his song, his dogs joining in with him: "Yo ho, yo ho, the scratching cat, Its tails are nine, you know, And when they're writ upon your back— What was the last line will never be known, for of a sudden the song was stayed by a dreadful screech from the cabin. It wailed through the ship, and died away. Then was heard a crowing sound which was well understood by the boys, but to the pirates was almost more eerie than the screech. "What was that?" cried Hook. "Two," said Slightly solemnly. The Italian Cecco hesitated for a moment and then swung into the cabin. He tottered out, haggard. "What's the matter with Bill Jukes, you dog?" hissed Hook, towering over him. "The matter wi' him is he's dead, stabbed," replied Cecco in a hollow voice. "Bill Jukes dead!" cried the startled pirates. "The cabin's as black as a pit," Cecco said, almost gibbering, "but there is something terrible in there: the thing you heard crowing." The exultation of the boys, the lowering looks of the pirates, both were seen by Hook. "Cecco," he said in his most steely voice, "go back and fetch me out that doodle-doo." Cecco, bravest of the brave, cowered before his captain, crying "No, no;" but Hook was purring to his claw. "Did you say you would go, Cecco?" he said musingly. Cecco went, first flinging up his arms despairingly. There was no more singing, all listened now; and again came a death-screech and again a crow. No one spoke except Slightly. "Three," he said. Hook rallied his dogs with a gesture. "S' death and odds fish," he thundered, "who is to bring me that doodle-doo?" "Wait till Cecco comes out," growled Starkey, and the others took up the cry. "I think I heard you volunteer, Starkey," said Hook, purring again. "No, by thunder!" Starkey cried. "My hook thinks you did," said Hook, crossing to him. "I wonder if it would not be advisable, Starkey, to humour the hook?" "I'll swing before I go in there," replied Starkey doggedly, and again he had the support of the crew. "Is it mutiny?" asked Hook more pleasantly than ever. "Starkey's ringleader!" "Captain, mercy," Starkey whimpered, all of a tremble now. "Shake hands, Starkey," said Hook, proffering his claw. Starkey looked round for help, but all deserted him. As he backed Hook advanced, and now the red spark was in his eye. With a despairing scream the pirate leapt upon Long Tom and precipitated himself into the sea. "Four," said Slightly. "And now," Hook asked courteously, "did any other gentleman say mutiny?" Seizing a lantern and raising his claw with a menacing gesture, "I'll bring out that doodle-doo myself," he said, and sped into the cabin. "Five." How Slightly longed to say it. He wetted his lips to be ready, but Hook came staggering out, without his lantern. "Something blew out the ght," he said a little unsteadily. "Something!" echoed Mullins. "What of Cecco?" demanded Noodler. "He's as dead as Jukes," said Hook shortly. His reluctance to return o the cabin impressed them all unfavourably, and the mutinous sounds again broke forth. All pirates are superstitious; and Cookson cried, "They do say the surest sign a ship's accurst is when there's one on board more than can be accounted for." "I've heard," muttered Mullins, "he always boards the pirate craft at last. Had he a tail, captain?"

"They say," said another, looking viciously at Hook, "that when he comes it's in the likeness of the wickedest man aboard." "Had he a hook, captain?" asked Cookson insolently; and one after another took up the cry, "The ship's doomed." At this the children could not resist raising a cheer. Hook had well-nigh forgotten his prisoners, but as he swung round on them now his face lit up again. "Lads," he cried to his crew, "here's a notion. Open the cabin door and drive them in. Let them fight the doodle-doo for their lives. If they kill him, we're so much the better; if he kills them, we're none the worse." For the last time his dogs admired Hook, and devotedly they did his bidding.

The boys, pretending to struggle, were pushed into the cabin and the door was closed on them. "Now, listen," cried Hook, and all listened. But not one dared to face the door. Yes, one, Wendy, who all this time had been bound to the mast. It was for neither a scream nor a crow that she was watching; it was for the reappearance of Peter. She had not long to wait. In the cabin he had found the thing for which he had gone in search: the key that would free the children of their manacles; and now they all stole forth, armed with such weapons as they could find. First signing to them to hide, Peter cut Wendy's bonds, and then nothing could have been easier than for them all to fly off together; but one thing barred the way, an oath, "Hook or me this time." So when he had freed Wendy, he whispered to her to conceal herself with the others, and himself took her place by the mast, her cloak around him so that he should pass for her. Then he took a great breath and crowed. To the pirates it was a voice crying that all the boys lay slain in the cabin; and they were panic-stricken. Hook tried to hearten them; but like the dogs he had made them they showed him their fangs, and he knew that if he took his eyes off them now they would leap at him. "Lads," he said, ready to cajole or strike as need be, but never quailing for an instant, "I've thought it out. There's a Jonah aboard." "Ay," they snarled, "a man wi' a hook." "No, lads, no, it's the girl. Never was luck on a pirate ship wi' a woman on board. We'll right the ship when she's gone." Some of them remembered that this had been a saying of Flint's. "It's worth trying," they said doubtfully. "Fling the girl overboard," cried Hook; and they made a rush the figure in the cloak. "There's none can save you now, missy," Mullins hissed jeeringly. "There's one," replied the figure. "Who's that?" "Peter Pan the avenger!" came the terrible answer; and as he spoke Peter flung off his cloak. Then they all knew who 'twas that had been undoing them in the cabin, and twice Hook essayed to speak and twice he failed. In that frightful moment I think his fierce heart broke. At last he cried, "Cleave him to the brisket," but without conviction. "Down, boys, and at them!" Peter's voice rang out; and in another moment the clash of arms was resounding through the ship. Had the pirates kept together it is certain that they would have won; but the onset came when they were all unstrung, and they ran hither and thither, striking wildly, each thinking himself the last survivor of the crew. Man to man they were stronger; but they fought on the defensive only, which enabled the boys to hunt in pairs and choose their quarry. Some of the miscreants leapt into the sea; others hid in dark recesses, where they were found by Slightly, who did not fight, but ran about with a lantern which he flashed in their faces, so that they were half blinded and fell an easy prey to the reeking swords of the other boys. There was little sound to be heard but the clang of weapons, an occasional screech or splash, and Slightly monotonously counting five—six—seven—eight— nine—ten—eleven. I think all were gone when a group of savage boys surrounded Hook, who seemed to have a charmed life, as he kept them

at bay in that circle of fire. They had done for his dogs, but this man alone seemed to be a match for them all. Again and again they closed upon him, and again and again he

hewed a clear space. He had lifted up one boy with his hook, and was using him as a buckler, when another, who had just passed his sword through Mullins, sprang into the

fray. "Put up your swords, boys," cried the newcomer, "this man is mine." Thus suddenly Hook found himself face to face with Peter. The others drew back and formed a

ring round them. For long the two enemies looked at one another; Hook shuddering slightly, and Peter with the strange smile upon his face. "So, Pan," said Hook at last,

"this is all your doing." "Ay, James Hook," came the stern answer, "it is all my doing." "Proud and insolent youth," said Hook, "prepare to meet thy doom." "Dark and

sinister man," Peter answered, "have at thee." Without more words they fell to, and for a space there was no advantage to either blade. Peter was a superb swordsman, and

parried with dazzling rapidity; ever and anon he followed up a feint with a lunge that got past his foe's defence, but his shorter reach stood him in ill stead, and he could not

drive the steel home. Hook, scarcely his inferior in brilliancy, but not quite so nimble in wrist play, forced him back by the weight of his onset, hoping suddenly to end all

with a favourite thrust, taught him long ago by Barbecue at Rio; but to his astonishment he found this thrust turned aside again and again. Then he sought to close and give

the quietus with his iron hook, which all this time had been pawing the air; but Peter doubled under it and, lunging fiercely, pierced him in the ribs. At sight of his own blood,

whose peculiar colour, you remember, was offensive to him, the sword fell from Hook's hand, and he was at Peter's mercy. "Now!" cried all the boys, but with a magnificent

gesture Peter invited his opponent to pick up his sword. Hook did so instantly, but with a tragic feeling that Peter was showing good form. Hitherto he had thought it was

some fiend fighting him, but darker suspicions assailed him now. "Pan, who and what art thou?" he cried huskily. "I'm youth, I'm joy," Peter answered at a venture, "I'm a

little bird that has broken out of the egg." This, of course, was nonsense; but it was proof to the unhappy Hook that Peter did not know in the least who or what he was,

which is the very pinnacle of good form. "To't again," he cried despairingly. He fought now like a human flail, and every sweep of that terrible sword would have severed

in twain any man or boy who obstructed it; but Peter fluttered round him as if the very wind it made blew him out of the danger zone. And again and again he darted in and

pricked. Hook was fighting now without hope. That passionate breast no longer asked for life; but for one boon it craved: to see Peter's bad form before it was cold for ever.

Abandoning the fight he rushed into the powder magazine and fired it. "In two minutes," he cried, "the ship will be blown to pieces." Now, now, he thought, true form will

show. But Peter issued from the powder magazine with the shell in his hands, and calmly flung it overboard. What sort of form was Hook himself showing? Misguided man

though he was, we may be glad, without sympathising with him, that in the end he was true to the traditions of his race. The other boys were flying around him now, flouting,

scornful; and as he staggered about the deck striking up at them impotently, his mind was no longer with them; it was slouching in the playing fields of long ago, or being

sent up for good, or watching the wall-game from a famous wall. And his shoes were right, and his waistcoat was right, and his tie was right, and his socks were right. James

Hook, thou not wholly unheroic figure, farewell. For we have come to his last moment. Seeing Peter slowly advancing upon him through the air with dagger poised, he

sprang upon the bulwarks to cast himself into the sea. He did not know that the crocodile was waiting for him; for we purposely stopped the clock that this knowledge might

be spared him: a little mark of respect from us at the end. He had one last triumph, which I think we need not grudge him. As he stood on the bulwark looking over his

shoulder at Peter gliding through the air, he invited him with a gesture to use his foot. It made Peter kick instead of stab. At last Hook had got the boon for which he craved.

"Bad form," he cried jeeringly, and went content to the crocodile. Thus perished James Hook. "Seventeen," Slightly sang out; but he was not quite correct in his figures.

Fifteen paid the penalty for their crimes that night; but two reached the shore: Starkey to be captured by the redskins, who made him nurse for all their papooses, a melancholy

come-down for a pirate; and Smee, who henceforth wandered about the world in his spectacles, making a precarious living by saying he was the only man that Jas. Hook had

feared. Wendy, of course, had stood by taking no part in the fight, though watching Peter with glistening eyes; but now that all was over she became prominent again. She

praised them equally, and shuddered delightfully when Michael showed her the place where he had killed one; and then she took them into Hook's cabin and pointed to his

watch which was hanging on a nail. It said "half-past one"! The lateness of the hour was almost the biggest thing of all. She got them to bed in the pirates' bunks pretty

quickly, you may be sure; all but Peter, who strutted up and down on deck, until at last he fell asleep by the side of Long Tom. He had one of his dreams that night, and cried

in his sleep for a long time, and Wendy held him tight. CHAPTER XVI *The Return Home* By three bells that morning they were all stirring their stumps; for there was a big

sea running, and Tootles, the bo'sun, was among them, with a rope's end in his hand and chewing tobacco. They all donned pirate clothes cut off at the knee, shaved smartly,

and tumbled up, with the true nautical roll and hitching their trousers. It need not be said who was the captain. Nibs and John were first and second mate. There was a woman

aboard. The rest were tars before the mast, and lived in the fo'c'sle. Peter had already lashed himself to the wheel; but he piped all hands and delivered a short address to

them; said he hoped they would do their duty like gallant hearties, but that he knew they were the scum of Rio and the Gold Coast, and if they snapped at him he would tear

them. His bluff strident words struck the note sailors understand, and they cheered him lustily. Then a few sharp orders were given, and they turned the ship round, and

nosed her for the mainland. Captain Pan calculated, after consulting the ship's chart, that if this weather lasted they should strike the Azores about the 21st of June, after

which it would save time to fly. Some of them wanted it to be an honest ship and others were in favour of keeping it a pirate; but the captain treated them as dogs, and they

dared not express their wishes to him even in a round robin. Instant obedience was the only safe thing. Slightly got a dozen for looking perplexed when told to take soundings.

The general feeling was that Peter was honest just now to lull Wendy's suspicions, but that there might be a change when the new suit was ready, which, against her will, she

was making for him out of some of Hook's wickedest garments. It was afterwards whispered among them that on the first night he wore this suit he sat long in the cabin with

Hook's cigar-holder in his mouth and one hand clenched, all but the forefinger, which he bent and held threateningly aloft like a hook. Instead of watching the ship, however, we must now return to that desolate home from which three of our characters had taken heartless flight so long ago. It seems a shame to have neglected No. 14 all this time;

and yet we may be sure that Mrs. Darling does not blame us. If we had returned sooner to look with sorrowful sympathy at her, she would probably have cried, "Don't be

silly; what do I matter? Do go back and keep an eye on the children." So long as mothers are like this their children will take advantage of them; and they may lay to that.

Even now we venture into that familiar nursery only because its lawful occupants are on their way home; we are merely hurrying on in advance of them to see that their beds

are properly aired and that Mr. and Mrs. Darling do not go out for the evening. We are no more than servants. Why on earth should their beds be properly aired, seeing that

they left them in such a thankless hurry? Would it not serve them jolly well right if they came back and found that their parents were spending the week-end in the country?

It would be the moral lesson they have been in need of ever since we met them; but if we contrived things in this way Mrs. Darling would never forgive us. One thing I should

like to do immensely, and that is to tell her, in the way authors have, that the children are coming back, that indeed they will be here on Thursday week. This would spoil so

completely the surprise to which Wendy and John and Michael are looking forward. They have been planning it out on the ship: mother's rapture, father's shout of joy,

Nana's leap through the air to embrace them first, when what they ought to be preparing for is a good hiding. How delicious to spoil it all by breaking the news in advance;

so that when they enter grandly Mrs. Darling may not even offer Wendy her mouth, and Mr. Darling may exclaim pettishly, "Dash it all, here are those boys again."

However, we should get no thanks even for this. We are beginning to know Mrs. Darling by this time, and may be sure that she would upbraid us for depriving the children

of their little pleasure. "But, my dear madam, it is ten days till Thursday week; so that by telling you what's what, we can save you ten days of unhappiness." "Yes, but at

what a cost! By depriving the children of ten minutes of delight." "Oh, if you look at it in that way." "What other way is there in which to look at it?" You see, the woman

had no proper spirit. I had meant to say extraordinarily nice things about her; but I despise her, and not one of them will I say now. She does not really need to be told to have

things ready, for they are ready. All the beds are aired, and she never leaves the house, and observe, the window is open. For all the use we are to her, we might go back to

the ship. However, as we are here we may as well stay and look on. That is all we are, lookers-on. Nobody really wants us. So let us watch and say jaggy things, in the hope

that some of them will hurt. The only change to be seen in the night-nursery is that between nine and six the kennel is no longer there. When the children flew away, Mr.

Darling felt in his bones that all the blame was his for having chained Nana up, and that from first to last she had been wiser than he. Of course, as we have seen, he was quite

a simple man; indeed he might have passed for a boy again if he had been able to take his baldness off; but he had also a noble sense of justice and a lion courage to do what

seemed right to him; and having thought the matter out with anxious care after the flight of the children, he went down on all fours and crawled into the kennel. To all Mrs.

Darling's dear invitations to him to come out he replied sadly but firmly: "No, my own one, this is the place for me." In the bitterness of his remorse he swore that he would

never leave the kennel until his children came back. Of course this was a pity; but whatever Mr. Darling did he had to do in excess; otherwise he soon gave up doing it. And there never was a more humble man than the once proud George Darling, as he sat in the kennel of an evening talking with his wife of their children and all their pretty ways.

Very touching was his deference to Nana. He would not let her come into the kennel, but on all other matters he followed her wishes implicitly. Every morning the kennel was carried with Mr. Darling in it to a cab, which conveyed him to his office, and he returned home in the same way at six. Something of the strength of character of the man will be seen if we remember how sensitive he was to the opinion of neighbours: this man whose every movement now attracted surprised attention. Inwardly he must have suffered torture; but he preserved a calm exterior even when the young criticised his little home, and he always lifted his hat courteously to any lady who looked inside. It may have been quixotic, but it was magnificent. Soon the inward meaning of it leaked out, and the great heart of the public was touched. Crowds followed the cab, cheering it lustily; charming girls scaled it to get his autograph; interviews appeared in the better class of papers, and society invited him to dinner and added, "Do come in the kennel."

On that eventful Thursday week Mrs. Darling was in the night-nursery awaiting George's return home: a very sad-eyed woman. Now that we look at her closely and remember the gaiety of her in the old days, all gone now just because she has lost her babes, I find I won't be able to say nasty things about her after all. If she was too fond of her rubbishy children she couldn't help it. Look at her in her chair, where she has fallen asleep. The corner of her mouth, where one looks first, is almost withered up. Her hand moves restlessly on her breast as if she had a pain there. Some like Peter best and some like Wendy best, but I like her best. Suppose, to make her happy, we whisper to her in her sleep that the brats are coming back. They are really within two miles of the window now, and flying strong, but all we need whisper is that they are on the way. Let's. It is a pity we did it, for she has started up, calling their names; and there is no one in the room but Nana. "O Nana, I dreamt my dear ones had come back." Nana had filmy eyes, but all she could do was to put her paw gently on her mistress's lap; and they were sitting together thus when the kennel was brought back. As Mr. Darling puts his head out at it to kiss his wife, we see that his face is more worn than of yore, but has a softer expression. He gave his hat to Liza, who took it scornfully; for she had no imagination, and was quite incapable of understanding the motives of such a man. Outside, the crowd who had accompanied the cab home were still cheering, and he was naturally not unmoved. "Listen to them," he said; "it is very gratifying." "Lot of little boys," sneered Liza. "There were several adults to-day," he assured her with a faint flush; but when she tossed her head he had not a word of reproof for her. Social success had not spoilt him; it had made him sweeter. For some time he sat half out of the kennel, talking with Mrs. Darling of this success, and pressing her hand reassuringly when she said she hoped his head would not be turned by it. "But if I had been a weak man," he said. "Good heavens, if I had been a weak man!" "And, George," she said timidly, "you are as full of remorse as ever, aren't you?" "Full of remorse as ever, dearest! See my punishment: living in a kennel." "But it is punishment, isn't it, George? You are sure you are not enjoying it?" "My love!" You may be sure she begged his pardon; and then, feeling drowsy, he curled round in the kennel. "Won't you play me to sleep," he asked, "on the nursery piano?" and as she was crossing to the day nursery he added thoughtlessly, "And shut that window. I feel a draught." "O George, never ask me to do that. The window must always be left open for them, always, always." Now it was his turn to beg her pardon; and she went into the day nursery and played, and soon he was asleep; and while he slept, Wendy and John and Michael flew into the room. Oh no. We have written it so, because that was the charming arrangement planned by them before we left the ship; but something must have happened since then, for it is not they who have flown in, it is Peter and Tinker Bell. Peter's first words tell all. "Quick, Tink," he whispered, "close the window; bar it. That's right. Now you and I must get away by the door; and when Wendy comes she will think her mother has barred her out; and she will have to go back with me." Now I understand what had hitherto puzzled me, why when Peter had exterminated the pirates he did not return to the island and leave Tink to escort the children to the mainland. This trick had been in his head all the time. Instead of feeling that he was behaving badly he danced with glee; then he peeped into the day-nursery to see who was playing. He whispered to Tink, "It's Wendy's mother. She is a pretty lady, but not so pretty as my mother. Her mouth is full of thimbles, but not so full as my mother's was." Of course he knew nothing whatever about his mother; but he sometimes bragged about her. He did not know the tune, which was "Home, Sweet Home," but he knew it was saying, "Come back, Wendy, Wendy, Wendy;" and he cried exultantly, "You will never see Wendy again, lady, for the window is barred." He peeped in again to see why the music had stopped; and now he saw that Mrs. Darling had laid her head on the box, and that two tears were sitting on her eyes. "She wants me to unbar the window," thought Peter, "but I won't, not I." He peeped again, and the tears were still there, or another two had taken their place. "She's awfully fond of Wendy," he said to himself. He was angry with her now for not seeing why she could not have Wendy. The reason was so simple: "I'm fond of her too. We can't both have her, lady." But the lady would not make the best of it, and he was unhappy. He ceased to look at her, but even then she would not let go of him. He skipped about and made funny faces, but when he stopped it was just as if she were inside him, knocking. "Oh, all right," he said at last, and gulped. Then he unbarred the window. "Come on, Tink," he cried, with a frightful sneer at the laws of nature; "we don't want any silly mothers;" and he flew away. Thus Wendy and John and Michael found the window open for them after all, which of course was more than they deserved.

They alighted on the floor, quite unashamed of themselves, and the youngest one had already forgotten his home. "John," he said, looking around him doubtfully, "I think I have been here before." "Of course you have, you silly. There is your old bed." "So it is," Michael said, but not with much conviction. "I say," cried John, "the kennel!" and he dashed across to look into it. "Perhaps Nana is inside it," Wendy said. But John whistled. "Hullo," he said, "there's a man inside it." "It's father!" exclaimed Wendy. "Let me see father," Michael begged eagerly, and he took a good look. "He is not so big as the pirate I killed," he said with such frank disappointment that I am glad Mr. Darling was asleep; it would have been sad if those had been the first words he heard his little Michael say. Wendy and John had been taken aback somewhat at finding their father in the kennel. "Surely," said John, like one who had lost faith in his memory, "he used not to sleep in the kennel?" "John," Wendy said falteringly, "perhaps we don't remember the old life as well as we thought we did." A chill fell upon them; and serve them right. "It is very careless of mother," said that young scoundrel John, "not to be here when we come back." It was then that Mrs. Darling began playing again. "It's mother!" cried Wendy, peeping. "So it is!" said John. "Then are you not really our mother,

Wendy?" asked Michael, who was surely sleepy. "Oh dear!" exclaimed Wendy, with her first real twinge of remorse, "it was quite time we came back." "Let us creep in," John suggested, "and put our hands over her eyes." But Wendy, who saw that they must break the joyous news more gently, had a better plan. "Let us all slip into our beds, and be there when she comes in, just as if we had never been away." And so when Mrs. Darling went back to the night-nursery to see if her husband was asleep, all the beds were occupied. The children waited for her cry of joy, but it did not come. She saw them, but she did not believe they were there. You see, she saw them in their beds so often in her dreams that she thought this was just the dream hanging around her still. She sat down in the chair by the fire, where in the old days she had nursed them. They could not understand this, and a cold fear fell upon all the three of them. "Mother!" Wendy cried. "That's Wendy," she said, but still she was sure it was the dream. "Mother!" "That's John," she said. "Mother!" cried Michael. He knew her now. "That's Michael," she said, and she stretched out her arms for the three little selfish children they would never envelop again. Yes, they did, they went round Wendy and John and Michael, who had slipped out of bed and run to her. "George, George," she cried when she could speak; and Mr. Darling woke to share her bliss, and Nana came rushing in. There could not have been a lovelier sight; but there was none to see it except a strange boy who was staring in at the window. He had ecstasies innumerable that other children can never know; but he was looking through the window at the one joy from which he must be for ever barred. CHAPTER XVII *When Wendy Grew Up* I hope you want to know what became of the other boys. They were waiting below to give Wendy time to explain about them, and when they had counted five hundred they went up. They went up by the stair, because they thought this would make a better impression. They stood in a row in front of Mrs. Darling, with their hats off, and wishing they were not wearing their pirate clothes. They said nothing, but their eyes asked her to have them. They ought to have looked at Mr. Darling also, but they forgot about him. Of course Mrs. Darling said at once that she would have them; but Mr. Darling was curiously depressed and they saw that he considered six a rather large number. "I must say," he said to Wendy, "that you don't do things by halves," a grudging remark which the twins thought was pointed at them. The first twin was the proud one, and he asked, flushing, "Do you think we should be too much of a handful, sir? Because if so we can go away." "Father!" Wendy cried, shocked; but still the cloud was on him. He knew he was behaving unworthily, but he could not help it. "We could lie doubled up," said Nibs. "I always cut their hair myself," said Wendy. "George!" Mrs. Darling exclaimed, pained to see her dear one showing himself in such an unfavourable light. Then he burst into tears, and the truth came out. He was as glad to have them as she was, he said, but he thought they should have asked his consent as well as hers, instead of treating him as a cypher in his own house. "I don't think he is a cypher," Tootles cried instantly. "Do you think he is a cypher, Curly?" "No, I don't. Do you think he is a cypher, Slightly?" "Rather not. Twin, what do you think?" It turned out that not one of them thought him a cypher; and he was absurdly gratified, and said he would find space for them all in the drawing-room if they fitted in. "We'll fit in, sir," they assured him. "Then follow the leader," he cried gaily. "Mind you, I am not sure that we have a drawing-room, but we pretend we have, and it's all the same. Hoop la!" He went off dancing through the house, and they all cried "Hoop la!" and danced after him, searching for the drawing-room; and I forget whether they found it, but at any rate they found corners, and they all fitted in. As for Peter, he saw Wendy once again before he flew away. He did not

exactly come to the window, but he brushed against it in passing, so that she could open it if she liked and call to him. That was what she did. "Hullo, Wendy, good-bye," he

said. "Oh dear, are you going away?" "Yes." "You don't feel, Peter," she said falteringly, "that you would like to say anything to my parents about a very sweet subject?"

"No." "About me, Peter?" "No." Mrs. Darling came to the window, for at present she was keeping a sharp eye on Wendy. She told Peter that she had adopted all the other

boys, and would like to adopt him also. "Would you send me to school?" he inquired craftily. "Yes." "And then to an office?" "I suppose so." "Soon I should be a man?"

"Very soon." "I don't want to go to school and learn solemn things," he told her passionately. "I don't want to be a man. O Wendy's mother, if I was to wake up and feel

there was a beard!" "Peter," said Wendy the comforter, "I should love you in a beard;" and Mrs. Darling stretched out her arms to him, but he repulsed her. "Keep back, lady,

no one is going to catch me and make me a man." "But where are you going to live?" "With Tink in the house we built for Wendy. The fairies are to put it high up among

the tree tops where they sleep at nights." "How lovely," cried Wendy so longingly that Mrs. Darling tightened her grip. "I thought all the fairies were dead," Mrs. Darling

said. "There are always a lot of young ones," explained Wendy, who was now quite an authority, "because you see when a new baby laughs for the first time a new fairy is

born, and as there are always new babies there are always new fairies. They live in nests on the tops of trees; and the mauve ones are boys and the white ones are girls, and

the blue ones are just little sillies who are not sure what they are." "I shall have such fun," said Peter, with one eye on Wendy. "It will be rather lonely in the evening," she

said, "sitting by the fire." "I shall have Tink." "Tink can't go a twentieth part of the way round," she reminded him a little tartly. "Sneaky tell-tale!" Tink called out from

somewhere round the corner. "It doesn't matter," Peter said. "O Peter, you know it matters." "Well, then, come with me to the little house." "May I, mummy?" "Certainly

not. I have got you home again, and I mean to keep you." "But he does so need a mother." "So do you, my love." "Oh, all right," Peter said, as if he had asked her from

politeness merely; but Mrs. Darling saw his mouth twitch, and she made this handsome offer: to let Wendy go to him for a week every year to do his spring cleaning. Wendy

would have preferred a more permanent arrangement; and it seemed to her that spring would be long in coming, but this promise sent Peter away quite gay again. He had

no sense of time, and was so full of adventures that all I have told you about him is only a halfpenny-worth of them. I suppose it was because Wendy knew this that her last

words to him were these rather plaintive ones: "You won't forget me, Peter, will you, before spring-cleaning time comes?" Of course Peter promised; and then he flew away.

He took Mrs. Darling's kiss with him. The kiss that had been for no one else Peter took quite easily. Funny. But she seemed satisfied. Of course all the boys went to school;

and most of them got into Class III., but Slightly was put first into Class IV. and then into Class V. Class I. is the top class. Before they had attended school a week they saw

what goats they had been not to remain on the island; but it was too late now, and soon they settled down to being as ordinary as you or me or Jenkins minor. It is sad to have

to say that the power to fly gradually left them. At first Nana tied their feet to the bed-posts so that they should not fly away in the night; and one of their diversions by day was to pretend to fall off buses; but by and by they ceased to tug at their bonds in bed, and found that they hurt themselves when they let go of the bus. In time they could not even fly after their hats. Want of practice, they called it; but what it really meant was that they no longer believed. Michael believed longer than the other boys, though they jeered at him; so he was with Wendy when Peter came for her at the end of the first year. She flew away with Peter in the frock she had woven from leaves and berries in the Neverland, and her one fear was that he might notice how short it had become, but he never noticed, he had so much to say about himself. She had looked forward to thrilling talks with him about old times, but new adventures had crowded the old ones from his mind. "Who is Captain Hook?" he asked with interest when she spoke of the arch enemy. "Don't you remember," she asked, amazed, "how you killed him and saved all our lives?" "I forget them after I kill them," he replied carelessly. When she expressed a doubtful hope that Tinker Bell would be glad to see her he said, "Who is Tinker Bell?" "O Peter," she said, shocked; but even when she explained he could not remember. "There are such a lot of them," he said. "I expect she is no more." I expect he was right, for fairies don't live long, but they are so little that a short time seems a good while to them. Wendy was pained too to find that the past year was but as yesterday to Peter; it had seemed such a long year of waiting to her. But he was exactly as fascinating as ever, and they had a lovely spring cleaning in the little house on the tree tops. Next year he did not come for her. She waited in a new frock because the old one simply would not meet; but he never came. "Perhaps he is ill," Michael said. "You know he is never ill." Michael came close to her and whispered, with a shiver, "Perhaps there is no such person, Wendy!" and then Wendy would have cried if Michael had not been crying. Peter came next spring cleaning; and the strange thing was that he never knew he had missed a year. That was the last time the girl Wendy ever saw him. For a little longer she tried for his sake not to have growing pains; and she felt she was untrue to him when she got a prize for general knowledge. But the years came and went without bringing the careless boy; and when they met again Wendy was a married woman, and Peter was no more to her than a little dust in the box in which she had kept her toys. Wendy was grown up. You need not be sorry for her. She was one of the kind that likes to grow up. In the end she grew up of her own free will a day quicker than other girls. All the boys were grown up and done for by this time; so it is scarcely worth while saying anything more about them. You may see the twins and Nibs and Curly any day going to an office, each carrying a little bag and an umbrella. Michael is an engine-driver. Slightly married a lady of title, and so he became a lord. You see that judge in a wig coming out at the iron door? That used to be Tootles. The bearded man who doesn't know any story to tell his children was once John. Wendy was married in white with a pink sash. It is strange to think that Peter did not alight in the church and forbid the banns. Years rolled on again, and Wendy had a daughter. This ought not to be written in ink but in a golden splash. She was called Jane, and always had an odd inquiring look, as if from the moment she arrived on the mainland she wanted to ask questions. When she was old enough to ask them they were mostly about Peter Pan. She loved to hear of Peter, and Wendy told her all she could remember in the very nursery from which the famous flight had taken place. It was Jane's nursery now, for her father had bought it at the three per cents. from Wendy's father, who was no longer fond of stairs. Mrs. Darling was now dead and forgotten. There were only two beds in the nursery, now, Jane's and her nurse's; and there was no kennel, for Nana also had passed away. She died of old age, and at the end she had been rather difficult to get on with, being very firmly convinced that no one knew how to look after children except herself. Once a week Jane's nurse had her evening off, and then it was Wendy's part to put Jane to bed. That was the time for stories. It was Jane's invention to raise the sheet over her mother's head and her own, thus making a tent, and in the awful darkness to whisper:—

"What do we see now?" "I don't think I see anything to-night," says Wendy, with a feeling that if Nana were here she would object to further conversation. "Yes, you do," says Jane, "you see when you were a little girl." "That is a long time ago, sweetheart," says Wendy. "Ah me, how time flies!" "Does it fly," asks the artful child, "the way you flew when you were a little girl?" "The way I flew! Do you know, Jane, I sometimes wonder whether I ever did really fly." "Yes, you did." "The dear old days when I could fly!" "Why can't you fly now, mother?" "Because I am grown up, dearest. When people grow up they forget the way." "Why do they forget the way?" "Because they are no longer gay and innocent and heartless. It is only the gay and innocent and heartless who can fly." "What is gay and innocent and heartless? I do wish I was gay and innocent and heartless." Or perhaps Wendy admits that she does see something. "I do believe," she says, "that it is this nursery!" "I do believe it is!" says Jane. "Go on."

They are now embarked on the great adventure of the night when Peter flew in looking for his shadow. "The foolish fellow," says Wendy, "tried to stick it on with soap, and when he could not he cried, and that woke me, and I sewed it on for him." "You have missed a bit," interrupts Jane, who now knows the story better than her mother. "When you saw him sitting on the floor crying what did you say?" "I sat up in bed and I said, 'Boy, why are you crying?'" "Yes, that was it," says Jane, with a big breath. "And then he flew us all away to the Neverland and the fairies and the pirates and the redskins and the mermaids' lagoon, and the home under the ground, and the little house." "Yes! Which did you like best of all?" "I think I liked the home under the ground best of all." "Yes, so do I. What was the last thing Peter ever said to you?" "The last thing he ever said to me was, 'Just always be waiting for me, and then some night you will hear me crowing.'" "Yes." "But, alas, he forgot all about me." Wendy said it with a smile. She was as grown up as that. "What did his crow sound like?" Jane asked one evening. "It was like this," Wendy said, trying to imitate Peter's crow. "No, it wasn't," Jane said gravely, "it was like this;" and she did it ever so much better than her mother. Wendy was a little startled. "My darling, how can you know?" "I often hear it when I am sleeping," Jane said. "Ah yes, many girls hear it when they are sleeping, but I was the only one who heard it awake." "Lucky you!" said Jane. And then one night came the tragedy. It was the spring of the year, and the story had been told for the night, and Jane was now asleep in her bed. Wendy was sitting on the floor, very close to the fire, so as to see to darn, for there was no other light in the nursery; and while she sat darning she heard a crow. Then the window blew open as of old, and Peter dropped on the floor. He was exactly the same as ever, and Wendy saw at once that he still had all his first teeth. He was a little boy, and she was grown up. She huddled by the fire not daring to move, helpless and guilty, a big woman. "Hullo, Wendy," he said, not noticing any difference, for he was thinking chiefly of himself; and in the dim light her white dress might have been the nightgown in which he had seen her first. "Hullo, Peter," she replied faintly, squeezing herself as small as possible. Something inside her was crying

"Woman, woman, let go of me." "Hullo, where is John?" he asked, suddenly missing the third bed. "John is not here now," she gasped. "Is Michael asleep?" he asked, with

a careless glance at Jane. "Yes," she answered; and now she felt that she was untrue to Jane as well as to Peter. "That is not Michael," she said quickly, lest a judgment should

fall on her. Peter looked. "Hullo, is it a new one?" "Yes." "Boy or girl?" "Girl." Now surely he would understand; but not a bit of it. "Peter," she said, faltering, "are you

expecting me to fly away with you?" "Of course; that is why I have come." He added a little sternly, "Have you forgotten that this is spring-cleaning time?" She knew it was

useless to say that he had let many spring-cleaning times pass. "I can't come," she said apologetically, "I have forgotten how to fly." "I'll soon teach you again." "O Peter,

don't waste the fairy dust on me." She had risen; and now at last a fear assailed him. "What is it?" he cried, shrinking. "I will turn up the light," she said, "and then you can

see for yourself." For almost the only time in his life that I know of, Peter was afraid. "Don't turn up the light," he cried. She let her hands play in the hair of the tragic boy.

She was not a little girl heart-broken about him; she was a grown woman smiling at it all, but they were wet smiles. Then she turned up the light, and Peter saw. He gave a

cry of pain; and when the tall beautiful creature stooped to lift him in her arms he drew back sharply. "What is it?" he cried again. She had to tell him. "I am old, Peter. I am

ever so much more than twenty. I grew up long ago." "You promised not to!" "I couldn't help it. I am a married woman, Peter." "No, you're not." "Yes, and the little girl in

the bed is my baby." "No, she's not." But he supposed she was; and he took a step towards the sleeping child with his fist upraised. Of course he did not strike her. He sat

down on the floor and sobbed, and Wendy did not know how to comfort him, though she could have done it so easily once. She was only a woman now, and she ran out of

the room to try to think. Peter continued to cry, and soon his sobs woke Jane. She sat up in bed, and was interested at once. "Boy," she said, "why are you crying?" Peter rose

and bowed to her, and she bowed to him from the bed. "Hullo," he said. "Hullo," said Jane. "My name is Peter Pan," he told her. "Yes, I know." "I came back for my mother,"

he explained, "to take her to the Neverland." "Yes, I know," Jane said, "I've been waiting for you." When Wendy returned diffidently she found Peter sitting on the bed-post

crowing gloriously, while Jane in her nighty was flying round the room in solemn ecstasy. "She is my mother," Peter explained; and Jane descended and stood by his side

with the look on her face that he liked to see on ladies when they gazed at him. "He does so need a mother," Jane said. "Yes, I know," Wendy admitted rather forlornly; "no

one knows it so well as I." "Good-bye," said Peter to Wendy; and he rose in the air, and the shameless Jane rose with him; it was already her easiest way of moving about.

Wendy rushed to the window. "No, no!" she cried. "It is just for spring-cleaning time," Jane said, "he wants me always to do his spring cleaning." "If only I could go with

you!" Wendy sighed. "You see you can't fly," said Jane. Of course in the end Wendy let them fly away together. Our last glimpse of her shows her at the window, watching

them receding into the sky until they were as small as stars. As you look at Wendy you may see her hair becoming white, and her figure little again, for all this happened long

ago. Jane is now a common grown-up, with a daughter called Margaret; and every spring-cleaning time, except when he forgets, Peter comes for Margaret and takes her to

the Neverland, where she tells him stories about himself, to which he listens eagerly. When Margaret grows up she will have a daughter, who is to be Peter's mother in turn and thus it will go on, so long as children are gay and innocent and heartless. THE END. PETER PAN IN KENSINGTON GARDENS | Chapter I *The Grand Tour Of The Gardens* You must see for yourselves that it will be difficult to follow Peter Pan's adventures unless you are familiar with the Kensington Gardens. They are in London, where the King lives, and I used to take David there nearly every day unless he was looking decidedly flushed. No child has ever been in the whole of the Gardens, because it is so soon time to turn back. The reason it is soon time to turn back is that, if you are as small as David, you sleep from twelve to one. If your mother was not so sure that you sleep from twelve to one, you could most likely see the whole of them. The Gardens are bounded on one side by a never-ending line of omnibuses, over which your nurse has such authority that if she holds up her finger to any one of them it stops immediately. She then crosses with you in safety to the other side. There are more gates to the Gardens than one gate, but that is the one you go in at, and before you go in you speak to the lady with the balloons, who sits just outside. This is as near to being inside as she may venture, because, if she were to let go her hold of the railings for one moment, the balloons would lift her up, and she would be flown away. She sits very squat, for the balloons are always tugging at her, and the strain has given her quite a red face. Once she was a new one, because the old had let go, and David was very sorry for the old one, but as she did let go, he wished he had been there to see. The Gardens are a tremendous big place, with millions and hundreds of trees; and first you come to the Figs, but you scorn to loiter there, for the Figs is the resort of superior little persons, who are forbidden to mix with the commonalty, and is so named, according to legend, because they dress in full fig. These dainty ones are themselves contemptuously called Figs by David and other heroes, and you have a key to the manners and customs of this dandiacal section of the Gardens when I tell you that cricket is called crickets here. Occasionally a rebel Fig climbs over the fence into the world, and such a one was Miss Mabel Grey, of whom I shall tell you when we come to Miss Mabel Grey's gate. She was the only really celebrated Fig. We are now in the Broad Walk, and it is as much bigger than the other walks as your father is bigger than you. David wondered if it began little, and grew and grew, until it was quite grown up, and whether the other walks are its babies, and he drew a picture, which diverted him very much, of the Broad Walk giving a tiny walk an airing in a perambulator. In the Broad Walk you meet all the people who are worth knowing, and there is usually a grown-up with them to prevent them going on the damp grass, and to make them stand disgraced at the corner of a seat if they have been mad-dog or Mary-Annish. To be Mary-Annish is to behave like a girl, whimpering because nurse won't carry you, or simpering with your thumb in your mouth, and it is a hateful quality; but to be mad-dog is to kick out at everything, and there is some satisfaction in that. If I were to point out all the notable places as we pass up the Broad Walk, it would be time to turn back before we reach them, and I simply wave my stick at Cecco Hewlett's Tree, that memorable spot where a boy called Cecco lost his penny, and, looking for it, found twopence. There has been a good deal of excavation going on there ever since. Farther up the walk is the little wooden house in which Marmaduke Perry hid. There is no more awful story of the Gardens than this of Marmaduke Perry, who had been Mary-Annish three days in succession, and was sentenced to appear in the Broad Walk dressed in his sister's clothes. He hid in the little wooden house, and refused to emerge until they brought him knickerbockers with pockets. You now try to go to the Round Pond, but nurses hate it, because they are not really manly, and they make you look the other way, at the Big Penny and the Baby's

Palace. She was the most celebrated baby of the Gardens, and lived in the palace all alone, with ever so many dolls, so people rang the bell, and up she got out of her bed,

though it was past six o'clock, and she lighted a candle and opened the door in her nighty, and then they all cried with great rejoicings, "Hail, Queen of England!" What

puzzled David most was how she knew where the matches were kept. The Big Penny is a statue about her. Next we come to the Hump, which is the part of the Broad Walk

where all the big races are run; and even though you had no intention of running you do run when you come to the Hump, it is such a fascinating, slide-down kind of place.

Often you stop when you have run about half-way down it, and then you are lost; but there is another little wooden house near here, called the Lost House, and so you tell

the man that you are lost and then he finds you. It is glorious fun racing down the Hump, but you can't do it on windy days because then you are not there, but the fallen

leaves do it instead of you. There is almost nothing that has such a keen sense of fun as a fallen leaf. From the Hump we can see the gate that is called after Miss Mabel Grey,

the Fig I promised to tell you about. There were always two nurses with her, or else one mother and one nurse, and for a long time she was a pattern-child who always

coughed off the table and said, "How do you do?" to the other Figs, and the only game she played at was flinging a ball gracefully and letting the nurse bring it back to her

Then one day she tired of it all and went mad-dog, and, first, to show that she really was mad-dog, she unloosened both her boot-laces and put out her tongue east, west

north, and south. She then flung her sash into a puddle and danced on it till dirty water was squirted over her frock, after which she climbed the fence and had a series o

incredible adventures, one of the least of which was that she kicked off both her boots. At last she came to the gate that is now called after her, out of which she ran into stree

David and I have never been in though we have heard them roaring, and still she ran on and would never again have been heard of had not her mother jumped into a 'bu

and thus overtaken her. It all happened, I should say, long ago, and this is not the Mabel Grey whom David knows. Returning up the Broad Walk we have on our right th

Baby Walk, which is so full of perambulators that you could cross from side to side stepping on babies, but the nurses won't let you do it. From this walk a passage calle

Bunting's Thumb, because it is that length, leads into Picnic Street, where there are real kettles, and chestnut-blossom falls into your mug as you are drinking. Quite commo

children picnic here also, and the blossom falls into their mugs just the same. Next comes St. Govor's Well, which was full of water when Malcolm the Bold fell into it. H

was his mother's favourite, and he let her put her arm round his neck in public because she was a widow; but he was also partial to adventures, and liked to play wit

chimney-sweep who had killed a good many bears. The sweep's name was Sooty, and one day, when they were playing near the well, Malcolm fell in and would have be

drowned had not Sooty dived in and rescued him; and the water had washed Sooty clean, and he now stood revealed as Malcolm's long-lost father. So Malcolm would r

let his mother put her arm round his neck any more. Between the well and the Round Pond are the cricket pitches, and frequently the choosing of sides exhausts so m

time that there is scarcely any cricket. Everybody wants to bat first, and as soon as he is out he bowls unless you are the better wrestler, and while you are wrestling with the fielders have scattered to play at something else. The Gardens are noted for two kinds of cricket: boy cricket, which is real cricket with a bat, and girl cricket, which is with a racquet and the governess. Girls can't really play cricket, and when you are watching their futile efforts you make funny sounds at them. Nevertheless, there was a very disagreeable incident one day when some forward girls challenged David's team, and a disturbing creature called Angela Clare sent down so many yorkers that—However, instead of telling you the result of that regrettable match I shall pass on hurriedly to the Round Pond, which is the wheel that keeps all the Gardens going. It is round because it is in the very middle of the Gardens, and when you are come to it you never want to go any farther. You can't be good all the time at the Round Pond, however much you try. You can be good in the Broad Walk all the time, but not at the Round Pond, and the reason is that you forget, and, when you remember, you are so wet that you may as well be wetter. There are men who sail boats on the Round Pond, such big boats that they bring them in barrows, and sometimes in perambulators, and then the baby has to walk. The bow-legged children in the Gardens are those who had to walk too soon because their father needed the perambulator. You always want to have a yacht to sail on the Round Pond, and in the end your uncle gives you one; and to carry it to the pond the first day is splendid, also to talk about it to boys who have no uncle is splendid, but soon you like to leave it at home. For the sweetest craft that slips her moorings in the Round Pond is what is called a stick-boat, because she is rather like a stick until she is in the water and you are holding the string. Then as you walk round, pulling her, you see little men running about her deck, and sails rise magically and catch the breeze, and you put in on dirty nights at snug harbours which are unknown to the lordly yachts. Night passes in a twink, and again your rakish craft noses for the wind, whales spout, you glide over buried cities, and have brushes with pirates, and cast anchor on coral isles. You are a solitary boy while all this is taking place, for two boys together cannot adventure far upon the Round Pond, and though you may talk to yourself throughout the voyage, giving orders and executing them with despatch, you know not, when it is time to go home, where you have been or what swelled your sails; your treasure-trove is all locked away in your hold, so to speak, which will be opened, perhaps, by another little boy many years afterwards. But those yachts have nothing in their hold. Does any one return to this haunt of his youth because of the yachts that used to sail it? Oh no. It is the stick-boat that is freighted with memories. The yachts are toys, their owner a fresh-water mariner; they can cross and re-cross a pond only while the stick-boat goes to sea. You yachtsmen with your wands, who think we are all there to gaze on you, your ships are only accidents of this place, and were they all to be boarded and sunk by the ducks, the real business of the Round Pond would be carried on as usual. Paths from everywhere crowd like children to the pond. Some of them are ordinary paths, which have a rail on each side, and are made by men with their coats off, but others are vagrants, wide at one spot, and at another so narrow that you can stand astride them. They are called Paths that have Made Themselves, and David did wish he could see them doing it. But, like all the most wonderful things that happen in the Gardens, it is done, he concluded, at night after the gates are closed. We have also decided that the paths make themselves because it is their only chance of getting to the Round Pond. One of these gypsy paths comes from the place where the sheep get their hair cut. When David shed his curls at the hair-dressers, I am told, he said good-bye to them without a tremor, though his mother has never been quite the same bright creature since; so he despises the sheep as they run from their shearer, and calls out tauntingly, "Cowardy

cowardy custard!" But when the man grips them between his legs David shakes a fist at him for using such big scissors. Another startling moment is when the man turns back

the grimy wool from the sheeps' shoulders and they look suddenly like ladies in the stalls of a theatre. The sheep are so frightened by the shearing that it makes them quite

white and thin, and as soon as they are set free they begin to nibble the grass at once, quite anxiously, as if they feared that they would never be worth eating. David wonder

whether they know each other, now that they are so different, and if it makes them fight with the wrong ones. They are great fighters, and thus so unlike country sheep tha

every year they give my St. Bernard dog, Porthos, a shock. He can make a field of country sheep fly by merely announcing his approach, but these town sheep come towar

him with no promise of gentle entertainment, and then a light from last year breaks upon Porthos. He cannot with dignity retreat, but he stops and looks about him as if lo

in admiration of the scenery, and presently he strolls away with a fine indifference and a glint at me from the corner of his eye. The Serpentine begins near here. It is a love

lake, and there is a drowned forest at the bottom of it. If you peer over the edge you can see the trees all growing upside down, and they say that at night there are al

drowned stars in it. If so, Peter Pan sees them when he is sailing across the lake in the Thrush's Nest. A small part only of the Serpentine is in the Gardens, for soon it pass

beneath a bridge to far away where the island is on which all the birds are born that become baby boys and girls. No one who is human, except Peter Pan (and he is only ha

human), can land on the island, but you may write what you want (boy or girl, dark or fair) on a piece of paper, and then twist it into the shape of a boat and slip it into t

water, and it reaches Peter Pan's island after dark. We are on the way home now, though of course, it is all pretence that we can go to so many of the places in one day

should have had to be carrying David long ago, and resting on every seat like old Mr. Salford. That was what we called him, because he always talked to us of a lovely pl

called Salford where he had been born. He was a crab-apple of an old gentleman who wandered all day in the Gardens from seat to seat trying to fall in with somebody w

was acquainted with the town of Salford, and when we had known him for a year or more we actually did meet another aged solitary who had once spent Saturday to Mon

in Salford. He was meek and timid, and carried his address inside his hat, and whatever part of London he was in search of he always went to Westminster Abbey first

starting-point. Him we carried in triumph to our other friend, with the story of that Saturday to Monday, and never shall I forget the gloating joy with which Mr. Salf

leapt at him. They have been cronies ever since, and I noticed that Mr. Salford, who naturally does most of the talking, keeps tight grip of the other old man's coat. The

last places before you come to our gate are the Dog's Cemetery and the chaffinch's nest, but we pretend not to know what the Dog's Cemetery is, as Porthos is always w

us. The nest is very sad. It is quite white, and the way we found it was wonderful. We were having another look among the bushes for David's lost worsted ball, and ins

of the ball we found a lovely nest made of the worsted, and containing four eggs, with scratches on them very like David's handwriting, so we think they must have been

mother's love-letters to the little ones inside. Every day we were in the Gardens we paid a call at the nest, taking care that no cruel boy should see us, and we dropped cru and soon the bird knew us as friends, and sat in the nest looking at us kindly with her shoulders hunched up. But one day when we went there were only two eggs in the nest, and the next time there were none. The saddest part of it was that the poor little chaffinch fluttered about the bushes, looking so reproachfully at us that we knew she thought we had done it; and though David tried to explain to her, it was so long since he had spoken the bird language that I fear she did not understand. He and I left the Gardens that day with our knuckles in our eyes. CHAPTER II *Peter Pan* If you ask your mother whether she knew about Peter Pan when she was a little girl, she will say, "Why, of course I did, child;" and if you ask her whether he rode on a goat in those days, she will say, "What a foolish question to ask; certainly he did." Then if you ask your grandmother whether she knew about Peter Pan when she was a girl, she also says, "Why, of course I did, child," but if you ask her whether he rode on a goat in those days, she says she never heard of his having a goat. Perhaps she has forgotten, just as she sometimes forgets your name and calls you Mildred, which is your mother's name. Still, she could hardly forget such an important thing as the goat. Therefore there was no goat when your grandmother was a little girl. This shows that, in telling the story of Peter Pan, to begin with the goat (as most people do) is as silly as to put on your jacket before your vest. Of course, it also shows that Peter is ever so old, but he is really always the same age, so that does not matter in the least. His age is one week, and though he was born so long ago he has never had a birthday, nor is there the slightest chance of his ever having one. The reason is that he escaped from being a human when he was seven days old; he escaped by the window and flew back to the Kensington Gardens. If you think he was the only baby who ever wanted to escape, it shows how completely you have forgotten your own young days. When David heard this story first he was quite certain that he had never tried to escape, but I told him to think back hard, pressing his hands to his temples, and when he had done this hard, and even harder, he distinctly remembered a youthful desire to return to the tree-tops, and with that memory came others, as that he had lain in bed planning to escape as soon as his mother was asleep, and how she had once caught him half-way up the chimney. All children could have such recollections if they would press their hands hard to their temples, for, having been birds before they were human, they are naturally a little wild during the first few weeks, and very itchy at the shoulders, where their wings used to be. So David tells me. I ought to mention here that the following is our way with a story: First I tell it to him, and then he tells it to me, the understanding being that it is quite a different story; and then I retell it with his additions, and so we go on until no one could say whether it is more his story or mine. In this story of Peter Pan, for instance, the bald narrative and most of the moral reflections are mine, though not all, for this boy can be a stern moralist; but the interesting bits about the ways and customs of babies in the bird-stage are mostly reminiscences of David's, recalled by pressing his hands to his temples and thinking hard. Well, Peter Pan got out by the window, which had no bars. Standing on the ledge he could see trees far away, which were doubtless the Kensington Gardens, and the moment he saw them he entirely forgot that he was now a little boy in a nightgown, and away he flew, right over the houses to the Gardens. It is wonderful that he could fly without wings, but the place itched tremendously, and—and—perhaps we could all fly if we were as dead-confident-sure of our capacity to do it as was bold Peter Pan that evening. He alighted gaily on the open sward, between the Baby's Palace and the Serpentine, and the first thing he did was to lie on his back and kick. He was quite unaware already that he had ever been human, and thought he was a bird, even in appearance, just the same as in his early days, and when he tried to catch a fly he did not understand that the reason he missed it was because he had attempted to seize it with his hand, which, of course, a bird never does. He saw, however, that it must be past Lock-out Time, for there were a good many fairies about, all too busy to notice him; they were getting breakfast ready, milking their cows, drawing water, and so on, and the sight of the water-pails made him thirsty, so he flew over to the Round Pond to have a drink. He stooped and dipped his beak in the pond; he thought it was his beak, but, of course, it was only his nose, and therefore, very little water came up, and that not so refreshing as usual, so next he tried a puddle, and he fell flop into it. When a real bird falls in flop, he spreads out his feathers and pecks them dry, but Peter could not remember what was the thing to do, and he decided rather sulkily to go to sleep on the weeping-beech in the Baby Walk. At first he found some difficulty in balancing himself on a branch, but presently he remembered the way, and fell asleep. He awoke long before morning, shivering, and saying to himself, "I never was out on such a cold night;" he had really been out on colder nights when he was a bird, but, of course, as everybody knows, what seems a warm night to a bird is a cold night to a boy in a nightgown. Peter also felt strangely uncomfortable, as if his head was stuffy; he heard loud noises that made him look round sharply, though they were really himself sneezing. There was something he wanted very much, but, though he knew he wanted it, he could not think what it was. What he wanted so much was his mother to blow his nose, but that never struck him, so he decided to appeal to the fairies for enlightenment. They are reputed to know a good deal. There were two of them strolling along the Baby Walk, with their arms round each other's waists, and he hopped down to address them. The fairies have their tiffs with the birds, but they usually give a civil answer to a civil question, and he was quite angry when these two ran away the moment they saw him. Another was lolling on a garden chair, reading a postage-stamp which some human had let fall, and when he heard Peter's voice he popped in alarm behind a tulip. To Peter's bewilderment he discovered that every fairy he met fled from him. A band of workmen, who were sawing down a toadstool, rushed away, leaving their tools behind them. A milkmaid turned her pail upside down and hid in it. Soon the Gardens were in an uproar. Crowds of fairies were running this way and that, asking each other stoutly who was afraid; lights were extinguished, doors barricaded, and from the grounds of Queen Mab's palace came the rub-a-dub of drums, showing that the royal guard had been called out. A regiment of Lancers came charging down the Broad Walk, armed with holly-leaves, with which they jag the enemy horribly in passing. Peter heard the little people crying everywhere that there was a human in the Gardens after Lock-out Time, but he never thought for a moment that he was the human. He was feeling stuffier and stuffier, and more and more wistful to learn what he wanted done to his nose, but he pursued them with the vital question in vain; the timid creatures ran from him, and even the Lancers, when he approached them up the Hump, turned swiftly into a side-walk, on the pretence that they saw him there. Despairing of the fairies, he resolved to consult the birds, but now he remembered, as an odd thing, that all the birds on the weeping-beech had flown away when he alighted on it, and though this had not troubled him at the time, he saw its meaning now. Every living thing was shunning him. Poor little Peter Pan

He sat down and cried, and even then he did not know that, for a bird, he was sitting on his wrong part. It is a blessing that he did not know, for otherwise he would have lost faith in his power to fly, and the moment you doubt whether you can fly, you cease for ever to be able to do it. The reason birds can fly and we can't is simply that they have perfect faith, for to have faith is to have wings. Now, except by flying, no one can reach the island in the Serpentine, for the boats of humans are forbidden to land there, and there are stakes round it, standing up in the water, on each of which a bird-sentinel sits by day and night. It was to the island that Peter now flew to put his strange case before old Solomon Caw, and he alighted on it with relief, much heartened to find himself at last at home, as the birds call the island. All of them were asleep, including the sentinels, except Solomon, who was wide awake on one side, and he listened quietly to Peter's adventures, and then told him their true meaning. "Look at your nightgown, if you don't believe me," Solomon said; and with staring eyes Peter looked at his nightgown, and then at the sleeping birds. Not one of them wore anything. "How many of your toes are thumbs?" said Solomon a little cruelly, and Peter saw to his consternation, that all his toes were fingers. The shock was so great that it drove away his cold. "Ruffle your feathers," said that grim old Solomon, and Peter tried most desperately hard to ruffle his feathers, but he had none. Then he rose up, quaking, and for the first time since he stood on the window ledge, he remembered a lady who had been very fond of him. "I think I shall go back to mother," he said timidly. "Good-bye," replied Solomon Caw with a queer look. But Peter hesitated. "Why don't you go?" the old one asked politely. "I suppose," said Peter huskily, "I suppose I can still fly." You see he had lost faith.

"Poor little half-and-half!" said Solomon, who was not really hard-hearted, "You will never be able to fly again, not even on windy days. You must live here on the island always." "And never even go to the Kensington Gardens?" Peter asked tragically. "How could you get across?" said Solomon. He promised very kindly, however, to teach Peter as many of the bird ways as could be learned by one of such an awkward shape. "Then I shan't be exactly a human?" Peter asked. "No." "Nor exactly a bird?" "No." "What shall I be?" "You will be a Betwixt-and-Between," Solomon said, and certainly he was a wise old fellow, for that is exactly how it turned out. The birds on the island never got used to him. His oddities tickled them every day, as if they were quite new, though it was really the birds that were new. They came out of the eggs daily, and laughed at him at once; then off they soon flew to be humans, and other birds came out of other eggs; and so it went on for ever. The crafty mother-birds, when they tired of sitting on their eggs, used to get the young ones to break their shells a day before the right time by whispering to them that now was their chance to see Peter washing or drinking or eating. Thousands gathered round him daily to watch him do these things, just as you watch the peacocks, and they screamed with delight when he lifted the crusts they flung him with his hands instead of in the usual way with the mouth. All his food was brought to him from the Gardens at Solomon's orders by the birds. He would not eat worms or insects (which they thought very silly of him), so they brought him bread in their beaks. Thus, when you cry out, "Greedy! Greedy!" to the bird that flies away with the big crust, you know now that you ought not to do this, for he is very likely taking it to Peter Pan. Peter wore no nightgown now. You see, the birds were always begging him for bits of it to line their nests with, and, being very good-natured, he could not refuse, so by Solomon's advice he had hidden what was left of it.

But, though he was now quite naked, you must not think that he was cold or unhappy. He was usually very happy and gay, and the reason was that Solomon had kept his promise and taught him many of the bird ways. To be easily pleased, for instance, and always to be really doing something, and to think that whatever he was doing was a thing of vast importance. Peter became very clever at helping the birds to build their nests; soon he could build better than a wood-pigeon, and nearly as well as a blackbird, though never did he satisfy the finches, and he made nice little water-troughs near the nests and dug up worms for the young ones with his fingers. He also became very learned in bird-lore, and knew an east wind from a west wind by its smell, and he could see the grass growing and hear the insects walking about inside the tree-trunks. But the best thing Solomon had done was to teach him to have a glad heart. All birds have glad hearts unless you rob their nests, and so as they were the only kind of heart Solomon knew about, it was easy to him to teach Peter how to have one. Peter's heart was so glad that he felt he must sing all day long, just as the birds sing for joy, but, being partly human, he needed an instrument, so he made a pipe of reeds, and he used to sit by the shore of the island of an evening, practising the sough of the wind and the ripple of the water, and catching handfuls of the shine of the moon, and he put them all in his pipe and played them so beautifully that even the birds were deceived, and they would say to each other, "Was that a fish leaping in the water or was it Peter playing leaping fish on his pipe?" And sometimes he played the birth of birds, and then the mothers would turn round in their nests to see whether they had laid an egg. If you are a child of the Gardens you must know the chestnut-tree near the bridge, which comes out in flower first of all the chestnuts, but perhaps you have not heard why this tree leads the way. It is because Peter wearies for summer and plays that it has come, and the chestnut being so near, hears him and is cheated. But as Peter sat by the shore tootling divinely on his pipe he sometimes fell into sad thoughts, and then the music became sad also, and the reason of all this sadness was that he could not reach the Gardens, though he could see them through the arch of the bridge. He knew he could never be a real human again, and scarcely wanted to be one, but oh! how he longed to play as other children play, and of course there is no such lovely place to play in as the Gardens. The birds brought him news of how boys and girls play, and wistful tears started in Peter's eyes. Perhaps you wonder why he did not swim across. The reason was that he could not swim. He wanted to know how to swim, but no one on the island knew the way except the ducks, and they are so stupid. They were quite willing to teach him, but all they could say about it was, "You sit down on the top of the water in this way, and then you kick out like that." Peter tried it often, but always before he could kick out he sank. What he really needed to know was how you sit on the water without sinking, and they said it was quite impossible to explain such an easy thing as that. Occasionally swans touched on the island, and he would give them all his day's food and then ask them how they sat on the water, but as soon as he had no more to give them the hateful things hissed at him and sailed away. Once he really thought he had discovered a way of reaching the Gardens. A wonderful white thing, like a runaway newspaper, floated high over the island and then tumbled, rolling over and over after the manner of a bird that has broken its wing. Peter was so frightened that he hid, but the birds told him it was only a kite, and what a kite is, and that it must have tugged its string out of a boy's hand, and soared away. After that they laughed at Peter for being so fond of the kite; he loved it so much that he even slept with one hand on it, and I think this was pathetic and pretty, for the reason he loved it was because it had belonged to a real boy. To the

birds this was a very poor reason, but the older ones felt grateful to him at this time because he had nursed a number of fledglings through the German measles, and they

offered to show him how birds fly a kite. So six of them took the end of the string in their beaks and flew away with it; and to his amazement it flew after them and went even

higher than they. Peter screamed out, "Do it again!" and with great good-nature they did it several times, and always instead of thanking them he cried, "Do it again!" which

shows that even now he had not quite forgotten what it was to be a boy. At last, with a grand design burning within his brave heart, he begged them to do it once more with

him clinging to the tail, and now a hundred flew off with the string, and Peter clung to the tail, meaning to drop off when he was over the Gardens. But the kite broke to

pieces in the air, and he would have drowned in the Serpentine had he not caught hold of two indignant swans and made them carry him to the island. After this the

birds said that they would help him no more in his mad enterprise. Nevertheless, Peter did reach the Gardens at last by the help of Shelley's boat, as I am now to tell you.

CHAPTER III *The Thrush's Nest* Shelley was a young gentleman and as grown-up as he need ever expect to be. He was a poet; and they are never exactly grown-up. They

are people who despise money except what you need for to-day, and he had all that and five pounds over. So, when he was walking in the Kensington Gardens, he made a

paper boat of his bank-note, and sent it sailing on the Serpentine. It reached the island at night; and the look-out brought it to Solomon Caw, who thought at first that it was

the usual thing, a message from a lady, saying she would be obliged if he could let her have a good one. They always ask for the best one he has, and if he likes the letter he

sends one from Class A, but if it ruffles him he sends very funny ones indeed. Sometimes he sends none at all, and at another time he sends a nestful; it all depends on the

mood you catch him in. He likes you to leave it all to him, and if you mention particularly that you hope he will see his way to making it *a boy this time,* he is almost sure to

send another girl. And whether you are a lady or only a little boy who wants a baby-sister, always take pains to write your address clearly. You can't think what a lot of babies

Solomon has sent to the wrong house. Shelley's boat, when opened, completely puzzled Solomon, and he took counsel of his assistants, who having walked over it twice,

first with their toes pointed out, and then with their toes pointed in, decided that it came from some greedy person who wanted five. They thought this because there was a

large five printed on it. "Preposterous!" cried Solomon in a rage, and he presented it to Peter; anything useless which drifted upon the island was usually given to Peter as a

plaything. But he did not play with his precious bank-note, for he knew what it was at once, having been very observant during the week when he was an ordinary boy. With

so much money, he reflected, he could surely at last contrive to reach the Gardens, and he considered all the possible ways, and decided (wisely, I think) to choose the best

way. But, first, he had to tell the birds of the value of Shelley's boat; and though they were too honest to demand it back, he saw that they were galled, and they cast such

black looks at Solomon, who was rather vain of his cleverness, that he flew away to the end of the island, and sat there very depressed with his head buried in his wings. Now

Peter knew that unless Solomon was on your side, you never got anything done for you in the island, so he followed him and tried to hearten him. Nor was this all that Peter did to gain the powerful old fellow's good-will. You must know that Solomon had no intention of remaining in office all his life. He looked forward to retiring by and by, and devoting his green old age to a life of pleasure on a certain yew-stump in the Figs which had taken his fancy, and for years he had been quietly filling his stocking. It was a stocking belonging to some bathing person which had been cast upon the island, and at the time I speak of it contained a hundred and eighty crumbs, thirty-four nuts, sixteen crusts, a pen-wiper, and a boot-lace. When his stocking was full, Solomon calculated that he would be able to retire on a competency. Peter now gave him a pound. He cut it off his bank-note with a sharp stick. This made Solomon his friend for ever, and after the two had consulted together they called a meeting of the thrushes. You will see presently why thrushes only were invited. The scheme to be put before them was really Peter's, but Solomon did most of the talking, because he soon became irritable if other people talked. He began by saying that he had been much impressed by the superior ingenuity shown by the thrushes in nest-building, and this put them into good-humour at once, as it was meant to do; for all the quarrels between birds are about the best way of building nests. Other birds, said Solomon, omitted to line their nests with mud, and as a result they did not hold water. Here he cocked his head as if he had used an unanswerable argument; but, unfortunately, a Mrs. Finch had come to the meeting uninvited, and she squeaked out, "We don't build nests to hold water, but to hold eggs," and then the thrushes stopped cheering, and Solomon was so perplexed that he took several sips of water. "Consider," he said at last, "how warm the mud makes the nest." "Consider," cried Mrs. Finch, "that when water gets into the nest it remains there and your little ones are drowned." The thrushes begged Solomon with a look to say something crushing in reply to this, but again he was perplexed. "Try another drink," suggested Mrs. Finch pertly. Kate was her name, and all Kates are saucy. Solomon did try another drink, and it inspired him. "If," said he, "a finch's nest is placed on the Serpentine it fills and breaks to pieces, but a thrush's nest is still as dry as the cup of a swan's back." How the thrushes applauded! Now they knew why they lined their nests with mud, and when Mrs. Finch called out, "We don't place our nests on the Serpentine," they did what they should have done at first—chased her from the meeting. After this it was most orderly. What they had been brought together to hear, said Solomon, was this: their young friend, Peter Pan, as they well knew, wanted very much to be able to cross to the Gardens, and he now proposed, with their help, to build a boat. At this the thrushes began to fidget, which made Peter tremble for his scheme. Solomon explained hastily that what he meant was not one of the cumbrous boats that humans use; the proposed boat was to be simply a thrush's nest large enough to hold Peter. But still, to Peter's agony, the thrushes were sulky. "We are very busy people," they grumbled, "and this would be a big job." "Quite so," said Solomon, "and, of course, Peter would not allow you to work for nothing. You must remember that he is now in comfortable circumstances, and he will pay you such wages as you have never been paid before. Peter Pan authorises me to say that you shall all be paid sixpence a day." Then all the thrushes hopped for joy, and that very day was begun the celebrated Building of the Boat. All their ordinary business fell into arrears. It was the time of the year when they should have been pairing, but not a thrush's nest was built except this big one, and so Solomon soon ran short of thrushes with which to supply the demand from the mainland. The stout, rather greedy children, who look so well in perambulators but get puffed easily when they walk, were all young thrushes once, and ladies often ask specially for them. What do you think Solomon did? He sent over to the house-tops for a lot of sparrows and ordered them to lay their eggs in old thrushes' nests, and sent their young to the ladies and swore they were all thrushes! It was known afterwards on the island as the Sparrow's Year; and so, when you meet grown-up people in the Gardens who puff and blow as if they thought themselves bigger than they are, very likely they belong to that year. You ask them. Peter was a just master, and paid his workpeople every evening. They stood in rows on the branches, waiting politely while he cut the paper sixpences out of his bank-note, and presently he called the roll, and then each bird, as the names were mentioned, flew down and got sixpence. It must have been a fine sight. And at last, after months of labour, the boat was finished. O the glory of Peter as he saw it growing more and more like a great thrush's nest! From the very beginning of the building of it he slept by its side, and often woke up to say sweet things to it, and after it was lined with mud and the mud had dried he always slept in it. He sleeps in his nest still, and has a fascinating way of curling round in it, for it is just large enough to hold him comfortably when he curls round like a kitten. It is brown inside, of course, but outside it is mostly green, being woven of grass and twigs, and when these wither or snap the walls are thatched afresh. There are also a few feathers here and there, which came off the thrushes while they were building. The other birds were extremely jealous, and said that the boat would not balance on the water, but it lay most beautifully steady; they said the water would come into it, but no water came into it. Next they said that Peter had no oars, and this caused the thrushes to look at each other in dismay; but Peter replied that he had no need of oars, for he had a sail, and with such a proud, happy face he produced a sail which he had fashioned out of his nightgown, and though it was still rather like a nightgown it made a lovely sail. And that night, the moon being full, and all the birds asleep, he did enter his coracle (as Master Francis Pretty would have said) and depart out of the island. And first, he knew not why, he looked upward, with his hands clasped, and from that moment his eyes were pinned to the west. He had promised the thrushes to begin by making short voyages, with them as his guides, but far away he saw the Kensington Gardens beckoning to him beneath the bridge, and he could not wait. His face was flushed, but he never looked back; there was an exultation in his little breast that drove out fear. Was Peter the least gallant of the English mariners who have sailed westward to meet the Unknown? At first, his boat turned round and round, and he was driven back to the place of his starting, whereupon he shortened sail, by removing one of the sleeves, and was forthwith carried backwards by a contrary breeze, to his no small peril. He now let go the sail, with the result that he was drifted towards the far shore, where are black shadows he knew not the dangers of, but suspected them, and so once more hoisted his nightgown and went roomer of the shadows until he caught a favouring wind, which bore him westward, but at so great a speed that he was like to be broke against the bridge. Which, having avoided, he passed under the bridge and came, to his great rejoicing, within full sight of the delectable Gardens. But having tried to cast anchor, which was a stone at the end of a piece of the kite-string, he found no bottom, and was fain to hold off, seeking for moorage; and, feeling his way, he buffeted against a sunken reef that cast him overboard by the greatness of the shock, and he was near to being drowned, but clambered back into the vessel. There now arose a mighty storm, accompanied by roaring of waters, such as he had never heard the like, and he was tossed this way and that, and his hands so numbed with the cold that he could not close them. Having escaped the danger of

which, he was mercifully carried into a small bay, where his boat rode at peace. Nevertheless, he was not yet in safety; for, on pretending to disembark, he found a multitude

of small people drawn up on the shore to contest his landing, and shouting shrilly to him to be off, for it was long past Lock-out Time. This, with much brandishing of their

holly-leaves, and also a company of them carried an arrow which some boy had left in the Gardens, and this they were prepared to use as a battering-ram. Then Peter, who

knew them for the fairies, called out that he was not an ordinary human and had no desire to do them displeasure, but to be their friend; nevertheless, having found a jolly

harbour, he was in no temper to draw off therefrom, and he warned them if they sought to mischief him to stand to their harms. So saying, he boldly leapt ashore, and they

gathered around him with intent to slay him, but there then arose a great cry among the women, and it was because they had now observed that his sail was a baby's

nightgown. Whereupon, they straightway loved him, and grieved that their laps were too small, the which I cannot explain, except by saying that such is the way of women.

The men-fairies now sheathed their weapons on observing the behaviour of their women, on whose intelligence they set great store, and they led him civilly to their queen,

who conferred upon him the courtesy of the Gardens after Lock-out Time, and henceforth Peter could go whither he chose, and the fairies had orders to put him in comfort.

Such was his first voyage to the Gardens, and you may gather from the antiquity of the language that it took place a long time ago. But Peter never grows any older, and if

we could be watching for him under the bridge to-night (but, of course, we can't), I dare say we should see him hoisting his nightgown and sailing or paddling towards us

in the Thrushes Nest. When he sails, he sits down, but he stands up to paddle. I shall tell you presently how he got his paddle. Long before the time for the opening of the

gates comes he steals back to the island, for people must not see him (he is not so human as all that), but this gives him hours for play, and he plays exactly as real children

play. At least he thinks so, and it is one of the pathetic things about him that he often plays quite wrongly. You see, he had no one to tell him how children really play, for the

fairies are all more or less in hiding until dusk, and so know nothing, and though the birds pretended that they could tell him a great deal, when the time for telling came, it

was wonderful how little they really knew. They told him the truth about hide-and-seek, and he often plays it by himself, but even the ducks on the Round Pond could not

explain to him what it is that makes the pond so fascinating to boys. Every night the ducks have forgotten all the events of the day, except the number of pieces of cake thrown

to them. They are gloomy creatures, and say that cake is not what it was in their young days. So Peter had to find out many things for himself. He often played ships at the

Round Pond, but his ship was only a hoop which he had found on the grass. Of course, he had never seen a hoop, and he wondered what you play at with them, and decided

that you play at pretending they are boats. This hoop always sank at once, but he waded in for it, and sometimes he dragged it gleefully round the rim of the pond, and he

was quite proud to think that he had discovered what boys do with hoops. Another time, when he found a child's pail, he thought it was for sitting in, and he sat so hard in it

that he could scarcely get out of it. Also he found a balloon. It was bobbing about on the Hump, quite as if it was having a game by itself, and he caught it after an exciting chase. But he thought it was a ball, and Jenny Wren had told him that boys kick balls, so he kicked it; and after that he could not find it anywhere. Perhaps the most surprising

thing he found was a perambulator. It was under a lime-tree, near the entrance to the Fairy Queen's Winter Palace (which is within the circle of the seven Spanish chestnuts),

and Peter approached it warily, for the birds had never mentioned such things to him. Lest it was alive, he addressed it politely, and then, as it gave no answer, he went nearer

and felt it cautiously. He gave it a little push, and it ran from him, which made him think it must be alive after all; but, as it had run from him, he was not afraid. So he stretched

out his hand to pull it to him, but this time it ran at him, and he was so alarmed that he leapt the railing and scudded away to his boat. You must not think, however, that he

was a coward, for he came back next night with a crust in one hand and a stick in the other, but the perambulator had gone, and he never saw any other one. I have promised

to tell you also about his paddle. It was a child's spade which he had found near St. Govor's Well, and he thought it was a paddle. Do you pity Peter Pan for making these

mistakes? If so, I think it rather silly of you. What I mean is that, of course, one must pity him now and then, but to pity him all the time would be impertinence. He thought

he had the most splendid time in the Gardens, and to think you have it is almost quite as good as really to have it. He played without ceasing, while you often waste time by

being mad-dog or Mary-Annish. He could be neither of these things, for he had never heard of them, but do you think he is to be pitied for that? Oh, he was merry! He was

as much merrier than you, for instance, as you are merrier than your father. Sometimes he fell, like a spinning-top, and from sheer merriment. Have you seen a greyhound

leaping the fences of the Gardens? That is how Peter leaps them. And think of the music of his pipe. Gentlemen who walk home at night write to the papers to say they heard

a nightingale in the Gardens, but it is really Peter's pipe they hear. Of course, he had no mother—at least, what use was she to him! You can be sorry for him for that, but

don't be too sorry, for the next thing I mean to tell you is how he revisited her. It was the fairies who gave him the chance. CHAPTER IV *Lock-Out Time* It is frightfully

difficult to know much about the fairies, and almost the only thing known for certain is that there are fairies wherever there are children. Long ago children were forbidden

the Gardens, and at that time there was not a fairy in the place; then the children were admitted, and the fairies came trooping in that very evening. They can't resist following

the children, but you seldom see them, partly because they live in the daytime behind the railings, where you are not allowed to go, and also partly because they are so

cunning. They are not a bit cunning after Lock-out, but until Lock-out, my word! When you were a bird you knew the fairies pretty well, and you remember a good deal

about them in your babyhood, which it is a great pity you can't write down, for gradually you forget, and I have heard of children who declared that they had never once

seen a fairy. Very likely if they said this in the Kensington Gardens, they were standing looking at a fairy all the time. The reason they were cheated was that she pretended

to be something else. This is one of their best tricks. They usually pretend to be flowers, because the court sits in the Fairies' Basin, and there are so many flowers there, and

all along the Baby Walk, that a flower is the thing least likely to attract attention. They dress exactly like flowers, and change with the seasons, putting on white when lilies

are in and blue for bluebells, and so on. They like crocus and hyacinth time best of all, as they are partial to a bit of colour, but tulips (except white ones, which are the fairy cradles) they consider garish, and they sometimes put off dressing like tulips for days, so that the beginning of the tulip weeks is almost the best time to catch them. When

they think you are not looking they skip along pretty lively, but if you look, and they fear there is no time to hide, they stand quite still pretending to be flowers. Then, after

you have passed without knowing that they were fairies, they rush home and tell their mothers they have had such an adventure. The Fairy Basin, you remember, is all

covered with ground-ivy (from which they make their castor oil), with flowers growing in it here and there. Most of them really are flowers, but some of them are fairies.

You never can be sure of them, but a good plan is to walk by looking the other way, and then turn round sharply. Another good plan, which David and I sometimes follow,

is to stare them down. After a long time they can't help winking, and then you know for certain that they are fairies. There are also numbers of them along the Baby Walk,

which is a famous gentle place, as spots frequented by fairies are called. Once twenty-four of them had an extraordinary adventure. They were a girls' school out for a walk

with the governess, and all wearing hyacinth gowns, when she suddenly put her finger to her mouth, and then they all stood still on an empty bed and pretended to be

hyacinths. Unfortunately what the governess had heard was two gardeners coming to plant new flowers in that very bed. They were wheeling a hand-cart with the flowers

in it, and were quite surprised to find the bed occupied. "Pity to lift them hyacinths," said the one man. "Duke's orders," replied the other, and, having emptied the cart, they

dug up the boarding school and put the poor, terrified things in it in five rows. Of course, neither the governess nor the girls dare let on that they were fairies, so they were

carted far away to a potting-shed, out of which they escaped in the night without their shoes, but there was a great row about it among the parents, and the school was ruined

As for their houses, it is no use looking for them, because they are the exact opposite of our houses. You can see our houses by day but you can't see them by dark. Well, you

can see their houses by dark, but you can't see them by day, for they are the colour of night, and I never heard of any one yet who could see night in the daytime. This doe

not mean that they are black, for night has its colours just as day has, but ever so much brighter. Their blues and reds and greens are like ours with a light behind them. Th

palace is entirely built of many-coloured glasses, and it is quite the loveliest of all royal residences, but the queen sometimes complains because the common people will pee

in to see what she is doing. They are very inquisitive folk, and press quite hard against the glass, and that is why their noses are mostly snubby. The streets are miles long an

very twisty, and have paths on each side made of bright worsted. The birds used to steal the worsted for their nests, but a policeman has been appointed to hold on at th

other end. One of the great differences between the fairies and us is that they never do anything useful. When the first baby laughed for the first time, his laugh broke into

million pieces, and they all went skipping about. That was the beginning of fairies. They look tremendously busy, you know, as if they had not a moment to spare, but if ye

were to ask them what they are doing, they could not tell you in the least. They are frightfully ignorant, and everything they do is make-believe. They have a postman, b

he never calls except at Christmas with his little box, and though they have beautiful schools, nothing is taught in them; the youngest child being chief person is always elect

mistress, and when she has called the roll, they all go out for a walk and never come back. It is a very noticeable thing that, in fairy families, the youngest is always ch person, and usually becomes a prince or princess; and children remember this, and think it must be so among humans also; and that is why they are often made uneasy when they come upon their mother furtively putting new frills on the bassinette. You have probably observed that your baby-sister wants to do all sorts of things that your mother and her nurse want her not to do—to stand up at sitting-down time, and to sit down at stand-up time, for instance, or to wake up when she should fall asleep, or to crawl on the floor when she is wearing her best frock, and so on, and perhaps you put this down to naughtiness. But it is not; it simply means that she is doing as she has seen the fairies do; she begins by following their ways, and it takes about two years to get her into the human ways. Her fits of passion, which are awful to behold, and are usually called teething, are no such thing; they are her natural exasperation, because we don't understand her, though she is talking an intelligible language. She is talking fairy. The reason mothers and nurses know what her remarks mean, before other people know, as that "Guch" means "Give it to me at once," while "Wa" is "Why do you wear such a funny hat?" is because, mixing so much with babies, they have picked up a little of the fairy language. Of late David has been thinking back hard about the fairy tongue, with his hands clutching his temples, and he has remembered a number of their phrases which I shall tell you some day if I don't forget. He had heard them in the days when he was a thrush, and though I suggested to him that perhaps it is really bird language he is remembering, he says not, for these phrases are about fun and adventures, and the birds talked of nothing but nest-building. He distinctly remembers that the birds used to go from spot to spot like ladies at shop windows, looking at the different nests and saying, "Not my colour, my dear," and "How would that do with a soft lining?" and "But will it wear?" and "What hideous trimming!" and so on. The fairies are exquisite dancers, and that is why one of the first things the baby does is to sign to you to dance to him and then to cry when you do it. They hold their great balls in the open air, in what is called a fairy ring. For weeks afterwards you can see the ring on the grass. It is not there when they begin, but they make it by waltzing round and round. Sometimes you will find mushrooms inside the ring, and these are fairy chairs that the servants have forgotten to clear away. The chairs and the rings are the only telltale marks these little people leave behind them, and they would remove even these were they not so fond of dancing that they toe it till the very moment of the opening of the gates. David and I once found a fairy ring quite warm. But there is also a way of finding out about the ball before it takes place. You know the boards which tell at what time the Gardens are to close to-day. Well, these tricky fairies sometimes slyly change the board on a ball night, so that it says the Gardens are to close at six-thirty, for instance, instead of at seven. This enables them to get begun half an hour earlier. If on such a night we could remain behind in the Gardens, as the famous Maimie Mannering did, we might see delicious sights; hundreds of lovely fairies hastening to the ball, the married ones wearing their wedding rings round their waists; the gentlemen, all in uniform, holding up the ladies' trains, and linkmen running in front carrying winter cherries, which are the fairy-lanterns, the cloakroom where they put on their silver slippers and get a ticket for their wraps, the flowers streaming up from the Baby Walk to look on, and always welcome because they can lend a pin, the supper-table, with Queen Mab at the head of it, and behind her chair the Lord Chamberlain, who carries a dandelion on which he blows when her Majesty wants to know the time. The table-cloth varies according to the seasons, and in

May it is made of chestnut blossom. The way the fairy servants do is this: The men, scores of them, climb up the trees and shake the branches, and the blossom falls like snow.

Then the lady servants sweep it together by whisking their skirts until it is exactly like a tablecloth, and that is how they get their tablecloth. They have real glasses and real wine of three kinds, namely, blackthorn wine, berberris wine, and cowslip wine, and the Queen pours out, but the bottles are so heavy that she just pretends to pour out.

There is bread-and-butter to begin with, of the size of a threepenny bit; and cakes to end with, and they are so small that they have no crumbs. The fairies sit round on mushrooms, and at first they are well-behaved and always cough off the table, and so on, but after a bit they are not so well-behaved and stick their fingers into the butter, which is got from the roots of old trees, and the really horrid ones crawl over the tablecloth chasing sugar or other delicacies with their tongues. When the Queen sees them doing this she signs to the servants to wash up and put away, and then everybody adjourns to the dance, the Queen walking in front while the Lord Chamberlain walks behind her, carrying two little pots, one of which contains the juice of wallflower and the other the juice of Solomon's seals. Wallflower juice is good for reviving dancers who fall to the ground in a fit, and Solomon's seals juice is for bruises. They bruise very easily, and when Peter plays faster and faster they foot it till they fall down in fits. For, as you know without my telling you, Peter Pan is the fairies' orchestra. He sits in the middle of the ring, and they would never dream of having a smart dance nowadays without him. "P. P." is written on the corner of the invitation-cards sent out by all really good families. They are grateful little people, too, and at the princesses coming-of-age ball (they come of age on their second birthday and have a birthday every month) they gave him the wish of his heart. The way it was done was this. The Queen ordered him to kneel, and then said that for playing so beautifully she would give him the wish of his heart. Then they all gathered round Peter to hear what was the wish of his heart, but for a long time he hesitated, not being certain what it was himself. "If I chose to go back to mother," he asked at last, "could you give me that wish?" Now this question vexed them, for were he to return to his mother they should lose his music, so the Queen tilted her nose contemptuously and said, "Pooh! ask for a much bigger wish than that."

"Is that quite a little wish?" he inquired. "As little as this," the Queen answered, putting her hands near each other. "What size is a big wish?" he asked. She measured it off on her skirt and it was a very handsome length. Then Peter reflected and said, "Well, then, I think I shall have two little wishes instead of one big one." Of course, the fairies had to agree, though his cleverness rather shocked them, and he said that his first wish was to go to his mother, but with the right to return to the Gardens if he found her disappointing. His second wish he would hold in reserve. They tried to dissuade him, and even put obstacles in the way. "I can give you the power to fly to her house," the Queen said, "but I can't open the door for you." "The window I flew out at will be open," Peter said confidently. "Mother always keeps it open in the hope that I may fly back." "How do you know?" they asked, quite surprised, and, really, Peter could not explain how he knew. "I just do know," he said. So as he persisted in his wish, they had to grant it. The way they gave him power to fly was this: They all tickled him on the shoulder, and soon he felt a funny itching in that part, and then up he rose higher and higher, and flew away out of the Gardens and over the housetops. It was so delicious that instead of flying straight to his own home he skimmed away over St. Paul's to the

Crystal Palace and back by the river and Regent's Park, and by the time he reached his mother's window he had quite made up his mind that his second wish should be to become a bird. The window was wide open, just as he knew it would be, and in he fluttered, and there was his mother lying asleep. Peter alighted softly on the wooden rail at the foot of the bed and had a good look at her. She lay with her head on her hand, and the hollow in the pillow was like a nest lined with her brown wavy hair. He remembered, though he had long forgotten it, that she always gave her hair a holiday at night. How sweet the frills of her nightgown were! He was very glad she was such a pretty mother. But she looked sad, and he knew why she looked sad. One of her arms moved as if it wanted to go round something, and he knew what it wanted to go round.

"O mother!" said Peter to himself, "if you just knew who is sitting on the rail at the foot of the bed." Very gently he patted the little mound that her feet made, and he could see by her face that she liked it. He knew he had but to say "Mother" ever so softly, and she would wake up. They always wake up at once if it is you that says their name. Then she would give such a joyous cry and squeeze him tight. How nice that would be to him, but oh! how exquisitely delicious it would be to her. That, I am afraid, is how Peter regarded it. In returning to his mother he never doubted that he was giving her the greatest treat a woman can have. Nothing can be more splendid, he thought, than to have a little boy of your own. How proud of him they are! and very right and proper, too. But why does Peter sit so long on the rail; why does he not tell his mother that he has come back? I quite shrink from the truth, which is that he sat there in two minds. Sometimes he looked longingly at his mother, and sometimes he looked longingly at the window. Certainly it would be pleasant to be her boy again, but on the other hand, what times those had been in the Gardens! Was he so sure that he should enjoy wearing clothes again? He popped off the bed and opened some drawers to have a look at his old garments. They were still there, but he could not remember how you put them on. The socks, for instance, were they worn on the hands or on the feet? He was about to try one of them on his hand, when he had a great adventure. Perhaps the drawer had creaked; at any rate, his mother woke up, for he heard her say "Peter," as if it was the most lovely word in the language. He remained sitting on the floor and held his breath, wondering how she knew that he had come back. If she said "Peter" again, he meant to cry "Mother" and run to her. But she spoke no more, she made little moans only, and when he next peeped at her she was once more asleep, with tears on her face. It made Peter very miserable, and what do you think was the first thing he did? Sitting on the rail at the foot of the bed, he played a beautiful lullaby to his mother on his pipe. He had made it up himself out of the way she said "Peter," and he never stopped playing until she looked happy. He thought this so clever of him that he could scarcely resist wakening her to hear her say, "O Peter, how exquisitely you play!" However, as she now seemed comfortable, he again cast looks at the window. You must not think that he meditated flying away and never coming back. He had quite decided to be his mother's boy, but hesitated about beginning to-night. It was the second wish which troubled him. He no longer meant to make it a wish to be a bird, but not to ask for a second wish seemed wasteful, and, of course, he could not ask for it without returning to the fairies. Also, if he put off asking for his wish too long it might go bad. He asked himself if he had not been hard-hearted to fly away without saying good-bye to Solomon. "I should like awfully to sail in my boat just once more," he said wistfully to his sleeping mother. He quite argued with her as if she could hear him. "It would be so splendid to tell the birds of this adventure," he said coaxingly. "I promise to come back," he said

solemnly, and meant it, too. And in the end, you know, he flew away. Twice he came back from the window, wanting to kiss his mother, but he feared the delight of it might

waken her, so at last he played her a lovely kiss on his pipe, and then he flew back to the Gardens. Many nights, and even months, passed before he asked the fairies for his

second wish; and I am not sure that I quite know why he delayed so long. One reason was that he had so many good-byes to say, not only to his particular friends, but to a

hundred favourite spots. Then he had his last sail, and his very last sail, and his last sail of all, and so on. Again, a number of farewell feasts were given in his honour; and

another comfortable reason was that, after all, there was no hurry, for his mother would never weary of waiting for him. This last reason displeased old Solomon, for it was

an encouragement to the birds to procrastinate. Solomon had several excellent mottoes for keeping them at their work, such as "Never put off laying to-day because you can

lay to-morrow," and "In this world there are no second chances," and yet here was Peter gaily putting off and none the worse for it. The birds pointed this out to each other,

and fell into lazy habits. But, mind you, though Peter was so slow in going back to his mother, he was quite decided to go back. The best proof of this was his caution with

the fairies. They were most anxious that he should remain in the Gardens to play to them, and to bring this to pass they tried to trick him into making such a remark as "I

wish the grass was not so wet," and some of them danced out of time in the hope that he might cry, "I do wish you would keep time!" Then they would have said that this

was his second wish. But he smoked their design, and though on occasions he began, "I wish—" he always stopped in time. So when at last he said to them bravely, "I wish

now to go back to mother for ever and always," they had to tickle his shoulders and let him go. He went in a hurry in the end, because he had dreamt that his mother was

crying, and he knew what was the great thing she cried for, and that a hug from her splendid Peter would quickly make her to smile. Oh! he felt sure of it, and so eager was

he to be nestling in her arms that this time he flew straight to the window, which was always to be open for him. But the window was closed, and there were iron bars on it,

and peering inside he saw his mother sleeping peacefully with her arm around another little boy. Peter called, "Mother! mother!" but she heard him not; in vain he beat his

little limbs against the iron bars. He had to fly back, sobbing, to the Gardens, and he never saw his dear again. What a glorious boy he had meant to be to her! Ah, Peter! we

who have made the great mistake, how differently we should all act at the second chance. But Solomon was right—there is no second chance, not for most of us. When we

reach the window it is Lock-out Time. The iron bars are up for life. CHAPTER V *The Little House* Everybody has heard of the Little House in the Kensington Gardens,

which is the only house in the whole world that the fairies have built for humans. But no one has really seen it, except just three or four, and they have not only seen it but

slept in it, and unless you sleep in it you never see it. This is because it is not there when you lie down, but it is there when you wake up and step outside. In a kind of way

every one may see it, but what you see is not really it, but only the light in the windows. You see the light after Lock-out Time. David, for instance, saw it quite distinctly far

away among the trees as we were going home from the pantomime, and Oliver Bailey saw it the night he stayed so late at the Temple, which is the name of his father's office

Angela Clare, who loves to have a tooth extracted because then she is treated to tea in a shop, saw more than one light, she saw hundreds of them all together; and this must

have been the fairies building the house, for they build it every night, and always in a different part of the Gardens. She thought one of the lights was bigger than the others,

though she was not quite sure, for they jumped about so, and it might have been another one that was bigger. But if it was the same one, it was Peter Pan's light. Heaps of

children have seen the light, so that is nothing. But Maimie Mannering was the famous one for whom the house was first built. Maimie was always rather a strange girl, and

it was at night that she was strange. She was four years of age, and in the daytime she was the ordinary kind. She was pleased when her brother Tony, who was a magnificent

fellow of six, took notice of her, and she looked up to him in the right way, and tried in vain to imitate him, and was flattered rather than annoyed when he shoved her about.

Also, when she was batting, she would pause though the ball was in the air to point out to you that she was wearing new shoes. She was quite the ordinary kind in the daytime.

But as the shades of night fell, Tony, the swaggerer, lost his contempt for Maimie and eyed her fearfully; and no wonder, for with dark there came into her face a look that I

can describe only as a leary look. It was also a serene look that contrasted grandly with Tony's uneasy glances. Then he would make her presents of his favourite toys (which

he always took away from her next morning), and she accepted them with a disturbing smile. The reason he was now become so wheedling and she so mysterious was (in

brief) that they knew they were about to be sent to bed. It was then that Maimie was terrible. Tony entreated her not to do it to-night, and the mother and their coloured

nurse threatened her, but Maimie merely smiled her agitating smile. And by and by when they were alone with their night-light she would start up in bed crying "Hsh! what

was that?" Tony beseeches her, "It was nothing—don't, Maimie, don't!" and pulls the sheet over his head. "It is coming nearer!" she cries. "Oh, look at it, Tony! It is feeling

your bed with its horns—it is boring for you, O Tony, oh!" and she desists not until he rushes downstairs in his combinations, screeching. When they came up to whip Maimie

they usually found her sleeping tranquilly—not shamming, you know, but really sleeping, and looking like the sweetest little angel, which seems to me to make it almost

worse. But of course it was daytime when they were in the Gardens, and then Tony did most of the talking. You could gather from his talk that he was a very brave boy, and

no one was so proud of it as Maimie. She would have loved to have a ticket on her saying that she was his sister. And at no time did she admire him more than when he told

her, as he often did with splendid firmness, that one day he meant to remain behind in the Gardens after the gates were closed. "O Tony," she would say with awful respect,

"but the fairies will be so angry!" "I dare say," replied Tony carelessly. "Perhaps," she said, thrilling, "Peter Pan will give you a sail in his boat!" "I shall make him," replied

Tony; no wonder she was proud of him. But they should not have talked so loudly, for one day they were overheard by a fairy who had been gathering skeleton leaves, from

which the little people weave their summer curtains, and after that Tony was a marked boy. They loosened the rails before he sat on them, so that down he came on the back

of his head; they tripped him up by catching his bootlace, and bribed the ducks to sink his boat. Nearly all the nasty accidents you meet with in the Gardens occur because

the fairies have taken an ill-will to you, and so it behooves you to be careful what you say about them. Maimie was one of the kind who like to fix a day for doing things, but

Tony was not that kind, and when she asked him which day he was to remain behind in the Gardens after Lock-out he merely replied, "Just some day;" he was quite vague about which day except when she asked, "Will it be to-day?" and then he could always say for certain that it would not be to-day. So she saw that he was waiting for a real good chance. This brings us to an afternoon when the Gardens were white with snow, and there was ice on the Round Pond; not thick enough to skate on, but at least you could spoil it for to-morrow by flinging stones, and many bright little boys and girls were doing that. When Tony and his sister arrived they wanted to go straight to the pond, but their ayah said they must take a sharp walk first, and as she said this she glanced at the time-board to see when the Gardens closed that night. It read half-past five. Poor ayah! She is the one who laughs continuously because there are so many white children in the world, but she was not to laugh much more that day. Well, they went up the Baby Walk and back, and when they returned to the time-board she was surprised to see that it now read five o'clock for closing-time. But she was unacquainted with the tricky ways of the fairies, and so did not see (as Maimie and Tony saw at once) that they had changed the hour because there was to be a ball to-night. She said there was only time now to walk to the top of the Hump and back, and as they trotted along with her she little guessed what was thrilling their little breasts. You see the chance had come of seeing a fairy ball. Never, Tony felt, could he hope for a better chance. He had to feel this for Maimie so plainly felt it for him. Her eager eyes asked the question, "Is it to-day?" and he gasped and then nodded. Maimie slipped her hand into Tony's, and hers was hot, but his was cold. She did a very kind thing; she took off her scarf and gave it to him. "In case you should feel cold," she whispered. Her face was aglow, but Tony's was very gloomy. As they turned on the top of the Hump he whispered to her, "I'm afraid nurse would see me, so I shan't be able to do it." Maimie admired him more than ever for being afraid of nothing but their ayah, when there were so many unknown terrors to fear, and she said aloud, "Tony, I shall race you to the gate," and in a whisper, "then you can hide," and off they ran. Tony could always outdistance her easily, but never had she known him speed away so quickly as now, and she was sure he hurried that he might have more time to hide. "Brave, brave!" her doting eyes were crying when she got a dreadful shock; instead of hiding, her hero had run out at the gate! At this bitter sight Maimie stopped blankly, as if all her lapful of darling treasures were suddenly spilled, and then for very disdain she could not sob; in a swell of protest against all puling cowards she ran to St. Govor's Well and hid in Tony's stead. When the ayah reached the gate and saw Tony far in front she thought her other charge was with him and passed out. Twilight crept over the Gardens, and hundreds of people passed out, including the last one, who always has to run for it, but Maimie saw them not. She had shut her eyes tight and glued them with passionate tears. When she opened them something very cold ran up her legs and up her arms and dropped into her heart. It was the stillness of the Gardens. Then she heard *clang*, then from another part *clang*, then *clang, clang* away. It was the Closing of the Gates. Immediately the last clang had died away Maimie distinctly heard a voice say, "So that's all right." It had a wooden sound and seemed to come from above, and she looked up in time to see an elm-tree stretching out its arms and yawning. She was about to say, "I never knew you could speak!" when a metal voice that seemed to come from the ladle at the well remarked to the elm, "I suppose it is a bit coldish up there?" and the elm replied, "Not particularly, but you do get numb standing so long on one leg," and he flapped his arms vigorously just as the cab-men do before they drive off. Maimie was quite surprised to see that a number of other tall trees were doing the same sort of thing, and she stole away to the Baby Walk and crouched observantly under a Minorca holly which shrugged its shoulders but did not seem to mind her. She was not in the least cold. She was wearing a russet-coloured pelisse and had the hood over her head, so that nothing of her showed except her dear little face and her curls. The rest of her real self was hidden far away inside so many warm garments that in shape she seemed rather like a ball. She was about forty round the waist.

There was a good deal going on in the Baby Walk, where Maimie arrived in time to see a magnolia and a Persian lilac step over the railing and set off for a smart walk. They moved in a jerky sort of way certainly, but that was because they used crutches. An elderberry hobbled across the walk, and stood chatting with some young quinces, and they all had crutches. The crutches were the sticks that are tied to young trees and shrubs. They were quite familiar objects to Maimie, but she had never known what they were for until to-night. She peeped up the walk and saw her first fairy. He was a street boy fairy who was running up the walk closing the weeping trees. The way he did it was this: he pressed a spring in the trunks and they shut like umbrellas, deluging the little plants beneath with snow. "O you naughty, naughty child!" Maimie cried indignantly, for she knew what it was to have a dripping umbrella about your ears. Fortunately the mischievous fellow was out of earshot, but a chrysanthemum heard her, and said so pointedly, "Hoity-toity, what is this?" that she had to come out and show herself. Then the whole vegetable kingdom was rather puzzled what to do. "Of course it is no affair of ours," a spindle-tree said after they had whispered together, "but you know quite well you ought not to be here, and perhaps our duty is to report you to the fairies; what do you think yourself?" "I think you should not," Maimie replied, which so perplexed them that they said petulantly there was no arguing with her. "I wouldn't ask it of you," she assured them, "if I thought it was wrong," and of course after this they could not well carry tales. They then said, "Well-a-day," and "Such is life," for they can be frightfully sarcastic; but she felt sorry for those of them who had no crutches, and she said good-naturedly, "Before I go to the fairies' ball, I should like to take you for a walk one at a time; you can lean on me, you know." At this they clapped their hands, and she escorted them up the Baby Walk and back again, one at a time, putting an arm or a finger round the very frail, setting their leg right when it got too ridiculous, and treating the foreign ones quite as courteously as the English, though she could not understand a word they said. They behaved well on the whole, though some whimpered that she had not taken them as far as she took Nancy or Grace or Dorothy, and others jagged her, but it was quite unintentional, and she was too much of a lady to cry out. So much walking tired her, and she was anxious to be off to the ball, but she no longer felt afraid. The reason she felt no more fear was that it was now night-time, and in the dark, you remember, Maimie was always rather strange. They were now loth to let her go, for, "If the fairies see you," they warned her, "they will mischief you—stab you to death, or compel you to nurse their children, or turn you into something tedious, like an evergreen oak." As they said this they looked with affected pity at an evergreen oak, for in winter they are very envious of the evergreens. "Oh, la!" replied the oak bitingly, "how deliciously cosy it is to stand here buttoned to the neck and watch you poor naked creatures shivering." This made them sulky, though they had really brought it on themselves, and they drew for Maimie a very gloomy picture of the perils that would face her if she insisted on going to the ball. She learned from a purple filbert that the court was not in its usual good temper at present, the cause being the tantalising heart of the Duke of Christmas Daisies. He was an Oriental fairy, very poorly of a dreadful complaint, namely, inability to love, and though he had tried many ladies in many lands he could not fall in love with one of them. Queen Mab, who rules in the Gardens, had been confident that her girls would bewitch him, but alas! his heart, the doctor said, remained cold. This rather irritating doctor, who was his private physician, felt the Duke's heart immediately after any lady was presented, and then always shook his bald head and murmured, "Cold, quite cold." Naturally Queen Mab felt disgraced, and first she tried the effect of ordering the court into tears for nine minutes, and then she blamed the Cupids and decreed that they should wear fools' caps until they thawed the Duke's frozen heart. "How I should love to see the Cupids in their dear little fools' caps!" Maimie cried, and away she ran to look for them very recklessly, for the Cupids hate to be laughed at. It is always easy to discover where a fairies' ball is being held, as ribbons are stretched between it and all the populous parts of the Gardens, on which those invited may walk to the dance without wetting their pumps. This night the ribbons were red, and looked very pretty on the snow. Maimie walked alongside one of them for some distance without meeting anybody, but at last she saw a fairy cavalcade approaching. To her surprise they seemed to be returning from the ball, and she had just time to hide from them by bending her knees and holding out her arms and pretending to be a garden chair. There were six horsemen in front and six behind; in the middle walked a prim lady wearing a long train held up by two pages, and on the train, as if it were a couch, reclined a lovely girl, for in this way do aristocratic fairies travel about. She was dressed in golden rain, but the most enviable part of her was her neck, which was blue in colour and of a velvet texture, and of course showed off her diamond necklace as no white throat could have glorified it. The high-born fairies obtain this admired effect by pricking their skin, which lets the blue blood come through and dye them, and you cannot imagine anything so dazzling unless you have seen the ladies' busts in the jewellers' windows. Maimie also noticed that the whole cavalcade seemed to be in a passion, tilting their noses higher than it can be safe for even fairies to tilt them, and she concluded that this must be another case in which the doctor had said "Cold, quite cold." Well, she followed the ribbon to a place where it became a bridge over a dry puddle into which another fairy had fallen and been unable to climb out. At first this little damsel was afraid of Maimie, who most kindly went to her aid, but soon she sat in her hand chatting gaily and explaining that her name was Brownie, and that though only a poor street singer she was on her way to the ball to see if the Duke would have her. "Of course," she said, "I am rather plain," and this made Maimie uncomfortable, for indeed the simple little creature was almost quite plain for a fairy. It was difficult to know what to reply. "I see you think I have no chance," Brownie said falteringly. "I don't say that," Maimie answered politely; "of course your face is just a tiny bit homely, but—" Really it was quite awkward for her. Fortunately she remembered about her father and the bazaar. He had gone to a fashionable bazaar where all the most beautiful ladies in London were on view for half a crown the second day, but on his return home, instead of being dissatisfied with Maimie's mother, he had said, "You can't think, my dear, what a relief it is to see a homely face again." Maimie repeated this story, and it fortified Brownie tremendously, indeed she had no longer the slightest doubt that the Duke would choose her. So she scudded away up the ribbon,

calling out to Maimie not to follow lest the Queen should mischief her. But Maimie's curiosity tugged her forward, and presently at the seven Spanish chestnuts she saw a

wonderful light. She crept forward until she was quite near it, and then she peeped from behind a tree. The light, which was as high as your head above the ground, was

composed of myriads of glow-worms all holding on to each other, and so forming a dazzling canopy over the fairy ring. There were thousands of little people looking on,

but they were in shadow and drab in colour compared to the glorious creatures within that luminous circle, who were so bewilderingly bright that Maimie had to wink hard

all the time she looked at them. It was amazing and even irritating to her that the Duke of Christmas Daisies should be able to keep out of love for a moment: yet out of love

his dusky grace still was: you could see it by the shamed looks of the Queen and court (though they pretended not to care), by the way darling ladies brought forward for his

approval burst into tears as they were told to pass on, and by his own most dreary face. Maimie could also see the pompous doctor feeling the Duke's heart and hear him give

utterance to his parrot cry, and she was particularly sorry for the Cupids, who stood in their fools' caps in obscure places and, every time they heard that "Cold, quite cold,"

bowed their disgraced little heads. She was disappointed not to see Peter Pan, and I may as well tell you now why he was so late that night. It was because his boat had got

wedged on the Serpentine between fields of floating ice, through which he had to break a perilous passage with his trusty paddle. The fairies had as yet scarcely missed him,

for they could not dance, so heavy were their hearts. They forget all the steps when they are sad, and remember them again when they are merry. David tells me that fairies

never say, "We feel happy": what they say is, "We feel *dancey*." Well, they were looking very undancey indeed, when sudden laughter broke out among the onlookers, caused

by Brownie, who had just arrived and was insisting on her right to be presented to the Duke. Maimie craned forward eagerly to see how her friend fared, though she had

really no hope; no one seemed to have the least hope except Brownie herself, who, however, was absolutely confident. She was led before his grace, and the doctor putting a

finger carelessly on the ducal heart, which for convenience' sake was reached by a little trap-door in his diamond shirt, had begun to say mechanically, "Cold, qui—," when

he stopped abruptly. "What's this," he cried, and first he shook the heart like a watch, and then he put his ear to it. "Bless my soul!" cried the doctor, and by this time of course

the excitement among the spectators was tremendous, fairies fainting right and left. Everybody stared breathlessly at the Duke, who was very much startled, and looked as

if he would like to run away. "Good gracious me!" the doctor was heard muttering, and now the heart was evidently on fire, for he had to jerk his fingers away from it and

put them in his mouth. The suspense was awful. Then in a loud voice, and bowing low, "My Lord Duke," said the physician elatedly, "I have the honour to inform your

excellency that your grace is in love." You can't conceive the effect of it, Brownie held out her arms to the Duke and he flung himself into them, the Queen leapt into the

arms of the Lord Chamberlain, and the ladies of the court leapt into the arms of her gentlemen, for it is etiquette to follow her example in everything. Thus in a single

moment about fifty marriages took place, for if you leap into each other's arms it is a fairy wedding. Of course a clergyman has to be present. How the crowd cheered and leapt! Trumpets brayed, the moon came out, and immediately a thousand couples seized hold of its rays as if they were ribbons in a May dance and waltzed in wild abandon round the fairy ring. Most gladsome sight of all, the Cupids plucked the hated fools' caps from their heads and cast them high in the air. And then Maimie went and spoiled everything. She couldn't help it. She was crazy with delight over her little friend's good fortune, so she took several steps forward and cried in an ecstasy, "O Brownie, how splendid!" Everybody stood still, the music ceased, the lights went out, and all in the time you may take to say, "Oh dear!" An awful sense of her peril came upon Maimie; too late she remembered that she was a lost child in a place where no human must be between the locking and the opening of the gates; she heard the murmur of an angry multitude; she saw a thousand swords flashing for her blood, and she uttered a cry of terror and fled. How she ran! And all the time her eyes were starting out of her head.

Many times she lay down, and then quickly jumped up and ran on again. Her little mind was so entangled in terrors that she no longer knew she was in the Gardens. The one thing she was sure of was that she must never cease to run, and she thought she was still running long after she had dropped in the Figs and gone to sleep. She thought the snowflakes falling on her face were her mother kissing her good-night. She thought her coverlet of snow was a warm blanket, and tried to pull it over her head. And when she heard talking through her dreams she thought it was mother bringing father to the nursery door to look at her as she slept. But it was the fairies. I am very glad to be able to say that they no longer desired to mischief her. When she rushed away they had rent the air with such cries as "Slay her!" "Turn her into something extremely unpleasant!" and so on, but the pursuit was delayed while they discussed who should march in front, and this gave Duchess Brownie time to cast herself before the Queen and demand a boon. Every bride has a right to a boon, and what she asked for was Maimie's life. "Anything except that," replied Queen Mab sternly, and all the fairies echoed, "Anything except that." But when they learned how Maimie had befriended Brownie and so enabled her to attend the ball to their great glory and renown, they gave three huzzas for the little human, and set off, like an army, to thank her, the court advancing in front and the canopy keeping step with it. They traced Maimie easily by her footprints in the snow. But though they found her deep in snow in the Figs, it seemed impossible to thank Maimie, for they could not waken her. They went through the form of thanking her—that is to say, the new King stood on her body and read her a long address of welcome, but she heard not a word of it. They also cleared the snow off her, but soon she was covered again, and they saw she was in danger of perishing of cold. "Turn her into something that does not mind the cold," seemed a good suggestion of the doctors, but the only thing they could think of that does not mind cold was a snowflake. "And it might melt," the Queen pointed out, so that idea had to be given up. A magnificent attempt was made to carry her to a sheltered spot, but though there were so many of them she was too heavy. By this time all the ladies were crying in their handkerchiefs, but presently the Cupids had a lovely idea. "Build a house round her," they cried, and at once everybody perceived that this was the thing to do; in a moment a hundred fairy sawyers were among the branches, architects were running round Maimie, measuring her; a bricklayer's yard sprang up at her feet, seventy-five masons rushed up with their foundation-stone, and the Queen laid it, overseers were appointed to keep the boys off, scaffoldings were run up, the whole place rang with hammers and chisels and turning-lathes, and by this time the roof was on and the glaziers were putting in the windows. The house was exactly the size of Maimie, and perfectly lovely. One of her arms was

extended, and this had bothered them for a second, but they built a verandah round it leading to the front door. The windows were the size of a coloured picture-book and

the door rather smaller, but it would be easy for her to get out by taking off the roof. The fairies, as is their custom, clapped their hands with delight over their cleverness,

and they were so madly in love with the little house that they could not bear to think they had finished it. So they gave it ever so many little extra touches, and even then they

added more extra touches. For instance, two of them ran up a ladder and put on a chimney. "Now we fear it is quite finished," they sighed. But no, for another two ran up

the ladder, and tied some smoke to the chimney. "That certainly finishes it," they said reluctantly. "Not at all," cried a glow-worm; "if she were to wake without seeing a

night-light she might be frightened, so I shall be her night-light." "Wait one moment," said a china merchant, "and I shall make you a saucer." Now, alas! it was absolutely

finished. Oh, dear no! "Gracious me!" cried a brass manufacturer, "There's no handle on the door," and he put one on. An ironmonger added a scraper, and an old lady ran

up with a door-mat. Carpenters arrived with a water-butt, and the painters insisted on painting it. Finished at last! "Finished! How can it be finished," the plumber demanded

scornfully, "before hot and cold are put in," and he put in hot and cold. Then an army of gardeners arrived with fairy carts and spades and seeds and bulbs and forcing-

houses, and soon they had a flower-garden to the right of the verandah, and a vegetable garden to the left, and roses and clematis on the walls of the house, and in less time

than five minutes all these dear things were in full bloom. Oh, how beautiful the little house was now! But it was at last finished true as true, and they had to leave it and return

to the dance. They all kissed their hands to it as they went away, and the last to go was Brownie. She stayed a moment behind the others to drop a pleasant dream down the

chimney. All through the night the exquisite little house stood there in the Figs taking care of Maimie, and she never knew. She slept until the dream was quite finished, and

woke feeling deliciously cosy just as morning was breaking from its egg, and then she almost fell asleep again, and then she called out, "Tony," for she thought she was at

home in the nursery. As Tony made no answer she sat up, whereupon her head hit the roof, and it opened like the lid of a box, and to her bewilderment she saw all around

her the Kensington Gardens lying deep in snow. As she was not in the nursery she wondered whether this was really herself, so she pinched her cheeks, and then she knew it

was herself, and this reminded her that she was in the middle of a great adventure. She remembered now everything that had happened to her from the closing of the gates

up to her running away from the fairies, but however, she asked herself, had she got into this funny place? She stepped out by the roof, right over the garden, and then she

saw the dear house in which she had passed the night. It so entranced her that she could think of nothing else. "O you darling! O you sweet! O you love!" she cried. Perhaps

a human voice frightened the little house, or maybe it now knew that its work was done, for no sooner had Maimie spoken than it began to grow smaller; it shrank so slowly

that she could scarce believe it was shrinking, yet she soon knew that it could not contain her now. It always remained as complete as ever, but it became smaller and smaller,

and the garden dwindled at the same time, and the snow crept closer, lapping house and garden up. Now the house was the size of a little dog's kennel, and now of a Noah's

Ark, but still you could see the smoke and the door-handle and the roses on the wall, every one complete. The glow-worm light was waning too, but it was still there.

"Darling, loveliest, don't go!" Maimie cried, falling on her knees, for the little house was now the size of a reel of thread, but still quite complete. But as she stretched out her arms imploringly the snow crept up on all sides until it met itself, and where the little house had been was now one unbroken expanse of snow. Maimie stamped her foot naughtily, and was putting her fingers to her eyes, when she heard a kind voice say, "Don't cry, pretty human, don't cry," and then she turned round and saw a beautiful little naked boy regarding her wistfully. She knew at once that he must be Peter Pan. CHAPTER VI *Peter's Goat* Maimie felt quite shy, but Peter knew not what shy was. "I hope you have had a good night," he said earnestly. "Thank you," she replied, "I was so cosy and warm. But you"—and she looked at his nakedness awkwardly—"don't you feel the least bit cold?" Now cold was another word Peter had forgotten, so he answered, "I think not, but I may be wrong: you see I am rather ignorant. I am not exactly a boy; Solomon says I am a Betwixt-and-Between." "So that is what it is called," said Maimie thoughtfully. "That's not my name," he explained, "my name is Peter Pan." "Yes, of course," she said, "I know, everybody knows." You can't think how pleased Peter was to learn that all the people outside the gates knew about him. He begged Maimie to tell him what they knew and what they said, and she did so. They were sitting by this time on a fallen tree; Peter had cleared off the snow for Maimie, but he sat on a snowy bit himself. "Squeeze closer," Maimie said. "What is that?" he asked, and she showed him, and then he did it. They talked together and he found that people knew a great deal about him, but not everything, not that he had gone back to his mother and been barred out, for instance, and he said nothing of this to Maimie, for it still humiliated him. "Do they know that I play games exactly like real boys?" he asked very proudly. "O Maimie, please tell them!" But when he revealed how he played, by sailing his hoop on the Round Pond, and so on, she was simply horrified. "All your ways of playing," she said with her big eyes on him, "are quite, quite wrong, and not in the least like how boys play." Poor Peter uttered a little moan at this, and he cried for the first time for I know not how long. Maimie was extremely sorry for him, and lent him her handkerchief, but he didn't know in the least what to do with it, so she showed him, that is to say, she wiped her eyes, and then gave it back to him, saying, "Now you do it," but instead of wiping his own eyes he wiped hers, and she thought it best to pretend that this was what she had meant. She said out of pity for him, "I shall give you a kiss if you like," but though he once knew, he had long forgotten what kisses are, and he replied, "Thank you," and held out his hand, thinking she had offered to put something into it. This was a great shock to her, but she felt she could not explain without shaming him, so with charming delicacy she gave Peter a thimble which happened to be in her pocket, and pretended that it was a kiss. Poor little boy! He quite believed her, and to this day he wears it on his finger, though there can be scarcely any one who needs a thimble so little. You see, though still a tiny child, it was really years and years since he had seen his mother, and I dare say the baby who had supplanted him was now a man with whiskers. But you must not think that Peter Pan was a boy to pity rather than to admire; if Maimie began by thinking this, she soon found she was very much mistaken. Her eyes glistened with admiration when he told her of his adventures, especially of how he went to and fro between the island and the Gardens in the Thrush's Nest. "Ho romantic!" Maimie exclaimed, but this was another unknown word, and he hung his head thinking she was despising him. "I suppose Tony would not have done that?" he

said very humbly. "Never, never!" she answered with conviction, "He would have been afraid." "What is afraid?" asked Peter longingly. He thought it must be some splendid

thing. "I do wish you would teach me how to be afraid, Maimie," he said. "I believe no one could teach that to you," she answered adoringly, but Peter thought she meant

that he was stupid. She had told him about Tony and of the wicked thing she did in the dark to frighten him (she knew quite well that it was wicked), but Peter misunderstood

her meaning and said, "Oh, how I wish I was as brave as Tony!" It quite irritated her. "You are twenty thousand times braver than Tony," she said; "you are ever so much

the bravest boy I ever knew." He could scarcely believe she meant it, but when he did believe he screamed with joy. "And if you want very much to give me a kiss," Maimie

said, "you can do it." Very reluctantly Peter began to take the thimble off his finger. He thought she wanted it back. "I don't mean a kiss," she said hurriedly, "I mean a

thimble." "What's that?" Peter asked. "It's like this," she said, and kissed him. "I should love to give you a thimble," Peter said gravely, so he gave her one. He gave her quite

a number of thimbles, and then a delightful idea came into his head. "Maimie," he said, "will you marry me?" Now, strange to tell, the same idea had come at exactly the

same time into Maimie's head. "I should like to," she answered, "but will there be room in your boat for two?" "If you squeeze close," he said eagerly. "Perhaps the birds

would be angry?" He assured her that the birds would love to have her, though I am not so certain of it myself. Also that there were very few birds in winter. "Of course

they might want your clothes," he had to admit rather falteringly. She was somewhat indignant at this. "They are always thinking of their nests," he said apologetically, "and

there are some bits of you"—he stroked the fur on her pelisse—"that would excite them very much." "They shan't have my fur," she said sharply. "No," he said, still

fondling it, however, "No. O Maimie," he said rapturously, "do you know why I love you? It is because you are like a beautiful nest." Somehow this made her uneasy. "I

think you are speaking more like a bird than a boy now," she said, holding back, and indeed he was even looking rather like a bird. "After all," she said, "you are only a

Betwixt-and-Between." But it hurt him so much that she immediately added, "It must be a delicious thing to be." "Come and be one, then, dear Maimie," he implored her,

and they set off for the boat, for it was now very near Open-Gate time. "And you are not a bit like a nest," he whispered to please her. "But I think it is rather nice to be like

one," she said in a woman's contradictory way. "And, Peter, dear, though I can't give them my fur, I wouldn't mind their building in it. Fancy a nest in my neck with little

spotty eggs in it! O Peter, how perfectly lovely!" But as they drew near the Serpentine, she shivered a little, and said, "Of course I shall go and see mother often, quite often.

It is not as if I was saying good-bye for ever to mother, it is not in the least like that." "Oh no," answered Peter, but in his heart he knew it was very like that, and he would

have told her so had he not been in a quaking fear of losing her. He was so fond of her, he felt he could not live without her. "She will forget her mother in time, and be happy

with me," he kept saying to himself, and he hurried her on, giving her thimbles by the way. But even when she had seen the boat and exclaimed ecstatically over its loveliness,

she still talked tremblingly about her mother. "You know quite well, Peter, don't you," she said, "that I wouldn't come unless I knew for certain I could go back to mother whenever I want to? Peter, say it." He said it, but he could no longer look her in the face. "If you are sure your mother will always want you," he added rather sourly. "The

idea of mother's not always wanting me!" Maimie cried, and her face glistened. "If she doesn't bar you out," said Peter huskily. "The door," replied Maimie, "will always,

always be open, and mother will always be waiting at it for me." "Then," said Peter, not without grimness, "step in, if you feel so sure of her," and he helped Maimie into

the Thrush's Nest. "But why don't you look at me?" she asked, taking him by the arm. Peter tried hard not to look, he tried to push off, then he gave a great gulp and jumped

ashore and sat down miserably in the snow. She went to him. "What is it, dear, dear Peter?" she said, wondering. "O Maimie," he cried, "it isn't fair to take you with me if

you think you can go back! Your mother" —he gulped again—"you don't know them as well as I do." And then he told her the woeful story of how he had been barred out,

and she gasped all the time. "But my mother," she said, "*my* mother—" "Yes, she would;" said Peter, "they are all the same. I dare say she is looking for another one already."

Maimie said aghast, "I can't believe it. You see, when you went away your mother had none, but my mother has Tony, and surely they are satisfied when they have one."

Peter replied bitterly, "You should see the letters Solomon gets from ladies who have six." Just then they heard a grating *creak*, followed by *creak, creak*, all round the Gardens.

It was the Opening of the Gates, and Peter jumped nervously into his boat. He knew Maimie would not come with him now, and he was trying bravely not to cry. But Maimie

was sobbing painfully. "If I should be too late," she said in agony, "O Peter, if she has got another one already!" Again he sprang ashore as if she had called him back. "I

shall come and look for you to-night," he said, squeezing close, "but if you hurry away I think you will be in time." Then he pressed a last thimble on her sweet little mouth,

and covered his face with his hands so that he might not see her go. "Dear Peter!" she cried. "Dear Maimie!" cried the tragic boy. She leapt into his arms, so that it was a sort

of fairy wedding, and then she hurried away. Oh, how she hastened to the gates! Peter, you may be sure, was back in the Gardens that night as soon as Lock-out sounded,

but he found no Maimie, and so he knew she had been in time. For long he hoped that some night she would come back to him; often he thought he saw her waiting for him

by the shore of the Serpentine as his bark drew to land, but Maimie never went back. She wanted to, but she was afraid that if she saw her dear Betwixt-and-Between again

she would linger with him too long, and besides the ayah now kept a sharp eye on her. But she often talked lovingly of Peter, and she knitted a kettle-holder for him, and one

day when she was wondering what Easter present he would like, her mother made a suggestion. "Nothing," she said thoughtfully, "would be so useful to him as a goat." "He

could ride on it," cried Maimie, "and play on his pipe at the same time." "Then," her mother asked, "won't you give him your goat, the one you frighten Tony with at night?"

"But it isn't a real goat," Maimie said. "It seems very real to Tony," replied her mother. "It seems frightfully real to me too," Maimie admitted, "but how could I give it to

Peter?" Her mother knew a way, and next day, accompanied by Tony (who was really quite a nice boy, though of course he could not compare), they went to the Gardens,

and Maimie stood alone within a fairy ring, and then her mother, who was a rather gifted lady, said— My daughter, tell me, if you can, What have you got for Peter Pan? To

which Maimie replied— I have a goat for him to ride, Observe me cast it far and wide. She then flung her arms about as if she were sowing seed, and turned round three times. Next Tony said— If P. doth find it waiting here, Wilt ne'er again make me to fear? And Maimie answered— By dark or light I fondly swear Never to see goats anywhere. She also left a letter to Peter in a likely place, explaining what she had done, and begging him to ask the fairies to turn the goat into one convenient for riding on.

Well, it all happened just as she hoped, for Peter found the letter, and of course nothing could be easier for the fairies than to turn the goat into a real one, and so that is how Peter got the goat on which he now rides round the Gardens every night playing sublimely on his pipe. And Maimie kept her promise, and never frightened Tony with a goat again, though I have heard that she created another animal. Until she was quite a big girl she continued to leave presents for Peter in the Gardens (with letters explaining how humans play with them), and she is not the only one who has done this. David does it, for instance, and he and I know the likeliest place for leaving them in, and we shall tell you if you like, but for mercy's sake don't ask us before Porthos, for he is so fond of toys that, were he to find out the place, he would take every one of them. Though Peter still remembers Maimie he is become as gay as ever, and often in sheer happiness he jumps off his goat and lies kicking merrily on the grass. Oh, he has a joyful time! But he has still a vague memory that he was a human once, and it makes him especially kind to the house-swallows when they visit the island, for house-swallows are the spirits of little children who have died. They always build in the eaves of the houses where they lived when they were humans, and sometimes they try to fly in at a nursery window, and perhaps that is why Peter loves them best of all the birds. And the little house? Every lawful night (that is to say, every night except ball nights) the fairies now build the little house lest there should be a human child lost in the Gardens, and Peter rides the marches looking for lost ones, and if he finds them he carries them on his goat to the little house, and when they wake up they are in it, and when they step out they see it. The fairies build the house merely because it is so pretty, but Peter rides round in memory of Maimie, and because he still loves to do just as he believes real boys would do. But you must not think that, because somewhere among the trees the little house is twinkling, it is a safe thing to remain in the Gardens after Lock-out time. If the bad ones among the fairies happen to be out that night they will certainly mischief you, and even though they are not, you may perish of cold and dark before Peter Pan comes round. He has been too late several times, and when he sees he is too late he runs back to the Thrush's Nest for his paddle, of which Maimie had told him the true use, and he digs a grave for the child and erects a little tombstone, and carves the poor thing's initials on it. He does this at once because he thinks it is what real boys would do, and you must have noticed the little stones, and that there are always two together. He puts them in twos because they seem less lonely. I think that quite the most touching sight in the Gardens is the two tombstones of Walter Stephen Matthews and Phoebe Phelps. They stand together at the spot where the parish of Westminster St. Mary's is said to meet the Parish of Paddington. Here Peter found the two babes, who had fallen unnoticed from their perambulators, Phoebe aged thirteen months and Walter probably still younger, for Peter seems to have felt a delicacy about putting any age on his stone. They lie side by side, and the simple inscriptions read W. St. M. 13a P.P. 1841. David sometimes places white flowers on these two innocent graves. But how strange for parents, when they hurry into the Gardens at the opening of the gates looking for their lost one, to find the sweetest little tombstone instead. I do hope that Peter is not too ready with his spade.

It is all rather sad. THE END. PETER AND WENDY | Chapter I *Peter Breaks Through* All children, except one, grow up. They soon know that they will grow up, and the way Wendy knew was this. One day when she was two years old she was playing in a garden, and she plucked another flower and ran with it to her mother. I suppose she must have looked rather delightful, for Mrs. Darling put her hand to her heart and cried, "Oh, why can't you remain like this for ever!" This was all that passed between them on the subject, but henceforth Wendy knew that she must grow up. You always know after you are two. Two is the beginning of the end. Of course they lived at 14, and until Wendy came her mother was the chief one. She was a lovely lady, with a romantic mind and such a sweet mocking mouth. Her romantic mind was like the tiny boxes, one within the other, that come from the puzzling East, however many you discover there is always one more; and her sweet mocking mouth had one kiss on it that Wendy could never get, though there it was, perfectly conspicuous in the right-hand corner. The way Mr. Darling won her was this: the many gentlemen who had been boys when she was a girl discovered simultaneously that they loved her, and they all ran to her house to propose to her except Mr. Darling, who took a cab and nipped in first, and so he got her. He got all of her, except the innermost box and the kiss. He never knew about the box, and in time he gave up trying for the kiss. Wendy thought Napoleon could have got it, but I can picture him trying, and then going off in a passion, slamming the door. Mr. Darling used to boast to Wendy that her mother not only loved him but respected him. He was one of those deep ones who know about stocks and shares. Of course no one really knows, but he quite seemed to know, and he often said stocks were up and shares were down in a way that would have made any woman respect him. Mrs. Darling was married in white, and at first she kept the books perfectly, almost gleefully, as if it were a game, not so much as a Brussels sprout was missing; but by and by whole cauliflowers dropped out, and instead of them there were pictures of babies without faces. She drew them when she should have been totting up. They were Mrs. Darling's guesses. Wendy came first, then John, then Michael. For a week or two after Wendy came it was doubtful whether they would be able to keep her, as she was another mouth to feed. Mr. Darling was frightfully proud of her, but he was very honourable, and he sat on the edge of Mrs. Darling's bed, holding her hand and calculating expenses, while she looked at him imploringly. She wanted to risk it, come what might, but that was not his way; his way was with a pencil and a piece of paper, and if she confused him with suggestions he had to begin at the beginning again. "Now don't interrupt," he would beg of her. "I have one pound seventeen here, and two and six at the office; I can cut off my coffee at the office, say ten shillings, making two nine and six, with your eighteen and three makes three nine seven, with five naught naught in my cheque-book makes eight nine seven—who is that moving?—eight nine seven, dot and carry seven—don't speak, my own—and the pound you lent to that man who came to the door—quiet, child—dot and carry child—there, you've done it!—did I say nine nine seven? yes, said nine nine seven; the question is, can we try it for a year on nine nine seven?" "Of course we can, George," she cried. But she was prejudiced in Wendy's favour, and he was really the grander character of the two. "Remember mumps," he warned her almost threateningly, and off he went again. "Mumps one pound, that is what I have put down, but I daresay it will be more like thirty shillings—don't speak—measles one five, German measles half a guinea, makes two fifteen six—don't waggle your finger—

whooping-cough, say fifteen shillings"—and so on it went, and it added up differently each time; but at last Wendy just got through, with mumps reduced to twelve six, and the two kinds of measles treated as one. There was the same excitement over John, and Michael had even a narrower squeak; but both were kept, and soon you might have seen the three of them going in a row to Miss Fulsom's Kindergarten school, accompanied by their nurse.

Mrs. Darling loved to have everything just so, and Mr. Darling had a passion for being exactly like his neighbours; so, of course, they had a nurse. As they were poor, owing to the amount of milk the children drank, this nurse was a prim Newfoundland dog, called Nana, who had belonged to no one in particular until the Darlings engaged her. She had always thought children important, however, and the Darlings had become acquainted with her in Kensington Gardens, where she spent most of her spare time peeping into perambulators, and was much hated by careless nursemaids, whom she followed to their homes and complained of to their mistresses. She proved to be quite a treasure of a nurse. How thorough she was at bath-time; and up at any moment of the night if one of her charges made the slightest cry. Of course her kennel was in the nursery. She had a genius for knowing when a cough is a thing to have no patience with and when it needs stocking round your throat. She believed to her last day in old-fashioned remedies like rhubarb leaf, and made sounds of contempt over all this new-fangled talk about germs, and so on. It was a lesson in propriety to see her escorting the children to school, walking sedately by their side when they were well behaved, and butting them back into line if they strayed. On John's footer days she never once forgot his sweater, and she usually carried an umbrella in her mouth in case of rain. There is a room in the basement of Miss Fulsom's school where the nurses wait. They sat on forms, while Nana lay on the floor, but that was the only difference. They affected to ignore her as of an inferior social status to themselves, and she despised their light talk. She resented visits to the nursery from Mrs. Darling's friends, but if they did come she first whipped off Michael's pinafore and put him into the one with blue braiding, and smoothed out Wendy and made a dash at John's hair.

No nursery could possibly have been conducted more correctly, and Mr. Darling knew it, yet he sometimes wondered uneasily whether the neighbours talked. He had his position in the city to consider. Nana also troubled him in another way. He had sometimes a feeling that she did not admire him. "I know she admires you tremendously, George," Mrs. Darling would assure him, and then she would sign to the children to be specially nice to father. Lovely dances followed, in which the only other servant, Liza, was sometimes allowed to join. Such a midget she looked in her long skirt and maid's cap, though she had sworn, when engaged, that she would never see ten again. The gaiety of those romps! And gayest of all was Mrs. Darling, who would pirouette so wildly that all you could see of her was the kiss, and then if you had dashed at her you might have got it. There never was a simpler happier family until the coming of Peter Pan.

Mrs. Darling first heard of Peter when she was tidying up her children's minds. It is the nightly custom of every good mother after her children are asleep to rummage in their minds and put things straight for next morning, repacking into their proper places the many articles that have wandered during the day. If you could keep awake (but of course you can't) you would see your own mother doing this, and you would find it very interesting to watch her. It is quite like tidying up drawers. You would see her on her knees, I expect, lingering humorously over some of your contents, wondering where on earth you had picked this thing up, making discoveries sweet and not so sweet, pressing this to her cheek as if it were as nice as a kitten, and hurriedly stowing that out of sight. When you wake in the morning, the naughtinesses and evil passions with which you went to bed have been folded up small and placed at the bottom of your mind, and on the top, beautifully aired, are spread out your prettier thoughts, ready for you to put on. I don't know whether you have ever seen a map of a person's mind. Doctors sometimes draw maps of other parts of you, and your own map can become intensely interesting, but catch them trying to draw a map of a child's mind, which is not only confused, but keeps going round all the time. There are zigzag lines on it, just like your temperature on a card, and these are probably roads in the island; for the Neverland is always more or less an island, with astonishing splashes of colour here and there, and coral reefs and rakish-looking craft in the offing, and savages and lonely lairs, and gnomes who are mostly tailors, and caves through which a river runs, and princes with six elder brothers, and a hut fast going to decay, and one very small old lady with a hooked nose. It would be an easy map if that were all; but there is also first day at school, religion, fathers, the round pond, needlework, murders, hangings, verbs that take the dative, chocolate pudding day, getting into braces, say ninety-nine, three-pence for pulling out your tooth yourself, and so on, and either these are part of the island or they are another map showing through, and it is all rather confusing, especially as nothing will stand still. Of course the Neverlands vary a good deal. John's, for instance, had a lagoon with flamingoes flying over it at which John was shooting, while Michael, who was very small, had a flamingo with lagoons flying over it. John lived in a boat turned upside down on the sands, Michael in a wigwam, Wendy in a house of leaves deftly sewn together. John had no friends, Michael had friends at night, Wendy had a pet wolf forsaken by its parents, but on the whole the Neverlands have a family resemblance, and if they stood still in a row you could say of them that they have each other's nose, and so forth. On these magic shores children at play are for ever beaching their coracles. We too have been there; we can still hear the sound of the surf, though we shall land no more. Of all delectable islands the Neverland is the snuggest and most compact, not large and sprawly, you know, with tedious distances between one adventure and another, but nicely crammed. When you play at it by day with the chairs and table-cloth, it is not in the least alarming, but in the two minutes before you go to sleep it becomes very nearly real. That is why there are night-lights. Occasionally in her travels through her children's minds Mrs. Darling found things she could not understand, and of these quite the most perplexing was the word *Peter*. She knew of no Peter, and yet he was here and there in John and Michael's minds, while Wendy's began to be scrawled all over with him. The name stood out in bolder letters than any of the other words, and as Mrs. Darling gazed she felt that it had an oddly cocky appearance. "Yes, he is rather cocky," Wendy admitted with regret. Her mother had been questioning her. "But who is he, my pet?" "He is Peter Pan, you know, mother." At first Mrs. Darling did not know, but after thinking back into her childhood she just remembered a Peter Pan who was said to live with the fairies. There were odd stories about him, as that when children died he went part of the way with them, so that they should not be frightened. She had believed in him at the time, but now that she was married and full of sense she quite doubted whether there was any such person. "Besides," she said to Wendy, "he would be grown up by this time." "Oh no, he isn't grown up," Wendy assured her confidently, "and he is just my size." She meant that he was her size in both mind and body; she didn't know how she knew it, she just knew it. Mrs. Darling consulted

Mr. Darling, but he smiled pooh-pooh. "Mark my words," he said, "it is some nonsense Nana has been putting into their heads; just the sort of idea a dog would have. Leave

it alone, and it will blow over." But it would not blow over; and soon the troublesome boy gave Mrs. Darling quite a shock. Children have the strangest adventures without

being troubled by them. For instance, they may remember to mention, a week after the event happened, that when they were in the wood they met their dead father and had

a game with him. It was in this casual way that Wendy one morning made a disquieting revelation. Some leaves of a tree had been found on the nursery floor, which certainly

were not there when the children went to bed, and Mrs. Darling was puzzling over them when Wendy said with a tolerant smile: "I do believe it is that Peter again!"

"Whatever do you mean, Wendy?" "It is so naughty of him not to wipe," Wendy said, sighing. She was a tidy child. She explained in quite a matter-of-fact way that she

thought Peter sometimes came to the nursery in the night and sat on the foot of her bed and played on his pipes to her. Unfortunately she never woke, so she didn't know

how she knew, she just knew. "What nonsense you talk, precious. No one can get into the house without knocking." "I think he comes in by the window," she said. "My love,

it is three floors up." "Were not the leaves at the foot of the window, mother?" It was quite true; the leaves had been found very near the window. Mrs. Darling did not know

what to think, for it all seemed so natural to Wendy that you could not dismiss it by saying she had been dreaming. "My child," the mother cried, "why did you not tell me

of this before?" "I forgot," said Wendy lightly. She was in a hurry to get her breakfast. Oh, surely she must have been dreaming. But, on the other hand, there were the leaves.

Mrs. Darling examined them carefully; they were skeleton leaves, but she was sure they did not come from any tree that grew in England. She crawled about the floor, peering

at it with a candle for marks of a strange foot. She rattled the poker up the chimney and tapped the walls. She let down a tape from the window to the pavement, and it was a

sheer drop of thirty feet, without so much as a spout to climb up by. Certainly Wendy had been dreaming. But Wendy had not been dreaming, as the very next night showed,

the night on which the extraordinary adventures of these children may be said to have begun. On the night we speak of all the children were once more in bed. It happened

to be Nana's evening off, and Mrs. Darling had bathed them and sung to them till one by one they had let go her hand and slid away into the land of sleep. All were looking

so safe and cosy that she smiled at her fears now and sat down tranquilly by the fire to sew. It was something for Michael, who on his birthday was getting into shirts. The fire

was warm, however, and the nursery dimly lit by three night-lights, and presently the sewing lay on Mrs. Darling's lap. Then her head nodded, oh, so gracefully. She was

asleep. Look at the four of them, Wendy and Michael over there, John here, and Mrs. Darling by the fire. There should have been a fourth night-light. While she slept she

had a dream. She dreamt that the Neverland had come too near and that a strange boy had broken through from it. He did not alarm her, for she thought she had seen him

before in the faces of many women who have no children. Perhaps he is to be found in the faces of some mothers also. But in her dream he had rent the film that obscures the

Neverland, and she saw Wendy and John and Michael peeping through the gap. The dream by itself would have been a trifle, but while she was dreaming the window of…

Canterbury Classics

An imprint of Printers Row Publishing Group

10350 Barnes Canyon Road, Suite 100, San Diego, CA 92121

www.thunderbaybooks.com

Printers Row Publishing Group is a division of Readerlink Distribution Services, LLC. The Canterbury Classics and Novel Journal names and logos are registered trademarks of Readerlink Distribution Services, LLC.

All correspondence concerning the content of this book should be addressed to Canterbury Classics, Editorial Department, at the above address.

Publisher: Peter Norton

Publishing Team: Lori Asbury, Ana Parker, Laura Vignale, Kathryn Chipinka

Editorial Team: JoAnn Padgett, Melinda Allman, J. Carroll

Production Team: Jonathan Lopes, Rusty von Dyl, Lidija Tomas

A Novel Journal: Peter Pan

ISBN: 978-1-62686-603-4

Printed in China

20 19 18 17 16   2 3 4 5 6

$14.99 U.S.

ISBN 978-1-62686-603-4